AfroSF

SCIENCE FICTION
BY AFRICAN WRITERS

EDITED BY IVOR W. HARTMANN

"*AfroSF* will serve as an admirable antidote for all those who have to be reminded that Africa is a continent, not a country. Both the stories and the authors are as diverse as any reader could wish...Looking over this broad assortment...it's clear that this anthology has lived up to its ambition...highly readable and enjoyable stories that take the raw materials of science fiction and give them a different spin...Although it is coming from a small press, it would be lovely if this anthology were to get some of the wider attention it deserves." — Karen Burnham, *Locus* December 2012.

"Africa is in our future and *AfroSF* demonstrates that the same can be said of its authors. These stories have an energy and a vitality that is missing from much western science fiction today, and they're as varied as the continent itself. Read them and you'll find your new favourite authors. Recommended." — Jim Steel, *Interzone*'s Book Reviews editor and widely published short-story writer.

"I'd like the repurpose the title of an old anthropological study to describe this fine new anthology: 'African Genesis.' The stories in this unprecedented, full-spectrum collection of tales by African writers must surely represent, by virtue of their wit, vigor, daring, and passion, the genesis of a bright new day for Afrocentric science fiction. The contributors here are utterly conversant with all SF subgenres, and employ a full suite of up-to-date concepts and tools to convey their continent-wide, multiplex, idiosyncratic sense of wonder. With the publication of this book, the global web of science fiction is strengthened and invigorated by the inclusion of some hitherto neglected voices." — Paul Di Filippo, co-author of *Science Fiction: The 101 Best Novels 1985-2010.*

"The stories in *AfroSF* feature all the things fans of science fiction expect: deep space travel, dystopian landscapes, alien species, totalitarian bureaucracy, military adventure, neuro-enhanced nightlife, artificial intelligence, futures both to be feared and longed for. At once familiar and disarmingly original, these stories are fascinating for the diversity of voices at play and for the unique perspective each author brings to the genre. This is SF for the Twenty-first Century." — David Anthony Durham, Campbell Award winning author of *The Acacia Trilogy*

"This is a book of subtle refractions and phantasmic resonances. The accumulated reading effect is one of deep admiration at the exuberance of the twenty-first century human imagination." — A. Igoni Barrett, author of *Love is Power, Or Something Like That*.

"*AfroSF* is an intense and varied anthology of fresh work. Readers and writers who like to explore new viewpoints will enjoy this book." — Brenda Cooper, author of *The Creative Fire*.

"A ground-breaking anthology. I could not recommend it enough." — Lavie Tidhar, World Fantasy Award winning author of *Osama*.

AfroSF
Science Fiction by African Writers

Edited by Ivor W. Hartmann

A StoryTime Publication.

AfroSF Copyright © 2012 Ivor W. Hartmann.

Proofed by Elinore Morris.
Cover design by Ivor Hartmann.
(Ancient symbol for 'human' created by the Dogon people).

ISBN: 978-0-9870089-6-1 (Print Edition)

For more information, please contact StoryTime:
storytime.publishing@gmail.com

CONTENTS

Introduction

Ivor W. Hartmann

The *AfroSF: Science Fiction by African Writers* anthology has been a dream of mine for five years. In 2007, I returned to writing after sixteen years and the first story I completed was 'Earth Rise', a Science Fiction short story. As soon as I looked for somewhere to publish it, preferably an African publication, the harsh realities of African publishing, and publishing for African writers in general, in 2007, became quite apparent. Including the fact, a pan-African anthology of Science Fiction by African writers only had never been published, and thus the dream of *AfroSF* was conceived.

Long story short, I created the micro-press StoryTime that first published *StoryTime*: a weekly African literature online magazine, from June 2007 to June 2012. In 2010, StoryTime launched *African Roar*, an annual multi-genre anthology of African writers, co-edited by Emmanuel Sigauke and me, now in its third year. So, by late 2011, I felt ready to pursue the *AfroSF* dream.

If one looks at the last 50 years of publishing in terms of SciFi and African writers, some real gems have never been collected into one volume. Thus, the temptation to have a mix of reprints and original works was great, but the vision I had for *AfroSF* needed to include the forward thinking spirit embodied so well in SciFi as a genre. Therefore, in December 2011, I put out the call for submissions for original (unpublished) works only.

SciFi, like most fiction genres that aren't Contemporary except perhaps Romance and Crime to an extent, is highly underdeveloped in African literature as a whole. Now I could go into all the reasons why, but let's look to the future instead.

SciFi is the only genre that enables African writers to envision a future from *our* African perspective. Moreover, it does this in a way that is not purely academic and so provides a vision that is readily understandable through a fictional context. The value of this envisioning for any third-world country, or in our case continent, cannot be overstated nor negated. If you can't see and relay an understandable vision of the future, your future will be co-opted by someone else's vision, one that will not necessarily have your best interests at heart. Thus, Science Fiction by African writers is of paramount importance to the development and future of our continent.

The *AfroSF* stories have a bit of everything in the realm of SciFi, from Comic, Military, Apocalyptic, to Space Opera, Cyberpunk, Biopunk, Aliens, Time Travel, and more, and fairly liberal mixings thereof. The stories represent a diversity of voices and themes specifically rooted in the SciFi genre, from some stellar established and upcoming African writers.

Ivor W. Hartmann, Zimbabwean writer, editor, publisher, visual artist, and author of *Mr. Goop* (Vivlia, 2010). Nominated for the UMA Award ('Earth Rise', 2009), awarded The Golden Baobab Prize ('Mr. Goop', 2009), and finalist for The Yvonne Vera Award ('A Mouse amongst Men', 2011). His writing has appeared in *African Writing Magazine, Wordsetc, Munyori Literary Journal, Something Wicked Anthology: Volume One, The Apex Book of World SF V2*, and other publications. He runs the StoryTime micro-press, publisher of the *African Roar* annual anthology and *AfroSF*, and is on the advisory board of WINZ: Writers International Network Zimbabwe.

Moom!

Nnedi Okorafor

She sliced through the water imagining herself a deadly beam of black light. The current parted against her sleek smooth skin. If any fish got in her way, she would spear it and keep right on going. She was on a mission. She was angry. She would succeed and then *they* would leave for good. They brought the stench of dryness, then they brought the noise and made the world bleed black ooze that left poison rainbows on the water's surface. She'd often see these rainbows whenever she leapt over the water to touch the sun.

The ones who brought the rainbows were burrowing and building creatures from the land and no one could do anything about them. Except her. She'd done it before and they'd stopped for many moons. They'd gone away. She could do it again.

She increased her speed.

She was the largest swordfish in these waters. *Her* waters. Even when she migrated, this particular place remained hers. Everyone knew it. She had not been born here but in all her migrations, she was happiest here. She suspected this was the birthplace of one of those who created her.

She swam even faster.

She was blue grey and it was night. Though she could see, she didn't need to. She knew where she was going from memory. She was aiming for the thing that looked like a giant dead snake. She remembered snakes; she'd seen plenty in her past life. In the sunlight, this dead snake was the colour of decaying seaweed with skin rough like coral.

Any moment now.

She was nearly there.

She was closing in fast.

Nnedi Okorafor

She stabbed into it.

From the tip of her spear, down her spine, to the ends of all her fins, she experienced red-orange bursts of pain. The impact was so jarring that she couldn't move. But there was victory; she felt the giant dead snake deflate. It was bleeding its black blood. Her perfect body went numb and she wondered if she had died. Then she wondered what new body she would find herself inhabiting. She remembered her last form, a yellow monkey; even while in that body, she'd loved to swim. The water had always called to her.

She awoke. Gently but quickly, she pulled her spear out. Black blood spewed in her face from the hole she'd made. She quickly turned away from the bitter-sweet tasting poison. *Now* they would leave soon. As she happily swam away in triumph, the loudest noise she'd ever heard vibrated through the water.

MOOM!

The noise rippled through the ocean with such intensity that she went tumbling with it, sure that it would tear her apart. All around her, it did just that to many of the smaller weaker fish and sea creatures.

The water calmed. Deeply shaken, she slowly swam to the surface. Head above the water, she moved through the bodies that glistened in the moonlight. Several smaller fish, jellyfish, even crabs, floated, belly up or dismembered. Many of the smaller creatures were probably simply obliterated. But she had survived.

She swam back to the depths. She'd only gone down a few feet when she smelled it. Clean, sweet, sweet, SWEET! Her senses were flooded with sweetness, the sweetest water she'd ever breathed. She swam forward, tasting the water more as it moved through her gills. In the darkness, she felt others around her. Other fish. Large, like herself, and small… so some small ones *had* survived.

Now, she saw everyone. There were even several sharp-toothed ones and mass killers. She could see this well now

9

Moom!

because something large and glowing was down ahead. A great shifting bar of glowing sand. This was what was giving off the water that was so clean it was sweet. She hoped the sweetness would drown out the foul blackness of the dead snake she'd pierced. She had a feeling it would. She had a very good feeling.

The sun was up now, sending its warm rays into the water. She could see everyone swimming, floating, wiggling right into it. There were sharks, sea cows, shrimps, octopus, tilapia, codfish, mackerel, flying fish, even seaweed. Creatures from the shallows, creatures from the shore, creatures from the deep, all here. A unique gathering.

What was happening here? She wanted to know but remained where she was. Waiting. Hesitating. Watching. It was not deep but it was wide. About two hundred feet below the surface. Right before her eyes, it shifted. From blue to green to clear to purple-pink to glowing gold. But it was the size, profile and shape of it that drew her. Once in her travels, she'd come across a giant world of food, beauty and activity. The coral reef had been blue, pink, yellow and green, inhabited by sea creatures of every shape and size. The water was sweet and there was not a dry creature in sight. She had lived in that place for many moons before finally returning to her favourite waters.

When she'd travelled again, she'd never been able to find the paradise she'd left. Now here in her home was something even wilder and more alive than her lost paradise. And like there, the water here was sweet. Clean and clear. She couldn't see the end of it. However, there was one thing she was certain of: what she was seeing wasn't from the sea's greatest depths or the dry places. This was from far, far away.

More and more creatures swam down to it. As they drew closer, she saw the colours pulsate and embrace them. She noticed an octopus with one missing tentacle descending toward it. Suddenly, it grew brilliant pink-purple and straightened all its tentacles. Then right before her eyes, it grew its missing tentacle back and what looked like bony spokes erupted from its soft head. It spun and flipped and then shot off, down into one of the circular bone-like caves of the undulating coral-like thing below.

When a golden blob ascended to meet her, she still didn't move, but she didn't flee either. The sweetness she smelled and its gentle movements were soothing and non-threatening. When it communicated with her, asking question after question, she hesitated. Then she told it exactly what she wanted.

Everything was changing.

She'd always loved her smooth skin but now it became impenetrable, its colour now golden like the light the New People gave off. The colour that reminded her of another life where she could both enjoy the water and endure the sun and the air.

Her sword-like spear grew longer and so sharp at the tip that it sang. They made her eyes like the blackest stone and she could see deep into the ocean and high into the sky. And when she wanted to, she could make spikes of cartilage jut out along her spine as if she were some ancestral creature from the deepest ocean caves of old. The last thing she requested was to be three times her size and twice her weight.

They made it so.

Now she was no longer a great swordfish. She was a monster.

"Despite the FPSO Mystras' loading hose leaking crude oil, the ocean water just outside of Lagos, Nigeria was now so clean that a cup of its salty sweet goodness would heal the worst human illnesses and cause a hundred more illnesses yet known to humankind. It was more alive than it had been in centuries and it was teeming with aliens and monsters."

Moom!

Nnedi Okorafor is a novelist of Nigerian descent known for weaving African culture into creative evocative settings and memorable characters. 'Moom!' is a prelude to a forthcoming novel. Her novels include *Who Fears Death* (World Fantasy Award for Best Novel), *Akata Witch* (Andre Norton Award Nominee), *Zahrah the Windseeker* (Wole Soyinka Prize for African Literature), and *The Shadow Speaker* (CBS Parallax Award). Her children's book *Long Juju Man* is the winner of the Macmillan Writer's Prize for Africa. Her compilation of short stories, *Kabu Kabu* (Prime Books) and chapter book *Iridessa and the Secret of the Never Mine* (Disney Press) are due for release in 2013. Nnedi holds a PhD in Literature and is a professor of creative writing at Chicago State University. Visit Nnedi at: nnedi.com.

Home Affairs

Sarah Lotz

Pendi rubs the pad of her thumb where her blood was taken. That's it now. She's in the system. Her DNA stored forever. It's not as if she's planning on committing a crime in the near future, but it still makes her uneasy.

And really, she gripes to herself, these days you should be able to do all this bureaucratic crap online. But here she is, still shuffling along the rows of plastic chairs with the rest of the sheep who've booked the morning off work to get their lives in order. It's been years since she was last here, and she doesn't approve of the expensive revamp: the blinding white décor only serves to make the people queuing look grubbier and the chairs seem to have been specifically designed to numb her arse. Still, the Home Affairs office smells the same as she remembers—the air thick with the stench of chicken and nervous sweat. And at least she's nearly at the front of the queue. There's just one victim ahead of her now, a nervous, portly woman who keeps fiddling with her belongings. The woman lunges in her bag again, accidentally nudging Pendi with her elbow. "Sorry," she whispers.

"Don't worry about it," Pendi says.

The woman gestures at the row of Konabots poised behind the counter. "Can you believe this, eh? It wasn't like this in my day."

Pendi shrugs, not wanting to encourage her. She's not in the mood for small talk.

"The traffic department's the same," Pendi's neighbour continues undeterred. "Soon it's the banks. Taking our jobs. It's not right. They'll be running the government next."

Pendi snorts. Still, she thinks, that might not be a bad thing. She can't imagine the Konabots siphoning off taxpayers' money to buy BMWs and Boeings or taking kickbacks from arms manufacturers. Which is the point of them really: You can't bribe a machine, can you? You can't corrupt a robot.

The woman shivers. "Ag. They make me nervous."

Pendi read somewhere that the multi-racial holographic faces superimposed over the Konabots' smooth metal heads are designed to make the public less uneasy about dealing with them, but as far as she's concerned, they have the opposite effect. The machines' unwavering smiles have a tinge of lunacy about them, and there's a glitch on one that makes it look as if its mouth is opening too wide, as if it's planning on swallowing the fellow updating his status in front of it.

The klaxon sounds for the next victim. "DNA variable 79776 slash five," an automated voice croons from the ceiling: "Please go to station one."

"I think that must be you," Pendi says to the woman.

"Thank you, sisi."

The guy on Pendi's right—a twitchy, fiftyish man dressed in battered takkies and bizarre tartan trousers—coughs into his fist. Pendi turns to glance at him, but he drops his gaze.

The woman heaves herself up, hovers in front of the Konabot directly in front of where Pendi is sitting. Shame, Pendi thinks, watching as she fumbles her DNA disc out of her bag with shaking hands. She really is seriously nervous.

"Hello goeie more sawubona how are you today sir madam I'm fine thank you for asking," the Konabot greets the woman with its rictus grin. "In which language will you be communicating with us today? In a) English b) isiXhosa c) isiZulu we're sorry but these are the only three options available today. Please state the letter that corresponds to your language preference in three, two, one now."

The woman clears her throat. "Um... English."

14

Home Affairs

"I'm sorry sir madam I did not catch that. In which language will you be communicating with us today? In a) English b) isiXhosa c) isiZulu we're sorry but these are the only three options available today. Please state the letter that corresponds to your language preference in three, two, one now."

Jesus, Pendi thinks. She's been listening to this all morning. It's enough to drive you mad. She almost misses the snappish sadists who were lurking behind the counters the last time she was here.

"A," the woman falters. "English."

"English is your chosen language. Thank you sir madam. Are you a) updating your ID status b) passport status c) refugee status d) work permit status e) other status. Please state the letter that corresponds to your requirement preference in three, two, one now."

"None. I have a query."

"I'm sorry sir madam I did not catch that. Are you a) updating your ID status b) passport status c) refugee status d) work permit status e) other status. Please state the letter that corresponds to your requirement preference in three, two, one now."

"You don't understand. First I need to ask about my son's-"

"I'm sorry sir madam I did not catch that. Are you a) updating your ID status b) passport status c) refugee status d) work permit status e) other status. Please state the letter that corresponds to your requirement preference in three, two, one now."

"You're not listening!" The woman slaps the countertop and the Konabots all immediately stop talking. The sudden silence is made even more disturbing by the fact that their holographic faces continue to smile inanely.

"Not again," the twitchy man next to Pendi murmurs. He hunches his shoulders as if he's trying to appear smaller than he is.

The klaxon blares. "Attention," the smooth automated voice intones, and this time Pendi detects a sinister edge to it. "Attention. DNA variable 79776 slash five, please step away from the counter."

"No! I have queued here all morning. I have a query-"

"Attention. Attention. DNA variable 79776 slash five, please step away from the counter. This is your second warning."

The woman turns around and looks at Pendi pleadingly.

Dammit, Pendi thinks. She doesn't want to get involved, but she can hardly leave her there floundering.

As she stands up, the twitchy man grabs her arm. "Don't get involved, lady."

"I can't just sit here," she says to him.

"Don't do it," he hisses, shaking his head.

Pendi glares at him, yanks her elbow out of his grip and strides up to the counter. "Excuse me," she says to the Konabot. "This woman needs help. Can you call a supervisor or something?" The Konabot grins back at her blandly, the ear-splitting klaxon parps again. "And can you turn that bloody thing off?"

"Attention. Attention. DNA variable 89696 slash 12, please step away from the counter." Hang on, Pendi thinks—isn't that the DNA number she was assigned when she handed over her documents? "Attention. DNA variable 89696 slash 12, please step away from the counter."

Pendi looks up and into the dark eye of one of the cameras gazing down at her from the ceiling. "Is there anyone up there? Hello? I demand that you send a supervisor to-"

"Attention. Attention. DNA variable 89696 slash 12, please step away from the counter. Final warning. Final warning."

"Don't worry, sisi," the woman says, backing away from the counter. "It's fine."

Home Affairs

"It's not fine! Hey." She leans over the counter, jabs a finger at the Konabot. "You can't treat her like this. She's just having a problem understa-"

"Instituting protective mechanisms phase one."

There's a grinding sound, the floor vibrates under her feet and before Pendi has a chance to scream, she feels it disappear beneath her. Arms flailing, she drops, lands feet first on a soft uneven surface. Her knees buckle as she loses her balance and she rolls onto her side to catch her fall.

"Hey!" she screams, finding her voice. "Hey!"

She looks up, sees the woman she tried to help and that weird twitchy guy peering down at her. Then the small gap in the ceiling above her slides closed, leaving her in perfect darkness.

"Hey!"

Flushed with adrenaline, pulse juddering in her throat, she scrambles onto her hands and knees. Her palms sink into scratchy material—she's landed on some sort of cheap mattress.

What the hell just happened? She could have been hurt falling through that floor. It's ridiculous.

She waits for her eyes to adjust to the darkness, but there's no light source whatsoever and the blackness is impenetrable. The air in here smells musty and she can hear the skitter of rodent claws. Shuddering, she inches forward until she feels the mattress's edge, stands up, steps forward carefully, feels her shin connect with a hard edge.

"Hey!" she shouts at the top of her voice. Silence. Hands shaking, she fumbles her iPhone out of her pocket, finds the torch App she downloaded on a whim and hasn't, until now, had reason to use. The phone's glow struggles to penetrate the gloom, but from the little she can see she appears to be in some sort of junk room. The shadowy shapes of broken furniture and filing cabinets loom around her.

Sarah Lotz

So what now? Someone will be coming to fetch her, right? And she's got her cell, she can start by calling the Home Affairs office, insist that she be put through to the manager—someone with a pulse—let them know that she's going to sue their arses. She dials directory enquiries, requests the number, instructs the bored woman on the other end to put her straight through, listens to an automated voice saying: "Hello, you've reached the Wynberg Home Affairs Office. Our opening hours are nine a.m. to four p.m. Press one if you have a query about your ID or refugee status; two to enquire about passport renewal; three for more information on the current DNA legislation; four to hold for an operator."

Pendi presses four, holds her breath.

"Thank you. You have pressed four to hold for an operator. Please wait until one becomes available."

Musak plinks in her ear, a panpipe version of *Stuck in the Middle With You*. Ha, ha, very fucking apt, Pendi thinks. She sighs with relief as the song ends, grits her teeth as it begins again. She's about to hang up when the line beeps. "Hello you've reached... Home Affairs Wynberg," a heavily-accented voice drones. "Your call may be recorded for purposes of quality control this is Vikesh speaking please have your assigned DNA number ready how may I be of assistance to you?"

Although tempted to scream down the phone, Pendi tells herself she needs to keep her fury in check. She knows from experience that abusing call centre drones can backfire and make the situation worse. "Hi, look. I was just in the processing office, and... I fell through the floor."

A pause. "Excuse me?"

"I was in the queue at your office and the floor just like... opened underneath me. I'm in some kind of junk or storage room. Probably, I dunno, right below where you are. You need to get me the hell out of here."

Silence.

"Hello? Did you hear what I just said?"

18

Home Affairs

The man sighs. "Do you have your assigned DNA number, madam?"

"What's that got to do with anything?"

"Madam, I am trying to help you, please be remaining calm. Do you have your assigned DNA number?"

"You're not listening to me! You need to send security or whatever down here immediately to get me out of here!"

"Madam, I am trying to help you, please be remaining calm or I will have no choice but to disconnect this call. Please clearly state your assigned DNA number, madam."

Jesus. Pendi digs in her pocket, pulls out the disc the DNA scanner deposited into her palm, squints as she uses the light from her phone to read it. "89696 slash 12."

"Thank you, madam." She listens to the skitter-clack of fingers on a keyboard. "I am sorry, madam, but there is no record of you being in the system."

"What do you mean? I was just there."

"According to my computer, you do not exist, madam."

"Hello? I'm right here. How can I not exist?" Be cool, she tells herself, decides to try a different tactic and see if playing helpless and meek will help. 'I'm really frightened. Can't you just come and get me?"

Another pause. "I am not at liberty to do that, madam. I am not situated in South Africa."

"Well get a- what? What do you mean you're not situated in South Africa? Where are you?"

"Mumbai, madam. I am only at liberty to deal with queries regarding identity status where viable DNA information has been provided."

Awesome. "So what the fuck am I supposed to do now?"

"You'll have to bring your documents in and reapply, madam. Those regarding your birth, death, residence, tax, employment, and partner or single status. Copies are not acceptable at this time, madam."

"I've already done that! I handed in my documents—that was the bloody point! I don't have them anymore! I was told to come into your bloody office to update my fucking ID status, which I did, and the next thing I know, I'm stuck in some basement-"

"Madam, I cannot help you unless you remain calm."

"Sorry." Pendi can't believe she's apologising. "Please help me," she sniffs. She is actually feeling tearful, although more from frustration and anger than fear.

A sigh. "Hold on, madam, I am going to be trying to put you through to the supervisor on duty at the South African Home Affairs office where you are located."

Before Pendi gets a chance to say another word she's listening to a dire musak version of Cher's *Bang Bang, My Baby Shot me Down*. Mercifully, before it's run its course, there's another beep and a perfectly modulated voice comes on the line. "Hello goeie more sawubona this is supervisor seven slash nine in which language will you be communicating with us today? In a) English b) isiXhosa c) isiZulu we're sorry but these are the only three options available today. Please state the letter that corresponds to your language preference in three, two, one now."

"You have *got* to be kidding me."

"I'm sorry sir madam I did not catch that. In which language will you be communicating with us today? In a) English b) isiXhosa c) isiZulu we're sorry but these are the only three options available today. Please state the letter that corresponds to your language preference in three, two, one now."

"Put me back to that call centre guy-"

The call dies.

Brilliant. Pendi presses redial, this time hears nothing but a serious of empty beeps. She tries again, almost hurls the phone onto the floor when she gets a 'Network Busy' message.

There has to be a way out of here. She'll find a way, yeah, then heads will roll.

She steps forward carefully, using the meagre cell phone glow to help her navigate the minefield of broken chairs, overturned tables, and filing cabinets. Reaching the wall, she finally locates a light switch. She flicks it on, blinking as strip lights stutter into life. The place really is a dump; the floor strewn with crumpled paper. She makes out several ripped ID books and ancient passports tossed amongst the debris.

"Ha!" she punches the air in relief when she spots a door half-hidden behind a metal shelf. She picks her way over to it and tries the handle. Half expecting it to be locked, she almost falls through it as it opens smoothly onto a piss-stinking passageway lit by a naked swinging bulb. Spotting the green glow of an emergency exit sign to her right, she runs up to the heavy fire door, pushes the bar to open it and steps out into a barrage of traffic noise and bright sunlight.

It takes her a few seconds to get her bearings. She's on Wynberg high street, metres away from the corner of the block housing the Home Affairs building.

A passer-by shoots her a dubious look. She glances down, sees that her suede jacket is dusted with cobwebs, shredded paper, and what look horribly like rodent droppings. It will cost a fortune to dry-clean, but no way in hell is she going to be shelling out for that.

She brushes herself down, breathes in, breathes out.

Right, she thinks, flushed with a fresh spurt of fury, time to kick some serious Home Affairs arse.

She jogs past the seemingly endless queue of people waiting to be let into the building and checked through security. Everyone wears the same expression of resigned boredom; several have even come equipped with camping chairs and large buckets of fried chicken. But she isn't going to be joining them—she's already queued once; she got up before dawn this morning for a reason.

She shoulders her way up the steps and through to the front of the queue, ignoring the irritated grunts around her.

The security guard lounging outside the glass doors looks her up and down. "Join the back of the queue, lady."

"I need to talk to the manager."

He yawns. "Join the back of the queue, lady."

"You don't understand. I was just in there. In the processing office or whatever you call it and... something happened. I need to make a complaint."

The man sighs. "Did you attempt to bribe one of the Konabots, ma'am?"

"What? No! I fell through the floor—I could have been hurt! Look at my jacket, it's fucking ruined. Have you any idea how much it cost?"

"Did you cause a disturbance in the office ma'am?"

"No! Are you deaf? Let me in."

"Other people are waiting. Go to the end of the queue and you can come in and make your complaint when it's your turn."

She makes a show of staring at his name badge. "Look. Listen to me very carefully, Mr Traverso. I was just *in* there. I've already queued. I need to see a manager immediately."

"Ma'am," he says, fiddling with his walkie-talkie, "If you do not go to the back of the queue I will have no choice but to call the cops."

"*You* call the cops? Are you kidding? Have you any idea what I've just been through?"

"Just do as he says, sisi," a woman behind her says. "We've all got problems."

"You haven't heard the last of this," Pendi snaps, pointing a finger in the security guard's face. Trying to draw the strands of her fraying dignity together, Pendi pushes her way back to the pavement. There's no way she's going to the back of that queue. She'll go to the cops, report Home Affairs for... kidnapping or abuse or something.

She strides away from the building, pausing as a figure emerges from an alcove and steps out in front of her. She recognises him immediately as the twitchy guy in the tragic tartan trousers who told her not to help the woman.

Home Affairs

"Hey, lady," he says.

"What do you want?"

He nods to the queue behind her. "You're wasting your time. Even if you do get back in there, you've lost your status."

"My what?"

"Your status. Your identity. It is gone. I told you not to help that lady."

"Thanks. That's really helpful." She is about to tell him to go screw himself when something strikes her. "Hang on, how did you know that would happen?"

He sighs. "Because it happened to me."

"When?"

"Three weeks ago. I have only just got my life back."

"Are you saying that you also fell through the floor?"

"Ja. They kept asking me the same question... I just snapped. Next thing I knew I was ejected."

"But why would they do that? They're just robots. Machines."

"The Konabots don't like confrontation. You shouldn't have threatened them."

"Threaten them? I didn't threaten them!"

"You only have one choice now-"

"Yeah. I'm going to the cops."

"When was the last time you went to a police station, lady? Who do you think does all the admin there? Takes the statements?"

"Seriously? They're there too?"

"Of course."

Pendi supposes it's possible. She's hardly been keeping her finger on the pulse of the new anti-corruption measures, has she? "But... there were witnesses. You saw what happened, it also happened to you. You can come with me; we need to put a stop to this."

He shakes his head. "I promise you, there is nothing you can do. There is no record of you now. You have been wiped from the system."

23

Pendi remembers what that guy from Mumbai told her. That according to his records, she doesn't exist. The thought of sorting out this particular bureaucratic nightmare fills her with nausea. "So what can I do?"

"You have money?"

"What?"

"You have money?"

"I'm not giving you any money."

"It's not for me. Listen, lady, I'm just trying to help. If you want your life back, then come with me."

He turns, starts weaving through the passers-by.

What should she do? She imagines trying to explain her situation to a cop shop Konabot. She's not sure she'll be able to keep it together without punching it; and God knows where she'd end up then. No, she'll see where this leads her first. Slinging her bag over her shoulder, she stalks after him, keeping her distance in case he tries anything.

He rounds the block, heading towards the parking lot where she left her car. He stops and gestures at a peeling door sealed by a rusty security gate, set into the alleyway between the Home Affairs building and a cut-price shoe shop.

"That door. Ask for Busi. Say Lucas sent you." He turns to leave.

"Hey," she calls after him. "How come it took you three weeks to get sorted?"

He smiles ruefully and slaps his fraying trousers. "Look at me, lady. You think I'm like you?"

Feeling a tinge of shame, Pendi scrabbles in her bag for twenty rand to give to him for his trouble, but when she looks up, he's gone.

She steps into the alleyway and presses the grubby intercom button next to the security gate. There's a static crackle and then: "Ja?"

"Hi. Um, Lucas sent me."

A pause. "Wait."

Home Affairs

Pendi pulls out her iPhone, intent on phoning her boyfriend and venting her frustration, but there's only one bar of battery life left. She'd better preserve it in case she needs to call for help—for all she knows this whole thing could be some kind of elaborate ruse to lure her into a compromising position.

The door finally creaks open, and an elderly man with yellowed eyes peers distrustfully at her through the gate's bars. He looks her up and down, seems to come to some sort of decision. "Ja?"

"You Busi?"

"Ja. What did you do?"

"Do? Nothing."

"You must have done something if you are here."

Jesus. "How much is this going to cost me?"

"Five hundred."

"Five hundred? Are you serious?"

He shrugs.

"Okay, okay." Pendi tries to remember if she has that much in her wallet. She should do—she drew cash yesterday to pay the Malawian guy who does her ironing.

Busi slinks a palm through the bars of the gate.

Pendi snorts. "You think I'm stupid? How do I know you can even help me?"

He cackles, unlocks the gate and leers at her. He's small, barely comes up to her shoulder—Pendi thinks she could take him if she had to; she can't see any sign of a weapon on him. Besides, he's dressed in a crumpled polyester suit and shirt; he looks more like a washed up office drone than a gangster. "How do I know you're not some con-man or rapist or whatever?"

He snorts a laugh. "You don't. Are you coming or not?"

Pendi hesitates, then slips through the gate before she changes her mind. The space is narrow and she's forced to press against the wall to avoid touching him. She winces as her palms brush against slimy brickwork.

He locks the door and steps forward, blasting her with stale coffee breath. "Follow me."

He limps down a murky corridor. Pendi covers her mouth with her hand, trying to block out the pungent odours of mould and urine. She hopes the puddles she's stepping in are just water; her boots weren't cheap.

The corridor leads down into a stairwell, equally ill-lit and festering, the putty-coloured walls scrawled with graffiti: 'Abandun hop all ye who enter hear,' 'I fuked a konabit and got AIDS,' and 'Skynet is NOW'.

Charming, Pendi thinks. Hanging back in case she needs to make a run for it, she follows Busi down three flights, the steps littered with cigarette butts, the paintwork bubbled and stained. 'Where are we going?'

"Into the bowels."

"The bowels of what?"

"Home Affairs of course."

Of course. "You the janitor?"

He snorts. "No, lady. I used to work here. Assistant manager. Before..." his voice trails off.

"Before your department became so corrupt you were all replaced by machines?" Pendi snaps.

"We were not all like that, lady."

But I bet *you* were, Pendi thinks. "So what's in the bowels, then?"

"You'll see."

He unlocks a door at the foot of the stairwell and leads her into a long, brightly-lit corridor that appears to be a conduit to empty cubicles and poky, windowless offices. They're all decorated in typical bland office-style—taupe carpeting and white walls—and after the fusty of the stairwell, even this soulless conformity is a welcome relief. Still, the aura of abandonment and neglect is palpable, the detritus of what was once a busy workspace littered throughout: the forlorn base of a broken ergonomic chair; a 'world's best boss' mug on a draining board in a stripped kitchen area; a 'please replace photocopying paper' notice still tacked up on the wall. Pendi feels another shiver of unease. No one knows she's here. She could get lost down here, disappear forever, absorbed by the ghosts of bureaucrats past.

She dips her head into what must once have been a separate, open-plan office space, hesitating when she spots large bundles of discarded fabric huddled behind the desk partitions. One of the bundles twitches and she yelps. 'Jesus!' She backs up, stares in disbelief as several women and an elderly man leaning on crutches emerge one by one from behind the partitions and start edging towards her. All are filthy; all wear identical expressions of desperation.

A white woman with greasy grey hair gazes at her imploringly. "Madam, can you help me?"

"Ignore them," Busi says.

"Who the hell *are* they?"

"The families of the ones erased from the system. Those like you. No status, no identity. Some tried to bribe the machines, others fought and argued."

"Why are the Konabots doing this? How can they get away with it?"

"They are cleaning up the system, getting rid of the bad seeds. That's their job. The powers that be don't care. Far as they're concerned, the system is now running smoothly. No corruption means no problems—at least from the media."

"You call this smoothly?' Pendi says, unable to drag her eyes away from the gathering group of identity refugees. "How long have these people been down here?"

"Some, a long time. They are waiting for the breadwinners to come back and sort out their status. I let them stay here until they bring the money."

"You're a real saint," Pendi says.

The guy chuckles. "It is better than being out on the street. It's safe, there is running water here, shelter."

Pendi pulls a five rand coin out of her pocket, drops it into the woman's palm. The others clamour forward.

Sarah Lotz

"Stay back," Busi snarls. "You know the rules."

The people retreat on a gale of sighs.

Busi hobbles on towards a glass-windowed door at the far end of the passageway. He cups his hand around a keypad and taps in a code. The door clicks open. He ushers Pendi through it and into yet another soulless corridor, pausing at the first door on the right. He unlocks it, opens it with a flourish.

Pendi gasps, stares in at a graveyard of dented, damaged Konabots. Some are nothing but decapitated torsos, their featureless heads thrown carelessly on the carpet next to them; most are missing at least one of the metal appendages that are supposed to resemble arms. Complex circuitry tumbles out of their bases like eviscerated innards.

"This is where they dump the broken ones," Busi says.

"So how does this help me?"

"The one you need is in here. The corrupted one."

"The corrupted what?"

"Konabot, of course."

An image of surreptitiously handing over a flash drive full of illegal Apps to one of these things in exchange for her identity pops into her mind. "What do you mean corrupted? Like rusty or something? I mean, you can't corrupt them, that's the point of them, isn't it?"

Busi laughs as if she's said something hilarious. "Everything can be corrupted, lady."

"So what did you do to it? Hack it?"

"No," he says. "No one has yet managed to hack them. Some people are born bad. This one was just manufactured bad. You go in, I will wait out here."

She steps forward tentatively. There have to be at least thirty of the things packed in here; she catches a glimpse of her warped reflection in the curved surface of a severed head. "How do I know which one it is?"

"You'll know. Choose E."

He shuts the door behind her, locks it.

Home Affairs

Pendi clears her throat. "Hello?"

Pendi jumps as a Konabot shoved in the corner of the room beeps. The scanner on the front of its chest clicks and its holographic face—which appears to be that of a middle-aged white man—stutters into life. Unlike the others in here, it looks intact; it's merely covered in a shroud of dust and shredded paper. And like the creepy Konabot she saw in the processing office, there's something wrong with its mouth—it's blurred with static and looks more like it's snarling than grinning.

"Um. Hello," Pendi falters. "Can you help me?"

There's another flurry of beeps, and then: "Hello sir madman I'm fine thank you for aching. In which linger will you be consuming with us today? In a) entrails b) isiklot c) isizoom we're sorry but these are the only three opinions available to die. Please snake the litter that corresponds to your linger preference in three, four, one now."

"What the hell?" The automated voice drags at half-speed; its too-low timbre sounds almost demonic.

"I'm sorry sir madman I did not cabbage that. In which linger will you be consuming with us today? In a) entrails b) isiklot c) isizoom we're sorry but these are the only three opinions available to die. Please snake the litter that corresponds to your linger preference in three, four, one now."

"A", Pendi says. "Um ... Entrails."

"Entrails is your chosen linger. Thank you sir madman. Do you require a) eaten b) filed c) erased e) reset. Please snake the litter that corresponds to your rehirement predicament in three, two, six now."

Christ, Pendi thinks. "Um, E. E—reset."

"Thank you sir madman. You have selected C reset. Please snake your DNA number so that I can reseat you."

"Reseat?"

"I'm sorry sir madman I did not cabbage that. Please clearly snake your DNA number so that I can reseat you."

Pendi digs out her DNA disc, reads out the numbers as clearly as she can, fighting to control the wobble in her voice.

"Thank you sir madman. You have been successfully reset. Have a good die."

The face snaps off. Pendi shivers with relief and thumps on the door. She hears it unlock, then steps out into the corridor to join Busi.

"That's it?" she asks.

Busi shrugs. "That's it."

"Now what?"

He points towards a doorway at the other end of the corridor. "Go through there, head upwards and you'll reach the corridor outside the processing office. You can go back and join the queue."

"So I'm sorted?"

"Ja. You've been reset into the system. Just don't cause any more trouble."

Pendi turns away.

"Ahem," Busi says, holding out his palm. "Aren't you forgetting something?"

Pendi digs in her bag, hands over the five hundred rand. "Aren't you ashamed of yourself? Taking money for this? While those people back there are suffering?"

He shrugs again.

She shoots him a loaded look of disgust and heads for the stairwell, trying not to dwell on the lost souls crammed in that office.

"If I didn't do it, someone else would!" Busi calls after her.

Yeah, yeah, she thinks, steeling herself for the long afternoon of queuing ahead of her. The more things change, the more they stay the same.

Sarah Lotz is a screenwriter and novelist with a fondness for the macabre and fake names. She writes urban horror

Home Affairs

novels under the name S.L. Grey with author Louis Greenberg and a YA pulp fiction zombie series with her daughter, Savannah, under the pseudonym Lily Herne. Her latest solo novel, *The Three*, will be published by Hodder in the UK and Reagan Arthur in the US in 2014. She lives in Cape Town with her family and other animals.

The Sale

Tendai Huchu

The sale was yet to be finalised, and Mr. Munyuki was rushing about frantically in his brown suit that he wore only on major occasions—the last time was at his father's funeral. He'd bought it at Robert Gabriel Retailers in HaCity—as it was now rebranded by the Asian entrepreneurs who'd swapped it for a bad debt sometime in the late 21st century. HaCity was an appropriate name, something in between a laugh and K-pop trendy. Sweat dripped down Mr. Munyuki's side, his blue shirt was damp. He wore a yellow tie and the breast pocket of the suit had chicken soup stains on it he'd tried to wipe off with little success that morning.

He entered the tall glass building, formerly the reserve bank building, and told the heavy at the door that he had an appointment. A lift took him up to the top floor with sweeping views of the city. A TV screen in the lobby was tuned to the Voice of Truth. The PA for the Minister for Native Affairs, Anna Kansasian picked up her apparat, spoke into it, and told Mr. Munyuki that the minister was going to be tied up much longer than anticipated. His appointment had been rescheduled for tomorrow afternoon.

"But this is a matter of great urgency, there is no time. It's about the sale," he pleaded in his mouse-like voice—the CorpGov hormones did that to the voice, every man in his quarter spoke as if they'd permanently swallowed a helium balloon.

"The minister is a busy man. You really should have Facebooked it, if it was that important," she replied.

"I'm old fashioned. I prefer Face2facing," he said, thinking, Facebook, face to face, get it? No of course not. She wouldn't get it.

Tendai Huchu

"Well, you'll just have to wait." She was a thin woman with a long neck, and Mr. Munyuki thought she was probably fucking the minister—male intuition.

"But it's to be moved tomorrow morning," he cried out in despair, burying his head in his hands.

"Everyone knows about the sale. It's on the news every day," she said. There was no getting through to her, no hint of emotion or human empathy behind the business-like tone. The CCTV whirled round and focused on Mr. Munyuki. She continued, "Look, for what it's worth, the deal was done a long time ago. Your people sold out ages ago. You started with mineral concessions, agricultural rights. It's not the minister's fault if you can't pay your debts."

He bit his tongue and tasted sweet salt.

Anna narrowed her eyes a little. "Are you on your meds, buddy?" Her hand reached for the panic button under her desk.

"Of course, of course," Mr. Munyuki smiled, "tomorrow it is. You've been very helpful."

He made his way out, walking under the sign hanging by the door that said, Ministry of Native Affairs Pvt Ltd— Serving the Nation One Country at a Time.

Outside, back in the bright sun obscured by a thin film of toxic brown haze, he paused on the pavement. Around him were men in suits carrying briefcases. Men from around the world. Businessmen, the only type of men still allowed freedom to come to the centre of the city like this. The apparat worn on a chain round his neck bleeped a warning that his visa-pass had one hour left. Up above drones flew watching, recording everything. The businessmen walked past him as if he did not exist. He made his way to the ticketdrome, walking on the spotless streets, failing to avoid looking at the electronic advertisement boards that surrounded them.

In many ways, the city was cleaner. It had water and electricity, but it'd lost its soul, or so his father had told

The Sale

him during, the great sell-out. He was too young then to understand but now he did. Third World nations heavily under debt were sold off piecemeal to Corporations or *voluntarily* placed in caretakership as Zimbabwe was. They were the lucky ones. Some countries had to sell people to make up the difference that kept rising with the interest rates. The sign at the ticketdrome read:

:) The Natives Are Happy and Prosperous (:
:) The Future Must Be Magnificent (:

The woman at the checkout asked for his passport and checked his visa-pass, which was still valid. "Only twenty minutes left on this, you're cutting it pretty close. You know what they'll do to you if they catch you expired?" It was a rhetorical question, everyone knew. She was a fat, red haired woman with a wobbly chin that animated her face as she moved. He noticed her long nails, painted red. A native policeman, hand on Taser, passed by, double checked his passport, looked him up and down, and walked away.

"Was it like this in the old days before the Chimerica?" He found himself thinking aloud.

"Excuse me?" the checkout woman asked.

"Nothing, it's nothing. I need an extension for one more night."

"You had an interview with the minister for native affairs… The computer tells us it was for this afternoon." The contempt in her Cockney accent barely disguised.

"I did."

"Then you have to travel back and reapply for your pass in Mas-ving O." Some of the old names had been kept by CorpGov, with minor phonetic changes to reflect the language of the new administrators. They couldn't be bothered to learn the old names.

Tendai Huchu

"He rescheduled for tomorrow morning, first thing. I've literally just come from his offices where I had to wait all day whilst he was in and out of meetings."

"We can't help you here. The rules are very clear that visa-passes can only be applied for at your local native office."

"This is important. I have to stay in the city."

"Sir, maybe you are not hearing me. Go back to Masving O and reapply."

"I'm not..." Before he could finish his statement, a public health drone descended from the steel strutted ceiling where it was hovering. It made a buzzing sound, almost bee-like but with a hint of steel in the harmony. The light on its monocam at the front slowly changed from green to bright red as it hovered around his head, sampling pheromones and body odour.

Public health was a major concern for CorpGov and drones were deployed in major cities, always sampling, ever vigilant. They were egg-shaped, metallic machines with a red cross underneath that people could see as they walked about. Life expectancy was up 100% thanks to CorpGov's *unwavering* commitment to native health. Mr. Munyuki stood very still while it scanned him. Ordinance 32e: failure to comply with public health drones is a felony.

"PROSCRIBED LEVELS OF TESTOSTERONE
PROSCRIBED LEVELS OF TESTOSTERONE
PROSCRIBED LEVELS OF TESTOSTERONE."

It kept repeating with loud wailing reminiscent of old order police sirens. People stopped to look at the man who'd failed to efficiently manage his hormonal balance. It was true, he'd neglected taking his NeustrogenAlpha™, but only so he'd have the nerve to fight the sale; the sort of nerve that ended at the PA's desk. The drone reminded Mr. Munyuki that under CorpHealth directive 706.22.1438, section V, subsection II, all native males were required to maintain low testosterone levels in public

The Sale

unless otherwise authorised as in the role of native policeman and/or bouncer. The checkout woman chewed gum nonchalantly, watching everything, savouring his humiliation.

The drone hovered around him, its spectrometer measuring every conceivable detail about him, height, weight, BMI, blood pressure, pulse rate, sampling the air for any trace hormones emanating from him. It automatically linked into his apparat and downloaded previous medical records, sifting through relevant medical data, allergies, inoculations, dental appointments. Its calculations complete, the top opened and a capsule held by a mechanical arm emerged. "Comprehensive diagnosis complete," it announced. Mr. Munyuki knew what to do. He unbuckled his belt, dropped his trousers and bent over. The drone hovered zeroing in on the sphincter and pumping the off-white suppository until it was safely, deep inside his cavity.

It pulled back and said, "CorpGov thanks you for your co-operation, please remember your six monthly dental appointment is due in 21 days. Have a nice day." Then it flew back to the ceiling from where it scanned other native males in the ticketdrome.

Mr. Munyuki pulled his trousers up, avoiding the condemning stares of the masses walking back and forth. Humanity, were they even human at all with their daily diet of NeustrogenAlpha™, and the mood stabilisers and anti-depressants pumped into the water supply? He wondered this knowing full well that within minutes he would be incapable of such thoughts, that he would turn back into a docile robot. He turned to the woman. Something inside of him was happening, a rebalancing of brain chemistry. He felt light and happy for the first time that day. As if his very soul itself was lifted up to heaven. Balance restored in a chaotic world.

"I shall be going back to Mas-ving O, as you suggested," he said, and smiled at the checkout woman.

Tendai Huchu

"A wise decision. We'll make sure you get a nice window *seeeeaaat*," the woman replied, emphasising seat like one would talking to a toddler.

He left for the transport, a small part of him, unable to understand why despite his every desire to make a stand, he found himself co-operating, wanting to co-operate. The part of him pharmacologically altered was winning over his true self but it still lingered somewhere inside him, he could feel it. He never told his physician this, though under some health ordinance or the other he was fully obliged to.

He returned to the boys' hostel on the northern outskirts of the town. It was called 'Sponsored by Investco Perpetual' with the sub-tag, 'Ensuring Better Homes for the Earth's Native Population'. All the hostels were sponsored by some corp or the other. He swiped his apparat, the door opened, and he went up the steps to his room on the third floor.

"Jimmy!" his workflatmate John shouted out, a weak, subdued call coming from the depths of a NeustrogenAlpha™ haze.

"Hey, John."

"I've got something for you. A letter." John hid it behind his back. "You have to guess where it's coming from."

He knew straight away. There's only one place where decisions are so important they have to be printed out and sent the old-fashioned way.

"My answer from PopPlan," he replied hesitantly. He took the envelope, opened it very slowly, and took a deep breath.

PopPlan—Population Planning didn't send these replies out by apparat because they wanted them to be intimate. Its advertisements on television featured a muscled, smiling man, receiving his letter through the post, opening it, reading it and then looking at the television, mouthing, "Thank you PopPlan," with Tchaikovsky's Serenade for

The Sale

Strings in C Major playing in the background. The tune was stuck in his head. The advert played every day, on repeat.

"Do you want me to read it for you," said John.

"Hang on a minute, will you." His head was spinning. The future counted on this.

"Come on, read it already, you've been waiting five years for this."

"Dear Mr. Jimmy Munyuki," he began reading the piece of paper that had the PopPlan Logo on top and pink hearts dotted all round. "Thank you for your application to sire, which the committee has considered in great detail. We regret…" he stopped and froze.

John took the letter from him and continued. "We regret to inform you that we will not be accepting you for the sireship program. While your health is impeccable, the rearfoot valgus presented in your lower limb anatomy may be detrimental to the quality of future stock… We wish you the best for the future…"

"And commend you for being a loyal, hardworking citizen. Your's Sincerely MM Mcguire (head of PopPlan C-DIV)." He finished it off by heart. He knew the words by rote. Everyone he knew who'd made the application from Sponsored by Investco Perpetual had been declined.

"I guess when mine comes through, it'll be the same," John said, resigned and weary.

"What on earth is a rearfoot valgus anyway?"

Jimmy Munyuki lay on his bed and slept, a deep black sleep.

He woke in the middle of the night feeling thirsty, and poured himself a glass of water. John was snoring on the bunk above. Mr. Munyuki undressed, removing the suit he'd fallen asleep in. A mosquito buzzed in his ear. In his underpants, he fiddled behind his back to remove his 36 A bra. He moved his hands to feel his boobs, a known side effect of the daily doses of NeustrogenAlpha™. He lay on top of the covers, feeling the stifling summer heat. He looked up on the ceiling where a screen played nonstop advertisements. He watched them, they were better than counting sheep, for after an hour or so, he fell back to sleep.

Morning came with the singing of winter birds and the chatter of monkeys in the vast wilderness surrounding Mas-ving O. A handful of natives came wearing worn resigned looks, and amassed outside the monument offices. They'd heard word spreading of some resistance to the sale, but nothing had so far materialised. They looked like vegetables, walking zombies. As soon as they appeared, four health drones appeared from the sky, sampling, testing, checking. One of the drones played a loud, recorded broadcast: "Since Health Ministry Pvt Ltd a subsidiary of CorpGov took over this sector, Native Population has stabilised to a replacement rate of 1:1, life expectancy has doubled, free sanitation, jobs for all, Life, Liberty, Happiness for all. CorpGov is better than OldGov. Life is better. Life is good. You are Happy. One world, One people, United at last."

The hydrogen-fuelled trucks started rolling in, a large convoy that stretched out past the horizon. Their mirrors and windshields glistened in bright morning sun. Mr. Munyuki saw the hieroglyphs that marked them as CorpGov property. Everything was owned by CorpGov or the little Ltds that found a niche in the gigantic corporate macrocosm. He watched their slow progress as though they were appearing from behind a screen, or he was the one under a glass jar insulated from it all, or maybe the layer was on his eyes, a thin film covering them.

The first trucks were the removers and behind them followed heavy, earth moving equipment. Diggers, bulldozers, caterpillars, all moving silently, a vapour trail of clean H2O trailing as they went. The surveyors had been and gone already. For months, they took photographs, made detailed measurements and noted

The Sale

everything down on their apparats that transmitted terabytes of data to the twin capitals—Washington-Beijing. 'One world, two capitals,'—that was what the adverts said. The adverts said a lot of things.

This was the new order of stability. Since Nial Gerson, the 21st century historian, had discovered the doctrine of Consumption=Manufacturing, shortened to ConMan, which was enshrined in the eternal treaty, peace and order prevailed. In this order, China manufactures=America consumes. It has always been this way; it will always be this way. A stable equilibrium combining free markets, scientific rationale, and central planning, was created by the 2059 ConMan treaty that founded Chimerica as the pillar of GloSta. Every nation on the planet now had a ranking and a function from which no deviation was allowed unless CorpGov or one of its franchises ordered it. 'A better world for all. Eternal Growth,'—more slogans in his head.

The hundreds of workmen in white jumpsuits waited, sprawled across the grounds surrounding the monument. These were native workmen. Strong men. The sort of men with strong bodies and low IQs that were valued above all else by CorpGov. Loyal men who followed orders, the first of a new breed. A call came in to their supervisor who wore a red and blue jumpsuit. He spoke briefly on his apparat and gave the signal. Mr. Munyuku watched silently from the open window at the heritage offices. This is where he worked, a subsidiary of the Ministry of Native Affairs. He clenched to hold in his morning suppository, which felt like it was slipping out. Obviously, drones do the job better, they don't get distracted by the physical contortion required to slip the fingers in and push the capsule, they just do, pushing deep into the cavity.

He looked at the holographic blueprint for where Great Zimbabwe (Property of Ling Lee Antiquities Enterprises and Debt Recovery) would be finding its new home. The theme park on the outskirts of the Eastern capital,

Tendai Huchu

alongside the Cholula Pyramid and Great Pyramid of Giza, the Taj Mahal, British Museum, and a host of other antiquities from nations that had failed to meet their quota, failed to pay their debts. He read the information hailing the theme park as yet another example of how the world was moving towards greater unity, integration and a new era of unlimited growth. Strangely, he thought, it looked good there. He imagined the businessmen and their families drifting round the ancient world and enjoying the wonders all put together in one place.

Mr. Munyuki almost felt like laughing at the history of the monument. The first European adventurers had ransacked it, tearing down the carefully crafted granite walls searching for gold in the nineteenth century. But nothing like when palladium had been discovered under it in the twenty second. He felt tears swell up in his eyes, but he understood this was the chemical balance telling him all was for the best. Yet, deep inside him, a more primeval feeling of rage stirred up. The morning air had a tinge of time and pollen in it. This is the last time it will ever smell this way here, he realised. A message came through on his apparat, reassigning him from antiquities to his new role as a mine clerk. Under the scorching sun, he ran outside, past the small watching group of natives and the workmen. He ran faster than he'd ever run before and placed his body between the old stone walls and the bulldozers.

Tendai Huchu, author of *The Hairdresser of Harare* was born in Bindura, Zimbabwe. He has a great love of literature, and currently lives in Edinburgh, Scotland.

Five Sets of Hands

Cristy Zinn

Their hands linked, shadows forming a perfectly integrated circle on the resin floor. Njort crouched in the nearby darkness, watching the pale silhouettes as they leaned in towards each other, whispering. She was beginning to understand their language, the cadences and lilt of their tongues, their over-vowelled words.

"Did you find anything today?" Raafi asked them.

"I found something," said Mounk, his voice slow and deliberate. "I found a disk; sliver thin and circular. Not like the processors. It *reflected* light."

"Wish you'd kept it, Uncle," said Nald. She was the youngest, her skin the palest, like a ghost in the air. "I would have liked to see that."

"And you Nald? Did you find much of anything?" Raafi asked.

"Just more of the same. This poisoned earth is death to my fingers. It is difficult to pry the tech out of this hard ground. What is this ground they make us dig in?"

"Who knows," said Raafi. "It's a graveyard of sorts; compacted earth, tech fossils. It belonged to the first settlers, before the disaster. Who knows what they want with it all."

"They want to regain their intellect," said Cronje. He was the most distant of the five, even when attached to them like this. He was the least hopeful, the least amused. "Clearly they have lost it. Silly place to look for lost intellect, I say. Minds do not grow from the ground."

They all nodded solemnly, as they always did when he spoke. Njort wondered what was so magical about him that they bowed to his every thought like that.

Cristy Zinn

"And you, Raafi? Did you find anything today?" asked Pinta, her long neck craning towards her sister with interest.

Raafi did the unthinkable and unhitched her hand from their circle to pull something from her pocket. Njort could not see Pinta's face as she leaned towards the thing in her hands. The others gravitated towards her, their voices silenced, their faces hidden in each other's shadows.

"Impossible," whispered Cronje, taking a step away from the group. They were startled by his reaction and sudden separation. "If you were caught taking this..."

Njort heard the circle murmur but she did not catch the words.

"Is it a sign?" asked Mounk.

"A sign that we should flee..." said Cronje. "We should run and suffer the bitter consequences rather than stay here. *That* we might survive, but this... We may not keep Wuntyan artefacts."

No one spoke for a moment and then Njort heard the distant clomp of boots along the corridor. The five peeled their shadows from one another, disengaging in one smooth motion and climbed back in their cots where they pretended to sleep. The Nognagel guard did little more than glance over the slow rise and fall of their chests, and walk away.

He did not see Njort crouched in the corner, her deep red Nognagel skin blending with the darkness. Neither did Raafi as she lifted her blanket to take one last look at her treasure.

Njort tiptoed away; it would not do to be caught watching the affairs of adults, even alien ones who did not belong here.

Unlike the domed World Houses across the planet, which contained lush forests produced by manufactured water, the Borderland was an arid quadrant of hard, black dirt. It stretched between the eastern wastelands, with its grey

Five Sets of Hands

mud-sea and the yellow-rocked canyons in the west where a recently failed World House was being levelled by mammoth machines. Both of those places were a day's walk away; a walk none survived. The Borderland was naked and lifeless, its only allure the old tech buried deep within its filthy, poisoned folds.

Even the Nognagel, especially modified for a life on Mars, were not strong enough to work the fields as relentlessly as the Wuntya were made to. Though their pale Wuntyan skin seemed fragile, it was strong enough to withstand the unterraformed atmosphere outside the World Houses with minimal protection. It was yet another reason for them to be assigned to the Work Houses, and forced to churn the ground to find relics from before the terraforming disaster.

Pinta felt her sister's glare from where she worked. Pinta had been stretching for too long and the guards were beginning to notice. There were nine Wuntya on the ground today and nine guards on the platforms. The ground was already churned up but bore very few gifts. The guards would not be happy.

Mounk, Cronje, and Nald, worked the far side of the field. As always, Pinta felt that distance keenly—it was as if her very shadow longed to draw her nearer to the others. She wondered how the remaining four bared being so far from their fifth, hard at work in a distant field. She was thankful to have Raafi so close, to calm her and keep her from doing something she would regret. However, it was not only for their sakes that she did not turn her tool into a weapon and kill the nearest guard. Raafi's treasure had given her such hope; all night Pinta had barely slept for thinking of what it meant.

"Work," Raafi whispered.

Pinta slouched over her trowel and swiped a mostet from the visor of her helmet. The tiny bio-mechanical pests loved the hum of the tanks that bore healthier air but their bites left itching welts and bruises on the skin if they got inside the suit. They were another by-product of the Nognagel's tampering with the planet, another reason why Pinta hated the place. Raafi moved closer, pretending to inspect the earth at Pinta's feet.

"If you keep daydreaming you'll get the shovel in your back. Those guards are looking for an excuse to hurt one of us—you know that. You must work."

Pinta scowled at her sister. Her coolant had expired a few minutes ago and she was sweating and chaffing in her suit, worsened by how little the ground had yielded that day.

"When did we become the dirt under the Nognagel fingernails?" she asked.

"Haven't we always been this way?" sighed Raafi.

"I remember something else, something other than this digging. I remember sharing a room with you where we played..."

A small Nognagel sap yanked on the elbow of Pinta's suit, holding out a ladle of water from a faded green bucket. Little Njort was one of the few Nognagels who was considered low enough to serve the Wuntya because of her muteness. She was considered damaged, less-than, broken; which in Nognagel opinion made her very like the Wuntya. Pinta found Raafi's fondness for the child irritating.

"Njort," smiled Raafi. "You crept up on us. You're always lurking aren't you?"

Njort beamed up at them, nodding. Even though the nanofibre of her suit kept the atmosphere out, it was still baggy around elbows and legs, and the helmet seemed too heavy for her small shoulders. Each day Pinta saw the child up on the small domed towers that surrounded the tech field, staring through the aluminium slats as though she would rather be with the workers. She was often awarded unjustified blows or unwarranted kisses for taking too long on the ground, and yet, whenever Pinta saw her, she was smiling.

Five Sets of Hands

Njort shoved the ladle into Pinta's face and the woman coughed out a laugh.

"Thank you, Njort," said Pinta, lifting her visor and taking a long drink before passing it to her sister.

Pinta noticed Njort watched each of them intently, shuffling from foot to foot as if she were desperate to say something. When Raafi dropped the ladle back into the bucket Njort grabbed her hand and pressed a small stone into it. She nodded emphatically at it.

Raafi looked down at the shining black rock. It was nothing more than compressed earth but in the sun's light, it was beautiful. "Thank you, Njort," said Raafi.

Njort only looked frustrated. She took the stone back and pressed it again into Raafi's hand nodding sternly at the closed fist.

Pinta glanced up at the guards. There were two standing against the railings now, watching them. "What is it you want?" she asked.

"She wants you to treasure it," said Raafi.

Njort jumped up and clapped her hands, nodding her head.

"Treasure?" asked Pinta.

Njort nodded again. She mimed opening a pocket, putting something inside and patting it, smiling all the while.

"She's been spying on us again," said Pinta.

Raafi looked at her sister in surprise. "What do you mean?"

"She's seen the treasure. The one you found yesterday," said Pinta.

Raafi's hand flew to her pocket in horror. "*Have* you been spying on us, little one?"

Njort took a moment to respond and then nodded slowly, clasping the handle of the bucket and looking as though she were ready to run. Pinta grabbed the back of small girl's neck in her gloved hand, lifting her slightly from the floor.

46

Cristy Zinn

"It's rude to spy," she said, staring down the child.

Njort's red Nognagel skin flamed at Pinta's touch and her body cringed away as if she were awaiting a blow. She squeezed her eyes shut and hung there in Pinta's hand.

Raafi slapped at her sister when she saw one of the guards begin the long descent down the tower.

"Leave her," said Raafi, her warning tone enough to set Pinta on edge.

Pinta dropped the girl in a heap on the earth. "She shouldn't spy."

Njort nodded her agreement, looking shameful. Then she patted Raafi's hand that still held the rock.

"That treasure is not for Nognagel," said Pinta sternly.

"No. I'm afraid it isn't," said Raafi. "Now be on your way before you get us into trouble."

Njort nodded and scurried off towards the others at the far end of the field. Cronje was leaning on his shovel, staring at them with his usual scrutiny. He would have questions later, and admonishments.

"Get back to work, Pinta," said Raafi. "That guard is coming down and we'd better be working by the time he gets his suit on."

In the distance, Mounk saw the black clouds of mosterts hovering in patches of hot, shimmering air. The field crew's work was almost done for the day and Mounk only hoped the swarm would hold off until they made it back to the safety of the Work House. His back ached. He'd found nothing of use which meant his rations would be less tonight. Just the thought of it made his stomach growl.

He watched Cronje scowl at the ground where he dug, brows furrowed beneath his visor and beads of sweat collected on his temples. Mounk knew Cronje would work himself to death but he was determined to be the best at everything, even slavery.

Mounk caught sight of Njort hobbling away from Pinta and Raafi with her water bucket. The child was an oddity

Five Sets of Hands

on the Borderlands—accepted by neither Nognagel nor Wuntyan but tolerated with much amusement by both. As he yearned for the five to be joined together again, he wondered how the child survived so alienated. He wondered what a person was without a unit, though the Nognagel did not consider it a necessity.

The Borderland stretched out in every direction, bleak and shimmering in the late afternoon light with the small domed Work House seeming to waver on the horizon. The Nognagel guards emerged from the towers in their white suits, looking almost Wuntyan, and bound the workers with chains so that they could all make their way to the Work House three kilometres west. Chained together like that made Mounk feel better; they were connected again. He noticed the brief, weary smiles of the other workers as they reunited with their five-fold unit.

He saw Njort trotting ahead, her bucket lighter, trying to keep close to the guards. One of them swatted her away with such force that she was bowled over. Mounk winced at the thought of her pain. She jumped up, unaffected, and retrieved her bucket. She was as resilient as a Wuntyan, enduring much without complaint. No wonder the Nognagel hated her.

In her small cot, shrouded by carbon-fibre cut-offs from old cafeteria tables and holey blankets, Njort counted her stones. She had collected them for months, stuffing them into her pockets when the guards were busy. They were her treasures—the only things she owned. There were blisters on her palms again, from carrying the bucket, but she could no longer feel them. She stared down at her fingers as they tapped out a counting rhythm over her stones. Five fingers, just like the Wuntya, but darker. She wondered what those red Nognagel fingers of hers would look like woven between the pale ones of a Wuntya.

It was no good thinking things like that. She had been taught that she should despise the Wuntyan. They looked washed out and sickly beside the robustness of the Nognagel. Instead of hard, tall bodies, they were made of over-flexible stuff and had the propensity to lean towards their own kind. Worst of all, their need for one another was their greatest weakness—and Njort knew better than most how the Nognagel detested weakness.

No, it was no good thinking like that. Anyway, the Wuntya only needed five sets of hands.

"We made a mistake coming here," whispered Pinta over her small portion of rehydrated food. Thanks to their bad yield on the tech fields, their dinners were all severely undersized.

The five sat around a cafeteria table in the glass-domed garden of the Work House. They could have had worse accommodation on the Borderland but that had never been much of a consolation for the life they led there and Pinta refused to let herself feel too grateful for the Nognagel's dismal attempt at hospitality.

"What? To the Borderland?" asked Nald.

"Yes, that too. But I was referring to the planet. Mars was a mistake."

"Speak for yourself. I was born here. This is home more than Wunta," said Cronje.

"Really?" Pinta laughed. "Nice way for your brothers to treat you then," she said, lifting up his wrist where a tracking device glowed red just beneath the surface of his skin.

Cronje yanked his arm away. "Yes, well, this home may be corrupted but it's still home. Maybe if those Nognagel could just see that…"

"They would what?" Mounk interrupted. "Welcome us with open arms as brothers? They have no concept of community. No need for contact."

Pinta patted the old man's hand. Their pale skin was darkening despite the suits, which meant more than just sunlight was getting through.

Five Sets of Hands

"We have hope, now," whispered Raafi. "We have something they cannot steal from us."

"No, they wouldn't know it if they saw it anyway," Nald smiled.

"Not that we know what to do with it yet either," said Cronje, looking away from them. "Our treasure is a puzzle."

"But a treasure none the less," said Raafi. "Let us not forget that. Any remnant of our home will always be a treasure."

As if the room had heard them, every Wuntyan raised their heads in unison. All eyes turned to where the sun was almost lost beneath the horizon. As one, every Wuntyan stood and made their way to their cots. Pinta sighed with relief—it was time for the Communal.

Njort had watched the Communal many times. She knew she shouldn't. She knew it was a sacred, intimate time, shared only by Wuntya, but she felt a delicious warmth in her chest whenever she saw it and she yearned for it. The guards always disappeared during the Communal, the one time of day when the Wuntya were left unguarded.

It was at a Communal, over a century ago when the first Wuntyan were stranded on Mars, that they were captured. They did not resist until disconnected from one another. Their rage then was unexpected and despite their small stature, they fought valiantly and with great strength. Many Nognagel died. From then on, the raids were done more sensibly, keeping the Wuntya connected and transporting them in their circles. By the time the Communal was over it was too late for them to fight; they were already prisoners.

Yet, as vulnerable as they were, they never stopped the Communal, even in captivity. This was the premise for the Nognagel classing them as 'lesser beings' because they chose ritual over reason. Njort watched them and saw something else, something foreign and beautiful.

Cristy Zinn

She followed Raafi and her unit to their room and hid in her shadowed corner. They joined their five sets of hands and each of them took a turn looking into the eyes of another, speaking a blessing. Njort could feel her breathing slow and her mind calm as she listened to their gentle whispers. They noticed nothing but each other in that moment. Then they pulled their circle closer, so that their faces were hidden from Njort. She leaned forward but still she could not make out what they were saying, it was the one part of the ritual she did not understand.

Just as the night before, Raafi pulled the treasure from her pocket.

"We will discover how to use this," she vowed.

They all nodded sombrely, eyes fixed on the treasure—except for Cronje, who turned his head imperceptibly to the window and the sky outside. As he did, the circle opened slightly and Njort caught a glimpse of the small disk of three interlinking circles, covered in symbols, before Raafi pocketed it again. As the sun finally set, the five unhitched their hands and set about their evening activities of reading, sewing, and playing foreign games that Njort could not comprehend. Even separated she could see how they looked for one another, how Raafi would occasionally walk past Pinta and stroke her sister's arm as she went by, or how Nald squeezed Mounk's shoulder, or Cronje ruffled Nald's hair. They obviously loved these small contacts.

Njort's hand went to her neck and she rubbed where Pinta had pulled her up. No one touched Njort, no one at all, not Wuntya, not Nognagel. Her neck was slightly chaffed from Pinta's gloved hand. It was Njort's proof that she was real; that she was not as invisible as she felt.

There was strange weather on the Borderland. The broad solar panelled window that looked out towards the tech fields was darkened by thick purple clouds. Mounk stood looking out the window, one hand pressed against the

Five Sets of Hands

glass. The clouds looked as though they carried rain, though he had never seen it rain on the Borderland. Rain was a rumour, water a commodity, produced and packaged for those who could afford more than their daily rations. These clouds however, promised something free.

"Must be the treasure," Mounk whispered as Raafi joined him at the window.

"The clouds?" she asked. He could not see her face but he could hear her smile. "I don't think the treasure works like that."

"Why not? Have you ever seen this before?" he asked.

She shook her head and said, "No. Never."

"The sky is so full," said Mounk, his face lit up with childlike wonder.

They both gasped as a finger of light struck out from the cloud and pierced the ground. Seconds later the air was split by a deafening crack that shuddered the window. The others looked up from their tasks in surprise.

"What *was* that?" Nald asked, grabbing hold of Pinta's hand as they rushed to the window.

Mounk watched more light pierce the ground as the clouds swept towards the Work House. Some of the light moved in between the clouds, brightening the Borderland as though it were day.

"What's happening to the sky?" asked Pinta.

"I don't know but it's beautiful," said Mounk. His eyes had taken on a strange light as he stared into the storm.

"It sounds like explosions," said Nald.

"But look," said Mounk, "where the light touches it doesn't hurt the ground at all."

Pinta laughed. "And here I was hoping it would dig up some of the ground in the fields for us."

The others laughed too but Mounk thought it sounded tainted with the anxiety of seeing something powerful for the first time; they didn't know if they should be afraid.

Cristy Zinn

Mounk was no longer watching with the five. He pulled himself away and slipped out through the door, his brow furrowed with purpose.

Njort knew what it was. She didn't know how. It was as though the idea were an implanted memory that did not belong to her. The word *storm* sprang into her mind unbidden and she knew it was right. When the second terraforming attempt had failed, the planet was wracked with storms and when they had abated, a newly formed landscape left behind, they were never seen again. It was too expensive to try again and the Nognagel had to settle for the paraterraformed cities within the domes spread out over the planet.

Njort had never seen a storm for herself but somewhere in her memory, she felt that nothing good could come from them.

She watched as Mounk slipped out the door with something on his mind. When he headed for the outer garden she ran to cut him off. He looked down at her in surprise, his pale brows rising.

"Excuse me little one," he said.

Njort shook her head, pointing outside and crossing her arms in front of her in an adamant 'no'. A panic had risen in her, deep and desperate.

"What's wrong?" he asked, but his eyes were already off her and glancing out the dome, to where the latest lightening strike hit.

Njort grabbed his hand and he jerked away, surprised by the alien contact. When his eyes met hers, she shook her head again, wishing desperately that she could find her voice from somewhere inside her.

"Don't be afraid, little one. It's only weather. I just want to have a look," he said. There was a lusty look in his eyes. "I think it came to see the treasure."

Njort closed her eyes in frustration, squeezing his hand again, shaking her head.

Five Sets of Hands

He did not listen. Her hold on him was nothing like the other four. He slipped out the door just as a bolt of lightning struck the frame of the dome and electrified every inch of metal in the place. Mounk's hand, still clasping the door's handle, absorbed the electric overload with a horrifying sizzle. His eyes widened and his pale skin turned a sickly purple as he crumpled to the ground, his hand half melted onto the handle.

The four must have sensed their loss because they were there before Njort could make her way to him. They pushed her aside and crowded around him, their keening blending with the vicious storm outside. Neither one abated for many hours.

It did not rain. The lightning bearing clouds swept over the Borderland, leaving little to show for their presence but a death. The remaining four mourned Mounk as though he had been an arm or a leg. Njort watched them with a heavy heart, wondering how much her voice might have saved them if only she had one. She felt Mounk's death almost as keenly as they did, seeing his dying face in her dreams and smelling his burning skin as she woke.

Like others she had seen before them, the absence sent the remaining four into sickness. Njort knew it wouldn't be long before they gave up entirely—the medics had already left them to their deaths. But Njort couldn't. She visited the medical centre daily, stroking their hands and foreheads with cool sponges and helping to feed them. In their various states of grief, they did not resist her small, gentle hands.

It was late in the night when Raafi remembered the treasure. Her throat was raw with disuse and her tongue thick with thirst. At her feet lay the small, curled figure of Njort. Raafi kicked gently and Njort sat up, sleepy eyes glancing around the room to find who had woken her.

"Njort," called Raafi in a hoarse whisper.

Njort stared at her in surprise, a delighted smile on her lips.

"Please," Raafi said, trying to raise her voice to be heard.

Njort shuffled towards Raafi, so that she was close-by, inclining her head to listen.

"I need my treasure," Raafi said.

Njort frowned in confusion and Raafi's heart fell. It had been foolish for her to expect the girl to remember; what significance would it have to her after all? Then suddenly, Njort's mouth popped open and her face lit up. She clasped Raafi's hand in her own and nodded her head emphatically before jumping off the cot and disappearing.

Raafi let her head fall back on her pillow and closed her eyes. That small effort had drained her. Now that she was fully conscious, she felt the ache of Mounk's death again and her chest grew heavy with the pain of the memory. She wondered how long she had slept and then longed to go back into that oblivion. In the corner of her eye, she could see the prostrate bodies of the others, just as sapped by their grief as she was.

Then, Njort was at her side, prying open her hands and placing the cool disk in her palm.

"You found it," whispered Raafi.

Njort nodded and put her small hands around Raafi's closed one.

"I wish it had saved us," Raafi whispered. "I wish we had discovered what it meant before..."

Njort looked curiously at the disk so Raafi placed it in the girl's small hands. Njort looked up at her as though she expected a rebuke.

"It's alright, Njort. It's no use to us now, you may as well look at it," said Raafi with a defeated sigh.

Njort turned the disk over again and again, running her fingers over the repeated pattern on the three circles, her brows knitting together intensely as if she were trying to unlock a puzzle.

Five Sets of Hands

"Little one, do you really think *you* could figure it out when none of us could?" Raafi asked.

Njort sighed and shook her head mournfully. Her shoulders slumped and she let her head drop onto Raafi's chest. Raafi felt the child's body heave with silent crying and wondered how it was that this small enemy felt such empathy for them.

Raafi brought her hand to the child's head and stroked her strange black hair. When Njort lifted her head she had a strange look of hope. She glanced down at Raafi's hand and then looked over the other three stretched out in the nearby cots. She jumped down again and began an enormous effort to push them, moving them into a haphazard circle, with their heads close together. When she began to link their hands, Raafi understood what she was trying to do.

"It won't work with only four, Njort," Raafi said. Her voice broke with despair but Njort ignored her. "Little one, please. Don't do this. There has to be five sets of hands."

Njort continued her work until she reached Raafi again. The four Wuntya were linked, not letting go of each other's hand in an unconscious need to be connected. Njort paused at Raafi and looked her deeply in the eyes. She smiled apologetically, her hand still holding Cronje beside her and then took hold of Raafi's hand.

There was an instant response from the four. Raafi's eyes widened and she gasped as their link was re-established.

Njort was only a child. She had not lived a long life and being mostly alone and silent, she had not had much experience other than the occasional abuse from her Nognagel brothers and the wariness of the Wuntya. Nevertheless, she knew that this was not an ordinary feeling coursing through her chest.

Through both hands ran a current that felt oddly like a piece of string tying her to the others. She could *feel* them as she had never felt another person, and she could sense who they were; who they *really* were. She could feel Pinta's strength, Cronje's wisdom, Nald's trust, and Raafi's kindness. And somehow she knew they could feel her faith.

Raafi was staring at her with her large pale eyes. "This is not possible," she breathed.

The others seemed to need no further convincing; they were already beginning to speak their blessings. Njort had once watched a digital re-creation of the ancient Earth theory of growing nerves that could repair broken connections by acting like tentacles that reattached themselves to the spinal nerves. That was what she imagined in her mind's eye when she heard the blessings spoken, and they connected like old friends.

Then came the part of the ritual that Njort had never been able to hear; they began telling stories of their home, they were remembering. They whispered about the trees and fields, about what their homes would look like, how they would see family and reunite with their rulers. Their words were so evocative that even though there were many she had never heard before, and could not interpret, she could *see* Wunta in her mind. Light, foreign, and beautiful. No Nognagel words would sufficiently describe it.

When they eventually let go of Njort's hand the connection was not severed as she had imagined it would be. Instead, there was a lingering tingle in her fingertips and her heart quickened when she looked into the eyes of her new friends.

"How is this possible?" Pinta asked. "She is Nognagel."

"It's never been done before... perhaps it's always been possible," Nald said, looking at Njort as though she were seeing into her soul rather than just her face.

Njort nodded enthusiastically, wanting to grab up their hands again.

"It shouldn't be possible," said Cronje, "and yet, here we are, *connected* to a Nognagel."

Five Sets of Hands

"They are not as we thought," said Pinta. "*You* are not what we thought, are you little one?"

Njort shook her head but then she suddenly remembered her original purpose for joining them in the Communal again—she had wanted to wake them from their stupor so they could figure out the treasure. She held up the disk, lifting her hand high into the air, and shook it around.

"You know how it works?" asked Nald. "You know what to do with it?"

Njort shook her head but pointed emphatically towards the doors and the corridor that led to the other Wuntyan quarters.

"You want us to ask the others?" Nald asked.

Njort nodded and clapped her hands together excitedly.

"No," said Cronje. Everyone turned their eyes on him in surprise. "We cannot use it. It's not safe."

Pinta narrowed her eyes at him. "You know what it is?"

Cronje nodded reluctantly. "I recognised it as a Transposer the first time Raafi showed us."

"And you never said anything?" asked Pinta, her voice breaking. "You never told us that there was a way out of here?"

"Because we would not survive it," he said sternly."Who knows how old this device is? It probably came with the first Wuntyans. Do you honestly think it could transpose us to Wunta after all this time?"

Njort had never seen them angry with one another, their faces challenging and hard. After such closeness, it did not sit well with her.

"Who are you to decide that? Being dead may be better than this," said Pinta.

Raafi put her hand on both of theirs and looked deeply at them. "We've kept this treasure to ourselves for too long, friends. It is not our decision alone to make."

"Where would it transpose us, Raafi?" asked Cronje. "There is no ship waiting for us in orbit and Wunta is light years away. It is not fair to give the others false hope."

Cristy Zinn

"How many Wuntya are here?" Nald asked suddenly. She was standing a little way off, looking at the door in a distracted way.

"Thousands," said Cronje.

"How many fives?"

The room went so still that Njort felt as though she were also holding her breath. The current in the air seemed to change direction and understanding lit their eyes one by one.

"Hundreds," said Cronje softly. "Yes. I understand. It might not have worked a hundred years ago but now..."

The others were nodding, lost in thought. Njort tugged on Raafi's arm and raised her hands in a silent question.

"We're going to go home, Njort," she said softly. "All of us."

"The more of us there are, the more powerful the device," said Nald. "With so many, surely we will make it all the way home."

"That, or die trying," said Cronje but even his cynicism was tainted with hope now.

At sunset, the Wuntya did not go back to their rooms. Instead, they walked out into the large domed garden where Mounk had died; it was as close to outside as they could get. They made their Communal circles but this time, each circle integrated with another, surrounding the Transposer disk Raafi had found. Njort saw Raafi and her three standing apart from the forming pattern, listening at the door for the sound of boots in case the guards decided to pay them a visit.

Nald was crying. "Is there no way?" she was asking Raafi.

"How? There has to be five sets of hands, Nald. Our four might diminish everything and then we don't know what would happen."

"Then use her," Nald cried, pointing at Njort who was in the doorway, half in shadow and silent as always.

Five Sets of Hands

All four turned to look at Njort. Njort could not tell what they were thinking but she felt her connection to them still. She yearned for it. She nodded.

"But I don't know what will happen to her," said Raafi. "She might not be able to survive Wunta, let alone the journey. She wasn't made for it."

"It seems she wasn't made for this place either. Perhaps she was made for us," said Cronje.

As usual, the weight of his opinion carried them all and as the sun was almost gone, he grabbed little Njort to form their circle, and they integrated into the last of the Wuntyan fives.

They heard shouting down the corridor, curious at first but escalating into alarm. Boots stomped down the corridor, the sound of aluminium batons smacking against the walls, drawing nearer and nearer. The guards were coming.

Njort looked over her shoulder, to the faces of the confused guards. This strange pattern was nonsense to them, but being out of the ordinary, they decided it must be some kind of rebellion. They descended on the quiet circles of Wuntyan, raising their batons, ready to fight, warnings on their lips.

And then their enemies were gone. Only Njort stood in the domed garden looking victoriously into the stars, oblivious to the chaos that followed.

Even now, years later, Njort cannot explain what happened. The Wuntya were quietly there and then they were not. She will never know the outcome of their journey; whether they survived or died. She likes to imagine them alive on their planet, reuniting with lost family and enjoying their own air.

What she can say is that she feels their loss very deeply because even though she is not Wuntya, they are the closest thing she ever had to family. She was a fifth in their five sets of hands, and even that one day had great impact on her.

The Wuntya were not ungrateful for her small part though, they left her a gift, a marvellous gift as mysterious as their vanishing. They left her a voice.

Much happened in those hundreds of years that the Wuntya had been slaves on Mars. The atrocities were too great to be ignored. But the Wuntya knew that the Nognagel would forget quickly, that they would find another race to enslave. Many have already tried to enslave Njort for the things she is saying, they do not like to be confronted with their own evil.

Njort is the Wuntya's voice of memory, their living memory that spreads through the Nognagel like a miracle. Though some refuse to believe such things, there are some who are enraptured by her story and continue to record it so that no one will forget.

Cristy Zinn lives in Durban where she is a graphic designer by day and speculative fiction writer by night. Though she has won several SF writing competitions, her story in AfroSF will be her first published work. You can see more of her unpublished work at cristyzinn.com where she also interviews writers and blogs about writing.

New Mzansi

Ashley Jacobs

A bass-line pounded from a nearby nightclub invading the window on the fourth floor of a decrepit high-rise in downtown Tshwane, South Africa. The inner city, Sunnyside, had a way of blurring night into day with its perma-blanket of noise and light. KG brought himself to his feet from the haggard red carpet doubling as his mattress.

KG glanced out the window as he grabbed his phone from the windowsill. The opposite flats were barely visible and lights like a fairy town pierced the veil laid down by fires and industrial pollution during the political turmoil of the late second decade of the century. The low-level incandescence of the streets below was a comforting sight to one of their own.

KG flicked out his phone from his jeans pocket on his way out. The edges of the thin, transparent polymer just shorter than his palm glowed green indicating a new message.

<check you soon bra? Lion>

"Let's first check my feeds from last night," KG muttered, downloading a song sent to him from a local philosopher of the streets—the communication medium of the new era of renegade dilettantes the world over.

<Streaming 'Science of Inequality' by S'fiso"...>

<Found the Higgs boson, did it prove anything?

Fix inequality? Did it improve anything?>

The steps down the wooden stairs dropping off to street level once again blended into an eclectic mix of philosophy, science, and hip-hop, in KG's mind. He slid on his Breather and popped up his hoodie before stepping out. Vapour whipped across the pavement, and music grew louder with each step. Both warmed him up to the day ahead.

Bright holographic screens blinked and scrolled at eyelevel on KG's left, scrounging off nearby social media accounts wirelessly and displaying them for the world to see. The power arcs for the screens became known as trajectories for their ability to throw freeware opinions across the streets in real-time. KG wasn't entirely against the whole movement, and besides, he had a few opinions of his own...

The nearby trajectory latched onto his personal account as he made his way across the road and scrolled one of his notes across Skinner Street Corner.

<Screw X-Cell>

<Tshwane, political capital of 'Mzansi'—the nation of South Africa. The City takes on a new artificial bloom. Instead of the Jacaranda trees that used to brighten up the city on spring mornings, we now have X-Cell on every street corner. Weren't those trees an invasive alien species that choked up all the local plants over the years?>

The thought that he should probably reply to Lion's message was what brought his phone back to life. The sheet illuminated with auto-annotation across his Wernicke's Lobe Link and sent his deciphered neurochemistry across X-Cell's network.

<On my way mfwethu...>

He still felt alone in the slums compressed with locals—along with Nigerians, Indians, and the odd remaining white person—gathered together unwillingly like the ingredients of a pungent atchar and polony roll. At least the one friend he did have was expecting him.

"*Heita,*" KG greeted under his breath, pushing his chin further into the dark hoodie to conceal his eyes, the guy just another makwerekwere, foreigner, he thought.

One of the local girls was being chatted up by the guy, posing with her hips tilted, voice lilted, and heels stilted, whilst playing with her red plastic hair extensions—

luminous like a mane on a lioness. The guy looked nervous as he scanned the nearby alleyway and couldn't hide his intentions towards her or his fear of the South African dark.

The last trajectory before KG's one-stop back alleyway hooked onto him.

<What is up with these masks?>

<It still looks strange to see people actually wearing the Breathers. It seems no one in Tshwane wants to die except through violence and stupidity, and besides the masks keep the vapour and extremely drug-resistant tuberculosis from damaging lungs better left for inhaling the latest in chemical fashion, 'Strike'.>

The back entrance to where Lion stayed lit up the dim alleyway that formed a cleft in the vertical amalgamation of oddly shaped apartments and shacks. Both forms of accommodation liberally adorned with illegally erected graffiti trajectories. The asphalt hemmed in by the opposite wall that depicted Mandela sporting a Breather: 'LONG WALK TO FREEDOM' tagged underneath.

He turned into the familiar doorway and pushed through the Aggression Scanner into 'Labuschagne's Books'. Mr. Labuschagne, working behind the till, caught a glimpse of KG as he slipped into the store.

KG looked up at the dusty shelf of books he thought no one would ever buy. He considered the grey-haired man benignly insane to stay behind and open his personal collection of books, DVDs, and stray forms of data, to a city that lived to extract survival from the lives of easy prey.

"KG, Lion's in the spare room next to the kitchen, told me you were definitely coming..." Labuschagne said.

"Thanks Mr. Labs," KG answered stiffly, offended that his loyalty would be questioned.

"Don't walk away yet! Where's my last copy of Steve Biko? Books aren't like your bloody trajectories and feedslates. There's only one left in the whole of the province!"

KG gave half-smile. A different and peculiar sense of duty clearly bound Labuschagne to stay when people had flocked out of the country during the journo-dubbed '2023 Exile'—after which Mzansi had curled inwards like a shongololo millipede protecting itself.

"Thanks for the free books, history lessons and stuff Mr. Labs, but seriously I've got to get to Lion..." KG rattled off to evade more questions.

"Always in a hurry, ok, go see him," Mr. Labuschagne said in a warm and hopeful manner.

KG knew Labuschagne thought of him as possible successor to Labuschagne's book kingdom, but he wasn't in any hurry to claim it.

KG swore when he took off the Breather to see better in the spare room. "Should never make promises to help people that I actually have to keep," he mumbled.

The room's trajectory threw a music video on the wall across the room from where Lion turned fitfully. KG had made the promise that he'd help Lion get his meds if the need ever arose, in exchange for staying in Lion's father's apartment block for free. It had all been easy, until now.

Barely anyone KG knew had a university degree. A formal education wasn't the roadblock to success it used to be, a curious mind could be enough. The kind of mind that left KG feeling emotionally detached as he noted how gaunt Lion's temples had become; how Lion's rapid breathing made his neck muscles strain almost pulsatile underneath the white vest covering the prominent assembly of his ribcage. The vapid reality of the portrait in front of him sublimated into comprehension and drained heavily into the pit of his stomach.

<My friend Lion>

<When you're born with HIV you're expected to live the life of a saint, and that's pretty much what you have done. Lion, so wildly dubbed for his habit of evergreen optimism

New Mzansi

(read annoying) but if you asked him, he's named after the brand of matches his dad used to navigate the shack he was conceived in.>

Every year these kids go for the Breath of Life to re-kindle a dead immune system. They cram themselves into a ward and wait for someone to open the gas canisters. Fifteen minutes later the nano-particulate inhalant has given them another year. Locals here call it the Mula, from the Zulu verb pephumula that means to breath. Conveniently, it also means hard cash on the streets—mula the icy currency of living.

Maybe drug-resistant TB had finally found him, mass-murderer of the nation stabbing lungs all over South Africa. KG ran his fingers over the grate of the mask in his hand, covering the 40-nanometre filtration slits he'd spray-painted his initials on last week. It felt cold and heavy in his hands, but being able to speak properly to Lion was worth it.

I'll take my chances. Doing this won't make it onto the social feeds anyway—boring. HIV is a boring way to die if you've seen it happen so many times, KG thought.

"Lion, brother, what's wrong with you?" KG finally bought himself to ask.

His friend's eyes were half-open and glazed from the battle for air against his thick cough. "Bra, they want double the cash for the Mula now..." Lion answered.

"Seriously? How long have you been like this then?"

"Had an appointment for last month... Been trying to get the cash but I've been feeling a bit crap recently you know."

KG let out a stunted laugh. When death becomes common it also becomes easier to deal with. "Alright friend, let's go get you that Mula."

KG knew Lion didn't want to be carried all the way to the city centre so he paced ahead of him pensively. Enough eyes pawed on you here to make anyone grow self-conscious, even if those eyes had fallen on a hundred other hopeless cases in the same day. He wondered how Lion was handling the attention, but realised that he was probably the one who felt more embarrassed about making the journey. Awnings of corrugated iron sheltered cowering old women sitting with their stewing pots, surveying the streets as fires burnt on each corner, and music clattered in from every direction. Street vendors sold data bundles and pap meal from mobile stalls, competing with each other using faded digital displays.

The gravel itself was strewn with history, and as they walked, he caught a glimpse of an election poster from before Nelson Mandela's death: WE PROMISE JOBS AND NO CRIME IN TSHWANE. Lion must have noticed as well because he let out a weak "ha", which transformed into yet another fleck of blood hastily wiped on the back of his jeans.

Somewhere a screechy feminine voice jumped out at them. "We voted this year to finally get rid of trash like your friend." KG did his best to brush off the offense as he walked, but eventually twisted around and glared.

Tshwane Central had sunken subterranean roots as if a giant earthworm had scoured Sunnyside for necrotic vegetation. Tunnels sprung up from Gautrain extensions as a way for the existing businesses to expand in the congested city centre. The eastern suburbs of Tshwane were visible in the distance; sleek ivory towers surrounded by digital security like moats that sealed in the surrogate slices of Europe, complete with one mall per sector. The actual tunnels, although similar to those found in cities like New York, London, and Paris, doubled as home for many of the HIV orphans, and a disposal site for political excretion. KG looped his arm around Lion's waist as they descended the stairs into Sammy Marks Square, Entrance 14 underneath the old State Theatre. Lion mutely leaned on his shoulder for support.

The stairs gave way to a wide hall yawning at least a kilometre in, with exits snaking away ahead. The walls were smooth, layered concrete illuminated via trajectories scrolling 'DJ SBU TONIGHT' and 'CAGE DISKI LIVE. COME TO ZAKE'S BAR'.

They were instantly welcomed by the panoply of Africa's finest fong kong, Chinese knock-off wares, being peddled from discreet curtained-off stalls filling the market sprawl. A tide of odours rolled towards the entrance where they were standing, carrying the surf of sweat, spice, and smoke from the shisa nyama barbeques crackling between the stalls. Infectious drumming came from the troupes of tunnel dancers fused together in hypnotic concerto as their bodies shook to grinding afro-house. The market was bustling with people browsing for bargain technology or clothes, its edges lined with friends eating and reading each other's social feeds displayed above the public tables.

"Hello my friend! You... ah, you want this? You want Strike?" asked a towering giant in ornate purple and green with skin like soot. He pushed himself into KG's path and reached into his coat to bring out a packet of yellow powder.

"Doctor Zingi got the best Strike for you!" Zingi said, leaning down and whispering spittle into KG's face.

Bastards, KG thought, he's like a hijacker sitting behind a bush. He tucked his head further into the hoodie to avoid the vitriol in his eyes earning him trouble. Looping his arm around Lion's waist, he pulled away from the good doctor.

"You know what the drug *Tik* did to the Cape Flats Lion..." KG said into Lion's ear.

<I hate Strike>

<Nothing against the tsotsis huddled next to the fires using Strike to bore their way out of Tshwane through their own skulls, but I hate Strike. I hate that it seems to be the only way out of here.>

Strike, the drug Efavirenz, was originally used as part of the most effective HIV treatment regimens when the old style of treatment was at its peak. Even though doctors knew it could cause madness in rare circumstances. If you ground it up, singed it with a match, and inhaled the smoke your mind would shoot off into the sky. The drug was abandoned after the influx of nano-inhalants, yet expired surplus still made its way into places like Sammy Marks Tunnel by demand.

As they moved further down the cold tunnels, the density of the shops and bars lining the walls lessened. Several children were idling around fires lit in barrels. They stared at Lion, figuring they probably shouldn't ask for money this time, given the current visible circumstances.

"Bra... you give money to those kids and you only donate... enough... to separately buy the lighter, bottle, and Strike," Lion expelled, another speckle of red escaping onto his chin.

"Lion, I know what'll make you feel better!" KG said, as he figured a way to lift Lion's spirits and assuage his growing guilt for not being there to help sooner.

The chicken joint they collapsed into was one of at least twenty branches in Sunnyside. Tattered red couches belied the novelty of the transparent service chutes lining the circular walls.

Three Cage Diski players, shirtless mounds of muscle, smirked at them from the opposite booth. The table lit up as KG sat down next to Lion, revealing a touchscreen menu underneath the congealed greasy memoir of previous customers. The batter-wrapped drumstick next to CHICKEN FEAST 2 did an awkward jive under KG's finger.

"Hey, what's a skinny laaitie like you doing ordering two pieces? You sure you don't want that free toy with the kiddies meal?" said one of the Cage Diski players who was wearing a cap with the baby blue colour of the provincial team. He's big enough to be a defender KG thought, before he realised whose attention he'd caught.

"Stuff off man, can't you see he's sick?" KG answered, after a moment of calculating risk against loss of dignity.

New Mzansi

"Do you know who I am small boys? I'm the Mamba! I'm the king of the Loftus Stadium Cage!" Mamba shouted back across the room. He extended his sculpted arm, pointing to the trajectory.

"Sorry, never heard of you, I guess you Cage Diski guys who aren't good enough for mixed-martial arts just aren't popular enough yet?" KG replied feeling offended on Lion's behalf.

Mamba returned to his bucket of chicken in front of him, his ego deflated.

KG knew of Mamba; renowned for his ability to slam opponents on the way to the goalmouth, cheered for his wrestling ability, but derided for not knowing what to do with the ball. The trajectory was showing a promo of Mamba entering Loftus Rugby Stadium alone, the pride of Tshwane. The arena was square-shaped with spectators in stands peering steeply down onto the cage's astroturf. Cage Diski was mixed martial arts combined with the local love of Diski soccer into a gladiator sport, merely a lion or two short of its ancient Coliseum counterpart.

KG placed his phone by the empty meal carton waiting for the map to stream while he wiped his hands and watched Lion gag down the last of his chips. He'd hoped the meal would cheer up Lion and give him some strength to make it through the next part of his plan.

"How far are we from the clinic?" Lion asked.

"Don't worry about that Lion, you'll make it there," KG replied.

"You don't understand, they don't just give the Mula without money there... it's expensive. It's like someone stole one of the private hospitals and left it there to hide."

"Don't worry gazi, I know this girl that can help us. She owes me. Finish your chips, take it easy."

The smallest of the three Cage Diski players shouted to KG, as he hoisted Lion off the couch. "Howzit brother! Forgive Mamba here; they pay him to be huge and a bit stupid. Us zinger wingers are small so we must be smart hey." The other player tapped his skull in solidarity, above his cauliflower-ear badge of apprenticeship in the business of pain. "Lekker Muay Thai and shooting skills hey! Take care of your mate bro!" he added as KG and Lion walked out the sliding doors. It was good to hear some optimism.

By now, Lion was heaving from somewhere deep within his chest and his forehead was searing hot. An attenuated gagging noise made KG glance at Lion, who met his gaze with wide eyes expectant of some great hope to appear. What KG wanted was to be as far away from the situation as possible. He wanted to wake up and realise he had all of his life to himself with none of the weight of another human life on his shoulders. But finally caring, finally risking his heart and mind for something, made him feel alive. Standing up to the Mamba for Lion's sake meant that he could do this, he could get Lion the Mula.

A memory jarred his thoughts as they waited for a robo-taxi to take them out of Sunnyside. He recalled a pavement lined with dirty shopping bags, a copy of the Sun newspaper splayed open, and sun beating the street like a Zulu dancer's feet. He was a little boy watching his father bellowing into a taxi rank in Soweto. Fat taxi mammas were about their business cramming into the box-cart Toyota sixteen-seaters. Vagrants gazed at the familiar sight of the politician-turned-preacher, loved by some, hated by most. That was the official day of the roll-out of the Amended South African Constitution and the street was starting to fill with supporters that CNN would later dub as rioters and looters.

KG let the memory fade.

Outside the taxi window, the riptide Tshwane wind was now heralding a coming Highveld storm, the passion-orange sky contrasting puffy charcoal harbingers tumbling onto the cityscape from the mountainous Magaliesberg region. As he helped Lion out of the taxi, the air felt ominous around KG, simultaneously cold and humid with distant thunder rumbling towards them.

New Mzansi

They swam through multi-coloured reflective beads that made up the door to Ubuntu in downtown Stanza Bopape Street. Ubuntu was one of the older cafés in the flattened east area of the metropolis, located just before the city thinned into isolated suburbia leaning off super-highways.

The entrance foyer was dim and lined with couches and bookshelves on the three opposite walls. A current of coffee and blues swirled gently around them, inviting them into the main area divided by more beaded partitions for privacy. In the centre of the room were touchscreen tables with 8x8 grids and holographic chess pieces linked to trajectories broadcasting the games and social blurbs around the café. Staccato bursts of applause came from behind the furthest partition indicating a tournament was in progress. KG scrunched his eyelids searching for Pumi. She'd know what to do, he hoped.

<Nompumelelo Luthuli>

<She wears all black with black nails and a slightly charred soul that hides a heart soft and gooey. The garish neon pink Breather she uses is just to spite the rest of her apostate appearance. Pumi is the Cloud Storage where I keep my understanding of ethics behind her impregnable dreadlocked firewall.>

Pumi was wedged into her favourite corner with a purple cushion, mug of roobois tea, and the backside of a transparent feedslate constructing a fortress to dissuade interested gamers. Not that she minded engaging in the odd conversation, as KG well knew, it's just that she did mind the odd idiot who tried—they normally had about twenty seconds to say something profound before she'd place them in her 'non-stimulating pile'.

When she saw KG she asked, "KG, you seen this yet?"

Pumi held up the transparent slate and switched it to reverse display so that he could read the headline: NOVEL VIRUS OUTBREAK SPREADS TO CAPE TOWN FLOOD DISTRICT.

"Three thousand dead already," she stated.

Ashley Jacobs

"You can't put work away can you? Probably feel sorry for all those people you'll never even meet," KG hastily responded.

A split-second motion of her eyes to seek solace behind her dreads covering her face meant he'd hit home. Her arms folded around the pinstripe-patterned trench-coat firm enough to crease the tough fabric. "Well between the two of us has someone has to actually give a-" Pumi began.

KG interrupted. "Look, you're doing a good job with the HIV counselling here in Sunnyside... for all you know there's someone just like you working the outbreak, so it's going to be ok, but only for those *bergies* who've learn to swim hey."

She lowered her gaze at him as her arms slowly unfolded. Her posture softened and she placed her mug of rooibos tea on an unoccupied chess slate. They both watched the steam dissipate from the mug as her precious tea edged away from optimal drinking temperature. With that, KG knew he'd made it into the 'you have two minutes' pile.

"Ok Pumi, I need your help... It's my friend Lion. I need to get him into your clinic's ward for the Mula. Mahala, for free. And he doesn't have much time, he's in the bathroom now, but I'm worried about what will happen if he doesn't get the Mula," KG said.

"What about your whole only-looking-out-for-yourself thing you're always on about?" Pumi replied, sounding sceptical.

"Ja well... maybe I do care about Lion," KG trailed off. "I had a plan to use your pass to break into the clinic and get him the Mula myself."

"KG, I'm just the neurocounsellor, and I'm not even supposed to be there today... So you're planning to break into a clinic and steal the treatment, isn't that both illegal and stupid?"

"There isn't another way... At least, I can't think of one."

New Mzansi

"KG... What if you get caught? The head of the clinic, Dr. Singh, will kick my ass and then fire me. I actually like my job you know."

"You like sticking people into scan chambers and stuffing around in their heads? What happened to just sitting down and talking like the old days you know?"

"Hey, did you read that article I sent you about the neurobiological approach compared to traditional counselling, was it too confusing for you?"

Lion staggered out from the bathroom interrupting the argument. His jeans were dirty, crusted and ludicrously oversized. KG saw her shift her gaze to Lion eyeing the holes in his tattered vest with disbelief, moisture showed in her eyes.

"Alright, before I change my mind, here's my ID key," Pumi finally said.

KG softened his posture, which had grown uncomfortably tense, grateful that she'd risk her job for him, actually more for Lion who she hadn't even met before.

"The main entrance has credit analysis, so you're going to have to sneak around the back to the staff entrance," she added.

Pumi helped them to the entrance and watched as they reattached their Breathers before stepping outside. The now brick-coloured sky assaulted KG's eyes with flashes of lightning bolts in the distance. KG said goodbye silently, the two locking eyes for a second. Pumi let out a pained sigh and turned on her heels back towards her corner. KG wondered, as he got into the taxi, whether her tea was still warm enough to drink or not.

The path to the clinic was inside a fenced-off area in downtown Sunnyside. A pervading odour of caked blood and vomit came from the people queuing for the main entrance. Friends and families tended to the sick as they lay waiting for access to the physicians inside the clinic. Dr. Singh's face flickered on the display above the clinic.

Ashley Jacobs

"Dr. Singh's Clinic is the best place to get your treatment. We offer a comprehensive HIV and TB program where for just 10 000 Rands you can have your HIV cured for the year!" He had a Bollywood quaff perched above eyes glinting with deception and a moulded white-tooth smile. "Nowhere else in this city can you get this special offer and if you bring your friends you can even get half-price for next year!"

Who is this man, KG wondered. By now, the whole day was starting to piss KG off. The queue stretching ahead towards the mesmerising neon Clinic sign made the voyage seem endless. Mr. Labuschagne had told him how the healthcare crisis had gotten so bad hospitals would have signs saying: estimated waiting time nine hours please be patient. But what that must have felt like hadn't occurred to him until now.

Closer to the entrance he could see walls garrisoning off a single front gate. The walls were made of solid concrete, bleak totalitarian regime style, making a large crescent that disappeared off into darkness on either side. It was lit by a row of streetlights and light raindrops from the earlier storm were visible in the soft glow.

Feed trajectories ran health education info on either side of the gate reflecting on two guards stationed at the clinic entrance.

<What is The Breath?>

<The Breath, or Mula as you know it, is a particular form of medicine based on a class of drugs known as HIV Integration Inhibitors. Scientists from the University of Cape Town discovered it after an outbreak of Avian Flu in 2025 when aerosolised nano-antivirals were distributed all around the world to combat the pandemic. The Mula was created when it was realised that the anti-HIV drugs would work better in the new nano-particulate form and could be given to whole wards at a time. Our special formula is up to three times as effective at increasing CD4 cell counts as before!>

New Mzansi

<Why must you pay for The Breath every year?>

<Of course everyone would like there to be a permanent cure, but the Mula only suppresses the virus until the effect of the medicine wears off. Without coming to us every year, the virus will re-emerge, this time far quicker, and may kill you. Please do not forget to make your appointment for next year, and ask us about our specials for your friends and family!>

KG picked Lion up to get him through to the entrance of the clinic. However, he hesitated as he remembered the last words of his father: 'We were given freedom by our mothers and fathers, and we have given them back the gift of sickness, apathy, and crime! We have inherited corruption from our leaders, but if we allow it to continue then is the corruption not us? What we need now is a new Mzansi!' Directly afterwards, a panga struck the back of his father's skull and his body rushed to greet his shadow on that dusty street.

One of the guards looked down on KG. "You don't look like you and your friend can afford Dr. Singh's Clinic? You sure the credit scanner will let you through?" He asked, and was not angry, merely quizzical with well-disguised concern KG realised. The guard let them through the metal gate leading to the main entrance of the Clinic.

They came to the side entrance, fortunately shielded from the guards by a large yellow dumpster branded with a DR. SINGH CLINIC sign above a biohazard logo. KG held Pumi's ID key to the scanner at the single door. 'WELCOME NEUROCOUNSELLOR LUTHULI' scrolled across the door display.

They pushed through into a long corridor top-lit by swirling blue lights. KG's heart raced, and Lion clutched onto him. The bright blue UV lights on the ceiling used to kill airborne micro-organisms were disorientating. The only sound was the faint plod of KG's worn shoes and the sweeping of Lion's red sneakers across the smooth floor. The clinic corridor that led to BREATH - WARD ONE was sparsely decorated and lined with linoleum benches punctuated by plastic plants. The ceilings were still lit by trajectory feeds even though this ward wasn't in use at night.

"Almost there friend, this was easier than what I thought..." KG whispered to Lion.

The ward had one entrance with an ID feed linked to credit status on it. Pumi's card automatically registered her presence: COUNSELLOR LUTHULI, YOUR HIV STATUS IS NEGATIVE. ARE YOU SURE YOU WANT TO PROCEED TO THE WARD?

KG pushed 'yes' on the decontamination chamber door, which opened into a blinding blue light. For a second, he held Lion and gazed upwards, blinded by the spotlights, deafened by the roaring negative pressure vacuum. He felt caught up in a transcendent moment as if awaiting a triumphant reincarnation on the other side.

"Good evening, can I help you?" a voice from inside the ward resonated.

KG made out the visage of Dr. Singh pushing his fingers together, smiling with only the left side of his mouth before straightening out the cuff of his grey suit.

"I believe you two will need me to activate the four gas canisters you see in the corners, yes?"

"Look Dr. Singh, I know what this looks like... All I want is to get my friend the Mula just this once... I think he's going to die if he doesn't get it tonight," KG stammered.

"Let me ask you this, young man, do you think he's the only one? Do you think this is the first time someone weaves me such a sad tale of terrible tragedy? This clinic is the only thing that survived the collapse of the National Health Initiative in the heart of Tshwane for a reason."

KG was silent, left defenceless. Dr. Singh continued, "Every day the desperate come here after having their Wernicke's Lobe Links cut out for hard cash, or after selling their Gautrain passes; anything to get into Dr. Singh's clinic!"

He could see Dr. Singh seated in an oversized chair behind a luminescent control station.

"You know what we are here? We are the new plague doctors, and these tanks are my precious fresh leeches. Do you think we have enough for every piece of rubbish like your friend here?"

KG felt a sudden loss of weight on his shoulder as the grate in the centre of the ward clanged. He looked down to see Lion sprawled, staring upwards with a frantic look in his eyes. A trickle of blood made its serpentine way to a flawlessly reflective black shoe. Humiliated, KG grabbed Lion's hand, squeezed it and pulled him back onto his knees in front of Dr. Singh.

"Dr. Singh... Please..." KG managed to ask, bending down to gather Lion into his arms.

"Let me ask you this, do you really think the Mula, as you scum call it, really only works for one year? A cure of mine that only works for one year? Ha! Saving your friend's life here will change nothing; I don't even think it would change one of you kids for the better."

KG felt sick and dizzy taking in Dr. Singh's words, which struck him as horrific but close to the logic he might have employed if he were in those shiny black shoes. With that, Dr. Singh walked calmly past them as the ward lights flashed red and the air was cauterised by blaring alarm horns. KG loaded Lion onto his shoulders, put his head down, and ran down the corridor to the main entrance. The guard who spoke to him earlier made a move towards him but only pretended to reach out to stop them. Outside the clinic, the storm had arrived in full force.

"KG..." Mr. Labuschagne gasped as KG tumbled through the door with Lion.

"I tried Mr. Labs..." KG choked, still breathless from the journey.

Ashley Jacobs

"It's ok my boy, get some rest. I'll take care of Lion for now."

The sun finally awoke KG sleeping in Mr. Labuschagne's store. Lion... he thought, and the previous night's events came back to him.

KG stumbled downstairs grabbing onto the banister to stop from falling. Mr. Labuschagne was kneeling next to the bed. The happy cartoon figures on the bed sheet contrasted Lion's wide, white eyes staring back at him, his face pulled gaunt and sucked of all life. A deep rift widened in the depths of KG's soul when his eyes met with Mr. Labuschagne's and locked there in fragile horror. He crashed out the store knocking shelves to the ground.

Days later, the Skinner Street trajectory hooked onto a young man walking through Sunnyside next to a girl with dreadlocks.
<New Mzansi>
<What we need is...>

Ashley Jacobs is a young South African doctor on a quest to write Science Fiction in his spare time. Ha, spare time. 'New Mzansi' is his first published short story. He has a love of international Science Fiction and various eclectic subjects such as hip-hop, philosophy, and combat sports. Both career and future story interests include weird diseases and nanobots.

Azania

Nick Wood

I'd never been very cold before—not until I headed into
space. Deep space I'm talking, not a joyride to the moon.
So deep, we go on and on, past suns and planets, moons
and nebulae—deep, deep space, through the coldest of
empty places that hang between the stars.

So cold, it penetrates our star-ship TaNK, infiltrating the
dreams of my long sleep; for I see nothing of all we pass.

Instead, I lie encased in ice, too cold to scream.

For twelve years...

And still more.

It is time for the last lesson but thunder rumbles over the
sound of the bell. I laugh and run, finding myself in a
strange field, far from home and school. The ground is
bitten red-rock dry and marked only by redder crumbling
fragments of dried out anthills. No trees, no grass, no
houses or sounds. Above me, the sky roils in with darkness
and lightning sheets that spark my blood. I laugh and tilt
my head backwards, flicking my hair so that it tumbles
down my back. I close my eyes, opening my mouth as the
wind sweeps in great water blasts that sting my face and
lips. I suck greedily, as the dust churns to muddy rivulets
beneath me, shifting my footing, muddying my feet. The
warm water slakes my throat, turning cold and then, to ice.
I choke, mouth frozen open, unable to breathe. I am pinned
tight in a latticed cage of ice. I open my eyes. There is
nothing else around me; nothing, till a flash in the
darkness. I turn, but too late. The arrow pierces my right
ear and bores into my brain. I can only gag on ice.

I wake shivering.

Above me, there is a large overhanging tree trunk. Frosty
edges of the dream-cage melt around me and I track the
blurred branch to the huge trunk and overhanging canopy.

80

Nick Wood

Muuyo—the African baobab. The soft green leaves swirl and shake, always just out of my frozen reach. I struggle to stretch out painful fingers, searching for warmth in the green. But the organic patterns shift and reform, distant as stars, untouchable.

She watches me through the leaves, wearing the face of Wangari Maathai. Is it in identification with me that She is mostly female?

I sigh. So...

Not my Copperbelt home then, nor my old school.

Not even Earth.

Planet XA- I've lost the numbers in my cold, waking head-fog—or, as we prefer to call it, Azania. (A planet partially mapped by the African Union Robotic Missions with (just) breathable air and water and no known advanced life forms—a veritable waiting Eden).

The baobab branch bending and swaying above me, however, is but a digital shadow on our domed roof—a shape without texture, form without life.

Wangari, She smiles, with richly red lips: <Mangwanani, Aneni.>

"Morning," I grunt, sitting up and casting a glance at grandfather's rough, reddish-brown stone sculpture, dimly but decoratively placed near the screened window, as if keeping alien forces at bay.

Besides me, Ezi stirs.

I sign to She to keep quiet and swivel clumsily out of bed; bracing my stomach muscles for the pull of serious gravity. The room spins beneath the canopy of faux leaves and my feet fail to find floor.

Instead, my face, fists, and breasts, do, hands barely in place quick enough to protect my teeth.

I spit blood from a cut lip, concerned about one thing.

There is something in my ear.

It's a faint tickle in the right ear, deep inside, but followed by a sputtering burst of popping noises, as if my ear is protesting and trying to expel something. Then a

Azania

pain lances through the right side of my face and I grunt and clasp my ear.

I sway.

Ezi is starting to snore, low and rasping, as she has rolled onto her back. I watch her for the barest of moments, sealing the pain within me so that I don't wake her, reacquainting myself with my old adversary.

It's been many, many years—but, almost without thinking, I rate the pain five out of ten and akin to a bright blue candle burning inside my ear. I close my eyes to pour cooling imaginary water onto it, but it continues to burn just as brightly, just as painfully.

I'm out of practice, my spine now comfortably straight, even stiffened and dulled by the passing years. Pain pulls me back to thirteen again, my last spinal surgery sharpened by anxiety around my first period.

This time, though, there is no mother to hold me.

Instead, I need to see <u>She</u> in the Core Room.

Firstly though, I cover Ezi with the scrambled thermo-sheet to keep her warm. (Always, she kicks herself bare).

I manage the corridor with my left hand braced against the wall, following etched tendril roots, past the men's door and on into the heart of our Base, where <u>She</u> sits.

Or squats—her heavy casing hides her Quantum core, scored with bright geometric Sotho art—her flickering holographic face above the casing is now the usual generic wise elder woman, grandmother of all.

<u>She</u> straddles the centre of the circular room, like a Spider vibrating the Info-Web.

<u>She</u> smiles again, but this time with pale and uncertain lips.

"I need help," I say, "A full medical scan. My ear feels painful and my balance has gone."

<A <u>full</u> scan?>

I swallow, appreciating the caution in her emphasis, but strip off my night suit with a shaky but firm certitude: "Yes."

Nick Wood

And so I am needled, weighed, poked, sampled, scraped, and gouged, until I shrink with exhaustion from the battery of bots she has whizzing around me. I finally take refuge in a chair near the door and gulp a cup of my pleasure, neuro-enhanced South Sudanese coffee.

She calls off her bots and they swing back into fixed brown brackets raised around the edge of the room, as if pots on shelves in an ancient traditional rondavel. She has her eyes closed, soaking in the analysis.

I finish the cup and rub my stinging lip where it's cut.

She speaks: <Not detecting any pathogen nor otological dysfunction, but I do see diffuse activated pain perception across your somato-sensory cortex.>

"Show me." I am a doctor after all, even if many years a psychiatrist now, specialised in space psychosis and zero-G neurosurgery.

I watch my rotating holographic brain in bright blue, with red traces glowing in the anterior insula and cingulate cortex—sensory, motor, and cognitive components, involved then: a dull, all-encompassing pain, no identifiable specificities tracing a direct neural link to the ear. There's new pain merged and mixed with old memories perhaps, fudging and blurring my experiential pathways? I scan the data that She scrolls condescendingly before me—no, there are no clear signs of dysfunction clearly emanating from my inner ear that I can see either.

I stand and sway. Surely it can't all be in my head?

"Aneni?" It's Ezi on our room screen, frowning from the bed, thermo-sheet clutched to her chin. "There's something sore in my right ear."

Dhodhi! As always, I keep the expletive hidden inside me. "I'm on my way, Ezi."

I lurch back down the corridor, just as the men's door slides open. Petrus is on his hands and knees and startles as I stop and lean against the wall opposite him. I watch the corridor light bounce off his brightly tattooed scalp as he bends his head to look up at me.

Azania

"Sorry Cap'n," he says. "Can't seem to stand upright anymore... and my ear's *fokkin'* sore."

I'm always cold, whatever temperature we set here, but now this coldness bites almost as deeply as my pain.

We meet where we eat, genetically diverse, even though we number just four. It is dull but honest food, the cassava and eddoes Anwar had saved on arrival, holding starvation at bay on this alien planet.

I nibble and long for a pineapple or banana.

Finishing up quickly, the others look shaken, unwell, with little appetite.

She has sprinkled the table and walls with swathes of savannah grass and shimmering pools of blue water. They bleed into my vertigo. I ask her for plain reality. She gives us a brown table, flanked by opposing brown seat-bunks, ergo-green kitchen neatly splayed behind with heaters and processors. She has the windows sealed white against the planet's night, keeping the focus on our preparatory tasks within.

I steady myself with a firm grip on the table—tension is building—I don't need my psychiatric training to tell me that. The men sit opposite us. Ezi and I exchange the briefest of encouraging glances and brace our selves. At least some vestibular stability has returned for us all.

Sure enough, it's Petrus who sits opposite me; brown head and hairless, smooth face lined by late middle age and constant earnestness. "So... *Captain*, what is responsible for our ear pain and dizziness?"

He has not used my name nor looked at me directly since three Earth days after we arrived; certainly not since I moved in with Ezi. That's six weeks and rising now, in Earth time.

Azanian time, though, it's been just four days.

I shrug and gesture to the ceiling, where leaves still hang heavily over us: "She doesn't know."

Nick Wood

Anwar chuckles at me; his white teeth sharply offset against his trimmed black beard and moustache, his ashen grey skin obviously short of sunlight. His teeth look sharp, conveying little of his humour; but perhaps it's just my mood.

"<u>She</u> is not omniscient though, am I correct, Aneni?"

I nod and smile: "<u>She</u> wants to check all of us thoroughly. She's learned literally nothing from me."

All three of them groan and I let slip a smile.

"Is it the same ear for all of us?" asks Ezi. Both men turn to look at her; Petrus gesturing right, Anwar left.

"Random, then?"

Ezi ignores me. "Mine's the right ear like Aneni and Petrus," she says, leaning forward, right hand grasping the cream, circular utilities remote. With a flick of her wrist, she sends it straight towards Anwar's midriff. He stops it with his left hand.

"Maybe your dominant ear is left," says Ezi, "but then, what do I know? I'm only the engineer." (Why does she look at me? We all know she is a special engineer, simply the best on antimatter rockets. More to the point now, her genius resides in having gotten our waste recycling going again, such a welcome respite for our noses.)

"Neurologically targeted?" I ask.

Ezi shrugs, coiled corn-plats flicking across her shoulders. "What do you think, <u>She</u>?"

<I cannot speculate without sufficient evidence, but I can confirm a full physical is needed for all of you.>

They eye each other with reluctance; the full physical on waking from years of enforced hibernation six weeks earlier no doubt still fresh in mind. A rigorous exam followed by even more rigorous exercises to recondition our severely weakened bodies—we still struggle against the pull of this planet, even though it is barely five percent more than full Earth gee.

Azania

I smile again, despite the ear-pain, having done my time. "We'll stay here until we've all been assessed. Alphabetical order, first name."

Anwar scowls at me as he gets up to go through to the Core-Room.

Petrus looks at the cup of coffee in front of me. "So, what do you suspect, Captain?"

I look at his scalp, feeling inexplicably sad. Two human figures are etched in sub-dermal nano-ink on his skull. They've not moved since we've woken from our Star-Sleep, their micro-programmed motility messages seemingly degraded and destroyed by his prolonged, lowered neural activity. His head used to show the Mandelas walking endlessly free from prison in the late twentieth century—now; it's just two faded humanoid shapes frozen together, smeared like an ancient Rorschach blot across his scalp. I can't explain it, but the still and fading images continue to cool my early desires for him.

"Aneni?" Petrus is looking at me, green eyes fierce and I am reminded of his rough Cape Town Flats roots.

"At this point I can't say, but there has to be some foreign pathogen, despite all our precautions. We can't all be ill with the same symptoms simultaneously."

He raises his eyebrows and leans forward, "Foreign?"

For some reason, I can't take my eyes off the Mandelas on his head, "From Azania perhaps, although we can't rule out a hidden, mutated infectious agent from Earth."

Anwar stomps in and Ezi sighs as she stands up.

It's strange to sit alone again with the two men, both who appear to keep smouldering with residual resentment at my authority and unexpected relationship with Ezi. Strange too, to think it's a full sixty years now since the African Gender and Sexuality Equality Act. Laws we were all born with—but still for some, slow to shape trans-generational attitudes around queer sexuality—despite credible arguments they are internalised residues of negative colonial views. (In the end though, nothing is so neatly

86

separated, unless you're an exceptional surgeon. As for me, my words are my customary tools, blunter than any scalpel, so I keep my thoughts private.)

The men mutter briefly and inaudibly to each other. I smile behind my hands, for I am used to masculine silence; fifteen years in the Zambian army is preparation enough.

Ezi comes back and Petrus leaves. We stare with discomfort at the table; we have silently avoided this threesome.

I am startled when Anwar breaks it. "I've made a holo-disk of Yakubu Chukwu."

It's Ezi's favourite West African Federation footballer. "Really?" she smiles.

I stand to halt a surge of emotions. Ridiculous really, as if physical actions can stop feelings—I should indeed know better. Walking over to the blinds that hide this planet from us, I grasp their metal slats, ready to claw them away.

This is why we are here.

This is where we need to survive.

But Ezi's eyes do not follow me, so I hesitate.

Ezi's from South of the Tenth Parallel, an old fracture line Anwar may not find so easy to cross—Africa harbours exacting fault lines, both ancient and modern.

Still, the AU is—was?—a powerful, if fragile and fast ripening fruit of i-networked Lion economies, ready to burst across the burnt out husk of the Earth—if it survives the gathering heat. We are indeed the first of its more ambitious and widely dispersed seeds...

A further ten missions have been planned, but spread across a number of promising solar systems. None follow us here. We will remain alone.

I look at the others and suddenly begrudge them nothing. This will be a hard place to survive.

As if on cue, Petrus returns. He looks at me and I turn away to the window—thinking of seeds, I thumb the shutter button.

Azania

The slats rise on darkness. An almost impenetrable blackness, with both moons yet to rise. I press my nose against the cold-treated quartz—against the faint starlight and the reflected light from within; I make out huge trunked shapes swaying in a light nocturnal breeze.

It's *always* windy here; circulating air continuously ensuring temperatures are not excessively varying across the long days and nights.

In the reflected window, I can see Petrus is standing quietly behind me. He glances up.

She is back amongst the canopy of leaves over our heads: <There are no clear biological markers I can identify as yet, I'm afraid—but I can offer you all a blunt neural painkiller. Our scheduled venture onto the planet surface will be set back indefinitely. We are, in effect, quarantined. I will also ask Kwame Nkrumah for His thoughts.>

Ah, Kwame Nkrumah, the Father-ship that circles above our head, He who watches from above.

More waiting, more cages, quarantine shuts me in, like the ice cage of my dream.

So many people left behind too, of whom I miss my daughter the most. Anashe, she was barely twenty-three when we launched from Kinshasa. As a child, she had loved to sit under the baobab.

I look up at She's swaying branches and '*tccchhh!*' with irritation, "I am tired of baobabs, She, give me a fever tree."

Above us, a yellowish tree with fern like leaves billows, photosynthesising through the pale bark—an odd tree indeed, but somehow more suitable for this strange planet we still try to hold at bay with walls and shutters.

I stare into the darkness again, no longer hungry.

I wake.
It is worse.
Much worse.

Nick Wood

I look pleadingly at <u>She</u> but there is nothing for my gaze to hold onto, just a rumbling, tumbling vertiginous splash of browns and greens and yellows. I sway and spin even though I am lying still and wait quietly for the vomit urge to die, sweating out my fear.

Blurred colours sharpen and take shape.

Chinanga—the fever tree.

Cautiously, I lift my head.

Chikala! Of course, my bed is empty too.

Slowly, I swing my legs out of the bunk and anchor them on ground. I sit and earth my feet on synthi-steel, one by one.

The pain shreds my ear.

I close my eyes and isolate it. There is only one arrow. It is nine out of ten and ice cold, bright blue-white. I send my spirit to stroke it, warm it, but it cuts at my hands. I blow my warm breath onto it, steaming it red in my mind. My breath runs out. Blue it burns again.

I ask for help from grandfather, holding his rough-hewn sculpture, warm Shona stone, but all I hear is silence—the silence that leaks from vast and cold interstellar distances. We are alone here. Only the wind speaks, but in what a strange and empty tongue.

I stand and move before the pain burns too brightly, eyes open, anchoring my swaying body and shaking ankles with step-by-step focused visual cues, to help stabilise my proprioceptors.

There, door button, now press... root tendril designs, pick one, follow along the hall to <u>She's</u> heart; ow, get up, get up, focus, follow and lean on that root, don't lose sight, don't think ahead, not of <u>She</u>; get up, damn it, again, same root, that's it, ow, that's it, up again, the root's thickening, approaching CR, door button, press, collapse...

The floor is cold beneath my back.

I look upwards, feeling sick as my ear burns more and more. What on Earth is happening? No, *not* Earth; is that indeed the point?

Azania

Don't fight it; it's just one Buddhist arrow. No thoughts and emotions to make a second arrow, a second and deeper wound. Examine it; inspect it. This arrow is seven out of ten—steel grey, but pulsing blue. It's only pain. It will shift; it will change. Everything does.

Eventually.

Above me, <u>She's</u> face is a familiar old bald white man in a white coat. He's got a stethoscope draped around his neck. I remember him, old Doctor Botha from my childhood. He'd been one of the South African émigrés, moving north for new opportunities, new challenges. Why has <u>She</u> become him?

<u>She</u> speaks slowly, words pulsing with warmth: <You seem ill Aneni, what can I do?>

I cough, but my throat is clear, I am not choking. "Make it go away <u>She</u>... please!"

The old man shakes his head. <I still don't know the cause, although I can maybe dull the pain.>

Yes... and no. Fuck it; I don't want to just *ease* things. There's a job to do. There's always a job; but how can we live and work if this world is somehow poisoning us, sickening us? I lever myself slowly into a sitting position and slide against the wall. "Open all room channels, <u>She</u>."

Two screens flicker on as the wake-alarm sounds.

Ezi is hanging head down, retching over the side of her mattress, now stacked on top of a black bench-press in our tiny Gym-room. Every day, she must pack her bed away, for all of us still need to bulk up our bodies with exercise there, ever-fighting against this planet's enervating pull.

Petrus is lying in his bunk, body still, limbs twitching and eyes open. Anwar is strapped to a Smart-chair facing skywards, a chair that constantly cranks itself towards our solar system. He must have been praying, even though Mecca itself is too blunt a target at this distance.

"Aneni here, how are you all doing?"

Ezi is in no state to talk and the men can only groan, although Petrus makes a fist of it. "*Kak*!" is all he says.

Nick Wood

I look at my old Doctor, whose face is now filling the room with concern. "Is this terminal?" I ask.

She looks at me long and hard before shrugging: <I'm afraid I don't know, Aneni.>

I sigh, gathering in strength for more words, hard words, "I'm taking a vote on Procedure F76."

She's eyes widen with simulated shock: <That would breach our Primary Mission Goal.>

"If we're going to die, we should at least have the choice of *where* that is."

Silence.

I look down. The arrow is eight and rising; purple now, steady and aching. Wrap it tight with the words you must say. "All in favour of F76, special emergency protocol I am empowered to authorise, just say 'me'; voice recognition certification on full, She."

The old man looks disappointed and puts on a pair of glasses, black horn-rimmed archaic ones. I don't remember *those*.

"This is to return to Earth, no?"

It takes me some moments to realise it is Petrus speaking, his body twitching but stilling in his bunk.

I nod, suddenly feeling cowardly.

"I think Allah has brought us safely here for a reason."

Confused momentarily, I suddenly realise Anwar has followed up on Petrus's question. (His face averted skywards; I had not seen his lips move.)

The old man She looks up at me, smiling.

"And...," continues Anwar, panting after each brief rush of words: "Do we really want to... to bring back with us... dare I say it... a plague of ...of possibly Biblical proportions?"

His words shame me and remind me of time, both ancient and future. "If we do leave, She, when will we arrive back on Earth?"

She is no longer my doctor, but has morphed into a small, elderly and sharp featured brown woman in a bright

Azania

orange sari. I immediately recognise Indira Moodley, my teacher, the great Kenyan psychiatrist who revised Fanon, integrating his theory with genetic neuro-physiology into a marvellous psychiatric Theory of Everything. (From the mindfulness of cells to the Minds within politico-cultural events and back down again.)

<It'll be 2190 when we get back.>

I realise I'm looking at a long dead woman.

Seventy years gone! I'm freezing fast on this icy surface. I close my eyes. The arrow is Ten and vivid fucking violet. Out of the darkness I see the second arrow coming, but I am too cold to move, ice forming around me like a casket.

There is no way home. There never was. I'd known that in my head when we'd left—we all had, but not to the core of our cells and selves.

There is nothing else to do but whisper goodbye to my family, to Earth, although my voice is broken: *"Sarai zvakanaka."*

Anashe will be dead too—perhaps *long* dead, my beloved daughter. My eyes sting, so I close them, coughing out words I hope can be heard. "Shall we vote?"

I knuckle my eyes and open them, but She doesn't even bother to wait for us—swelling, shifting, and swaying... Finally bursting into a huge windstalk above us, a thick-stalked purple plant with splayed giant leaves hanging from the apex—but swirling to the sound of alien winds we cannot hear.

As for the arrow of pain, now drilling through my head and into my left ear, there is only one thing left I can do.

I hold it, my fingers cupping my ears, burning and melting into the white-hot shaft of pain. I hold and don't let go, as if my hands have fused across my ears.

Tonight, please let me dream of the Copperbelt again, even just fleeting fragments of places I don't recognise. (Huge rainy season droplets on my tongue will be enough, toes curled into reddish-brown earth. No, anything will do...)

Nick Wood

Later on, though, I dream of nothing.

We gather for the Sun-Show meal, warming up first with my Zambo-Chinese tai chi lessons—short form, the long form can come later. Petrus has proved himself a natural master in waiting, moving with a slow grace. So too have I taught them to harness their visual attention and their muscle proprioception, in order to compensate for now periodic vestibular disturbance.

She opens the blinds as daylight gathers above the rocking purple windstalks, standing ten to twenty metres tall. We watch them sway as we eat, our balance strangely bolstered in the pending dawn. Anwar has prepared a glorious meal indeed—tested on the five mice that survived the trip—spliced and pummelled purple cereal lifted from   'bot samples, with a sharp, but curiously pleasant tang.

At the end, we all look at him and he smiles: "It is our first safe combination of Earth and exo-plants." (He'd been thrilled to find a workable genetic compatibility, Allah seeding the Universe.)

So. We will greet the new day with a hope of real sustainability—perhaps we shall not starve, nor die, anytime soon. As for our ear pain, it both fluctuates and hovers, like a random and ghostly wasp who has been angered.

Perhaps it is here to warn us, that here too, we also need to bend our ways of working to survive? I have banned religion from the table—Western tables must be really dull without politics as well—but for once I relent.

It is that afterwards, with thanks, I hold a truncated ceremony of *kurova guva*—welcoming the spirits of the deceased, although Anwar leaves to say his own prayers. I know remembrance rituals differ across the continent, so I keep it brief and generic. "We leave a bowl for those who travel to new places and hunger in the holes between. May you all find your way to new joys... and just perhaps a few of you may even make it here."

Ezi has no belief, but still she cries, quietly. (Hers was a close family indeed, her grandmother a Hero of the Oil Wars; the start of Africa reclaiming her resources.)

The sky is paling fast, the windstalks bending before the heat of this sun's heralding winds. We stay quarantined; the First planned Walk is no longer taking place.

But I am tired of waiting. Still the pain bites deep in my ear, but I feel there are no answers here.

I bow to the others and leave the room, making my way to the airlock. (We're just about breathing native air by now anyway, sterilised and incrementally added into our closeted atmosphere.)

I pick up a head-suit with visor; there is no reason to take unnecessary risks on the eyes. The scalp cap peels on with a sticky tightness and I flip the visor down, the small room darkening instantly.

Flicking a switch, an inner door seals the small room, lined with built in benches in case of prolonged emergency use. I pick up a walking rod too.

<Is this wise, Aneni?> She warbles into the ear-speaker.

"Since when have I been wise, She? Open the external door please."

<And if I deem this a breach of safety protocol, given our quarantined status?>

"We're humans. We *do* things. I am tired of cowering from this place."

The door remains shut. I turn and lever the walking rod through the handles of the inner door, effectively locking it.

<What are you doing, Aneni?>

I sit. "Just waiting for you to open the external door."

<We don't know enough yet about the biological risks.>

"Perhaps we never will," I say. "Life is a biological risk. Open the door."

Nick Wood

<You're not ready for all possible challenges that may arise, in your physically compromised state.>

"I am a woman."

The external door light glows green, but it remains shut. I make a note to ask Petrus whether quantum She can have two different minds at the same time.

"I am an *African* woman!"

A green light flickers on and I hear a hiss from the ceiling as odourless but penetrating and sterilising nanoparticles descend, seeping through my overalls, cleansing me in readiness for a new place. Slowly, the door grinds open and I gasp and cough at the acrid, burning air. Gradually my breathing eases and I'm able to raise my head. The ground outside our Base is rough, uneven, with tightly latticed blue grass of sorts.

As my gaze lifts, I sweep past the Lander-Plane that spring-loaded our base, down a rough, uneven slope towards indigo reeds lining a patch of dark water. The water is partially obscured by towering windstalks that seem to be circling the small lake, like giants rearing above us and emitting a stench that seems part sulphur, part acid. My eyes stream under the visor and I cough again, but pull the walking rod free and step forward, moving slowly around our circular base.

The others are pressed against the wide kitchen window and wave, but I'm too engrossed with the sparkle of orange-red rays amongst heavy grey clouds overhead.

"Azania," I breathe.

She must have patched the suit-speaker into the kitchen.

I recognize Ezi's voice, groaning: "Ahhhh, mmmmm!"

"What?" I turn to the shadowed shapes behind the window; Ezi is etched thinner and taller than the men.

"Ahhhhh, mmmmmm," she repeats. "The sound of this place. We're not going to repeat the same shit that happened to us, we're not going to do a Shell Oil or Cecil Rhodes on this place!"

Azania

I laugh, coughing at the burning, almost peppery air. "Good point, although if we're going to change the name of this planet, wouldn't 'Euromerica' be a more easily pronounceable name?"

"Look," says Petrus, and I see him pointing high behind me.

The first rays of the young new sun are flashing through the windstalks, now shimmering a deep violet. Below them, the ground sways with rustling purple reed ferns. Shadows shrink, hiding nothing but vivid variegations of purple and movement—as well as purpose? Have our projections onto the landscape begun? Or are there some things or beings hidden and active amongst the vegetation? TaNK has seen nothing so far, but He is not God.

Still, could there be things so small they invade our ears undetected—even now, the pain is five and... I forget the numbers, there are too many beautiful colours flowing down the groaning windstalks as I brace myself against a blast of hot and pungent air.

And then it comes again. A high-pitched keening sound, but more modulated, subtler.

"Ahhhhhh, mmmm," Ezi repeats in my painful ears, but she's not even close.

The atmospherics amplify and fracture the sound, enhancing into a multitude of varying tones, polyphony of sounds and calls. It's as if the windstalks are talking.

<Aneni,> I know from the intimacy of her tone, She has secured this communication just for me. <I'm picking up a slight neuronal rewiring throughout your auditory cortex, a hint of neurogenesis.>

"Ah!" I say. So it's my brain, not my ear. Have we been colonised so deeply too, from within? Or is this the consciousness of cells responding to a new and alien call?

I take grandfather's sculpture out of my baggy jacket pocket, stoop with bended knees and braced back, placing it carefully on the ground. It's not a spirit or a person, not a totem or God—Grandfather Mapfumo prided himself on

Nick Wood

being a modern man—his grandfather before him driving regime change in Zimbabwe with Chimurenga music. Instead, it's a Zanoosi, Zimbabwe's first Eco-car, running on degraded organic waste, not someone else's food, like maize. The car he helped design, which powers the Southern African Federation lion economy. This sculpture was of the same car he drove us all up to Mufulira in, where he traded with the Chinese and we settled, establishing new factories. (And it was he alone who never laughed at me, when I spoke of going into space as a little girl.)

I straighten, stiffening my spine against the pull of the planet. I taste the sour but balmy breeze on my tongue, knotted, blue grass closing around the sculpted stone, sealing it from view.

I believe the rain here is a little heavier, a little saltier.

Out of Africa and now out of Earth...

No, not Earth, but a new... place. Home is a hard word. Why couldn't I have just gone back some several hundred k's to my old familial roots in Mutare, instead of trillions of miles here? Of course, the signs were closing in, as Earth heated up and disasters grew worse and I'd never been able to convince myself, unlike mother, that it all meant the Rapture was indeed near.

So, here we are, with biological seeds from Earth, including a frozen egg from my very own daughter. It is here we must make our heaven.

I stand stiffly, locked into the planet in a left bow stance, as the bright new sun burns its heat into me. 'This is the same sun imbued with illusions/the same sky disguising hidden presences'— words from an old Leopold Senghor poem that circulate my head.

But—this is a *new* sun and I have no idea what lies beneath it; whether voices or spirits, plants or animals.

"Salaam Aleichem."

Behind me there are racking coughs. I turn—all three have followed me out, arms around shoulders as they

Azania

walk, bracing themselves against the whipping wind. Ezi, thin, but as strong as rope, is in the middle.

"Don't tell me you want to hog this planet's air all to yourself, Aneni?" she chides me: "Wasn't stealing my sheets bad enough?"

An old joke, but who knows the barb beneath? The English have a saying about dirty laundry—but as for us, all is public, all is shared.

I smile; the new Sun shines on Petrus' scalp; almost making the Mandelas dance. He gestures at me to join them. I smile at him again but move next to Anwar, who stiffens at my touch.

We can't afford to lapse too quickly into neat and convenient relationships, however fecund. Not yet. This world has hurt and shaken us, perhaps for a reason, perhaps not. But for now, we must stay on our toes and learn new things, new ways of being.

At the end of the line, Petrus breaks into a slow tai chi stepping motion, moving from a left bow stance. But his left arm is still anchored around Ezi. Down the line, we echo and ripple his motions, the line dipping and rising with the flow of movement.

So it is, we dance African tai chi in our first real alien dawn. As we move, I note the pain—neither an adversary, nor a friend. Like rain and bananas, mice and joy, it just is.

We move slowly in a clumsy, lurching and stumbling dance—I laugh as Ezi bursts into a song, in words I don't understand.

Finally, I am warm again.

Nick Wood is a Zambian born, but naturalised South African clinical psychologist currently living and working in the UK. He has a Young Adult SF book published under the 'Young Africa' series in South Africa entitled *The Stone Chameleon*. He also has about a dozen short stories

Nick Wood

published in magazines such as *Interzone*, *PostScripts*, *Albedo One* and *Redstone Science Fiction*.

Notes from Gethsemane

Tade Thompson

Tosin's last stroke closed the curve of the horizon, separating meadow from sky, completing the drawing. He turned to Bayo, who nodded, and they both watched as condensation filled out the lines traced on the fogged-up window obliterating the drawing. The bus lurched once as it swapped from solar to internal combustion, and the noise from the engine increased with an accompanying speed boost. Tosin noted this must be an early model, as its cells did not store much energy, so as soon as it got dark the power source switched. He wrinkled his nose as exhaust fumes filtered in.

"Think perhaps you should take captures of your art?" asked Bayo, eyes closed.

"Why?"

"Dunno. Other people will get to see them."

Tosin grunted. "Perhaps I don't want other people to see them."

"So what's the use of drawing?"

"All art is useless," said Tosin. "A smarter man than I said that once."

"Yeah, and I bet he died in poverty," said Bayo. He pressed the bell for the next stop. "Sure you're up to this?"

Tosin nodded to reassure him.

They pulled their hoods up when the doors of the bus whooshed shut behind them. The rain was a steady misery-inducing presence that varied from fine spray to hail over the course of the day. Close to midnight and it still hadn't let up. This was the worst rainy season Tosin could remember, but he preferred it to the Harmattan with its red dust haze, and the water cleaned the streets when nobody else would.

Tade Thompson

He spotted Bayo's foot soldiers emerging from doorways and alleys, clustering around. They all touched fists but reserved a handshake or smile for Tosin. He was not one of them but received reflected respect for being their leader's brother, and for what he was about to do.

Lightning flashed and in his mind Tosin started counting. The thunder peal came soon after and he hissed under his breath. He hated being wet. If you didn't count Bayo's firm, the streets were empty, and Tosin imagined that even the police would stay indoors on a night like this. Under normal circumstances he would have been home studying. He trotted over to a storefront, out of the rain, and stared at old mannequins and his own reflection.

Tosin heard his brother giving last minute instructions— how far behind to stay, the absolute boundaries of no-man's-land, how long to wait, when to check radiation patches, how often to keep in touch. Bayo repeated himself, something Tosin knew his brother did when he was nervous, but the boys wouldn't notice. It gave Tosin a twinge of disquiet.

"It's simple," Bayo had said the night before. "I need you to pick up a package for me."

Up until that point Tosin had been ignoring him, attention locked into the lecturecast he was attending. He killed the sound and flipped the hemi-visor up into his cap. Developed countries had screens on contact lenses, but, as they say, *This is Lagos*. He sat up on his bed and gaped at Bayo, who looked back, deadpan.

"It's simple," said Tosin, "I do college, I do books, I do seminars. You and your pack do burglary, bootlegging, and street crime."

Bayo was serious, though.

One of his many streams of income was an underground courier service. It was mostly drugs and money, although sometimes it would be body parts from kidnappings or reprisal mutilations. It paid well. The section of town they lived in was too close to The Pit and surrounding

Notes from Gethsemane

exclusion zone for regular police patrols, but the danger of discovery during random checks did exist. Policing in Nigeria was in part a moneymaking exercise. A checkpoint was a tollgate for both the innocent and guilty. Setting up a random one around Christmas or Ileya would pay for a Superintendent's house party. One day, Loop, a member of Bayo's firm, was carrying a package and came across an unexpected checkpoint. It turned out he had several pending warrants and no money for bribes. Bye-bye Loop. He had however ditched the package before arrest; the protocol for such situations was carved in stone.

"The carrier stashes the package, and whoever controls the area in which the carrier gets caught is responsible for its safety until it's picked up. Two problems though." Bayo was like a lecturer, pacing the room, a master of his topic. "The protecting firm gets a token payment, for goodwill. And it's gotta be picked up by a civilian."

"What does the civilian get?" Tosin pulled down the hemi-visor and turned his lecturecast volume back on.

"He gets to live." Bayo opened the door to go. A thin wedge of light leaked into the dark corridor, but only his sneakers were visible. "Don't worry, I won't let you get hurt, little brother."

And so, he found himself in the rain with scintillation counter readings from The Pit borderline dangerous for biological systems. Tosin shivered, but not from the cold; he was excited in spite of himself. He felt a hand on his shoulder.

"You still okay with this?"

Tosin nodded.

"Remember: get in, get the parcel-"

"Get out. I know. Don't worry about it."

"Then go. These guys will escort you up to a point and wait. I'll be up at Salako Flats."

Only Bayo called it Salako Flats anymore. Tosin and the rest of Lagos knew it as Gethsemane.

Tade Thompson

Bayo's area extended up to the central mosque on Oluwadare Street. Beyond that due north on Church Street was neutral until it crossed Igbobi College Road, marked by the defunct evangelical building.

The rain had settled into a drizzle by the time Tosin got to the end of Church Street, and he was yet to meet a single soul. What did that old Rod Stewart song say? *In a Broken Dream.* People were asleep before nine o'clock if they were good. Tosin had never liked the song, but his father had played it often. He checked the signal on his portable and the glowing medium strength bar calmed him. He flicked down his hemi-visor and pulled an online street map of the area. Fortified with a surer route he ducked into an alley that led him to Market Street. He stopped, wordlined Bayo of his arrival, took off his key-glove, and sat on an upturned drum under a dead tree. Most of the buildings were two or three storey residential, some with shop fronts on the ground floor, all blasted and burnt out.

A dot of red light appeared on the crotch of his chinos.

"Are you armed?" A voice, female, from behind and close to Tosin's ear. He hadn't heard her walk up. "Don't move, just answer."

"I'm not armed." Could a laser sight affect his gonads? His groin felt tight, and he expected his genitals to erupt in blood and shreds of cloth any minute.

"Get up."

He did.

He could see them now. Hidden in the shadows they marched out slowly from awnings, doorways, and kiosks, in the same manner as Bayo's men. Tosin found the similarity interesting from an anthropological perspective and thought he would return to it later; perhaps write an essay about the loss of distinction between gendered street gangs. They were all girls, dressed in black tops, blue jeans, and wearing black scarves over the lower part of their faces Dick Turpin style, which rendered them anonymous.

Notes from Gethsemane

Tosin tagged them with attributes other than facial features. He used the gait, body shape, height, even the smells when they came closer. He counted four, five if one included the person giving him the laser treatment.

"I have an envelope for you," he said, as one of them patted him down. She found and took it. "You'll find a payment chip which you can confirm on a portable. Do you have something for me?"

"Come with us," said the one he had dubbed Narrow-Hips.

"That's not what I was told," said Tosin. "The protocol…" The laser dot crawled up his trunk and came to rest on the tip of his nose. He thought it would be a good idea to stop talking.

Bayo closed the door of the abandoned house, took off his rain-soaked jacket, sat on a pile of rolled-up carpets in the corridor, and lit a cigarette. First time he came into the house ten years earlier it was elegant. Now the walls were grey-black with fungus growth that always came off on his clothes when he leaned on it. Somewhere in the house, water dripped a dull metronome. His portable beeped and he plugged-in the hemi-visor and read the wordline. His brother was in place and waiting to make contact. Bayo disconnected without responding.

He had only ever been up the stairs once. Even now, all he could do was look at the landing, and on some days not even that. He couldn't come to Salako Flats without thinking of Conrad.

Unlike most people in Lagos, The Pit did not change Bayo's life much. He remembered the day he had gone to Ojota Motor Park to pick up Tosin, then six years old, who had arrived from Ilesha in an interstate taxi, bewildered with a country edge to his Yoruba. *Ara oko.* They got on a bus to their uncle's place and when he heard the first explosion Bayo thought it was a Boko Haram incident since that group was active back then. The second explosion upturned the bus. There were more, but by then Bayo was confused. He got Tosin out of the black smoke, twisted ruins, away from the terror, as people ran for cover from the fires, and above all, the radioactive fireworks display from Crater-191. Rumour was rife, but Bayo did not concern himself with the cause of chaos, just the opportunity it presented. Looting was lucrative in the first couple of weeks, then ferrying people out from behind the barricades.

While everybody was struggling to get out, Conrad bribed his way in, past the police and military, past the spiky black-on-yellow biohazard signs. With a loping walk, lanky frame, and nonchalant attitude, Conrad sought Bayo out even before he had a place to stay. Bayo had a reputation even before the catastrophe, and at first, he took Conrad for one of those trying to escape. He was wrong.

"There's something we can do in this place," said Conrad, that smiling stranger. The smile extended to his eyes and demanded absolute loyalty while promising great reward.

The beep of Bayo's portable interrupted the memories.

"Yeah?"

"Your brother's three minutes late," said Vandal, one of Tosin's guardians.

"My brother's a stop-and-smell-the-roses kind of guy, so don't break out the nine mills just yet," said Bayo.

"Should we go in?"

"No. Wait for him." Bayo disconnected and banged out a line to Tosin.

<Are you on your way back yet? Things are tense out here>

Something dripped on to the back of his neck and he swore. The whole damn house was leaking. He got up and rubbed it off, planning to move to another spot, but then stopped. The water seemed sticky and dark.

He flipped his lighter on and almost dropped it when he saw the blood smear on his palm.

Notes from Gethsemane

To their credit, they were not heavy-handed, and Tosin didn't get the impression of being kidnapped. The streets this far from The Pit had a different character—cleaner, with more signs of occupancy. The signs were more reality congruous, too. Instead of the years-old speed limit lollipop signs there were panels stating the time of sunset, the location of recharge stations, credit chip exchange rates, and food drop-off points. There were no scintillation counter readings, but then, at this distance it was probably not a life-or-death matter.

The six of them walked in a wedge formation in the middle of the road with Tosin front-centre and the girls on both sides of him, like strange land-based migratory birds walking south instead of flying. They didn't speak, but looked to Narrow-Hip for cues and surreptitious gestures before taking specific alleys or routes. They entered an unpaved path between two tower blocks. On the ground, a steady stream of inch-deep water made its lonely way nourishing the profuse weed growth on both sides. Posters of the current politicians were on the walls. Each either a chief or alhaji, sometimes both, and they all promised to sort out the question of The Pit. The adverts pasted over the yellowed corpses of previous posters making the same promise.

Narrow-Hips stopped him in front of a doorway and they were soon inside a sparsely furnished apartment where nobody invited him to sit. She exchanged muted words with the girls they met there before turning to him.

"What was in the package?" she asked.

"I don't know," said Tosin.

"What was in the package?"

It was like he hadn't spoken. "I just told you, I have no clue." In the light, he could see her eyes above the mask, and they didn't seem to hold malice or malevolence. "Come on, I'm not involved in your gangs. Your rules state that the exchange should be done with a non-member, right? How would I know?"

Narrow-Hips pulled a revolver out from under her jacket, but said nothing.

"Do you want me to ask my brother? I have a portable-"

She silenced him with a raised hand and went into conference with the others. While he watched their fevered whispering he wished Bayo had told him more about them, or indeed that he had paid more attention to his brother's activities, which were criminal, yes, but had ensured Tosin's survival over the last decade. He didn't judge. A gift horse is accepted as if it has pristine teeth. What makes a good brother does not necessarily make a good person.

They finished and Narrow-Hips beckoned. She took him down a corridor, handed him a state-issue gas mask, and put one on too. He didn't notice where she put her gun but did wonder. She came to a makeshift airlock—polythene wrapped around the edges of an ordinary door. Tosin heard fans going a full blast somewhere and the hum of a generator. He found the precautions unsettling, crude, and inadequate. Many lethal gases did not require access to the respiratory system and could be absorbed just as well through the skin, a Hazmat suit would be better. If it was a biological agent on the inside there needed to be a negative pressure isolation room. They had neither, and Tosin felt his heart rate increase. The hiss of his breath through the mask did nothing to calm him.

The room had been a lounge in another life Tosin was sure. A thick slab of glass divided it into two with an amorphous blue sealant lining the edges. Narrow-Hips walked up to the glass and placed her palms on it. There was another member of her firm reading a paperback on a chair in the room, also wearing a gas mask. Tosin moved to Narrow-Hips' side. There were three people behind the glass. They lay in narrow cots along each wall. All

Notes from Gethsemane

writing and the grimaces on their faces left no doubt in Tosin's mind that they were in excruciating pain.

Each had multiple eruptions on their skin. Judging from the linear streaks Tosin figured they were itchy, and from the pus, that they were infected. The lesions covered every strip of exposed skin, scabbed in some areas, bleeding in others. The woman on the left appeared to be in the most severe condition, and her skin seemed to Tosin like a freeze-frame of boiling water. She was naked, her nipples obliterated, and everything else matted together. On the floor, he noticed plates half-full of food, glasses, clothes, water, and some pills. The lights were dim on that side of the room, and there was a small port close to the ground, presumably for exchange.

"What is this?" he asked. "Who are these people? Shouldn't you get them to a hospital?"

Narrow-Hips didn't talk at first, and he followed her lead out of the room.

"These 'people' are Shonda, Claire, and Fatimah." She took off the gas mask and the bandanna, so he could see her face. "They are three of the four girls who came in contact with your precious package, the one Loop dropped."

"And the fourth?"

Hesitation. "We incinerated her body yesterday."

In the wobbling halo of yellow flame from his lighter Bayo saw a word on the wall in front of him.

PESTILENCE

Written in blood, the C and E had dripped and smeared where he had rested his head when he sat down. Bayo backed away and controlled his fear. Someone had written the word and escaped pretty fast, unless they were still in the house…

He drew his gun and swept through both floors, wraithlike, silent, but found nothing. It was real blood, too. He could smell it, knew the odour well.

Tade Thompson

His portable rang.

"Bro," said Tosin.

"Where are you?"

"No time for that. Listen, did you talk to Loop?"

"What are you talking about? Do you have the package?"

"There's been a complication. Did you talk to him or not?"

"Why?"

"I need to know what the package was and where it was going."

"Is anyone listening in on this conversation?"

"You have to trust me, Bayo. This is important. Tell me what you know."

"Oh, man. This was a no-brainer. How could you possibly have mucked it up?"

"Are you feeling all right? You sound distracted, not nearly as annoyed as I would have expected."

Bayo glanced at the wall, and then looked away. "I'm fine. Are you?"

"Yeah. They're not happy about that package, though, and I don't blame them. You have to tell me where it was going. I'll explain later."

Bayo gave him a name and address. Tosin hung up only after extracting a promise: he wanted the guardians assigned to him called off. Bayo called Vandal as soon as he got a clear line.

"Yeah?"

"Cross the mosque. Hunt that little fool down and bring him home, you get me?"

"Do we have to be polite?" asked Vandal.

"Hell, no, they broke protocol first. Go." He cut the call, lit up another cigarette, and looked at the word on the wall again. He thought of accounts of bleeding statues, and of people seeing Jesus in cracker crumbs or something. "You," he said waving his cigarette at it, "are going to have to be a little more eloquent than that."

Notes from Gethsemane

Tosin sat behind the driver. It was an old internal combustion, no dual engine. Hard to believe they never used solar storage capabilities back then, but the Robinson Cell only came later in 2015, and the Robinson II changed everything a year later. Fully functioning petrol and diesel engines were only kept as conversation pieces in the developed world, not so in Nigeria.

The inner light was on since they wanted to keep an eye on him. He entertained them with scenes traced in the dust on the back of the driver's seat with his little finger—not that they acknowledged being entertained, he just assumed that they were. He sketched a lake and a forest before he ran out of dust. He drew from imagination and the memory of online photographs. He'd never seen a lake, but until the age of six, he had lived in the hilly and lush Ilesha with his mother and three sisters. The family sent Bayo south to Lagos when Tosin was a baby.

Tosin missed the countryside. Not to say life was easy in Ilesha. A political rival had assassinated his father, and to survive, his mother had provided catering for the local grammar school. A fierce, intelligent woman, she had been prevented from continuing to higher education by her father who thought she would never find a husband if educated. Tosin gorged himself on the books in the school library while his mother served akara, dundu, dodo, and eko, at the canteen. When she noted his precocity, she sent him to Lagos where there would be better opportunities. The day he arrived was the day the skies opened.

None of them wore masks this time. Narrow-Hips had introduced herself as Vendra, leader of the firm. She was in the back seat with him while two of her girls were in front, but Tosin couldn't remember their names.

"It was a ceramic doll," Vendra had said, before they left the house, "smashed to bits when your friend stashed it."

"He's not my friend," said Tosin.

"Whatever. Fatimah picked it up first. Shook it, handed it to Shonda. They both brought it back to base and reported to Claire. Then the rash appeared bright red on Fatimah's throat."

The spread had been both brisk and irresistible. Shonda and Claire were not far behind, within a few hours their skin covered over with pus-filled bullae. The fourth person was daft enough to open the package in a fit of curiosity. Tosin asked her name.

"That's a problem. We have people coming and going so it's difficult to keep track-"

"You didn't recognise her?"

"By the time we found her she didn't have a face."

They placed the infected in a jury-rigged isolation unit and, given the rapid deterioration, decided it would be best for all if they found out what exactly Bayo's firm was smuggling.

"At first I thought it was some biological warfare deal, but it didn't make sense. Such a thing would have military escorts and there is no reason to pass through the barricade. No way would the government move it this close to The Pit."

"Unless this is the target, what if they want to purge the population surrounding The Pit? No great loss to society, after all. Only those of us who had no other options stayed inside the barricade. Or what if it's an experiment and they couldn't find volunteers?"

"Would your brother be into that?"

"I have no clue what my brother would be into," Tosin said.

He was intrigued, and that he was still a captive seemed unimportant. He had asked many questions, went back for several looks at the infected and the broken bits of ceramic still contained in the isolation chamber. He spent time improving the quality of the air seal. Vendra seemed content to step aside and let Tosin prod and poke the problem, though only under guard.

"What exactly are you studying at university?" she asked.

Notes from Gethsemane

Tosin didn't know the most precise way to answer. He had drifted with the winds of his intellectual inquisitiveness, taken courses in everything from vitalism to vincristine. He had no major, no goal save the acquisition of knowledge in the most general forms allowed under the current academic curriculum.

"I have many interests, but nothing has seized my attention long enough for me to want to dedicate myself to it exclusively. My grade points are still good enough and the subjects are eclectic enough to get me into any specialty I want, but I do not know what that is yet. Perhaps I never will."

"How old are you?"

"Sixteen. How old are you?"

"Older than you."

The car bounced and Tosin's knee erased the lower half of the lake. The destination address turned out to be luxurious by The Pit standards. Formerly the concourse of a railway station, it was now residential and probably triple lead lined. All around the building severed rail tracks bent outwards away from the structure forming a radial barrier linked with barbed wire. Two freelancers guarded it—further evidence of the wealth of the occupier—and they regarded the approaching vehicle with hostility.

"Delivery," said Tosin. "We're expected."

The guards would only let two of them through, and even that was a compromise. They first said they'd only allow one and without any weapons, but Vendra pushed them for more, saying she didn't trust Tosin to go on his own.

Softly, she said, "Sorry, Tosin. I know you're the most qualified to get to the bottom of the problem and all, but Bayo *is* your brother."

"I understand," said Tosin. Sometimes people called Bayo, odale, which meant oath-breaker, because of what he did to Conrad.

Tade Thompson

After consulting with someone on a wireless, the guards ushered them into an antechamber where a man paced, agitated.

"There you are," he said, facing them. "It's been days. Can't you people get anything right? Where is it?"

Tosin studied him. He was small, with irregular tufts of white hair on his pate, a well-lined face, white goatee, and wearing rimless glasses. He was in a pink dressing gown of all things, but his movements were spry and he had an air of good health and youthfulness.

"Are you Mr. Adam?" Tosin asked.

"Who else would I be? Where's the delivery?" Adam asked.

"There's been a problem," said Vendra.

Adam's face went through several minute expression changes before it settled into a frown. "What kind of problem might that be? Wait, let me guess: some of your friends are sick? The ones who handled the package?"

"What exactly were you moving, Mr. Adam?" Tosin asked.

"Do you know what a fractal is?" Conrad had asked Bayo one day.

"Pretty computer pictures?"

"'Pretty computer pictures.' I suppose I'm asking the wrong brother."

Bayo told him to attempt sexual intercourse with himself.

"Think snowflakes, coastlines, mountains, and, yes, computer-generated pictures. I won't go into details of non-Euclidean geometry but fractals show something called self-similarity, which means all the component parts of something resemble the whole. In other words, let's say you showed self-similarity. If I were to cut you into little bits, each one would be a ruthless bastard, just like you. I want the whole area inside the barricade to show self-similarity. Every firm must operate like each other, and we will control the whole."

Notes from Gethsemane

"Never happen," said Bayo, but it did.

By the time they had that conversation Conrad had a four-mile circumference around The Pit under his control. The police didn't interfere—Conrad had controlled the riots that followed the government's announcement about not trying to fix The Pit anymore, so they thought his dominance of the roving gangs was a good thing. Conrad was insidious but decisive and brutal, and frighteningly intelligent, though not in the same way as Tosin who was book-smart. Between the two of them Bayo felt like a circus animal—clever in obeying specific instructions, but lacking any real initiative and dangerous without the proper controls.

The blood had all flaked off and the wall was back to mould and plaster. Bayo nodded, as if he had something to do with it, and he sat again, checked his messages. Nothing from either Tosin or Vandal. He queried them both and signed off.

He felt ill at ease and the environment kept bringing back memories of Conrad. This was not the ideal night, he thought, for Tosin to mess about and...

There was a new word on the opposite wall. Bayo blinked several times and rubbed his eyes. There was no mistake, and the metallic smell of blood reached him within seconds.

SACRIFICE

"Goddamnit, what does that mean?" Bayo yelled, but nothing answered him. "This isn't funny."

He emptied his weapon at the new text, chipping plaster, smashing a window, and then coughed in the cloud of gun smoke. He replaced the spent clip. Bayo was breathing heavy, but he had obliterated most of the letters, and the wall no longer bled.

Tosin rubbed a bronze statue of Shiva but Adam stopped him, and said, "You and your ilk have already disrespected one deity. You want to try another?"

Tade Thompson

"Explain," said Vendra.

Adam's quarters were full of altars, statuettes, and carvings of gods and goddesses from a thousand cultures. In the air, Tosin could detect old incense and cumin like the aftertaste from a spicy meal. There were animals too, caged rodents, exotic reptiles, pacing within their filthy confines. Underneath it all was the stench of decay and rot, a foundation of putrefaction.

Tosin noted dozens, perhaps hundreds of books, some open, some torn, none in the bookshelves lining the walls. The shelves instead contained bottles filled with liquids and powders. In the middle of the room, there was an hourglass the size of a grandfather clock, top bulb spilling its sand inexorably into the bottom one. Adam pushed a stack of paper off a stool and sat down, regarding them with naked suspicion.

"You haven't answered my question, Mr. Adam," said Tosin. "What were you moving?"

"For this pestilence to stop," said Adam, "one of you has to be prepared to die."

"One already has," said Vendra. "Three are still in the process."

"Those ones don't count. One of you has to elect to go into The Pit," said Adam.

"Can we do this from the beginning and in plain English, please?" said Tosin.

"Very well.

"There are a few interested parties who still care about The Pit, about neutralising it. I have been in contact with like-minded people outside the barricades: scientists, natural philosophers, thinkers from all schools. We have been working on a solution for years. My role has been to observe and theorise, transmitting my data to confederates around the world, correlating ideas. We came up with an organism, wholly artificial, with the single function of stereo-chemical conversion of radioactive isotopes. We called it Sopana-40 after a malevolent West African pox

Notes from Gethsemane

god who loved hunting for victims in hot areas. Liked to wear red too. In fact-"

"So Sopana-40 is a pox virus? DNA rather than RNA based?" Tosin asked, flipping down his hemi-visor to check online.

Adam laughed. "Son, a pox virus is a poor cousin to Sopana-40."

"What can we do to save our friends?" asked Vendra.

"Nothing," said Adam. "It's over for them."

"So why are we even talking to you?" asked Tosin.

"See that hourglass? When it empties, Sopana-40 will burn out provided it doesn't reach The Pit. The bugs will feed on their own proteins and self-destruct."

"You're saying we should just wait it out?" asked Vendra.

"No," said Adam. "Quite the opposite, actually..."

"Wait a minute. A virus won't have an effect on inorganic matter," said Tosin.

"Which should tell you that...?" Adam raised his eyebrows, looking expectant.

"Whatever is in The Pit is organic," said Tosin.

"I'm sorry, what?" said Vendra.

"The radiation from the pit has always been problematic for observing scientists. Even if a meteor fell with natural unstable elements, the emissions don't seem to follow expected patterns of radioactive decay," said Tosin. "Mr Adam is saying that The Pit is alive."

Bayo stood in the centre of the dining hall on the first floor, away from all the blood-writing on the level below. He did not believe in ghosts, but he was more than spooked. It was a mind thing, something to do with guilt, not real at all, but an unreliable mind was not reassuring.

Near the end, Conrad owned most of the area around The Pit. He knew the gangsters who controlled the rest and asked Bayo to set up a meeting in the house at Salako Flats.

Tade Thompson

"We settle this thing with a quiet relocation," said Conrad, "We pay them to move out. No death, no loss of face, everybody happy, right?"

Bayo had nodded. There was no reason to handle it otherwise; it had worked well in the past. By then Conrad was comfortable with cash flowing in, a trusted lieutenant in Bayo, and the final settlement coming up. He had the respect of the firm and the struggling, marauding police. He left Bayo to handle the details of the meeting for the first time, electing to resolve another insignificant matter. This was a mistake.

Bayo quietly murdered all the potential attendees of the meeting and when Conrad arrived at Salako Flats, Bayo was waiting, holding the same gun that he now held in the empty room.

"I knew you were going to do this, man," said Bayo to the empty room, echoing the words replaying in his memory, words from a bleeding Conrad. He hadn't replied, and the other members of their firm said nothing when he told them of their leader's death. Of course, he retold the legend of Conrad in his own words. Their leader had killed off the rivals. Of course though he knew they renamed Salako Flats, Gethsemane, and why. Gethsemane, the place where Judas betrayed Jesus, a comparison Bayo found excessive. Conrad was no saviour, and had done none of the legwork.

"You're dead, Conrad," said Bayo to the room. "What do you want from me?"

His phone rang; it was Vandal, but the signal was poor.

"I'm outside The Pit. A bunch of them just arrived with your brother," said Vandal.

"Is he hurt?"

"He's definitely not hurt. He's chatting with them. What's the word?"

Conrad, bleeding, shot in the back. Bayo standing over him with his empty pistol. He had searched Conrad's clothes and found no weapon.

Notes from Gethsemane

"Boss?" said Vandal.

"Go. Get my brother out of there."

The gunfight was short. Vandal fired one shot and had it returned in force by paramilitaries and police—bad timing, they were on patrol. As a result of the battle one officer got a glass splinter in his eye and was airlifted for emergency surgery, prioritised over the mortally wounded gang members.

None of Bayo's people survived.

Tosin waved Vendra back. "That's far enough. It's too dangerous from here."

"I agree," said Vendra.

Their scintillation counters were going mad. Tosin gave his portable to Vendra. "I've written a note to my brother. Wait a few weeks for him to cool down then give this to him. He'll understand."

"You're really going to do this?"

"Yes. I've always wanted to know what was in there," said Tosin.

"You don't even know if it'll work."

"No, I don't," said Tosin, and he started walking past the flashing lights and the warning signs in English, Yoruba, Hausa, Igbo, French, and Arabic. In the protective suit Adam had supplied it was slow going. There were fetish sacrifices, goat's heads, black eggs, and other charms on the ground, placed there by long dead babalawo who thought they could cure the land by magic.

When he was fifty feet away from Vendra he turned back. She waved.

"I feel like I should say 'I love you', like they do in the movies," she said.

"I'll settle for a wink," said Tosin.

She winked at him.

He stepped over the edge…

And fell…

118

Blinded.

Falling in darkness, surrounded by light...

BAYO

BAYO IT'S ALIVE

The dining room wall was like a display screen, with rapidly changing words in sanguineous splashes.

'Who are you?' asked Bayo.

HOLD ON

The blood flaked, fell off, and the wall was calm for a moment, then there was a bright flash. Bayo covered his eyes.

"It's all right, Bayo. It's only me."

Bayo blinked and standing there glowing like hot coals was his brother.

"Tosin?" He looked like a ghost. "Are you dead?"

"I'm not dead. I'm in The Pit, and it's alive." Tosin sounded excited.

"What do you mean?"

"Adam told us, Vendra and me. It's alive, and they wanted to kill it with an engineered virus. He wanted us to take one of the infected girls and dump her in The Pit, but I'd never do that. It's amazing. I know everything."

"Who's Vendra?" The boy had gone mad. How was he projecting the image?

"Never mind. It's not important. Bayo, I know about Conrad. Don't worry about it. It's done. Cannot be undone. The words, the blood on the walls, it wasn't only you. Six other people within the barricade saw the same thing. The being sensed Adam was trying to kill it and sent out a projection."

"Tosin-"

"No, listen. This thing, this being, it isn't from here. Its mind can reach out... I can hear everybody, even outside the barricade. It just could not understand the data and needed a mind to translate."

Notes from Gethsemane

"Get out of there. I'm coming to get you myself. Wait for me. We'll go back to Ilesha."

"Don't you get it? This thing needs my mind and I want to be part of it. There's so much to learn here. I'm... thanks for always protecting me, brother. Goodbye. I hope we meet again."

The image faded and Bayo was in the dark again. He scrambled outside and ran in the direction of The Pit, but he knew it was too late. The rain had stopped, and the night sky lit up bright, brighter than daylight and the ground shuddered.

A week later, a car rolled to a halt outside the family home. Bayo stepped out and paid the driver. In the yard, one of his sisters was shucking corn. She recognised him and screamed. While they hugged, he saw his mother open the front door. He prostrated himself in the traditional Yoruba greeting for elders.

"Mama," he said. "I have bad news about Tosin..."

Tade Thompson's roots are in Western Nigeria and South London. His short stories have been published in small press, webzines and anthologies. Most recently, his story 'Shadow' appeared in *The Apex Book of World SF 2*. He lives and works in South England and is old enough to remember watching Captain Scarlet on TV. He works under a unified influence field comprised of books, music, theatre, comics, art, movies, gourmet coffee, and amala. He has been known to haunt coffee shops, jazz bars, bookshops, and libraries. He is an occasional visual artist and tortures his family with his attempts to play the guitar.

Planet X

S.A. Partridge

The Russians found the new planet. Double the size of Earth, it was hiding in the shadows of Pluto all this time. At least, that's how I understand it.

We huddle inside Mzizi's with our eyes glued to the flatscreen TV to watch the Russian astronauts celebrate on the space station.

"Sisi, Sisi, look at them float?"

I squeeze my little brother's shoulder in warning. "Shh, Vuyo. Other people want to watch too."

Sometimes my little brother Vuyo doesn't realise that he isn't alone in his little universe, but then again, this is his first time inside the Shebeen. Any other day it would have been Strictly Forbidden, but tonight is a Special Occasion. At four, he's only starting to learn the difference.

A few people giggle when the globules of Champagne float inexplicably upwards on the screen, but they are quickly shushed into silence when the announcer begins talking in his thick European accent.

Ma Agnes, who is hard of hearing, pulls me closer with a thin, bony hand that is surprisingly strong. "What is he saying?"

I lean down till my lips are centimetres from her iron gray hair. I catch a whiff of Lavender and Sunlight soap, which is refreshing over the smoke and sweat of the bar. "He says the astronauts couldn't see it because there's no light in space that could reflect off it. They received an unusual radio frequency which led them there."

Ma Agnes sucks on her toothless bottom lip. "But there it is, on the screen."

I stare at the slick black orb floating in outer space. They've named it Planet X for now. Black on black; it's

S.A. Partridge

like one of those optical illusions where a shape appears the longer you stare at it. For some reason, the picture scares me. Goosebumps flare up my arms. "I don't understand either, Ma. Maybe it's a special type of photograph or something."

The picture switches to the white streets of Moscow where residents brave the cold to wave flags and shout things we can't understand into the camera. They clearly take the Russian space programme as seriously as we take our sport.

By this time Vuyo is bored. He leans his full weight against my legs and I have to grab hold of the side of the bar to steady myself.

He shoots his chubby arms in the air like he used to before Ma succumbed to the Virus, and I oblige, lifting him up onto my hip. "Oof, you're getting too big to be carried, bro."

He flashes me an uneven toothy grin. Two more milk teeth have fallen out and the Tooth Fairy left nothing underneath his pillow. I need to keep a closer eye on him.

As the news credits roll, a hundred different conversations begin at once. Vuyo's eyes take in the excited expressions around the crowded room. "Why is everyone here?" he asks.

I don't know how to explain the significance of what is happening to a toddler. I try anyway. "You know how we listen to the radio in the morning?"

He nods. So far so good.

"Who is our favourite DJ?"

"DJ Ama-Get-Down," he says gleefully.

"Ok, good. Now the Russian astronauts also listen to the radio, but it's always the same, boring static like when we search for a station, neh?"

He nods, a little slower this time.

"But one day, they found a station, and it came from this new planet, this Planet X."

"Do they have DJs there?"

122

Planet X

I think for a second before answering. "Yes, and that's why everyone is excited."

He accepts this explanation without question.

Out the corner of my eye I see Festus Shabalala passing around brown quart bottles of beer which is our cue to head home.

"Come, Baba, let's get you into bed."

He's having none of it. "No one else is going," he whines.

He struggles in my grip, but tonight I'm the big, bad, older sister.

"Don't push it," I say.

We shove our way through the crowd, which has thickened since we arrived. News travels fast in the townships.

Still, we get home very late as Vuyo attempts to count each and every star.

"Is that it, Sisi?" he asks.

"No, Vuyo," I say for the hundredth time. "Planet X is too dark to see."

Every face on the train is lost behind a newspaper, and those that don't have one read over their neighbour's shoulder. Headlines ask the questions we are all thinking. "WHO SENT THE MESSAGE? WHAT DO THEY LOOK LIKE? WHY HAVEN'T THEY TRIED TO CONTACT US BEFORE?"

The elderly man seated next to me catches my eye. He leans forward, and so does his smell.

I re-adjust my position on the hard plastic seat, but it's too late, he's already honed in on me.

"They're coming for us. Do you know what they do to people on their ships? Experiments." Saliva flies from his mouth when he speaks.

I edge away from him. I don't want to talk to him, but the reply forms on my lips automatically—it's a bad habit

S.A. Partridge

I'm trying to drop. "People do terrible things to each other all the time."

His eyes narrow. Clearly that wasn't the response he was looking for.

I'm relieved when he moves away to find someone else to bother. I'm even more relieved when the last of his smell dissipates.

I press my headphones closer to my ears and wait out the rest of the short journey to the City. Ever since Metrorail replaced the wasp coloured scrap heaps with new speed lines, it takes next to no time at all to get to work. Too bad it's double the price. If work didn't subsidise my travel costs I'd never be able to go anywhere.

High-speed trains or not, I'm still late. I run all the way up Riebeeck Street, pushing my way past street vendors setting up their stalls of cheap chips and cigarettes. People are hovering around them reading the papers. The new planet seems to be good for business. It's good for being late too. My colleagues are all too busy chatting excitedly about Planet X to notice me slip down the aisle to my desk. I log into my computer and pull up my schedule.

My task for the day is to come up with Ad Copy for our clients—today an Adult website, that will need to get past a browser's security nets. This involves a lot of creative thinking and a lot of copy pasting.

It takes a couple of minutes to come up with a few variations on 'Large collection of Adult films', which I'll alternate over a number of spreadsheets. Most of our clients are dubious websites. Yesterday, I had to come up with copy for an online Casino, and the day before that a Russian Bride catalogue.

It's hard to believe that the XXXs represent living breathing women subjected to the lowest kind of degradation. I try not to think about it and focus instead on the mindless task of filling the cells without actually taking in what I'm typing. It helps to focus on the first letter and ignore the rest.

Planet X

What also helps is the vast amount of pirated music on our data servers. A little Drum 'n Bass does wonders to deaden the guilt of trying to convince people to visit a website that sells Porn.

Towards the end of the day, I receive an email from my friend Azania that opens with, 'Nonhlanhla, this is sick. You must check it out!'

My first instinct is to click Delete, but my fingers hesitate over the keyboard. Azania isn't the type of person who would pass on those horrific SPCA newsletters featuring burnt and tortured animals. She's more the Amusing Cat type, which is a special type of torture in itself.

I open the mail. It's a news story that's only a few minutes old:

CATTLE MUTILATIONS SCAR WESTERN CAPE

Residents of the farming town of Porterville woke up this morning to the grisly discovery of a field of disembowelled livestock that appear to have been killed during the night.

Local farmer, Piet Wolmerans, was alerted by his staff in the early hours of the morning. Wolmerans told reporters that when he first approached the field, he saw a few hundred cows lying on their sides, seemingly unconscious, 'but when I approached the first animal I found a hole where its stomach should have been. There was no blood.'

Wolmerans is one of four farmers affected by the strange mutilations. Two thousand cows in the Western Cape were affected.

Farm worker Tertius September describes a strange light in the sky at around 2 am. 'At first I thought it was headlights, but when I opened the window I could see that it took up the whole sky.'

The National Department of Agriculture have quarantined the area in the likelihood that a dread disease has found its way to our shores. A spokesperson from the Department was unavailable for comment.

By Elias Khumalo.

S.A. Partridge

The article is accompanied by a colour photograph of a cow with its stomach spooned out. I delete it before I lose my lunch into the dustbin.

The sky has darkened by the time I arrive at the train station, and so has the mood. Azania waits for me on the platform in a short-short skirt and high-higher-highest heels. I have no idea how she walks around the city in them. Her look of nervousness was replaced with excitement when she spots me.

"Eish, Nonhlanhla, did you see that story? I'm not going to sleep after that."

My stomach heaves at the choice of topic. I don't remind her that she insisted I open the email in the first place. "What do you think did that to the animals, a lion?"

She laughs. "A lion. Where is your head, girl? It's the aliens, I'm telling you."

We find two seats on the train and settle in. "Why would they kill the cows, though? It doesn't make sense."

"Who knows? Maybe they're trying to find out what makes us tick or maybe to see what we taste like. Just as long as they stick to the cows, neh?"

I laugh, but it sounds strange and hollow in the too-quiet compartment. I quickly change the subject. We talk about work, and whether or not I should go on a date with Khaya, who's been arriving unannounced at my door with flowers all week.

"It takes more than flowers to like someone, Z."

"Who said anything about like? In these times you have to take what you can get."

"I have Vuyo to think about too."

"And that's exactly why you should go out with Khaya. Life is expensive and he's got big bucks. He can look after you both."

I'm glad she's studying her nails so she can't see my expression. Dating rich men may be fine and well for Azania, but I'm not that type of girl.

Planet X

She puts her hand on my knee. "It's hard to find a man who'll take you and your baggage. You see this?" she asks, waving a diamante studded purse. "This is nothing. A gift. When was the last time someone bought you a gift or took you to eat at an actual restaurant?"

I let her voice recede into a nondescript blah blah.

The train is about to depart when the doors are pried open by a pair of hands in fingerless gloves. It's a Train Preacher, sweaty and heaving from running. I lean back in my seat and avert my eyes. The travelling preachers are all fire and brimstone. This one holds a battered copy of The Daily Cape in his hands. He holds it up in his fist. The headline reads "VAMPIRES FROM SPACE: ARE WE THEIR PREY?"

His voice booms above the screech of the train. "There are those whose teeth are swords, whose fangs are knives, to devour the poor from off the earth, the needy from among mankind."

To my surprise, quite a few passengers lean forward to listen. Next to me, Azania, stops typing on her phone, and she too pays attention. Unease grows in my stomach like a snake uncurling itself.

"Their hair like women's hair, and their teeth like lions' teeth."

I don't want to listen. I want to press play on my MP3 player but he's standing too close to me and my hands remain folded helplessly in my lap.

His eyes bore into mine. "Sister, do you resign your soul to the keeping of the Lord?"

I turn my head slowly. All the passengers are looking at me expectantly. I nod quickly.

"Amen, brothers and sisters, Amen."

A woman to my right starts clapping her hands and singing. Others join in. It is the hymn, 'All is Right With My Soul'. I sing along with them. I don't want to be the only one that doesn't.

S.A. Partridge

Vuyo is sitting on his bed with his thumb in his mouth. He only ever does that when he's afraid.

I scoop him up in my arms and kiss his forward. "Hello, Baba. What's wrong? Did something scare you? Was it a spider?"

His eyes are as big as two-Rand coins. I unplug his thumb from his mouth.

"Sisi, is it true that vampires are coming to eat us?"

Goosebumps erupt all over my body. "Who told you that?"

"Goggo." *Grandma.*

I swallow the urge to swear. That woman and her stories. Instead I smile. "Nope, no alien vampires here. I promise. Besides, you know Will Smith won't let that happen. He's on the case, so you have nothing to worry about."

I kiss him again, and this time I get the right response. He pulls a disgusted face.

"What do you want for supper?"

"Chicken."

"And how do chickens go?"

"Cluck cluck!"

"And how do cows go?"

"Moo moo!"

"And sheep?"

"Baa baa!"

"And giraffes?"

His mouth opens and shuts. He breaks into a grin. "They don't make any noise, silly."

"They don't?"

"No!"

"You sure?"

"Yes!"

I warm up some chicken nuggets on the stove while he plays happily with his animals. Where is my grandmother getting these ideas from?

Planet X

The answer comes the following morning when I drop Vuyo at his Goggo for the day.

She holds herself straight, her lips pursed tight, poised for confrontation. She's purposely ignoring me. I wait until Vuyo has disappeared inside before I speak.

"Vampires, Ma?"

She challenges me with her eyes.

"Don't you understand? He's only a boy. He wets himself at night."

She clicks her teeth irritably. "Have you seen this?" she asks, pulling a folded newspaper from the front of her apron. Another outrageous headline.

FLATS MAN VISITED BY ALIENS is emblazoned on the front page.

"This is proof that they're coming for us."

I sigh. "Please, Ma, just for today, don't tell him any more of your stories."

She shakes her head. "Eish, you're a stubborn girl."

I roll my eyes. "Yes, Ma."

I pull my handbag over my shoulder and leave through the small wrought iron gate. On my way to the taxi rank I pass closed doors and drawn curtains. Washing flaps in the wind from makeshift lines.

It's never like this.

Today there are no children playing soccer before school. The park is empty save for a few pigeons pecking at the uncut grass.

Even the taxis are subdued. The gaatjies are hurrying their passengers into the mini buses. No screams of "Kep Toown!" that are better at awaking the senses than coffee.

This morning all eyes are on the white sky, the curtains of cloud closed so tight that not even a drop of rain can get through.

The day passes with my heart in my chest. Logan, the weird kid that comes to fix the copier, showed up with tin foil sticking out the sides of his peak cap. "It was something I saw in a movie," he said. No one laughed.

S.A. Partridge

On the train, Azania too, is uncommonly quiet. Her eyes dart to and fro, as if she's studying the other passengers. When she's sure no one is eavesdropping, she leans in close. Her perfume is rich and musky, with lingering vanilla. "They're saying there were bright lights above Jozi last night?"

My blood freezes. "Who's saying?"

"It was all over Twitter. People even posted pictures online."

"You sure? Do you know anyone that actually saw it?"

"Yes. Well, not personally. Thandeka Moloi said he was there and he's a proper journalist and he has over a thousand Followers. So it must be true."

I purposely keep off the Internet today. Some of the stories doing the rounds are too upsetting. One of the Russian scientists from the team that received the radio frequency was brutally murdered by someone who blamed him for discovering the new planet.

Worse, an American shuttle has disappeared. It's gone, along with all the astronauts on board.

I can't even imagine what my grandmother is telling Vuyo.

"A man was hijacked outside my building today. In broad daylight! These aliens are making people crazy."Azania shakes her head.

I stare straight ahead and don't reply. Someone has graffitied over the sign reminding passengers to wear their face masks. The End is Near, is written in blood red paint.

"It's not the aliens. Crime happens every day."

"Sho, Sisi, not like this."

"Maybe you've never noticed before."

The look Azania hits me with makes me zip-lock my lips. Some people don't want to hear what they already know but don't like to think about. For this reason I don't remind her that the reason she uses public transport is because her car was stolen, that fear is the reason we travel in pairs—some truths are best left unsaid.

Planet X

The whole city has caught this madness. I walk home like a tourist in a foreign city, unable to make sense of the people around me. There's a strange pressure in the air, like the expectant silence just before it rains. It is an infectious feeling. I hurry home, glad to close the front door behind me. Perhaps the stories are true and the aliens really are as bad as everyone says. As bad as us.

I wake up to the sound of shouting. I blink my eyes open. There's a bright light blazing outside my window.

Vuyo turns in his sleep. As I feared, his head had been poisoned with stories about alien vampires and he insisted on sleeping in my tiny bed.

I move my head from side to side to ease the cramp in my neck from sleeping at the wrong angle then get out of bed as slowly as I can so as not to wake him.

The shouting is louder now.

I open the door to an orange sky. My neighbours are running down the street towards the park. Their feet kick up an expanding cloud of dust.

Smoke chokes my throat and panic seizes me. Fire.

My fingers tremble as I unlatch the front gate. I didn't have time to put on my shoes, so the stones hurt my feet as I run after the others. My braids slap my skin hard. Ash cascades from the sky like confetti. I need to find out how bad it is.

I spin on the spot and see that the rows of shacks are dark and still. In front of me, a single cloud of smoke rises from the park.

Running feet make me turn. There are men chasing someone down the dusty street. I can't make out their faces so all I see are their silhouettes and the outline of make shift weapons in their hands. He stumbles, looks back and staggers on. They're herding him, cutting him off and steering him towards where the smoke is thickest.

As if hypnotised, my feet take me forward.

S.A. Partridge

My neighbours gather in a wide circle surrounding the fire. Many are shouting with their fists in the air; others are watching in silence with the golden flames reflecting in their eyes. I spot my grandmother, standing amongst a group of women. I force my way through, until my body is thrown into the empty space beside her.

"What's happening, Ma?"

She looks at me, a mixture of excitement and fear written clearly in her lined features.

"They caught an alien trying to sneak into Zama Khumalo's house."

She points to the centre of the circle where the men have forced their prey to his knees. I stand on my tiptoes to see, but their faces are still in shadow.

"There's blood on his clothes," someone is saying.

Ma nods her head. She needs no further confirmation of his guilt.

Through the wall of bodies, I see two smaller figures wheeling a rubber tyre towards the men. I know what they are going to do and I find myself unable to watch.

I bury my face into Ma's woollen cardigan, but she pushes me upright. A space opens up before us and my eyes move on their own, as if bewitched.

I see the face of the man about to be put to death. He is no older than twenty, and there is a scar on his cheek from some childhood accident. He's not an alien. He's a man. A scream travels up my throat and dies on my lips. My fear roots me to the spot and mutes my voice. I know if I say one word to save this man, utter one protestation to his killers, all eyes will turn on me. The thought of Vuyo asleep in his bed turns the key on the lock of my silence. He needs me.

I keep my eyes on the flames, wishing that they could burn away my sight.

I walk home, shuddering. My neighbours walk beside me. I cannot hear what they are saying. All I hear are the echoes of the screams of the dying man.

Planet X

I creep into bed beside Vuyo. My head is spinning and my hair smells like smoke, making me nauseous. I try to be still but my body continues to shake. I lie awake until the shouting stops, and silence once again descends on the night.

Only then do I find my voice, the words that I should have said but didn't. "It was just a man." My voice sounds scratchy and strange.

I wake once more to a blinding light through the window. It is so bright I'm convinced the whole Township must be burning. I nudge Vuyo but he doesn't stir.

"Vuyo, baba. Wake up."

My brother's head rolls from side to side. He's faraway in the deepest realms of sleep. I slip out of bed and peer out the window to gauge the danger, but the light is so bright I have to shield my eyes with my hand. It is like no fire I have ever experienced.

Only then do I notice the unearthly silence. As if in a dream, I part the curtain and watch the procession of a single figure walking in the narrow path between houses.

As if he can feel my eyes on his back, he turns around and faces me. His eyes are large and black, as black as Planet X in its cold corner of the galaxy.

I want to tell him to run, to get out of here before he's seen. Does he realise how dangerous it is out there?

Vuyo stirs in his sleep. I rush to his side to check if he's woken, but his eyes remain closed and his thumb is back in his mouth.

When I turn back to the window, it's dark again and the only movement outside is from the neighbour's gate swinging open and closed.

I should be afraid. I should be sounding the alarm, and rallying another mob to action. But I'm the furthest from afraid. I'm relieved.

S.A. Partridge

S.A. Partridge is a young adult novelist from Cape Town. Her work has won the MER Prize for Youth Fiction, the SABC I am Writer Competition, and made the IBBY Honour List. She was named one of the *Mail & Guardian*'s 200 Young South Africans for 2011 and one of South Africa's best up and coming authors by Women 24.

The Gift of Touch

Chinelo Onwualu

Bruno strode across the causeway, scanning the three land skimmers hanging from their docking harnesses with a critical eye. His footsteps echoed through the cavernous space of the docking bay. The diagnostic reader he held showed the surface vehicles were fuelled and in perfect mechanical condition. They were decades out of date, lacking the smooth, sleek designs of newer models, but they worked—and that was all that mattered.

Bringing passengers on board always set him on edge; they had a tendency to poke about in places they didn't belong. But running a haulage freighter doesn't pay much when there isn't much to haul. Now that the technology for instant matter transportation had improved movement between the five planets of the star system, work was becoming rarer. Bruno needed the money and he had to know that his ship, *The Lady's Gift*, was in perfect shape.

He keyed an all-clear code for the docking bay into his reader and sent the message to the main computer. Slipping the flat pad into his tool harness, he headed for engineering. Ronk, the ship's mechanic, met him at the entrance to the engine room. At almost seven feet of solid muscle, with skin a glossy brown so dark that it seemed to drink in light, Ronk was an intimidating presence. Bruno had no doubt the engineer could snap him in half. Luckily, Ronk was a pacifist.

"How's she looking?" Bruno asked, though he needn't have bothered. The burly engineer was scowling, which made Bruno smile. Ronk had grown up on a religious colony whose people believed that life was a burden and death was its only release. They frowned on anything meant to keep one comfortable.

Chinelo Onwualu

"We'll live," Ronk snapped. Bruno watched him lumber back into the dark recesses of the engine room, wondering, as usual, how a man so big could move so delicately.

Bruno continued towards the bridge. Passing through the mess hall, he saw his twin sister, Marley, sitting at the dining table. Her chestnut brown skin was a shade lighter than his and she liked to dye her black hair a vibrant orange, otherwise everyone said she was a female version of him. Which was unfortunate, because the square jaw and broad physique that gave him his rugged good looks, made her look homely.

Marley had taken up half of the dining table with an assortment of metal parts. Knowing her, she was reassembling some machine. He watched her work for a time.

"What's this?" Bruno picked up an unidentifiable bit of metal.

"This, fearless leader,"—he hated when she called him that—"is a V-26 Skyhammer with 10-volt action, 15-meg rounds and a zoom scope that could see Neptune—if it still existed."

"Try that again, this time in a language I can understand."

"It's a very big gun."

Bruno nodded and dropped the piece he'd picked up. He should have known. Marley had an intuitive grasp of machinery, focused exclusively on armoury, which made her the ship's default security officer.

"I'm trying to fix the balance, though. Thing's so top-heavy, you'd need to prop it over a barrel to shoot it straight."

"And what's wrong with the collection of very big guns you already have?"

"Nothing, but you never know when you might need a back-up. This baby could pop a hole in a military freighter—with the right modifications."

The Gift of Touch

"Marley, we're a trawler, not the Sixteenth Battalion. Why would we possibly need this?"

"You never know."

Bruno sighed. Sometimes it was like talking to a very small child.

"Just put that thing back together and stow it. I don't want any sign of it when the passengers board, got it?

"Aye, aye, fearless leader," Marley grinned and snapped him a salute.

"And stop calling me that!"

He continued towards the bridge. There, he found Horns, his navigator, frowning over a display console. She was small-boned, at full height she barely cleared his chest, with a round child-like face that dimpled when she smiled. It was rumoured that she was part Scion, the ancient race that had developed most of the technology that underpinned their world, but Bruno doubted it. The Scions had disappeared centuries ago. Still, given her porcelain pale skin, silver blonde hair, and almond-shaped gray eyes, it was clear that someone somewhere in her genealogy had fooled around.

"Did you look at this clearance ticket before you filled the passenger register?" asked Horns. Before a ship could take on passengers, clearance tickets were required from the Imperial Command certifying that none of the guests had outstanding warrants or, worse, unpaid bills.

"Yeah, they checked out. Why? What's wrong with it?"

"Nothing's wrong with it exactly," she said. "But take a look at the seal." Bruno leaned over her shoulder to stare at the screen. Her hair smelled like lemons. "Notice the extra cross over there? That's a top-level Imperial symbol. Only government brass use those."

"All we've got on the register are a widow and her kids."

"I know. Why would anyone that high up in the Imperial Command sign off for a farmer travelling on a broken-down freighter?"

Chinelo Onwualu

Bruno didn't like this. He and Marley had grown up on a smuggling scow in the rough waters of Moonlight Bay on Old Antegon, and it had been a long time since he had been on the wrong side of the law. They had worked hard to get off-planet and he wasn't eager to go back.

"Scrub them through the system again. If anything looks even remotely funny, flag 'em."

"Should I drop their booking, too?"

"Heck no! We need the money too badly for that. No, I'll have Marley keep her big gun handy. Anyone tries to start something on my ship, it won't be pleasant."

As soon as they walked on to the ship, Bruno knew they were trouble. They were dressed as farmers, but he knew none of them had ever seen a farm. The older woman was too straight. She moved like someone who was used to giving orders—shoulders thrown back and a steady, penetrating gaze. The young man was a soldier. Barefoot, dressed in a threadbare shirt and trousers two sizes too small, he carried nothing more dangerous than a cloth bag, but Bruno had seen too much of war to be fooled. The girl was something else entirely.

She could not have been older than fifteen. Her coal-black skin was so smooth it was luminous. She was bald as an egg with delicate features and a grace that made her seem as if she was gliding. She kept her gaze down for the most part, but for a moment, when she glanced up, Bruno saw that her eyes were as gold as the heart of a flame.

The woman called herself Ana. She introduced the young man and the girl as her children, Drake and Bella. She handed over their identification cards and Bruno checked them one last time. They were clean. Just like her clearance papers. But they had the same high-level seal he had seen on the manifest. Bruno hesitated over the cards, debating whether he needed this kind of trouble. There would be other passengers, surely. Then his eye fell on her

The Gift of Touch

payment receipt. The amount she'd paid was more than double what he had charged.

"Is there a problem, captain?" Ana asked softly.

"Not at all, ma'am," Bruno said. "Welcome aboard."

Usually, all the crew—except Ronk—would come out to the entrance of the docking bay to welcome new guests, but by the time they reached the loading bay only Marley had arrived. Bruno let out a relieved breath to see that strapped to her back was her big gun. He caught the young man's face when he saw Marley. His eyes had narrowed at the sight of the gun, but he had quickly smoothed his features into a careful blankness. Bruno resolved to watch him carefully.

"My, that *is* a big gun," Ana said after Bruno had made the introductions. She spoke as if she was talking to a slow-witted child. Luckily, Bruno's twin had no ear for sarcasm.

"Yeah, I call her Jane."

"That's a lovely name."

"Thanks! Hey, follow me, I'll show you where you'll be staying." Marley looked over at Bruno and mouthed: *I like her*. Bruno sighed inwardly. His sister was such a poor judge of character sometimes. As they headed into the heart of the ship, the intercom in his ear cackled to life.

"I need to talk to you." Horns' voice sounded strained.

"Can it wait?" Bruno wanted to keep an eye on his guests and he was in no mood to deal with any more strangeness.

"No, Bruno. It really can't." Horns only ever called him by his name when she was being serious. Otherwise it was 'Boss'.

When he got to the bridge he found Horns pacing. Her pale hands were fluttering like live things. He had never seen his hard-as-nails navigator so agitated.

"I didn't know, Bruno. I mean, I suspected something was shady, but I had no idea," she said.

"Horns, calm down. What are you talking about?"

"You've got to get them off the ship."

Chinelo Onwualu

"Our passengers? Are you crazy? They've already paid—and you should see how much. We can finally fix our hyperdrive, maybe even get one that was made in the last decade."

"Bruno, you don't understand," she took a deep breath to calm herself before she continued. "They're *Mehen*."

Bruno's smile froze on his face. The Mehen di Gaya were the highest class of priests in the Amethyst Order, the religious institution that controlled the Empire. There were rumours that the Mehen even operated a shadow arm of elite warrior monks who could make whole families disappear overnight.

"How can you be sure?" Bruno asked.

"Because I used to be one of them."

"You're Mehen? You never told me that."

"It's who I *was*, not who I am now," she said, waving her hand dismissively. "Besides, you never asked." She gave him a sad look.

"That's not fair, you could have said something if you wanted to. It's not like you talk about your past all the time. I mean, I don't even know your real name."

"Well, there never seemed a good enough time. It was always one crisis or another with you." She turned towards the control banks and stared out the giant windows. "It still is."

Bruno thought he heard a hint of tears in her voice. "What do you want me to say, Horns? I run haulage; if it's not someone trying to ship stolen goods off-planet, it's not having the right papers, or stowaways, or... there'll always be something."

"I know, but sometimes it's like you don't have space in your life for anything beyond this ship."

They had had this conversation a thousand times. He fought the urge to touch her, to wrap her in his arms and feel the way her body curved into his. He longed for the familiarity of her smell and her skin. He had never been good with words, but his touch could make her promises.

The Gift of Touch

Yet they had been down that path before. Only heartbreak lay that way.

"Doesn't matter anyway," she said, cutting into his thoughts. "We have bigger problems. I think the girl is in danger."

"What do you mean?"

"Most people don't know this, but the Order started out as the tenders of the fire pits in the old temples, back when people would burn sacrifices in the sacred flames. In those days, the priests would pick a child—a special child whom no one was allowed to touch—and when this child reached a certain age, it was sacrificed, burned in the Holy Fires. When I was a novice, they told me the Order stopped the practice hundreds of years ago." She turned. "But I don't think they have. I think they just took it off-planet."

"So you think they're going to kill that girl?"

"It's worse than that. I ran that symbol through the system and I found records going back nearly fifty years. Every fourteen years or so, this symbol would show up in the passenger manifests of a small M-class vessel—like ours—going to the moon of Osiris. The thing is, all the ships would go in... but none of them ever came back out."

A cold feeling settled at the base of Bruno's spine. "Are you sure?"

Horns nodded. "They didn't even bother to hide the records."

They were silent for a minute or two. "Well, no one's killing anyone on my ship," said Bruno. "It'll raise the insurance premiums."

"What are you going to do?"

"I'll figure out something, don't worry."

"I'm not worried," she said, and reached out to touch his cheek. He had forgotten how calloused her fingers were from gripping the navigation console. He closed his eyes and turned to brush his lips against them, but she withdrew her hand too quickly. Her touch lingered long afterward as if he had been burned.

Chinelo Onwualu

"I just don't see what the big deal is," Marley said.

"It's your eternal soul," growled Ronk.

"I know," she said quickly. "I just don't see why it matters. I mean, if I were an ant or a dog or a chimpanzee, nobody would care what my soul was up to. But just because I'm a person, suddenly my soul is important? I don't get it."

They had gathered at the dining table, all except the girl; Ana said she was ill and would be eating in her cabin. Tonight's dinner was a special treat, Ana and Drake had brought meat—dried strips of *real meat*. Between that and the greens and tomatoes—Horns grew them in a small hydroponic garden on the ship's abandoned leisure deck— it was almost a true meal. Almost.

Bruno had tried to ignore the increasingly heated conversation between Marley and Ronk, but in spite of himself, he found he was listening with growing interest. Besides, this was the most he'd heard Ronk say in one sitting in all the time he had known him.

"But we are better than animals or insects," Ronk snapped. "We made in the image of the Creator himself."

"See, that's the thing, how do you know that? How do you know what the creator looks like? No one's seen him. It's like we looked around and thought, 'hey no one else looks like us, we must be special.' But what if we're not?"

"We *are* special. We have reason and compassion," Ronk said in a low voice. His voice seemed calm, but Bruno noticed the engineer was gripping his knife tightly, as if to keep his fist from shaking. "It does not matter that no one has seen the Creator's face. We have seen the works of his hands. You have never seen the wind, yet you feel its power. Do you doubt *its* existence?"

"Oh come on, I'm not arguing about whether the Creator exists. I can't prove that and neither can you. What I'm saying is you can't know anything about what the Creator is thinking or what he wants just by looking at the

The Gift of Touch

universe. Just like you can't look at my fork and guess what I had for lunch."

"We do not need to guess. The Creator has told us what he wants of us through the words of his Prophet," Bruno's voice broke slightly at the mention of the Prophet. "Those who heed his words, follow in the path of truth."

"Oh! And that's another thing, how do you know the Prophesies are right? I mean, we're talking about a book collected from a bunch of other books, like, five thousand years ago. It's been translated and retranslated so many times that I'm pretty sure stuff's been lost. How do you know that what you're reading is even what was written in the first place? And why choose this book over any other ancient book? All you have is your belief. I'm sorry, man, that's just not enough for me."

Suddenly, Ronk stood up, knocking his chair over and juddering the table. He stared at Marley for a moment, his face unreadable. Then, without another word, he stalked off. Bruno watched him go, bemused.

"Oh no! Did I say something wrong?" Marley was immediately distraught and turned to each person at the table. "I didn't mean to offend him; I was just making a point."

"I'm sure he's ok." Bruno took the opportunity to look over at Ana at the opposite end of the table. "What about you? Do you think everything the Prophesies say are the 'unvarnished' words of the Creator?"

The older woman wiped her mouth deliberately before she spoke.

"Oh, I never discuss religion," she said. "Especially not over dumplings." She gestured at the young man beside her who produced an insulated food flask filled with dumplings—whose pork might possibly even have come from actual pigs. Amazingly, they were still hot. Bruno's mouth watered at the sight of them. Now, it was a real meal.

Chinelo Onwualu

"He hates me," said Marley.

"He doesn't hate you," said Bruno.

"Yes he does. I insulted his religion," she fingered the strap of the large gun she carried on her back. Bruno had asked her to keep it on her at all times.

"It's a big religion; it can take a little criticism," Bruno said, distractedly. He had not seen the girl since she arrived on the ship the day before. Their destination on the small moon formerly known as Ganymede—before it was terra-formed for human habitation and renamed Osiris—was only two days away. He had to draw the girl out and get her away from her captors before then. Once they landed, they'd be in the hands of the Mehen and there was no telling what would happen to them after that. A plan had started forming in his head. It was vague and dangerous, but it just might work.

They rounded a corner and Marley almost collided with Ronk as he emerged from the engine room. She ducked her head, unsure of what to do. They hadn't seen each other since the disastrous dinner the night before. The big engineer frowned and looked at his hands. He started to speak, but Marley spoke first.

"I'm sorry if I said anything blasphemous last night," she said. "It's just... I never think about that stuff—I mean, religion and all that—and you know me, sometimes when I open my mouth I don't know what comes out."

Ronk's frown deepened and he took a deep breath before speaking. "I am not insulted," he said. He spoke in his characteristic short, clipped sentences. Apparently, only religion brought out his loquacious side, Bruno observed wryly. "What you said last night made me think. I have never truly thought about my faith. When I left the colony, I wanted the freedom to do as I pleased. Now, you have given me the freedom to think as I please. For that, I thank you."

Marley blinked at him, owl-eyed. Ronk nodded curtly and retreated back into the gloom of the engine room. She

The Gift of Touch

stared after him for a moment, and then broke into a smile that made her beautiful.

"Did you hear that?" She turned to Bruno, beaming. "He thanked me. I think I'm going to die of happiness."

"We all have to die of something," Bruno said dryly. He continued on to the cargo hold, Marley skipped after him like a little girl. In the depths of the hold, he began moving boxes and crates.

"He said I freed his mind, can you believe that?" Marley chattered as she helped him move the detritus of past adventures. She stopped. "Hey, if we get married, will I have to convert?"

Bruno's cry cut her short. "Found it!"

"Wait, that's-"

"Yes, it is."

"You still have that? You can't be serious, Bruno. You use that and we'll be flagged for sure. Captain Moran warned us."

"We'll be fine. There's a lot more going on in this ship than some illegal smuggling."

"I hope you know what you're doing, fearless leader."

"Me too," said Bruno under his breath as he headed back to the bridge. "And stop calling me that!"

The young man called Drake was sitting alone in the small lounge in the cabin bay. It was less a lounge than two armchairs and a tiny table in the middle of a rounded cul-de-sac just off from the mess hall. From there one could see all the doors of every cabin in the bay. It was the perfect place to keep watch—if that was one's intention. He was examining his hands as if they belonged to someone else and looked up as Bruno stepped in.

For all his size, he was much younger than Bruno had initially thought. No more than fifteen, if that. "Drake, right? How's your sister?" he asked. "We haven't seen her since you all came aboard."

"She, she prefers to be alone."

Chinelo Onwualu

"Oh? Is she sick?" Bruno moved towards the door, but the boy—for that was what he was, really—stood up to block his way.

"No! I mean, well, she's just resting."

Bruno nodded sceptically. He had expected a hard-boiled veteran and had come prepared for a fight. This was not going as he had planned. He studied Drake a moment. "Is this your first time off-world?"

He nodded.

"How old are you?"

The boy blinked in confusion. It was clear he wasn't often asked personal questions. "Sixteen," he answered slowly, as if afraid of getting it wrong.

"That's a good age. You know, Marley and I were about that old when we first went off-planet, too."

"Yeah?" The boy was impressed, and Bruno could see he struggled not to show it. "How did you leave?" He asked too casually.

"We stowed away on a trade ship not much bigger than this one," Bruno chuckled at the memory. The captain had been so angry he threatened to put them both in an airlock and flush them out to space. Instead, for three years he had put the two orphans to work, caring for them like a father. It was tough, but they had been lucky. They could have been sold to slavers.

"What about your parents?" Drake asked.

"Never had any." That wasn't exactly true. Bruno and Marley had never known their father, but their mother had been a dockside runner on Moonlight Bay, selling charms and trinkets to sailors and spacers when the work was good and selling other things when it wasn't. One day, when the twins were ten, she'd told them she had found work on a smuggler's scow. She had Bruno and Marley wait for her on the deck of the ship while she went to see a man about some money he owed her. She never returned. For the next five years, the twins worked to earn their keep

The Gift of Touch

on the scow, running errands and hauling small loads to get by.

"But we survived, Marley and me. We had each other. It's important for family to stick together, isn't it?"

The boy shifted his weight at that, his eyes darting quickly to the door of their cabin. "That's important," he agreed reluctantly.

"Then tell me the truth, what's wrong with your sister? What's she got?"

"What? No, she's not sick."

"Look, she's been holed up in there since we've been space-borne. You're the only one who ever goes in there, so whatever she's got, you can't catch it. If it's the shakes, we've got ways to deal with it-"

"No, you don't understand, it's not like that, she's fine."

"Then, let me see for myself," Bruno made to shoulder past, but Drake remained firmly in his path.

"You can't go in there!" There was a note of desperation in his voice and a look on his face almost like fear. Otherwise, the rest of him was steel.

"You don't tell me where I can and cannot go on my ship," Bruno's voice was dangerously low. "Do you understand?"

"Is everything all right, Captain?" It was Ana.

"I want to see your daughter."

"Has she done something wrong?" The crackle of the overhead speakers interrupted his response.

"Boss, we've got company," Horn's voice was steady, but Bruno could hear the note of fear in it. "Big Brother is here." He cursed softly. It was too soon.

"I thought you said you didn't have any brothers," Drake said accusingly. The boy seemed hurt. He was so young, Bruno realised—younger than Bruno had ever been, even at that age.

"It's a literary reference, child, from a classic of Old Earth," Ana said. There was amusement in her eyes. "I didn't know you could read, Captain."

147

Chinelo Onwualu

"You'd be surprised what I can do," and with that, Bruno stalked off to the bridge.

Captain Alistair Moran was a grizzled veteran of half a hundred battles and you could see every one of them on his body. He wore smoked glasses to hide the cybernetic implants that had replaced his eyes and one of his hands was robotic, though it was impossible to tell which because he wore black gloves all the time. He was a small man, bald—whether by choice or from another accident, no one could say—with a clean-shaven face crisscrossed with scars from laser blades, and a jaw that seemed permanently clenched. He stood rod-straight in his gray Army Ranger uniform, black boots polished to a high shine. Bruno suspected that if anyone cared to measure, they would find that Moran stood at a precise 90-degree angle from the floor.

His ship, the *S.S. Gilgamesh* had overtaken *The Lady's Gift* easily and locked onto them with traction hooks. Twenty of his men had forced their airlock open and stormed the ship through an airtight bridge connecting the vessels. They rounded up the crew in the main hanger bay. Horns and Ronk both had looks of controlled fear, but Marley looked ready to beat someone's head in. They had confiscated her gun and her lip was bleeding, but otherwise she seemed unharmed. Bruno noted that they had not found his guests yet, but knew it was only a matter of time.

"Bruno Tertian," Moran's voice was hard as a leather whip. "What did I tell you about trawling contraband through my sky?"

Bruno chose his words carefully. He was in very dangerous territory; Moran did not like wrong answers. "We don't want trouble, we're just on a routine run to Osiris."

"Oh? And if I search this ship I won't find anything... untoward?"

148

The Gift of Touch

"We don't-"

But before he could finish, Moran's hand flashed out and pain bloomed across Bruno's face. Bruno fell to one knee in agony, blood pouring from his nose. He heard someone gasp—Marley or Horns, he could not tell whom. Moran had broken his nose with a casual flick of his wrist.

"Don't lie to me, Tertian," he said quietly. "You know how much I hate being lied to." He turned to his lieutenant, a big, pale-skinned man with a shock of red hair. "Search the ship."

It could not have been more than a few minutes, but it seemed like an eternity. Soon the big man returned carrying a sealed metal chest. It was very heavy, Bruno knew, but the lieutenant carried it with ease. Behind him, Ana and Drake followed. There was no sign of the girl. Ana showed no trace of fear; in fact, she had a small smile on her face. It grew larger when she saw Bruno on his knees trying to stanch the blood from his broken nose.

"I hope there is no problem Captain..." she hesitated to get his name and the captain supplied it. "Captain Moran," she finished.

"No problem, ma'am. Did you know this ship was carrying contraband goods?" He nodded to the sealed chest. "A serious violation of the law."

"I had no idea, captain. We are just humble farmers on our way to a homestead on Osiris."

"Of course, ma'am. But we're going to have to take you in for questioning. Just to be sure, you understand."

"Oh I don't think there'll be any need for that. If you just confiscate the contraband, you can let us go on our way."

"That won't be possible ma'am."

"I'm sure your command will understand," Ana said, and produced an ID disk that Bruno had never seen before. It was a dull metal grey with no holographs on it except for a strange symbol in one corner. She flashed it at the captain, smiling broadly.

"I'm sorry, ma'am, but rules are rules."

Chinelo Onwualu

Ana's smile died. "Who are you?" She demanded, but the truth had begun to dawn on her. "Where are your badges? What command do you belong to?"

Moran smiled thinly. He still wore his Ranger uniform and still flew his military-class schooner. He made sure all his men wore their uniforms and that they carried standard-issue ranger rifles, but it was all a ruse. Alistair Moran hadn't been an employee of the empire for a very long time.

He turned to Bruno. "I've warned you, Tertian. Don't let me catch you in my sky again. Next time, it won't be your nose I'll break," he nodded to his lieutenant. The big man tucked the chest under one arm and grabbed Ana with the other. She squealed in pain as he twisted her arm, marching her off towards the airlock.

Bruno almost felt sorry for her. "What are you going to do with her?" he asked.

"Whatever I want," Moran smirked. "The Red Priests are the reason I had to leave the army. They owe me."

"What about the boy?"

Moran examined Drake closely. The boy was expressionless, but the old pirate seemed to see something in his face.

"He's yours. Not my type anyway." With that, he marched off. His soldiers filed silently after him. They still retained their military discipline, Bruno noted.

He sighed with relief as the last of them walked through the airlock, sealing it shut behind him. He heard the metallic *thonk* as the traction hooks disengaged. Horns rushed to his side, helping him to his feet. The pain in his nose was now a dull throbbing. It was no longer bleeding, but he knew he had to tend to it soon.

"Everyone all right?" Bruno asked his crew.

"A bit roughed up, but fine," said Horns. Marley gave him a thumbs-up, grinning. A bruise was forming on her jaw, he saw. Ronk noticed it too. He touched it gingerly; she winced in pain but did not turn away.

150

The Gift of Touch

"Good, let's get out of here." Horns nodded. Reluctantly, she let him go and headed to the bridge. Ronk headed to the engine room while Marley went down to the hold to check to see how much of their supplies Moran had taken.

It was just him and the boy left. Drake looked lost and scared, but there was a determined cast in his jaw. He would be fine, Bruno knew.

"I'm sorry about your mother," Bruno said.

"She was not my mother," Drake's voice was hard.

"What happened to your sister? How come Moran didn't find her?"

Just as Drake opened his mouth to answer, the ship was rocked by a violent blast that that sent them both stumbling. High above them, the skimmers swayed dangerously in their harnesses.

Horn's voice crackled over the intercom. "Bruno, they're firing on us!" she cried.

"Get us out of here!"

"I can't," she said. "I can get the shields up, but nothing else is responding-"

Ronk's voice cut in. "Captain, they disabled the engine systems. They destroyed every control bank down here."

Bruno cursed under his breath. He knew it had been too easy. "Can you fix it?"

"It will be difficult, but I think so. Otherwise, we will all die," Ronk almost sounded pleased.

"Do it," he snapped. Haulage freighters were not usually equipped with weaponry, but then again, most haulage freighters didn't have Marley. "Sis? Tell me they left something behind."

"Never fear, fearless leader," Marley's voice was light. Chaos was her element. "They took our food, our meds and all our spares—they even took Martha—but Jane and the rest of the family are still here."

Another blast rocked the ship, but they held on to the walls for support and kept their feet.

Chinelo Onwualu

"Can you handle a gun?" Bruno asked. Drake nodded. "Good, follow me."

Bruno had never liked the bio-suits—they smelled like old bananas and they made him feel claustrophobic, though he would never admit that to anyone—but they were their last hope. Bruno and Drake met Marley in the ship's lowest cargo hold. Marley hadn't been exaggerating about her collection, Bruno realised. Over the years, she had collected and modified dozens of high-calibre weapons, making them lighter, more accurate, and above all, more powerful. She picked out the two largest. The gun she'd been modifying was big, but it was hardly the largest in her arsenal. That honour went to the one she gave Bruno; it was the size of a small cannon.

"I call her Bertha," Marley said, grinning.

There were more hideaways, pockets, and vents, on the ship than Bruno could count. It had been modified and refitted dozens of times and every time they wrenched out and replaced an old system with something smaller, faster, and more efficient, those old spaces would be closed off or converted to storage. One of these retrofitted spaces was the series of tanks from when the ship still used liquid fuel. They were massive carbon-fibre drums with two outlets: one at the top to allow for manual checks, and the other at the bottom where intake nozzles fitted. Located on the ship's underbelly, they were the perfect place to slip out unnoticed.

The tanks normally held the ship's extra water, but right now one of them was nearly empty. They climbed down into it and, amid an increasing barrage from Moran's ship, put on their bio-suits. The three of them slipped out of the ship through the intake valve. Marley immediately headed for the starboard side, while Bruno and Drake headed for the port side, the tiny air-jets on their suits propelling them through the zero gravity of space. Bruno tried not to look out at the vast blackness beyond the ship; it always made him dizzy.

The Gift of Touch

Soon, he could spy Moran's ship just over the bow. *The Lady's Gift* was facing the *S.S. Gilgamesh* directly and her front shields were taking most of the blasts. They were holding, but Bruno could see more sparks every time they took another hit. They would not last much longer. Bruno manoeuvred the large gun off his back. He snapped on the suit's magnetic boots and they held him fast to the hull. A few feet away, still near the underside of the ship, Drake did the same. Bruno knew that on the other side, Marley was doing it too.

"Ready?" Bruno called to the others through the suit's intercom.

"Aye, aye, fearless leader," sang Marley.

"Ready, sir," came Drake's voice. The boy had taken on a military precision that Bruno knew could have only come from long years of training—likely since childhood.

"Horns, on my signal, lower the shields. One... two... now!"

In a flash of light, Marley fired her gun. Moran had not been expecting return fire and hadn't bothered to raise his shields. A spot of fire bloomed on the other ship's hull and was quickly quenched by the vacuum of space. Marley was right; Jane really could pop a hole in a military freighter. Then, Bruno and Drake fired their guns. Their aim was true. Both rounds hit the same spot on the ship that Marley's had. Suddenly, all the lights on the *S. S. Gilgamesh* went out.

Bruno smiled grimly, snapped off the boots, and jetted towards the nearest airlock.

"Captain, I have made some adjustments," Ronk's voice crackled over the intercom. "We cannot go very fast or very far, but we can fly."

"Then let's get out of here."

The girl Bella was waiting for them when they returned. It was the first time Bruno had seen her since she arrived on the ship. Standing in the light, Bruno could see that her skin was darker than he'd first thought. She was coal-black—like something burned to a crisp—and she had no eyebrows. She was dressed in the same clothes she had worn when she boarded. But it was as if she was a different girl. Gone were the hunched shoulders and downcast eyes that had made her seem like some small, hunted, haunted thing. She stood straight, her red-gold eyes boring into him.

"The red woman, is she gone? Truly?" Her voice was low, almost masculine, and smooth as silk slipping through the fingers.

Bruno nodded.

A look of sadness passed over her face. "She was broken inside," she said quietly. "I could have fixed her, but she would not let me."

As Bruno took off the bio-suit's helmet, it brushed his broken nose, sending a lance of pain searing across his face. In all the excitement, he had completely forgotten about it. He let out an involuntary grunt.

Bella moved like silent lightening. Suddenly, she was in front of him, reaching out to touch him, ignoring Drake's shout. It was as if time slowed down for Bruno. He was aware of Drake's voice, of movement behind him, but somehow it did not matter. As her hand crept closer to his face, his skin began to prickle and his hair stood on end, as if he was too close to a high-voltage wire.

Her touch was electric. A searing light burned through him—as it passed he could feel the cartilage in his nose crunch back into place, the old laser blade wound on his shoulder melt away, the pitted scars on his hands from his childhood as a dockworker knit back up, the first beginnings of arthritis in his knees loosen—and then it was gone.

Bruno sagged to the ground; he would have fallen over had Marley not caught him in time. The girl stepped back, cradling her hand against her chest. Then she smiled and broke into a laugh. It was the most beautiful sound Bruno had ever heard.

The Gift of Touch

A few weeks later, as Bruno made his way up to the leisure deck, he passed Marley and Ronk sitting at the mess hall dining table. She was sitting on his lap.

"I did not leave the table in anger," Ronk was saying. "I just needed to think. So I went to down to the cooling vents in the engine room."

"Oh yeah, I think better when it's noisy, too. I like to go up to the main air turbine shaft. I have to be careful 'cause I could get sucked in if I stand too close."

Ronk laughed at that; it was deep and rich like soil. It was still strange to hear him do so, but Ronk was a man transformed. In some ways they all were.

"So, I've been meaning to ask you, what does 'Ronk' mean?"

"It's short for Aderonke. It's Yoruba..."

Bruno continued on.

Bella and Drake were in the cabin bay lounge talking heatedly in low tones.

"Captain!" Bella called out when she saw him and bounded down the short hallway to meet him. Dressed in a mix of Marley and Horns' hand-me-downs, she almost looked like a normal teenager. "I have the most wonderful news." She spoke like someone who had learned to speak out of a book—an old, old book.

"Yeah? What is it?"

"Have you ever heard of the Acolytes of Oshun?"

"Aren't they the priests who run a high-class prostitution scam?"

"No, no! They are honoured servants of the Goddess of Love," she said, her face animated by excitement. "They are priests and priestesses who dedicate their bodies to service; they spend years learning the intricate arts of pleasure, which they use to help bring devotees closer to divine. Their main temple is on Mars."

"That's nice, but what's that got to do with anything?"

Chinelo Onwualu

"I want to join them!" she burst out—and clapped her hands to her mouth as if she'd spoken without thinking. "Please, please, please may I join them?"

"I don't know Bel, you sure that's what you want?"

"Captain, I've spent my whole life craving the touch of others," she said. "The life of an Acolyte would be paradise for me."

"What about your... abilities?"

She shrugged and stuffed her hands in her pockets. "I can only fix those who want to be fixed," she glanced at Drake who folded his arms and turned away.

Bruno noted Drake's tense shoulders and obstinate scowl and resolved to talk to him later. He knew Drake had been trained as a warrior-priest. Though the warrior part had stuck long after the priest part had fled, he had spent his life keeping Bella safe from accidental contact. Would he be able to handle her new role? Bruno hoped so. The Amethyst Order was most likely still looking for them and she would need his protection.

It would be a few weeks before they wrapped up their current job and at least a week before they reached Mars. He had some time yet.

"If that's what makes you happy, Bel. Let's talk about this later, huh?"

She beamed and nodded.

Horns was waiting for him among the greenery of the hydroponic garden, tending a plant in the far corner of the room.

"You said you had some information for me," Bruno said, greeting her with a kiss.

"I've finally found Drake and Bella's files with the Order," she pointed at a reader on a nearby counter. Bruno thumbed through the different screens.

"Not a whole lot here," he said.

"I know, it's deep cover stuff. Most of it is Drake and Ana, really, all I managed to get on Bella is her name."

"Nefertiti? Huh. What kind of name is that?"

The Gift of Touch

"Well, once you become Mehen, you're given a 'true' name, something more spiritual."

"What was your true name?"

"I don't remember."

"Come on, Horns, if you don't want to talk about it..."

She laid a gentle hand on his arm. "Honestly, Bruno, I don't remember. I paid a guy in Qom 600 credits to have that memory erased."

"Why?"

"I didn't want to be reminded of my former self. I was an enforcer—like Drake. I did some pretty awful stuff."

"Did you torture people?" Bruno had been tortured once. A job had gone wrong and he'd ended up owing money to the wrong people. It had been the most hellish few hours of his life. He had often wondered about the blank-faced man, who had methodically pulled out his fingernails, who he was in the life outside that room.

"Torture doesn't work," Horns had gone curiously blank, as if something in her had closed off her true self. Bruno knew he was looking at the Enforcer she had once been.

"I'd disagree."

"Physical torture, I mean. The threat of pain will only get you so far. Once you start inflicting it, people will say anything to make the hurting stop, and it'll usually be lies. If you really want to find out the truth, you threaten what they love. And it doesn't always mean going after their families. You could go after their ideals or their sense of security. If they know anything, they'll tell you. If they don't, they'll be more than eager to help you find it."

There was a silence between them.

"You were good, weren't you?"

"I was the best."

"So why erase the one memory?"

"It was all I could afford. And by the time I got enough money for more treatments, I realised that I didn't want to forget my past. My memories make me who I am. Without

Chinelo Onwualu

knowing how bad it was then, I can't appreciate how good I have it now."

"You're amazing, you know that?" Bruno said, and Horns smiled. He watched the blankness dissolve and was filled with tenderness for her. The force of it hit him like a blow to the gut. There was an odd relief on her face and Bruno realised just how much she had risked in telling him about her past.

"I love you," she sighed and slipped into his arms.

Bruno smiled and wrapped her in his arms. He began to kiss her, slowly and softly. His touch could make her promises, and this time, he was sure he could keep them.

Chinelo Onwualu is former journalist turned writer and editor living in Abuja, Nigeria. She has a BA in English from Calvin College and an MA in journalism from Syracuse University. Her work has appeared in *Saraba Magazine*, *Sentinel Nigeria Magazine* and the *2010 Dugwe Anthology of New Writing*. Follow her on her blog at chineloonwualu.blogspot.com.

The Foreigner

Uko Bendi Udo

Edikan threw a stick a few yards in front of him. "Go get!" he said to Mboro, who froze in place and then turned his head sideways to show puzzlement. "Ke bin!" Edikan repeated in Milinan. Mboro hopped happily after the stick, fetched it, and returned it back to Edikan, his yellow eyes flashing brighter with pride.

Edikan's gaze strayed and he noticed that the security guard in front of the Lagos Ministry for Intergalactic Services building had moved from his spot. Edikan moved quickly. He accepted the stick from Mboro, touched a model car icon display on his gloved left palm, and then waved his right palm over Mboro, changing him into a toy car. Edikan pocketed the car and ran across the street.

"Yeye boy!" a motorist cursed as his vehicle missed Edikan by a hair. The motorist's outburst drew attention to him, so he squeezed behind the glass wall of the MIS building that faced Omotayo Street. Briefly distracted, he studied his image in the glass wall, and was reminded, sadly, of a few things about him that contributed to his 'foreignness'. His hair was a forest of dark-black, spiky locks, and his boyish, doll-like face bore eyes that were at once familiar but unearthly.

A worker in suit and tie walked up to the building's entrance, and pressed a thumb on a console. Edikan ran up and slipped into the building behind him. He walked briskly towards the glass door that led into a cavernous room with space travel and life-form monitoring equipment. A few workers in lab coats operated the equipment. A scanner checked an astronaut and his suit for alien particles. Seated three desks away from the scanner was Tolu Makinde, dressed in a suit and tie. Edikan ran up

159

to his desk and sat in front of him, making Tolu jerk back in surprise.

"How did you get in here?" Tolu said, looking around. "Where is the security guard?"

"Ayak no dok," Edikan said.

"Speak in English!"

"He let me come."

"You're lying."

"Go ask."

Tolu stood up and pointed at the door. "Get out!"

"Yem eti fok!" Edikan stood up. "My father Nigerian. You have proof!"

"I told you the last time you asked. We have no records to show that."

"Lie! Where paper from Milina?"

Tolu's brow squeezed tighter with more surprise. "What paper? What are you talking about?"

"NiMLAF say," Edikan said, and shoved a piece of paper at Tolu.

"The Nigerian-Milinan Legal Aid Foundation?" Tolu sat down as he read the paper.

"They help me. They say you have proof."

Tolu slowly ripped the paper in bits, fed them to the shredder, and leaned closer to Edikan. "Since you have friends like this on your side, why don't you tell them to buy you a one-way ticket back to Milina where you belong? This case is closed, as far as the government is concerned. You're an illegal alien."

"I am Nigerian-Milinan. I belong here!"

"There's nothing here for you, Edikan. You have no proper papers, and no family."

"Nothing for me in Milina."

"But that's your home."

Edikan stood up. "Nigeria is home! My father born here!"

"Where's the security guard?" Tolu pressed a button on his desk, and then rose to his feet.

160

The Foreigner

"Give me paper!"

Tolu reached across the desk and shoved Edikan, who staggered backwards, spilling to the floor. "Get out of here!"

Mboro rolled out of Edikan's pocket and transformed into a great big bear with yellowish eyes. It growled loudly, prompting the other workers in the office to let out ear-splitting screams, and a mad dash for the exit ensued. Mboro charged after Tolu.

"Yak!" Edikan said.

Mboro froze, its sharp, big claws only inches away from Tolu's face. Edikan walked up to Mboro, and waved his right palm, reversing him back into a toy car, which he picked up and pocketed. Tolu remained frozen against the wall, his eyes bulging with fright.

A security guard burst through the door, gun drawn. Guided by Tolu's hysterical pointing, the guard turned to look. Edikan, however, was nowhere in sight. The guard ran around the office looking under desks and equipment.

Tolu pulled out a file from his desk labelled Edikan Usoro, and rifled nervously through it. He pulled out a document, folded and pocketed it. He replaced the file and then searched for his Galaxy phone.

"Freeze!" the guard barked as he spotted and then chased after Edikan, who had emerged from hiding headed for the back exit out of the office. Behind them, police officers with sophisticated weapons drawn entered the office.

"What took you people so long, eh?" Tolu said, and pointed in the direction Edikan and the security guard went, adding, "This is 2080, for God's sake. Not 1999!" Tolu found his phone and quickly exited the office.

"Open driver's door," Tolu Makinde commanded as he nervously approached his 2077 Moonray sports sedan. The car, recognising his voice, lifted up the driver's door like a butterfly's wing, exposing an interior dominated by a curvy touchscreen console that spewed relevant info-graphics.

Uko Bendi Udo

He looked around him and jumped when he heard another car's door open behind him. He should've requested a police escort, Tolu thought, that Edikan boy is dangerous. Where did he get that... thing? He'd heard of NiMi kids bringing strange toys back to Earth, but this one took the cake.

He entered the car, started it with another voice command, and drove out of the underground garage. When he emerged onto the surface streets, he saw that the security guard and the police officers had followed their quarry outside but were now looking around as if they'd lost Edikan.

Edikan must go, Tolu thought, as he gunned the car past his office building and onto Monsood Idowu Highway. He should've pressed on with the hire to eliminate the boy a month ago. He could've put this issue far behind him by now.

How did Edikan find out about the Milina Report? That lawyer group must have a snitch inside the government or perhaps right inside Tolu's office. *Kai!*

Tolu swerved sharply to avoid hitting the traffic pole signalling cars onto the highway entrance. He gunned the engine, but had to step on the brakes to avoid hitting another car in front of him, and became mired in a traffic jam.

His thoughts went to Edikan Usoro Snr., Edikan's father and Tolu's cousin. That old fool should've kept his zipper closed while up there on Milina. Though it did not surprise Tolu he had fathered a child up there with an alien as he was already a dedicated womaniser down here on Earth!

He must find a way to make Edikan go away. He would put in a forced deportation order on that boy. He must return to Milina, or die here on Earth. Either that or Tolu might as well kiss his plans and dreams good bye.

Tolu frowned as he gazed ahead and realised that the traffic was still tight. A 2080 Lunar Amphibian sedan lifted off the highway in front of him and slowly flew

The Foreigner

away, leaving the traffic jam behind. Tolu wished that he could afford that car. Maybe with Edikan gone, everything—the houses, bank accounts, the whole estate left behind by his cousin—would be his. Then not only would he be able to afford the 2080 Amphibian, but he could actually buy one of the just-listed houses on Callaway Moon, the new galactic moon approved for settlement by MIS.

"Music," Tolu said, triggering a blast of atmospheric music in the car. He leaned back on his seat and sighed deeply, but the car's phone rang, the music faded away, and Chinyere Oduma's face appeared on the console screen.

"Mr. Makinde, where are you?" she asked.

Tolu sat up straight on his seat. "Boss. On break, madam."

"What happened here, Tolu? The police are looking for you?"

"Don't mind them, jare. They are too slow! This NiMi boy eluded security and came into my office. Can you believe that?"

"*Enh*, but you needed to stay and help the police with their report. Come back to the office. This is a serious breach."

"Okay. I'm coming."

Tolu touched an icon on the screen, cutting off the call, and the music rose again. He frowned as he looked ahead for the next exit. Now he couldn't even quench the incessant hunger that was making his stomach growl.

A fly, with buggy yellowish eyes, landed outside on the car's windshield. Tolu leaned forward to study it, and then jerked back when he noticed the coloration of the fly's eyes. The windshield's eyelid of a wiper automatically nudged the fly off.

Just as he was about to lean back on his seat, the fly appeared inside the car and settled on the windshield, directly in front of him.

Uko Bendi Udo

He took wild swipes, but the fly zoomed directly at him, dodged his swipes, and settled on the exposed part of his neck. He felt a sharp sting just before he slammed his palm against his neck.

The car swerved sharply to the left and then quickly corrected itself by taking control. Tolu flailed, and the slumped forward in his seat, unconscious, as the car drove onto surface streets, and rolled to a gentle stop on a deserted street.

"Mr. Makinde, are you there?"

Tolu sat up in his seat and strained to see clearly. A pedestrian glanced curiously at Tolu as she strolled past the car.

Chinyere appeared on the car's console and said again, "Mr. Makinde, are you there?"

"Yes," Tolu replied. He frantically searched his pockets for the document he pulled out of Edikan's file in the office, found it, and sighed with relief.

"Where are you?"

"I don't know."

"You don't know?"

"I'm on Martins Street. Yes, I can see the sign now."

"Are you alright?"

"Yes. I'm fine."

"I spoke to you thirty minutes ago, asking you to return to the office. What happened?"

"I don't know."

"I'm sending the police."

"I'm fine! *Ah, ah*. I'm not a baby."

"We need you here immediately."

Tolu cut off the call, studied his reddened eyes in the visor mirror, and then said, "Start the engine." The engine did not start, he repeated the command but it failed again. He took out the car keys from his pocket, manually started the car, and then drove off.

The Foreigner

Edikan ran into the Nigerian-Milinan Legal Aid Foundation office and looked around, searching for John Obinna, a fellow NiMi and Edikan's legal counsellor. Spotting Edikan first, John got up from his chair and ran up to him.

"Aki bam o, where have you been?" John asked in Milinan as he embraced him.

"Mme niye, I have it!" Edikan exclaimed, jumping up and down with excitement.

"You have what?"

"The paper."

"What paper?"

"Come," Edikan said in English, grabbed John by the hand and turned around in a bid to lead him out of the office. John grabbed him instead and pulled him into an empty conference room.

"Where have you been?" John asked in Milinan, fright in his eyes. "The police are looking for you."

"Why?"

"Why? Where were you this afternoon?"

"I went to see Mr. Makinde."

"I told you not to go there. You don't listen!" John stood up and paced the room. "Now the police are looking for you."

"I didn't do anything wrong."

"How did you get into Mr. Makinde's building?"

"I just did!" Edikan stood up and kicked at the chair. "Nobody wants to help me. Not you, not anybody!"

John grabbed Edikan by the hand and yanked him around. "Listen. I've stuck my neck out for you because I care about you and your case. The deal was that you were not going to do anything we didn't tell you to do. This is not Milina."

"I see that. May be I should just go back as Mr. Makinde suggested and take my chances."

Uko Bendi Udo

"That is not a good idea either. They will surely kill you for joining the insurrection movement. And what were you doing joining that group?"

"They're killing NiMis like me on Milina, Mr. Obinna. Just because of our Earthling blood! Milina doesn't want us, and when we come here, Nigeria does not want us!"

"That is not so. Look at me."

"There are more of me than of you, Mr. Obinna."

"That's not true. The problem is that you came in without papers."

"And I'm trying to tell you that I have the papers."

John moved closer to him. "What papers?"

"The paper the government will not release. The paper you have been asking Mr. Makinde to show that proves that my father is Nigerian."

"Where is it?"

Edikan brought out Mboro, set him down, jabbed at an icon on his left palm, and waved his right hand over him, turning him into a computer tablet.

John jumped back. "Mboro is an Akan!"

Edikan beamed with pride. "Yes."

"How did you get one? I've asked people to bring back one for me, but they say the Milinan government banned its sales. I see why."

"You don't need it. You're not a kid."

"You're fifteen. That's three years removed from being an adult. Now what about this paper?"

Mboro beamed a video transmission from a pair of human eyes, while Edikan scrolled through video images on the tablet. "We need to find it. I saw it earlier. Then we need to print it."

John moved closer to the tablet as if approaching a spectacular phenomenon. "What is this?"

"Video from Mr. Makinde's eyes."

An urgent knock on the conference room door prompted John to guide Edikan and Mboro behind a cubicle partition. John tip-toed to the door and cracked it open.

166

The Foreigner

"The police are here," said a co-worker.

John grabbed Edikan and they escaped through the back of the office.

Tolu studied Edikan Usoro Snr.'s framed photo closely, and sighed. Yes, he had to agree, Edikan bore some resemblance to Edikan Snr. He remembered exactly the day of the photo. Edikan Snr.'s first trip into space, the family had been so happy. It silenced, at least for that day, the talk that Edikan Snr. was a misguided Nigerian astronaut who was more interested in chasing skirts than chasing his dreams.

Tolu had been happy that day for a different reason. His cousin, who had always overshadowed Tolu's accomplishments and made him seem inconsequential in the eyes of everybody—especially Tolu's father—was blasting away to a different world, and would be gone for a few years.

It gave Tolu the space to breathe, and the chance for his family to notice him, especially his father. It gave him the opportunity to suppress the suffocating inferiority complex he felt around his cousin. Tolu had hoped—although it made him uncomfortable—that Edikan Snr. would never return.

For if he never did, according to Nigerian law, and Tolu being the closest kin alive, Tolu would inherit everything Edikan Snr. owned, both here on Earth, and everywhere else in the galaxy. This house, the ones in the village and all the others on Milina, and all the other worlds his cousin had roamed in search of adventure. When his body returned back to Nigeria several years later, Tolu thought that his prayers had been answered.

Then, the NiMi boy showed up.

However, the little runt made a big mistake, and now was going to be forcibly removed from the country, and good riddance. Tolu rubbed his eyes, and then ran up to the bathroom to see what was causing his eyes to itch a lot lately.

In the bathroom, Tolu leaned closer to the mirror and noticed that his pupils reflected strange red dots that seemed to appear and disappear depending on how he tilted his head. He'd never seen such a thing before. He'd have to make an appointment with the eye doctor.

The doorbell chimed. Tolu touched the mirror and a projection of a video feed from the entrance showed Edikan standing at the front entrance with John.

"What do you want?" Tolu asked, irritation colouring his voice.

"Open the door, Tolu. We have something to show you," John said.

"Show it to the police."

"We have the document."

Tolu frowned. "What document?"

"Edikan is a citizen of Nigeria," John said, and held up the printed-paper to the camera.

Tolu's legs almost gave way under him as he leaned in to study the image projected on the mirror.

"You're lying! It's fake!"

"Your office has confirmed the existence of the original, Tolu. We need to talk."

Tolu swiped at the mirror, cutting off the image. He staggered out of the bathroom and flopped onto the couch in the living room. How did they get the document? He had the original! He stood up and ran to the door.

Tolu opened the door and yanked a document out of John's outstretched hand. Tolu studied the paper briefly, and then slowly sat down on the steps of the staircase.

"As of now, Mr. Tolu Makinde, this house belongs to Edikan, by virtue of him being the verified son of astronaut Edikan Usoro Snr., who died on Milina in the year 2069. If you wish to contest this fact, I suggest that you file an appeal in court within the next thirty days."

The Foreigner

Tolu sighed, stood up, and said, "Please come into the house."

Uko Bendi Udo has published works of fiction and feature articles in newspapers and magazines in the States and England. He's also contributed fiction to e-zines like *StoryTime* and *NaijaStories*. A radio play he wrote was produced and aired by Los Angeles radio station 90.7 FM (KPFK), and he currently reside in the US.

Angel Song

Dave de Burgh

"Get those fucking Blowers ready!" Ed screamed, buffeted on all sides by screaming, fighting soldiers. "I'm makin' a hole!" He rose, tossed the last of his S-grenades over the crest of the rise and collapsed to the dirt, throwing an armour-encased hand over his head.

A second later the pressure-wave reached him and his ears popped. The ground rose, then fell a foot below him and he thumped down, his teeth rattling.

Ed paused for breath and then engaged his helmet's IR-filters before pushing himself to his feet. With the IR activated he could see through the swirling dust, and what he saw was a crater, so smoothly hollowed out that it seemed the landscape had been replaced with some artificial depression. It glowed, the fiery orange of residual heat roiling above the crater like an air-shimmer. The power of singularity-grenades was terrifying. Ed understood why platoon-leaders were the only ones who were supplied with them, and then only five-a-piece.

Ed thanked humanity's myriad gods that he hadn't been in the middle of that blast. Somewhere in the air above that crater, a miniature black hole the size of a pinhead was dying away, sucking into compressed oblivion who-knew-how-many of the enemy. He scanned the space behind him and then moved forward. His troops were getting to their feet too, but some, faces slack and eyes staring, didn't move—casualties of the Angel-advance they had died to halt.

"Come on, let's move it! Press them! Press the fuckers!"

Ed led his four-thousand and they rushed into the stillness of the grenade's aftermath. The digits in his HUD kept him updated on how many men he had left in his force. Twelve-thousand men had died already, and that

170

was just in his command. The current front line, which encompassed thirty square kilometres, had been filled with two-hundred-thousand soldiers just this morning. When the HUD's unit counter reached two-thousand he would abandon the attack, as ordered by High Command. Sometimes it seemed to him that High Command thought massive casualties were somehow sustainable in this war, and that leaving a core of shell-shocked veterans was good for the war's continuation. Ed didn't understand it, but it was what he had to work with. He also didn't understand why this planet, so far from Earth that Earth was just a dim star in the night sky, had been targeted by the Angels. It was well off their invasion vector, so out-of-the-way that it didn't have a name, only a designation that he had already forgotten.

One of his men, a lieutenant who'd been on the job for precisely forty-five minutes, ran up beside him and shouted, "The Blowers are offline, sir! The Techs were hit!"

"By what?" Ed screamed back, although it was obvious; when someone died in this war, they weren't hit, they were touched. Caressed.

They had to shout above the distant thunder of surrounding engagements—four groups of similar size hitting the kilometres' long front-line of advancing Angels. Ed hadn't even noticed that the Techs had fallen.

He was losing focus.

As one they streamed down the side of the crater, jump-running. Thirty yards ahead Ed could see the sky begin to fill with the radiance of another advancing wave.

More of the Angels were coming. How many people must have died to make so many Angels?

That thought, more than the numbers who had died trying to push the Angels back, staggered Ed.

"Get the Blowers up here! We'll make-do without the Techs!"

Angel Song

The lieutenant stumbled and Ed's arm shot out, supporting him until he regained his footing. Ed saw his face reflected in the lieutenant's face-plate—haggard, red-eyed, in desperate need of a shave, but he no longer saw the face that Lena had loved, once. He had been round-faced, jowly, eyes hardly visible behind folds of skin, but all the fat had burned away. It didn't matter—Lena was gone, among the millions killed when New Rome fell.

"Right away, Sir!" the lieutenant said.

Ed would have given anything for a moment's rest himself, but there just wasn't time right now, not with another wave of Angels coming right at them. They had to advance across the ground they had captured and then hold it.

He scanned the ground ahead. There were small outcroppings of what the Geo-Techs had named organo-regolith, probably what remained of something that had once lived, existed; the landscape was so battered by continuous bombings that nothing, not a tree, nor clump of shrubs, still stood. They could set up the Blowers there, and would probably command a field of fire fifty meters all around with just one Blower. Multiply that by three... They had a slim chance of holding out until support arrived.

If it ain't nothing, said the voice of Ed's long-dead Barracks-instructor, *it's better than fuckall*. Yes, it could be done.

Now to find three men who could man the Blowers. They wouldn't be able to sync-link, of course—only Techs could do that, with their enhanced minds—but they could pound the Angels' advance. Hopefully.

Ed pointed at each of the outcroppings in turn. "There, there, and there! I want three volunteers! Set up the Blowers, ASAP!"

"Yes, Sir! But whoever mans the Blowers-"

Dave de Burgh

"Dies, I know that! Three volunteers!" The Blowers worked amazingly well but they were also prime targets for the Angels.

The soldier hurried away and Ed put all his effort into reaching the section of ground he knew would probably be their last stand. It was flat, marred by rubble, but with a clear line-of-sight all around. It would do. Support would have to come from the regiments that enjoyed at least three-fourths strength, and considering how the day had gone so far, it just seemed more likely that all regiments would be suffering the same casualties he had.

Ed began smiling as he accepted that he was going to die here. It seemed to him that he was now inseparably joined to the thousands throughout history who had found themselves in a similar situation—like Leonidas, that Spartan madman who had been in his sixties when he stood against the Persians at the Hot Gates. Still running, Ed barked a laugh. *Me wearing a red cloak and underwear...*

Moments later Ed stumbled to a halt, kicking up dust and coughing who-knew-what out of his lungs. Even his suit's filters were taking strain, their stuttering whine sounding like an air-cab with faulty mag-lev rotors.

Seconds after him the rest of his force arrived.

The three volunteers moved a couple of feet ahead of him and began pulling the sections of each Blower from the carry-cases. Thankfully, as soon as the Techs had gone down, someone had scrambled to disassemble the Blowers. As soon as one part of it touched the ground—*Deployment Area*, they were taught in the Barracks College—it began to unfurl and unfold itself. Spindly legs that were metal but had the look of some segmented insect-leg lengthened and spread to take the weight, a cylindrical body inflated and rose into view, one end of it telescoping outwards into a small nozzle that glinted with reflected light. Ed imagined these Blowers transported back in time and into a parallel reality where they became monstrous in size and strode through a city, destroying and killing with each three-legged step. He wondered if their designers had read any H.G. Wells.

Ed waited until each Blower was set up and ready, volunteers holding the directing-handles, then called out, "Soldiers! Shield and Box, people! Shield and Box, right now!"

The men obeyed, moving and blending together, becoming a sea of helmets that bobbed and weaved as everyone got into position. Sickly dust-polluted light reflected off their face-plates. When the last soldier had taken up his position Ed heard it.

A humming whine, pitched just high enough that it ached in the teeth and joints, giving birth to an insane mosquito-like *BURRRR* that couldn't be ignored.

The sound of advancing Angels.

The sound of trillions upon trillions of energetic particles vibrating.

A wave front of advancing, sentient energy, ovoids of achingly bright light haloed by the slow coil-uncoil of hundreds of light-tendrils.

Death.

The nutcases who had called the appearance of the Angels *The Great Baptism* should have been shot. There was nothing holy or biblical about this war. To Ed it was nothing but an extermination. Seemed like the initial reports of the meteorite strike on Gallimer's moon—which had destroyed the trans-portal there and effectively closed that section of the wormhole-network—had been forgotten, but Ed would have bet a year's salary that somehow the trans-portal's destruction was connected to this 'invasion'; that and the recently-settled planet that had been the first to go dark: New Rome. *Catholics were always warning everyone about the End of Days...*

"Get ready!" Ed called out. "Here they come!"

Dave de Burgh

Then they all heard it, swelling into the air as if the largest choir ever assembled was giving voice to the mad genius of an insane composer.

The singing, and otherworldly voices.

Numbers released to the general public six months earlier had put Angel-strength at upwards of seventeen-billion, spread across ten now-dark planets and six sectors. At the beginning of the war, no-one had reported anything about the singing. Back then, those who had heard the singing had put it down to battle stress and the effects of trauma.

After a while, though, when the hundreds of thousands of witnesses became millions, and every single one of them reported the same thing, only then had humanity realised that what they were hearing was a *weapon*.

Ed couldn't help but focus on one voice among the cacophony—it called out to him, so familiar that it broke his heart. It sounded like her, but he refused to believe that is was her—his sister calling out to him, the tone and timbre he had known so well spreading through his brain like the touch of gentle fingers.

She told him how wonderful it was in the Light, how it *wasn't* what he thought, that this was indeed the Angelic Host of the Lord God come to take His Flock up to Heaven. She told him that he didn't have to fight it. The Light was bliss, love, happiness, trust and peace, and it was painless. The Light was everyone who had ever died, and all were singing of God's glory and love.

His mother began calling too, as she did every time he stood against the Angels. His mother who had died ten years ago from a double-bang, simultaneous heart failure and stroke, back when he'd been one of the accountants at Virgin-Micro's Trans-Hub lunar headquarters. She was saying all the same things, with love and understanding and sympathy. His father chimed in, too, and then his little brother, then his aunts, uncles, cousins, nieces, and

Angel Song

nephews, every dead member of his family, even the ones he hadn't met before they had died.

Their voices blended, merging into a song that rose and rose in volume until it drowned everything else out.

Ed realised that he was screaming, spittle flying from his mouth, eyes bulging, but he couldn't hear his voice, or any of the voices of the men who surrounded him.

Light blossomed as the Blowers ignited and began singing in their own way. Ed aimed and opened up with his AM-rifle, already shaking off the effects of the singing, of the voices.

A Blower's 'song' was the emission of pressurised air from its nozzle, created when it sucked in the surrounding oxygen/nitrogen mix at a high rate before shunting it into a chamber that put the gases under immense pressure, and then released that pressure in an incredibly tight beam of air that cut through anything in its path.

Ed had seen the carnage that resulted when Blower-Techs fell in battle.

Two months ago, the second month of the war, a misaimed Anti-Matter shell hit the Tech team and in seconds, thousands of men literally lost their heads when the Blower's nozzle had swung in the wrong direction. The air had been full of dust that day, but the dust suddenly turned crimson as over three-thousand carotid arteries were instantly severed. The beam was so strong and so narrow that nothing could stand up to it—not armour, not rock, not diamond, and not even the strange unstable, kinetic-and-plasma mix energy that was an Angel.

Because when a Blower's beam struck Angel-energy, something strange happened. In hindsight, it should have been obvious, but it was still the only pleasant surprise of the war.

When the air-beam hit a flame, for instance, it created an explosion three times the collective size of the fire that birthed the flame. The Sci-Techs later figured out that the

176

Dave de Burgh

compressed air added fuel to the energy that caused combustion, and thought that the same result would occur if the Blower was used on an Angel; they were correct. The explosions of liberated energy were greater though, by quite a big margin.

The blossoming of light that Ed now witnessed was the Blower's beam cutting a swathe of pure annihilation through the advancing Angels.

Where the beam touched, Angels died. Their radiant forms obliterated on contact, releasing a firestorm of blinding white light that travelled outwards on the heels of a buffeting shockwave, jostling the closest Angels before dissipating. Ed had been told that the Angels seemed capable of absorbing the liberated energies of their fellows and that's why he was grimly pleased that the soldiers manning the Blowers were hitting as many Angels with each beam-pass as they could. The air itself recoiled at the explosions, shoving the soldiers backwards so that their boots dug small trenches in the ground.

Ed's light-shield dropped over his eyes as soon as the Angels began dying, and he now saw their deaths with the colours reversed—the explosions expanding black flowers against a lighter background. The energy released was equivalent to that of a mini-nuke in the one to two megaton range, but their suits could withstand any blast up to fifteen megatons.

Ed and his men were still pummelled by the force of the explosions. As more and more Angels died, the soldiers were shoved back further because there were just so many of the damned Angels, dying in their thousands as the Blowers 'sang'.

But there were too many of the things; they just kept advancing, filling the empty spaces among their 'ranks'. Soon, the volunteers manning the Blowers would be cut off, surrounded.

Ed knew that not many men would be able to stand there and fight. It took someone who had nothing, or someone who had *everything* and was bored to the point of death, to stand their ground in the face what advanced upon them. He hadn't always been one of those men—men like that only came into being if they had the luck, or lack thereof, to survive engagement after engagement. Sometimes fear fell away and the gibbering thing that was the soul crept into a corner and the *animal*, that life-greedy thing inside every human being, took over. His awakening had occurred on the carnal fields outside the sprawling, stinking slums that were New Mumbai, and his awakening had kept him alive while sixteen-billion souls had died, over a three-week period, further swelling the ranks of the Angels.

Fear would kill you, and if it didn't, it crept away into that same corner and gibbered.

Techs, being AIs, felt no fear. As soon as they 'died' their electronic 'souls' were shunted into a new body. No one knew where they began or ended, or cared. And Techs never made mistakes—their targeting was always tactically perfect, and not one beam-swathe was wasted. The soldiers, however, were men like any other—shitting their pants, thinking of family, ignoring hunger and ever-encroaching exhaustion, even as they screamed defiance at the Angels.

The first Blower-volunteer 'died', an Angel reached him and caressed him with a languid coil of pure light, and he dropped, his body now an empty shell. It would still breathe and shit and piss, but the essence, the soul, was gone, the mind wiped clean. The soldier crumpled onto the ground and then just lay there, as if sleeping.

Now Ed could hear that soldier's voice, too. <u>Don't be afraid, Sir. This is wonderful! This is Heaven! I'm with the Angels now!</u>

Ed blocked out the voice, screamed, "Get ready! Time to make our stand!"

Dave de Burgh

This was where the singing of the Angels became such a potent weapon. All around Ed, the soldiers were realising the same thing.

The only way to escape an Angel was to kill yourself before it reached you, and even then, there wasn't any guarantee that your *soul* would escape. The Baptists said that it was futile, that your soul would go to the Angels regardless of how you died, because they *came from God*, they had been *sent* by God to take everyone to Heaven. They urged everyone to release themselves to the Angels, to stop fighting. You could not, they said, fight the might of God and the Transubstantiation—the name they had given to this war against humanity. Those same Baptists who probably decided that since the Catholics were out of the game *they* might as well try and steal the spotlight.

Ed's answer was the same now as it had been then, though he knew that many of his men would choose to let the Angels reach them.

Some were afraid of nothing except being forced to take their own lives.

It would be easy, he knew, to follow those men, to just release himself. He was so tired and weary, exhausted from having to fight on three planets in three weeks. He had to think to remember the names of the combat theatres, and the details of the battles had become a blur of explosions and soldiers and Angels. His path to this place seemed a dream, as if he was an outsider peering into a room through dirty, opaque glass. It had been Lena's death on New Rome that had sucked him to the offices of the newly-created and incredibly-named Human Defence Force to get a speed-course in handling AR-rifles, S-grenades, Blowers, working with Techs... The first engagement—he pissed himself that day but didn't even notice—had shaken him badly, and it was only in his second battle that he had heard his mother's voice.

It hadn't been long after that that he had begun hearing the stories people were telling about him; that he was nuts,

Angel Song

that he kept on calling out to his mom, but that he seemed to carry some crazy kind of good luck along with him because no matter how many battles he walked into, he always walked back out.

Every place looked the same to him. Even the thousands of soldiers under his command had taken on one collective face—the only difference being the light, or lack thereof, in the eyes.

He knew what he would do, if it came down to it. One S-grenade could do the trick.

The numbers in his HUD were running down at such a speed that when he focused on them they were nothing but a blur. In seconds, four-thousand odd retreated into the three-thousands.

Ed tongued the amplifier-bud that had been drilled into a molar and screamed, "Retreat! RETREAT!" but it was too late. There was light all around them. He couldn't even see a single working Blower, and as he scanned around himself he saw how men were dropping, some soundlessly, others screaming wordlessly.

The singing of the Angels was a roar now, without words, huge and sustained, and as men died and became new Angels the radiance increased around the beleaguered force. Ed closed his eyes and then raised his hand, clamping it across his face, seeing for a second the shadows of bones.

He knew he was dead. *Choose the Hour*, one of the catechisms of the College went, but now even that choice had been taken from him. His armour could stand up to the explosive bolts of his AM-rifle, as if the tiny anti-matter particles were nothing but a caress of silk, and by the time he got his helmet off to send a bolt through his head it would be too late, anyway. The only way you survived Angels was if you were at the rear of the battle—front-siders, as they were fondly called, always carried one-way tickets.

Dave de Burgh

Keeping his eyes closed, Ed dropped his rifle and lowered his hand. He stood, buffeted on all sides by jostling men as they fought and died or stood still and died. His life didn't flash before his eyes—they did, in their billions, waves and tendrils of light advancing and spreading everywhere. Soon, he knew, there would never be darkness again.

Moments passed that became one long instant of time, and when the light surrounded him on all sides—devoid of the shadows of even one soldier—Ed nodded and said, "Alright, fuckers. What are you waiting for?"

Voices rose—his mother's, his father's, his sister's, those of the men who had died here with him—and they spoke, they spoke together, using one supreme Voice.

You are beloved of the Lord God Almighty, Edward. Take comfort in this certainty.

"You," he spat, "are nothing of God! Do it! End it!"

The light of His love has no end, Edward, neither did it have a beginning. Accept this and come into it, it said, with such calmness and such a depth of empathy.

Ed grimaced as doubt, finally, closed in on him. Was it even possible? Were they *real* Angels?

No. Real Angels wouldn't cause the destruction and death *these* 'Angels' had caused. God wouldn't *let* His Angels do that.

But what about Sodom and Gomorrah, whispered his own traitorous heart. *Hundreds of thousands were killed when God set loose one of His Angels. Those cities were wiped from the face of the world.*

But we've done nothing wrong! He railed at himself, hands contracting into fists. *Those cities were punished.*

Oh, and fathers don't punish their children? Fathers don't take children back home after they've been lost and alone?

"No, no, no, no," Ed muttered, shaking his head. "This is war. *War.* War is not from God."

181

Angel Song

You poor, poor pitiful thing, they said. You don't deserve the Light. The Angels moved in, pressing in around him, their song now one of thunder and insistence and futility. He thought they would just burn him, now, not *take* him, and as they surrounded him, he realised: *I don't know what I want anymore.* He stood rigid; jaws clamped shut, waiting for the feather-light touch of death. But instead he heard a voice.

LEAVE HIM. THIS ONE MUST YET COME TO UNDERSTAND. HIS SACRIFICE MUST BE SOMETHING *CHOSEN*, NOT ENFORCED.

Ed's eyes widened and his lips moved soundlessly. *Lena's voice.*

Then the Angels flowed around and away from him, retreating ever so slowly across the ground they had won. Ed could feel it, the sensation of being touched by light that had no heat; his body betrayed him, his knees unlocked and he sank to the ground.

When he opened his eyes the radiance was dimming, the Angels now a mass of distant, pulsing light. Silence hung heavy around him. Everywhere, it seemed, the Angels were retreating.

Ed's body began to shake, a tremor he couldn't control, and finally he dropped his head into his hands and began to sob.

Dave de Burgh is a bookseller and SFF fanatic from Pretoria, South Africa. He participated in the Random House Struik/Get Smarter Creative Writing Course, is revising his first Epic Fantasy novel for Mercury Retrograde Press, and wouldn't mind writing for the rest of his life. He is on Facebook, Wordpress, Blogger, and Twitter.

The Rare Earth

Biram Mboob

Finally, the Word was spreading. On an otherwise unremarkable morning in December, the very first pilgrims approached the stronghold at Kivu in the Congo.

Dora Neza was pulling her dying father on a hydraulic-steam litter. He lay motionless, his face a skeletal grimace, his skin a thinly congealed wax. She had pulled him for several days through forest thicket and marsh. In the dark and at the dawn he would rouse from his litter and cry out to her sharply. He would croak at her in the strange tongues of the void. Her reply to him was always the same, "We are nearly there Baba. Nearly there".

They approached the high, metal wall of the Nyungwe forest reserve. The wall stood twelve feet tall, featureless, alien, white morning mist roiling along its base like a trapped cloud. Dora observed the wall for a few minutes and then retreated from it. She found a nearby break in the thicket, set the litter down, and waited. She listened to the tortured breathing of her sleeping Baba, the warble and keen of a solitary hornbill, the rustle and bell of the early breeze. She waited. The Earth turned, bathing the glade about her with the muted lights of the morning sun.

More than an hour passed before the wall opened. A large metal panel creaked and then slid away. In the wall's new maw stood three Knights. They wore green armour, black crosses chiselled on their tabards. Heavy machetes hung from their waists in leather scabbards, rifles slung over their shoulders. It took a few moments for Dora to notice that there was a fourth figure, a giant zumbi lingering behind the Knights. At the sight of it, she scrambled to her feet, terror swelling in her like the tide. The zumbi wore nothing but a pair of transparent shorts, the attire of diamond miners and low domestics. It stopped

183

a few paces outside the wall, motionless, its manner somehow both limp and tense at the same time, its flat gaze fixated on some distant point beyond the glade.

"Unataka nini?" one of the Knights asked her, the largest of the three.

She began to reply, but the one who had spoken shoved her roughly. She realised he wanted no reply, so stayed silent while he admonished her for evading their checkpoints. From somewhere in the canopy, the hornbill sang its warble song one final time before rustling into flight.

The Knights lifted her sick Baba up to his feet and let him fall to the ground. They used their machetes to hack apart her litter and examined its innards, pistons, and joints. When their inspection was over, the largest Knight walked over to the zumbi and slapped it twice on the back of its head while pointing at her Baba. The zumbi gathered him up from the ground and easily slung him over its huge shoulder. The Knights walked through the opening in the wall, followed by the zumbi. Dora waited a few moments, and followed them through. The wall closed behind them, the scattered remnants of the litter contraption left outside like the metal bones of some unimaginable feast.

They walked through a forest, whose coppice grew thicker and it got darker as they walked. Then the forest trail widened, turning into a path. They soon began to walk past forest mahemas—camouflaged green canvas tents— among the trees. They began to encounter men and women along the path, some holding rifles, others holding axes and tools. Some were dressed in the foliage-like rags of forest dwellers, others in green ceremonial robes. Overhead in the arboreal, silvered arrays and antennae jutted into the sky. There were other machines parked between the trees: tri-wheeled jungle vifaru tanks, missile launchers, skyward pointing rail cannons.

They entered a large clearing. The biggest Knight turned to her, "Fuata," he said, pointing at the giant mahema that

The Rare Earth

stood at the clearing's centre. Unlike the other mahemas it was the size of a circus marquee, glossy white, with antennae and arrays protruding from its roof. A large wooden cross was planted before it alongside two armed sentries. The Knight slapped the zumbi on its broad shoulder blade and pointed at the mahema entrance, making it advance between the sentries and disappear inside. Dora followed.

Her eyes took a few moments to adjust to the darkness. The zumbi had deposited her father on the ground and retreated to the recesses of the tent. She looked around. A well-appointed leather suite, a plush carpet pile, and judging from the cooler air some form of air-conditioning mechanism. There were perhaps a dozen men in the mahema, some standing, others sitting. However, it was immediately obvious to Dora who among them was the Redeemer. He sat in an armchair at the focal point of the room. A tall man, muscled, stout, a warrior's build, not much older than thirty, but bald and hairless, except for a long beard. His face was oblong, severe, and he wore the stiffly contemplative frown of a man still settling into his role at the apex. Casually dressed in a simple white robe, his legs were crossed and displaying a pair of badly scarred knees.

Dora assumed that they had arrived at the conclusion of some disciplinary hearing, for a sobbing man lay prostrate before the Redeemer. Two sentries lifted the shuddering wretch by the arms and dragged him outside.

After the sentries left, the men in the mahema turned their attention to her. The Redeemer stared at her while the Knight who had spoken outside whispered something into his ear. She gazed evenly at him in return, her hands clasped behind her back. Despite the heat, she still had her orange kanga draped over her shoulders. Underneath she was wearing a ragged T-shirt and faded denims.

"Where are you from?" The Redeemer asked.

"From Cyangugu," she replied.

Biram Mboob

He nodded amiably. "That's a hard road that you've travelled. How did you know where to find us?"

"Everyone knows you are here. Everyone is talking about you."

"And what do they say about me?"

She kept her gaze on him as she spoke, "That you are *Yesu*. The Christ returned."

The Redeemer pursed his lips, as if hearing this for the first time. "What is your name?" he asked.

"Dora," she replied. "My father's name is Michael."

"Dora," he repeated. "What else do they say about me?"

"They say you have cured the blind and brought dead men to life. Before he stopped speaking my father told me that he saw you perform miracles in Ituri. He saw you summon fire from the sky with your finger. He saw you kill a hundred PLA without moving from where you stood."

The Redeemer nodded and smiled, pleased. He turned and glanced at one of the men seated near him.

A much older man wearing a Knight's uniform said with a smile, "The Word spreads."

The Redeemer turned back to her. "Tell me," he asked. "What name do I go by in your town?"

"Schwarzenegger," she said.

He frowned. "That was my war name," he said. "When you return to the town you will tell your people my true name. You will tell them that my name is Gideon. You will tell them that I am the Word made flesh."

Dora looked down at her Baba, who was lying still on the floor.

"Don't worry about your father," the Redeemer continued. "He will be made whole again. I will cure him. Does he hold faith in the Trinity?"

"Yes," she said, "he does."

"Then his faith will be rewarded. His faith in me will make him whole."

The Rare Earth

"PLA spies," Musa Kun said. "I guarantee it." The older man was Gideon's second in command, a trusted counsellor, and a thin shuffling man with a protruding jaw that gave him a deceptively gormless appearance. Musa set down his papers and stood up from his chair. He prodded Michael with his foot, making the stricken man groan. "Did you see her shoes?" he asked. "Nice boots like that?"

"I did," Gideon said. He looked down at Michael, observing his features, a man nearing sixty with grey temples and a painfully thin face. Beads of sweat ridged his forehead occasionally sliding down his nose. "They aren't spies. You wouldn't make a spy of a dying man."

Gideon stood up, bent down and touched the man's forehead. He could have been dying of any number of infections; there was no way to be certain. The superbugs evolved quickly enough that there was almost no point trying to catalogue them.

"We should still be careful though," Musa Kun said. "He might not be a spy, but the girl could be."

Gideon shrugged. The girl, Dora, was admittedly, a different matter. She might be employed to penetrate the camp, the sick old man merely a prop for her deception. But there were many reasons why he doubted this, the main one being that it wasn't the way the PLA usually worked—spending time on a subtle and elaborate ruse like this. The girl could do no serious damage on her own and if all they wanted was reconnaissance of his camp then they could have just flown one of their more expensive machines over the forest, something impervious to the rail cannons. However, perhaps things had changed since Ituri. Perhaps the kindoro were beginning to take him seriously. Perhaps they were beginning to understand.

A fortnight ago, Gideon dreamt of the final Uhuru. In his dream, he had cast down these forests and in their place raised up a towering city of cathedrals and spires. The dried Lake Kivu refilled again with crystal sweet waters. A bugle call had blown, shattering mountains. A winged doom had flown to his enemies. Before his very eyes, the towers of the Beijing Metropole crumbled to dust and salt; squadrons of PLA soldiers smote by lightning and swallowed up by the earth. The remaining kindoro knelt at his feet. They begged forgiveness, renouncing their pagan gods as the Israelites afore Moses on the mount. He had then turned his mind unto the new country. His new kingdom had stretched far and wide. He had built his church on the peak of the Kilimanjaro and there on the peak of the Oibor he had sat on a throne of white gypsum and bronze. Beside him, there had been a woman with golden braids in her hair, sitting as stiff and regal as an Abyssinian queen. As he recalled it now in his waking mind, he thought he saw Dora's face there. Was it? Had he been having premonitions again? Or had it been the face of some other woman, as yet unknown to him? He pinched his forehead, the clarity of the vision dangling just out of reach, tormenting and maddening. He shook his head clear and made his decision.

"I am going to heal this man," he said. "I will heal him and he will return to his town. They have heard about what happened at Ituri. Now they will hear of miracles too. The Ministry will grow. How else the Word?"

"How else the Word," Musa Kun echoed.

"Leave me with him," Gideon said. "And send for my cameraman."

Musa Kun stepped outside the mahema into the iron-forge of early afternoon. There had been a time when even he had doubted the Redeemer. But that was before he had seen Gideon walking straight through PLA divisions, making their guns fall silent with a wave of his hand, turning their hot bullets into harmless puffs of vapour and steam.

There were two sentries standing outside the tent. He sent one of them to find the cameraman and then approached the thatched lean-to that Dora was sitting

The Rare Earth

under. Alongside her were a small group of shackled workers, new captures from the forest. She stood up expectantly as he approached. Musa Kun eyed the good boots he had noticed earlier, military grade Kevlar with steel toes. He smiled and stretched out his hand. She shook it. Her palms were soft, pampered. He noticed a pale outline on her wrist, some watch or navigation device that she had taken off or lost before arriving. The girl was a spy. He was almost certain of it.

"You avoided every man we have on the Kivu road," Musa Kun said, "and from what I hear you came straight to a hidden gate on the wall. I'm going to have a few questions for you. I'll want to know who has been giving you information".

"And who are you?" she asked, without pause.

"I'll be asking the questions here. This is my camp."

Her eyes flicked over to the entrance of the large white mahema.

"Don't confuse yourself," Musa Kun said wearily. "He is the boss, but I run this camp. And when he's lost interest in you and your father, I'm still going to have questions for you."

"We can talk now if you want," she said with a shrug.

A sudden urge to seize her by the braids gripped Musa Kun, to teach her a lesson in respect. Instead, he smiled at her stiffly. "I expect you didn't bring any supplies with you?" he asked.

"I didn't know how long this was going to take."

"It will take as long as it takes."

"I have money," she added.

"Money? Marvellous." He pointed away from the clearing to the nearby tree-line. "If you head around there you will find we have quite a number of shops. You can take your pick. Anything you need."

Dora glared at him. Musa Kun didn't give her a chance to reply. He waved the remaining sentry over, "When he's finished with the old man set them up in a tent on the workers' row. Mark them down for worker rations only. Unless our princess volunteers to put in some work for a little bit more."

The sentry leered at her. Dora pulled her kanga about her more tightly. One of the shackled slave women started wailing, soon followed by another, their words in an obscure forest language soon to be lost.

The cameraman arrived at that moment, a tripod slung over his shoulder. Musa Kun gestured at the mahema. "Go in," he said. "Boss wants you." The cameraman went inside. Musa Kun turned his attention back to the girl. Dora was still standing with her kanga drawn about her upper body like a cloak, her glance, suspicious now, flittering between Musa Kun and the sentry.

"We will have a reward for you," she said.

Musa Kun waved at her dismissively. "We have enough money to buy that hole of a town of yours ten times over. The Lord's work won't need recompense from the likes of you. When you return to your town, you will tell them that freely ye received from God the Son."

"Our reward for the Redeemer is more than money," she said.

He eyed her again and frowned. Some elaborate trick she wanted to set in motion perhaps. There was no sense alerting her to his suspicions now though. "We'll see about that," he said. He turned away from her and faced the sentry standing outside the mahema. "And you. Either find a way to shut those workers up or move them somewhere else." He began to walk away.

"Wait," Dora said. "I want to speak to you."

"Later," Musa Kun said, not slowing down.

"We need to talk now. I want to make a deal."

"We have no need of deals, princess."

"My father has information from Bujumbura."

Musa Kun paused. He did not turn, but a twirl of his hand invited her to go on.

The Rare Earth

"A kindoro is being held hostage there," she continued. "The PLA are offering a reward for him. My father knows where he is.

Musa took his time turning around. When he did he was smiling. "I think that you are right," he said. "I think we do need to talk now."

"Our price is the Redeemer's cure and safe passage," she said. "Then my father will tell you everything he knows."

"What is wrong with this man?" the cameraman asked, standing uncertainly in the fore of the mahema.

"Stop being such a coward," Gideon said. He gestured at the camera impatiently. The cameraman stepped forward and quickly set up his tripod.

"Mark this then," Gideon said, looking into the camera. "This man you see lying here has been stricken with the bacteria. There is no earthly medicine that can help him. But for those who revere my name, I will take from thee all sickness."

Gideon knelt down beside Michael. He placed his hand on the dying man's forehead and he began to pray. It was not long before the Holy Spirit overwhelmed him. Tears came unbidden as he prayed and he no longer seemed conscious of the cameraman standing over him. Overtaken by The Tongue he began to babble. He rocked back and forth, tears streaming down his face at the glory. The mahema seemed to dim about him. A quickening of light shone from afar, some distant lantern. The numinous washed over him, stopping his heart momentarily, covering his body in goose-pimples. He swooned, shivered, and lost his Earthly consciousness, collapsing on top of Michael, convulsing, his spirit spent.

Two years ago, not long after the end of The Emergency, the Legion had been on the move, running short of supplies and morale. The Holy Ghost whispered to Gideon then, as it had done since. It whispered to him of a well-stocked PLA airship anchored in Arusha. It told him how to shoot it down without damaging its cargo bay. At great risk, he moved a large contingent of Knights to Arusha and found the airship exactly where the Holy Spirit said. A bolt to the tail and rail cannon shot to the Hull had sunk it to the ground, shedding its bounty upon them like manna. Amongst the food and munitions, he had found many strange medicines, all of which he had personally commandeered.

After the cameraman left, Gideon went to his personal store and removed a large plastic packet. He tore it open and removed a syringe filled with a thin black serum. There was a guidance leaflet wrapped around it. He unfolded the paper. On the one side was a single Mandarin character, on the other, much tiny writing. He read the paper slowly and carefully for a long time. Learning to read the language of the kindoro was the hardest thing that he had ever done in his life, but also perhaps one of the most fruitful.

The microzymic therapy was experimental. The paper said that it was to be used with extreme caution, as a last resort and only on low profile subjects. All results were to be reported through Medical Counsel Gateway Node 78. Gideon knelt down. Following the practical instructions carefully, he injected Michael in the neck with the syringe. After a few moments, the man shuddered, as if in the grip of some nightmare. Whatever infection he had would very likely be cleared out in the next few weeks. But the therapy was liable to be much worse than the disease. Man had squandered the Lord's gift of antibiotics and now resorted to these worthless poisons. The microzymic therapy was their latest creation. If the kindoro paper Gideon had read was accurate, then it was an attempt that was already doomed to failure. The cellular hyper-reaction that killed the infection would also tear down the essential fabric of all internal organs in a few years. But in those years, Michael Neza would have plenty of time to return to his home and spread the good news. The Ministry would grow. Gideon called out to his sentry and had Michael removed.

Six nights later, Gideon found himself in a dream he had never had before. He dreamt that the sea was on fire. Jet-black pterodactyls circled overhead, their reptile eyes fixed upon him like murder. He stood barefoot in green robes, cinder-black sand beneath his feet. There was a noxious hot breeze, and in the sky, the low pulsing embers of a dying sun. A black leviathan breached the burning water and roared.

He woke up with a start. It was nearly dawn. A black PLA banshee streaked across the sky, then a moment later a sonic boom erupted. The zumbi sleeping beside him woke up and began to make a desperate low keening.

"Be quiet," Gideon muttered, wiping the night's detritus from his face. He had slept badly. He did not like it here. There were no trees, no canopy, only the holes of the uprooted, as if a mob of giants had picnicked here and plucked them out by the trunks to use as toothpicks. They were in the abandoned rare earth fields that had encroached their way up to the very borders of Bujumbura. Huge mounds of red earth littered the Mars-like landscape about them. The old style mines were large craters in the ground, the largest of them stretching miles wide and miles deep. Slaves had dug these with bare hands and baskets. The by-products of their work were these new red mountains, the bowels of the Earth laid bare. The newer mines were deep straight shafts, machine-bored. The work of mining had cultured a certain strain of sadism in the hearts of men. As part of some intricate game, the miners had covered many of these deep holes with well-disguised sheeting. It would be easy to miss one and fall in. To be on the safe side Gideon had made the zumbi walk ahead and he followed behind in the creature's footsteps. Thankfully, the rare earth fields were beginning to thin out. He could already make out Bujumbura, its revolving rampart machines wheeling slowly on the horizon.

It was six nights ago that Musa Kun had burst into Gideon's mahema with the news.

"For this, it might be worth taking the city," Musa Kun said. "I've spoken to our man there. He says an entire PLA division was wandering the streets a couple of weeks ago checking door to door. They're handing out pictures of the missing kindoro, offering ten thousand Yuan for information on his whereabouts."

"And our man didn't think to inform us?" Gideon asked.

"Who? Yusufa? No. Reliable man, but not smart enough to realise the importance of what he was seeing. Not smart enough to know that the kindoro have never offered a ransom for defectors."

"Not even when that Major defected to the Indians last year," Gideon mused.

"Yes," Musa Kun said wistfully. "Not even then. This fish is one that they want very badly. If we have to take the whole city to find him, it will be worth it. It must be. They will pay good money to get him back. Supplies. Weapons..." Musa Kun was excited. He shifted his weight from one foot to the other, something uncharacteristically reckless about his manner.

"We could take the city, but you know we could never hold it," Gideon said.

"Yes, but we would only need it for a couple of days. Blow the airfield. Set up anti-air rail and make it impossible for anything to land. By the time a ground force comes in from Kinshasa we'll have had enough time to flush out this fish." Musa Kun paused, grinned hopefully. "And after what you did at Ituri, who knows what might be possible. Maybe they come. Maybe we give them a good beating."

Gideon shook his head. It was not yet time to take a city. He knew this instinctively. The PLA would strike back

The Rare Earth

quickly. And there, in that tidal crush of bodies, he would die.

"Taking the city is not the way," he said. "I will go in alone." That felt right, even as he said it. "But first we need to find out where the kindoro is. Is there a chance the girl actually knows?"

"I believe that she does," Musa Kun said. "But she wants to wait for her father to recover. Insurance. I can't see how we get the information out of her. Unless..." He left the question unasked.

"Her father will recover," Gideon said. "I am sure of it. But not for a time."

"The kindoro could get away while we wait."

Gideon nodded. "So we cannot wait then," he said. "Find out what she knows."

Musa Kun nearly ran out of the mahema, murderous intent present in his long hurried stride.

Gideon pulled out his microweb receiver from his pocket and carefully dialled Musa Kun garrisoned twenty kilometres away in the Kibira forest, well outside of the range of Bujumbura's rampart. Musa Kun had sixty Knights with him and the only two stealth vifaru tanks that the Legion possessed. In a tight situation, the vifaru might be able to pass the rampart undetected. But the Knights would need to secrete themselves through in small groups. It would take days for them to assemble. This was the reason why he had approached the city alone. On his own, he would be able to fool the kindoro machines easily. Bringing the zumbi with him had been Musa Kun's idea, and it had proven to be a good one. It wore a green cloak, its face hidden in a large hood. On its back, it carried their supplies, weapons, and the heavy microweb node. It walked silently, ate little, and did as it was told.

"Are you close?" Musa Kun asked.

"Two hours, maybe three," Gideon replied.

"Excellent. All is going to plan. Yusufa is ready to meet you outside the Interior Ministry building."

Gideon looked to the horizon. He could already make out the hazy black tower, sixty floors tall, rising from the cityscape like a premonition.

"He is certain to be waiting for me?" Gideon asked.

"Yes. Yusufa's reliable. He'll bring enough men to force into the building. They will have to search for the kindoro floor by floor."

Gideon snapped off the receiver and put it in his pocket. He clicked his fingers twice. The zumbi rose to its feet and began to pack up.

The Office of the Mayor of Bujumbura was on the fifty-third floor of the Interior Ministry Building. Gideon stood at the full-length window, taking in the view of the city. In the final years before The Emergency, there had been a furious spate of building work. With the profits from the burgeoning rare earth fields there had been an attempt to demolish the city and rebuild it. The work had only half started when The Emergency began. So everywhere, there were half-broken buildings interspersed with skeletal skyscrapers and huge rusting cranes. A series of collapsed tunnels ran through the centre of the city, a botched attempt at an underground metro system. The collapsed tunnels radiated outward towards the putrid Lake Tanganyika. From where Gideon stood, they looked like the decaying vertebrae of some ancient beast of red earth, steel, and stone.

Behind him, still sat at his desk, was Ndumana, the Mayor of the city. Yusufa's men had taken the building lobby with very little difficulty enabling Gideon to take the lift. He had left the zumbi outside in the Mayor's reception. There had been a receptionist there and a small number of city officials. At the sight of the zumbi they had all fled screaming down the stairs.

The Rare Earth

"This is needless," Ndumana said. "You'll start a panic in the streets."

Gideon didn't turn around. He kept looking down, into the streets of Bujumbura. The streets were flooded with people, hundreds of thousands of them. There was very little that frightened Gideon. He did not fear what men could do, for his power was greater still. He did not fear death, for even in death he would live. But he did fear the great unceasing crowd. As the rare earth fields had spread the great host had flooded into the city. They had come either to find work or to escape the casual sadism of the miners. Now, here they were, spread across every surface of the city. Shanties had grown even inside the abandoned metro tunnels, filling them with white plastic tents. The sight made him weary; man was not meant to live this way.

There was a muffled burst of gunfire from a lower floor of the building. While he had stood here, the melee had not stopped. Yusufa's men were searching the building, looking for the hostage kindoro. It was not proving easy. There was security scattered throughout the building. The fight was floor to floor, man to man.

"All this needless violence," Ndumana repeated. He cleared his throat and began to speak again. "As I said, we have sent you messages several times. Our men keep getting turned away at that wall of yours."

"He's telling the truth," Musa Kun whispered into Gideon's earpiece.

Gideon turned around and looked at Ndumana sat behind his desk. He was a fat, well-dressed man, in a linen Mao style suit and gold rings on his fingers. Behind him stood his security; five men, all of them holding PLA issue machine guns.

There was another burst of gunfire and the thud of a grenade explosion.

Biram Mboob

"You must stop this," Ndumana whined. "You might start a panic in the streets. And when it starts it does not stop."

Yusufa's thugs had done well so far. A handful of them were outside holding the Ministry's entrance, but they would not be able to hold the building for long once reinforcements arrived. This presumably was why Ndumana was trying to stall proceedings.

"Let me be clear," the Mayor said, tapping his finger on his desk as he so often did on television. "We want only friendship with the Legion. We have many proposals to discuss with you. The kindoro have found many new rare earth fields near Kivu—fields of antimony, tantalum, platinum—very good ones. They know that this is a time for peace with your Legion. If we work together then we can all prosper."

"As you have prospered here?" Gideon asked.

"We've done well here," Ndumana said dryly. "All things considered."

Gideon approached the Mayor's desk. "For the last time, where is he?"

Ndumana licked his lips. "You have to understand. The man that you speak of is not ours to give. If we let you take him then we'll find ourselves in a very difficult situation with the PLA. I cannot make such a decision without-"

"If the kindoro is here then you have been hiding him from the PLA," Gideon said. "If you have been hiding him then they don't know that you have him do they?" Gideon stepped closer to the Mayor's desk. "Is it the reward you are after? You would cross the Legion for the sake a few Yuan?"

A loud grenade explosion shook the floor. The Mayor glanced at his office door. "All this over such a simple misunderstanding."

The Rare Earth

"We found him," Musa Kun whispered excitedly in Gideon's ear. "Yusufa has him. They are on the twenty-second floor."

Gideon smiled and whispered back sub-vocally. "Tell Yusufa to bring him to the fifty-third. I'll meet them here."

Ndumana frowned at him.

"We have what we came for," Gideon said. "But I still have questions for you. I still need to know who he is."

Ndumana's lips curled into an uncertain sneer. "Shoot him," he said quietly. The lead security man levelled his machine gun. Gideon stepped forward to meet him. The man stepped back and then squeezed the trigger. Nothing happened. He shook his gun vigorously then squeezed his trigger once more. Again, there was nothing but dry clicking. Another two did the same, their faces contorting in confusion as they pointed their weapons at the Redeemer and fired. Gideon pointed out at the window. From the blue morning sky, a single white bolt rushed towards them and struck the ground near the Interior Ministry building. The building shook and swayed. The window of the Mayor's office shattered. There were screams from the street below, memories of The Emergency resurging in the great host. The panic had begun.

"Shoot him," the Mayor screamed, half-lunging over his desk as if to do the deed himself with nothing but his bare hands.

At that moment, the door of the Mayor's office opened and the zumbi appeared in its frame. As one, the Mayor's security bolted to the far wall of the office. One of them broke from his colleagues and went for the window where he paused and reconsidered his options. He joined the rest of the security at the far end of the office, their useless weapons pointed at the creature. The Mayor raised his hands and shrank back into his chair. The zumbi remained motionless in the doorway.

Biram Mboob

"You will not flee the Lord's work when you see it," Gideon said. "Yet you will flee this work of the Devil."

Ndumana ignored Gideon. His eyes fixed on the zumbi and with each passing moment, he shrank lower in his chair, as if his plan was to slide under his table and find safety there.

"Who is the kindoro?" Gideon asked.

"His name is John Lai," Ndumana said. "He's running from the Science Ministry. Life Medicine branch." The Mayor spoke briskly now, without pause, his eyes never leaving the creature in the doorway. The zumbi stared back at him, its arms motionless by its sides. At the far wall, the security men had not moved an inch.

"What does that mean?"

"Antibiotics," Ndumana murmured.

Musa Kun whistled in Gideon's ear.

"How did he fall into your dirty little hands?" Gideon asked.

"He was with a team that made a discovery," the Mayor said. "The big one. The one that they have been looking for all these years. The cure."

"A new strain," Musa Kun whispered in his ear. "Where? Ask him where?"

"Where?" Gideon asked.

"We don't know. We beat him, but he won't say. Somewhere in the bush. They found it and decided to keep it. They killed their military escorts and they ran. The rest of them died and but he made it here. He came to me for help."

"What were you planning to do?"

The Mayor shook his head slowly. "No plan. Beat him until he told us where. He told us that he already has a buyer. He says his buyer will pay us if we get him safely to the coast. He won't tell us anymore than that."

Musa Kun whistled again. "We're going to come in," he said. "I'll bring the vifaru. We'll break through the rampart. We're coming for you right now."

200

The Rare Earth

"No," Gideon transmitted. "Wait. We keep to the plan. I will come to you. Where is Yusufa?"

"Someone killed the lift and they don't know how to turn it back on. He's coming up the stairs now with the fish."

"Tell him to go back down. I'll meet him in the lobby. I'm coming."

Gideon walked slowly to the door, circling the zumbi on his way out. When he was behind it, he gripped the back of its head and pushed it forward roughly, then slammed the office door shut.

He waited outside the office. The zumbi was quick, efficient. There were a few half-hearted bursts of automatic fire. The security men had realised too late that once pointed away from the aura of the Redeemer their weapons worked again. But mostly the men in the office just screamed and screamed. It took two minutes, maybe three, and then there was complete silence. He opened the door. The zumbi stood there, its huge hands bright red, its large green cloak spattered with blood. Gideon clicked his fingers three times and ran to the fire exit. The zumbi followed.

They ran down the stairwell, all fifty-three flights. Each time Gideon felt himself flagging, the thought of the zumbi behind him kept him going, fearing the creature might crash into him and crush him to death. When he arrived at the ground lobby of the building, he doubled over, heaving. Yusufa's thugs were milling about, waving machetes and rifles, revelling in their victory. The lobby floor was strewn with bodies and the huge windows to the street were shattered. At the sight of the zumbi, most of Yusufa's thugs retreated outside. When he had caught his breath, Gideon approached Yusufa and the apprehended kindoro.

John Lai smiled at him and outstretched a hand. He had one arm in a dirty sling and his face was badly bruised, but he seemed surprisingly cheerful. Two of Yusufa's thugs flanked him, a third man had a machete pointed at his back. Wearing soiled linen trousers, torn shirt, and pair of damaged spectacles, he was younger than Gideon had expected.

"I understand that you are the man I owe my freedom to," John said.

Gideon shook the man's hand, and spoke to him in Mandarin. "I am. From now on you will speak to me only."

"Certainly," John said. If he was at all surprised then he didn't show it.

"You will go with Yusufa here and he will get you through the rampart. I will follow from behind." Without waiting for a response Gideon walked outside, feeling the kindoro's eyes burning into his back.

"On our way," he transmitted to Musa Kun.

It was dusk, and they were high up on a rare earth mountain, a particularly deep and yawning mining cavern beneath them. The mountain ridged with the ledges and walkways used by the miner slaves. Its top was perfectly flat, a high mesa. Gideon sat alone with John Lai. A few ledges down, Yusufa's men were making camp. They had made good ground and Bujumbura was many hours behind them. As the late Mayor Ndumana had predicted, a panic had indeed erupted in their wake. Gideon could see the orange haze of fire pulsing gently on the horizon. The great host had been stirred, and the city burned once more.

"There is one thing I don't understand," John said. "The satellite charge in the city, how did you do that? Where did you people get a weapon like that?"

"That was not a weapon. That was the Word. The Word is how I defeated your soldiers in Ituri. The Word is how I will drive you out of my kingdom."

John raised an eyebrow. "That may be what you think. But that charge was from a military orbital. Only PLA Space Ordnance has access to weapons like that."

The Rare Earth

Gideon laughed. He spread his arms and showed John his palms. A moment later, there was a white strike in the dusk sky, a lightning bolt that flashed noiselessly before striking the ground with a large thud a mile away. The rare earth mountain shuddered. Yusufa's men stirred, some shouted in mock terror, others sang praises.

John's eyes widened. He stood up, placed a hand over his mouth and stared at the smoking crater that the bolt had created.

"Behold then," Gideon said. "In his hand are the deep places of the earth. The strength of the hills is his also."

"All things are possible," John said thoughtfully. "Niàn Tou. Thought platform." He turned around and observed the Redeemer. "I've had men swear to me that the technology exists, but I'd never believed it. If it does exist then I imagine that there are governments that couldn't afford it. Who do you really work for? The Indians?"

"I work for God. Your petty squabbles do not concern me."

"Petty squabbles? Our nations will go to war soon Gideon. When it starts it will make The Emergency seem like a dinner party."

"If there is a war then you will lose," Gideon said. "You, the Indians, all of you. Only God will triumph here. Only God can. And I am his vessel."

John looked at him for a few more moments and then shook his head. "I see that there is more to you than meets the eye. Either that or you are at the centre of some grand mischief." He removed his broken glasses and rubbed the one good lens on his dirty trousers. "Tell me," he said. "Have you ever heard the story of a man named Kim Nam Ku, from North Korea?"

"No, I can't say that I have."

John put his glasses on, and smiled. "Remind me to tell you about him one day," he said. "You might find it familiar, and most instructive. But now I think we must focus on pressing matters."

Biram Mboob

"I would agree," Gideon said.

"I'm prepared to deal but time is of the essence."

"Time is always of the essence."

"May I make the broad assumption that the Mayor explained how I came to be a beneficiary of his rather rough hospitality for these past weeks?"

"You may."

"In which case he may have told you that I have a buyer, but he is unlikely to have been able to tell you just how powerful my buyer is. This for you will come as both good news and bad."

Gideon smiled, and crossed his legs. The zumbi approached, its arms laden with firewood. John stiffened. The zumbi dumped the firewood in a pile and then shambled away into the thickening gloom.

"It frightens you?" Gideon asked.

"Of course. It is a frightening thing."

"So why did you make them then?"

"I didn't make anything," John said irritably. "The army made them."

"Why?"

"I don't know. Ask them."

They sat in silence, the last of the dusk melting away into the true dark.

"You said that there was both good news and bad," Gideon said eventually.

When John replied, his voice was sullen. "The good news is that money is no object. There is no price that my buyer will not pay. There is nothing he will not give. You will be handsomely rewarded for your help. The bad news, for you, is that my buyer knows where I am. He's known for weeks. He has sent a warship for me. It is moored off Madagascar. He will not come for me until I give him the information that he wants." John leaned forward, something of a snarl on his lips now. "If you try what I think you might have in mind, then you will be crossing a very dangerous man. A man who probably already knows who you are. You were not exactly discreet back there in the city."

"No, I wasn't. So where does that leave us?" Gideon asked.

"I need a way to communicate with my buyer. To give him the information he needs and tell him I am ready to come in."

"We have microweb. Two-way. Secure."

John frowned. "That will have to do. I only need to a send a message. We'll deal with the remaining logistics later."

Gideon pulled a microweb receiver from his pocket and handed it over.

"You will understand if I ask for some privacy," John said.

Gideon stood up and walked away, towards the edge of the rare earth mountain. In the darkness, the orange haze over the city made it seem as if the sun was trapped beyond the horizon, unable to rise.

"He's sent the message," Musa Kun whispered in his ear. "My Durban man has intercepted it. They look like map co-ordinates. Should I send a reply?"

"Don't bother," Gideon said. He whistled for the zumbi and it came shambling up to him. He slapped it four times on the head and pointed at John who was still looking intently at the microweb receiver, waiting for his reply.

The creature moved quickly. In seconds, it had covered a hundred feet. John screamed and began to scramble backwards on his elbows and heels. The zumbi seized him by a leg and an arm and raised him clear off the ground. Gideon approached them.

"What are you doing? I told you-" John looked at the receiver that now lay on the ground, the realisation creeping over his face. "No," he whispered. "I can still help you."

"You've helped enough," Gideon said. "You've played your part."

Biram Mboob

John shook his head and opened his mouth to say something else. Whatever it was though, Gideon would never hear it. The zumbi flung him over the side of the rare earth mountain. He bounced four times off its sloping edge, his body breaking anew each time. After what seemed a long journey down, he came to a rest at the bottom of the deep mine cavern, his body twisted, the soft red earth caving in around him. On the lower ledge, Yusufa's men had fallen silent, and then gradually they started to murmur amongst themselves again. One of their number began to sing in a low husky voice.

"Is it done?" Musa Kun asked in his ear.

"It is done," Gideon replied.

Musa Kun sighed. "We'll strike camp and send a vifaru for you. We need to set out to these co-ordinates as soon as we can. My man in Durban cannot guarantee that the message did not reach its target. In fact, it probably did."

Gideon didn't reply. He had already turned his gaze from the yawning bottom of the mine and was again staring at the far city and the orange halo that glowed above it so brightly.

Yusufa joined him at the precipice and stood beside him quietly. Gideon turned and looked at him. The man was a fighter. Short, bow-legged, his face a criss-cross of scars.

"Have you been in the city long?" Gideon asked.

"I was born there," Yusufa said mildly.

"I'm sorry."

Yusufa shrugged. Gideon thought to ask him more, about his mother, his children if any. But he didn't. Instead, they stood there in silence, save the husky song that was carrying over the pitted red landscape.

"What does he sing?" Gideon asked. "I do not know his language."

"He mourns. For our men who died in the tower. His brother was among them."

"I'm sorry," Gideon said again. He could not remember the last time he had apologised to someone. Some strange

The Rare Earth

feeling had overtaken him. Something that John Lai had said, or perhaps Ndumana, he could not remember anymore. He looked at the zumbi that sat crouched alone at the far end of the mesa and came close to envying it. The creature would remember nothing of the day.

"He sings of how his brother will live again," Yusufa said. "In the glory of your kingdom. When it comes."

"When it comes," Gideon said.

The man continued to sing his lamentation. The city continued to burn. Gideon imagined that he could hear screams carrying on the wind. He thought then of Dora Neza, standing before him in his mahema, her orange kanga wrapped about her. He had not asked Musa Kun what had become of her, for he had not wanted to know. But he knew instinctively that her end would have been unpleasant. And whether he recovered or not, there was of course no question of allowing her father to leave the stronghold alive. He would return to his town and there would speak ill of the Legion. He thought of Ndumana and his security team; Yusufa's men who had died in the tower; John Lai; the rampaging host in the burning city and the ones who died now in the great crush.

"When it comes," Gideon repeated.

Biram Mboob was born in The Gambia in 1979. His short stories have appeared in a number of magazines, including *Granta* and *Sable*, as well as a number of anthologies including *Tell Tales* and *Dreams, Miracles and Jazz*. Biram earns a living as an IT Consultant and lives in South London.

Terms & Conditions Apply

Sally-Ann Murray

I wait and wait on the corner, conscious of being outdoors alone. While I wait, I pick up a thin iron spike and a shard of green glass. I wind my hair and skewer it with the spike. I finger the broken edge of glass, almost drawing blood, and lift it to my eye. A forest descends. I toss it.

The wind picks up, and a broken siding clanks. The stiff breeze raises a curtain in an alcove across the way: several staunch young Supers are sipping and shanking. One points lazily. In a wink, an informal posse has formed, and begins to slope in my direction.

Come on, Karl! I urge silently, getting ready to run. There's still no sign of him. A grating sound as a nearby manhole cover is eased up then shifted aside, and a head appears. A tunneller. He looks furtively at me, glances at the sound of feet, and gestures "Come!"

I'm nervous, conscious of the risk either way. Why would a complete stranger help me? *Me*? And the tunnels? Even while they're silicon lubed, even while I'm not what anyone would call a big girl, the entrance feels tight. I squeeze into the bung-hole, he yanks the hole shut, and screws it tight. Above, the Supers are beating on the cover with rocks and metal staves, stomping too with their heavy boots. I am shivering. The dark weighs heavily on my tongue. But the tunneller is poised, and runs his hands over me before I know it.

"Reckon a small should do it?" I'm in no condition to reply, and in the pitch he unwraps a pliable and passes it over, brushing against my body. "We must hurry," he urges, "so suit yourself!" In the same breath, he slides further down into the darkness, slippery as an eel. I cover myself and follow—a clumsy lubber.

Sally-Ann Murray

Deeper and deeper down a long metal ladder leading off into the shadows. Rung rung runng runnng clangs ring in my ears, echoing the Supers' recent clamour. Lights come on! Our feet and hands seem to cause pressure lights to glow, faintly at first, then more brightly. There must be sensors that gauge my fear.

Inside, it's pristine, a gleaming cavern with white painted walls. I half expect to see fantail pigeons or baby bunnies, maybe fresh snow. Against the whiteness, the blue water lapping below is a swimming pool, even without a sky.

"You expected what?" he asks. "Filth, dank, squalor? Just because we live down here?" He shakes his head. "And this section falls within my overview; I take personal pride in the commission. I'm sure you do the same, wherever it is you service."

I smile wanly. That will have to do.

Inside the tunnel, we reach the limit ledge and balance, the water purling below.

"Ready to hit?" he asks.

I nod, heart keeling.

"*Right!*" he says, and eases me tightly to him—for a second my skin aches. Webbed fingers deftly frog a mouthpiece between my lips, then he jumps us off the precipice and we fall.

It's an incredible rush, blending fast and slow, and we hurtle from air down into water, joined at the hips, liquid streaming along the fins of the protective inflatable. This, my body cries, this is what I've been missing.

The tunneller takes such care; nothing is too much trouble. At one point, I feel myself threatening to rip, and I squeeze, hoping to prevent a tear. He intuits and spots the pinprick of anxiety, a stream of tiny bubbles beginning to whoosh. Gathering himself to mask the puncture, he puts his mouth to the gap and breathes out so hard there's barely a pause. We keep streaming ahead. As one, my imagination plays, as one.

Terms & Conditions Apply

He is out of breath when we breach, his suit pulled tight as shagreen. Tactile. Breathlessly I stare at him, chest heaving, head dizzy. He has so many pupils, the irises blurring, that I think his eyes must be reflecting mine.

"Wow," I say, though I know it's inane.

He doesn't seem to mind, smiles and shrugs.

"I don't know what to say."

"Don't say anything! Words can only be relied on to fail us, don't you think? Well, I do. Which frees me to say it was my pleasure."

And mine, I'm thinking, looking at the gentle man's chest; smooth, hairless under the slick sheath, nipples tight and inviting as light switches in a dark passage. I almost reach out, but think better of it. Because now we're at the exit, and he's stooping, head cocked quizzically at the *D rogen* sign.

"You're sure this is you?" he asks.

"Yes."

"*Really?*"

I nod.

"Now *I'm* surprised," he says. "I could see you were in trouble, but I didn't take you for a Regular. You seemed… Well, let's just say I would never have guessed you were mixed up with the *D rogen* lot. *Big Pharma*."

I bite my lip, taste blood.

"I'm sorry, but you should have said."

"It seemed unnecessary. We were suited."

He slips abruptly beneath the water, as latent suddenly as he was recently manifest.

Perhaps I will see him again somewhere. Though now that we understand each other, the line is drawn.

And then Karl appears, jiggling impatiently at the foot of the steps. "Fuck was that?"

"Tunneller. Gave me a lift."

"You not supposed to go with anyone. Anyone else."

Sally-Ann Murray

"Then where were you, huh, leaving me in such a tight spot? I waited. These other Supers were making a move. You never came. And anyway, he *offered*."

"Doesn't make it right. You tell him?"

"I was in a hurry. I'm here now. Can we just leave it at that?"

"Lippy today, aren't we. A lot to say for yourself, girl. You looking for trouble again?"

"*No!*"

"Well, watch it. Otherwise."

Karl likes to leave his threats open-ended and powerful, suggestive of superior imaginative flair. Though with what I know of Karl, which by now is plenty, I think that even with his massive ego he's rather like any of us, often at a loss for words. Because there's no easy way to explain how things have turned out, fixed into camps and categories. Supers. Regulars. Supers over Regulars. And looming over it all, *D* rogen, the drug consortium that holds the carrots and the keys.

How to get out when it's all in?

That other little space, too risky even to think of it. Underneath. Water. Enough to wash it all away.

I think of the small rogue tribe of Tunnellers, spotted here, there, then gone. Always able to give the slip. My gentle man.

After our outburst, Karl and I walk silently, single file, up the narrow flight into the *D* rogen premises. I wish. I wish he would say sorry. I wish he would take my hand like a real girlfriend. I wish he could love me. I wish he wasn't Karl.

Wishing so hard (*whack*) I forget to duck near the top of the stairs, the overhang just before the waiting room.

"Always the same with you, hey. No pain no gain," Karl laughs as I rub my forehead.

Can't count how many times I've hit myself on that low blow beam. It's like the certified idiot who designed this complex shrank into a dwarf near the end of the job or something. Bad as pack shrinkage, and that threadbare Chinese glam the Supers chuck out once a year from the back of the monster truck. The way we Regulars hop, skip, and jump, running like crazy rabbits even though most of the kit turns out to be way too small, even at a stretch, whether it's one size fits all or supersized. XXL my foot. I'm skinny, been skinny since birth, and still it fits me too tight, that stuff, like suddenly I'm Mama Melons. That shit must've shrunk in the Supers' whitewash, the way they aim to keep us weak as children.

"They should be careful. Maybe one day we'll all just disappear, tits, arse, and all. What then? Who they find to fuck then?"

Karl laughs it off. "That'll be the day! You Regulars are always bound to get screwed, good and proper." He grabs me to emphasise the obvious point, grinding his boner against my increasingly bony rump. "What you say to that, hey?"

"What you say to that!" he shouts again, this time not a question. "Got anything to say to that?"

I don't know what to make of him. He gets hyped whether I answer him or not. Say nothing, say something. Spit it out. Hold it in. He's always ready to snap. It makes no difference. He needs the meds.

Now I'm nauseous too, starting to feel low. This is how it happens. A week between sessions is just long enough for you to recover, but by day six, you're worrying about the next visit. You don't stay chirpy for long, however hard you try. Next time quickly comes around to drag you down. This thing we're bound to. Sometimes it's burning, sometimes numbness. Blood, suddenly, seeping from anywhere. I have sores. I have scars. I have raw skin and ridges. Most of all, I have Karl, and like all the other Supers, he's obsessed with endless schemes to make good. Hit the big time, somehow. But for me, for the Regulars? For us things just get worse. There's no amount of ordinary suffering can break the grip of a Super who has bought in to *D* rogen's ambitious plans. Nothing and no one. Certainly not a female, that old, superfluous creature. No. They've attached us all to Super cells, scheduled fair and equal rotations, because it's important that every Superior has the chance to realise his opportunity, make the most of it. A bit of this. Some of that. Just another week, ok, then we'll see. That's the sort of crap they say.

"Stop moaning," Karl says. "Just get over it."

"Put your mind to it," he says, "your luscious little body".

And I do.

The waiting room in the medical complex has a glass screen for the staff, and black plastic chairs lined around the sides for all the Regular testers. Obligatory poster projections double as dicta and decoration. The wall facing the stairs has been papered with a huge mural of a forest; a retro-vinyl photo, supposed to be soothing. It's birch trees or something. Pin oaks? Trees, at any rate. At first, I reckoned it must've been summer, when it was taken, because the leaves are bright green, but it's probably been shopped. Looks so real it's a fairytale. But no way anyone could actually get lost in that: in the bottom corner, to the right, there's the familiar *D* rogen logo, a sphere halved horizontally by a needle that balances the Chairman's signature, a laser-cut flourish, *D*.

As per stipulation, Karl clocks me in using the keypad at reception. Gimme the code again, he lip syncs near my ear. He's supposed to remember. Never does. Me, I've got all that up here. I store things all the time, just in case: the sliver of iron that winds my hair, the memory of the tunnels. You never know. I'm a patient person. All this has taught me patience and fortitude. Often, I get through by pretending to be a saint. That faint glow? Hello, it's my halo.

The nurse correlates our reference against her schedule, and the machine prints a numbered slip. Then we hurry up and wait. I feel queasy, so I stand instead of moving and the nurse ticks me off—tells me curtly through the glass shield to take a seat and listen for my cue.

Take a seat? Where to?

"*Now!*" she shouts, "or the lines will get confused."

I snap out of my reverie and glare. Why that attitude *lady*? You're not so different. Look at you, all nice and dutiful under *D* rogen's Super thumb. Still, I can't stop myself from thinking: I'll give *you* lines, imagining the nurse on her starched knees in a nice little noose, the rope giddyup in one hand, the reared crop in the other. You won't be able to sit for a week you bitch. Not when I'm done.

The poster projections scroll, and change, illuminating the nurse in a mob of luminous bacteria, whipping multiple legs.

But that dies out as Karl surfaces into my consciousness. I'm left wondering how many lines he's done, or pills popped, because he's acting up. He says, "Madam, I'm Adam," to the nurse, in a sultry voice that brings down her blind, then swagger staggers to find a seat.

He wide-eyes the small, sex-kittenish girl and purrs "Hell*ow kew*tee". She's fidgeting on a chair, kicking her heels, pulling the diamante titty pasties off a new *D* rogen boob tube, eating pieces like Smarties. She squirms in her chair at Karl.

"Ants in your pants?" he asks, "or wriggle worms?"

Giggling, she licks another sparkle and slips it in her mouth. "Mr. Funny!" She offers him a taste.

Karl blows her a smoochy coochy kiss then bends down to suck a gem off her shiny index finger. Fucking Karl. Old habits, hey, he just can't keep it to himself. Always causing trouble. Already the girl's Super is narked; he makes a blunt, chopping gesture near his crotch for Karl's benefit, and swats the kid.

"*Dude,*" says Karl. "She's a *child*. Let's play nice. That's why we're here, right?"

The guy only glares like toughened glass.

214

Sally-Ann Murray

"No blubbing!" he says to Ms. PoutyPuss. "Just be good. Read a magazine or something."

There are other people we know from waiting. The Super with the big red suitcase, for instance. He's very careful, constantly adjusting and settling. He checks the straps and the buckles. Tugs. Makes sure the zip is still cable-tied. Amazing he hasn't thought to get it all bubble-wrapped, but then I suppose he'd have nothing to do. I didn't have the nerve to ask, but one day he'd caught me staring and murmured, "Just in case. I was a solicitor."

I nodded, feigning understanding. Mad as they come. Though he's quite entertaining, in his way, sits super straight, and keeps his eye on everything, brushes invisible specks from his jacket, and repeatedly smoothes his shiny trousers at the knee. Now and again, he strokes the red case like it's a good dog. Uncrosses and re-crosses his legs. Today he's jittery. He gets up, says to the shrunken Regular seated alongside, "A quick stretch is in order. But do not go in without me. I repeat, *Do not!*"

"Who's going anywhere at this rate?" asks the woman of no one.

Before he leaves for a breather, he unzips a little red side pouch from the luggage motherload and uses it to bag his chair. He pats it in place.

His Regular shakes her head, "Honestly. And I can't be trusted to do that for him? After all this time, what with everything else I do! I think I can keep a seat warm, don't you? That's the least of it!"

But he's trundled off hauling the suitcase, both taking strain. One of the wheels is wonky, and it wobbles like a bad drug reaction.

"The problem with Supers," she says quietly to me. "All those I've had, is they need to pretend. Take Rodney. I say he needs to get over it. His ex is ex. That's the nature of things. He can't carry that around with him forever. Rodney, I tell him—not that he listens—one day that's going to be me, and how will you manage then? But he's

215

Terms & Conditions Apply

such a dreamer, Rodney. Even after she died in D rogen before proper completion, he was willing to try again. When we were assigned, he straight away signed up, thinking we could get through and make enough to get out. You're stronger than she was, he said, much stronger. But what's this now, Round 5? I'm about ready to give up. I don't think I can take much more. Then he'll have case number two to deal with."

She looked helplessly at me. "You know what I mean?"

I nodded.

Karl had also dreamed big. "Nothing small about our man Karl," he'd boasted. "Not where it matters." He loved himself in the third person and the first person equally. "Check how she's walking," he'd laugh to the other Supers. "Last week I nearly tore her apart."

The doctor had examined me following Karl's opening gambit to D rogen, and then ignored me for the remainder of the interview. It was enough that I adequately embodied the research criteria. After much serious interlocution, Dear Dr. had wrapped up the interview with a conspiratorial whisper to Karl, "Some light reading," handing him a glossy manifold of materials marked 'Confidential: Supers Only'. The bullish brochures and persuasive pamphlets were intended to seal the deal. They detailed the procedures and fringe benefits, the overall outcomes. All of which were excellent, from Karl's point of view. Topping the generous once-off-payment was the major incentive: a free, lifetime supply of meds— Unlimited! Drugs of your choice!*

*Ts&Cs apply.

Karl needed no convincing. Shit was getting seriously expensive. He'd tried to stay independent, but could make it much bigger inside the official loops.

Though, when it came to the paperwork... well, Karl wasn't one for reading, and once we were outside the premises, he'd offloaded all the glossy logic onto me, which meant I was in on everything from the start, for better, or worse.

They used highly sophisticated equipment and products, which worked in bio-tandem with brain impulses. Once he was prepped, a Super simply had to think it, and he would engage. This instantaneity had caused some rough edges, in the beginning, some unfortunate glitches. But the personnel had tweaked and refined and titrated through four series of test protocols in order to engender in the Supers a necessary modicum of control. Rather too frequently, in D rogen Round 1, Regulars had been quickly eliminated; they couldn't stay the course long enough for useful data to be gathered about the test stimulants. By now, D rogen Round 5, systems were reliable if not failsafe—otherwise why experiment?—but the hypoallergenic factor was secure. All of this had been demonstrated by the extent of uptake and market penetration in geographic rim contexts not governed by restrictive legislation. When it came to the Regulars, the company was especially eager to access pure, raw data, as this was susceptible to the most favourable manipulation outcomes for D rogen purposes, hence the little girl. However, any Regular female would do. The job. The trick. The dirty.

The initial goal was to track the Super's behaviour as symptomatic, and then to extrapolate an extended model which could be routinely used to stimulate the Regular, but minus the drug impact. "Then," the Doctor summed up, "We will see what we will see!"

"In this phase of the experiment," he said—Doolittle, Spock, Zhivago, Who, or Whatever. "We have a better idea of the prognosis, how situations develop in response to random physical stressors. Regulars are signed in once a week by their Supers, they're hooked up, and the Super swings contact from there via voice drips and needle prompts emanating from our side. It's a valuable experience. The Regular doesn't ever really know what's

Terms & Conditions Apply

going on; it's a closed system, which works to our advantage. Ideally, we aim to extend indefinitely, or till Super exhaustion, but should problems occur...if we foreclose, the Regular won't know what hit her."

In the waiting room, still waiting, I study the new poster projections. The poster children freak me out, but that's good. They help me bone up so I know what's coming. Better to know what you're in for, I always say. Then you can face it.

Today—one minute each—I manage three close-up meditations before my stares start to tear and I have to blink—sixty seconds a shot isn't too bad when you're holding your breath with your eyes.

One is a flayed horse carcass, flanked in the shallows of a sandy sunset strip, the dunes pink and red, and muscled.

Two is a sharp, tight shot of a peeled eyeball, cornea nuzzled by a needle.

Three—oh little, last and least—is a raw gash gaping in the stirrups.

For the moment, that's all I can take, and when I sit it's a bit shakily, which Karl thinks is a gas.

"You still buzzing after your hot shot this morning?" he snipes. "Making it down the tunnels."

I think of him then, the gentle man. Slipping and sliding. How unlike Karl, Karl who just helps himself to me, while the tunneller had helped me without asking. I see us down there together. I can imagine dying in his arms.

"As if you're so good," I say quietly.

"What's that?" Karl snaps.

"You. You're why we're here. I waited, you know."

"Well, ex-*cuse me* for being in demand," he snips. "But you know how it works. Business is only business if it's a pleasure doing business with you, right. The Super comes if and when he's ready. Meaning *me*. The Regular comes when she's called. Meaning *you*. I got caught up this morning, ok, which has nothing to do with you. And anyway it's not my responsibility to get you from A to B.

Sally-Ann Murray

Life is dangerous, so big deal, we all know that. Your job
is to get on top of it. You know where you have to be, and
when. So get there, on time. And by the way—*please*
remind me—who said anything about getting possessive?"

This is a seriously long, complicated speech for Karl.
People are staring. It's considered neither polite nor politic
to speak so openly. The little girl after all, may be *D* rogen,
and her family will have been strategising the best possible
Super alliance from birth, but she doesn't have to *know*
about it. Not yet. Unless there's bigger than usual money
involved, they'll try to hold out for ten. Let her play for a
while still, grooming and petting, some sweet treats, and
bubble baths. Only then… Though it does depend on how
long her first Super's prepared to wait.

"Okay, okay. Karl, you're right," I shush him, scared that
next thing he'll erupt, come clean across the reception and
then the girl will start to show cracks.

As always, it's better to appease him. Though the mood
seems already to have spread, for a tall, dark Super is
muttering to his Regular attachment, "Don't think you can
just go back. It's not like anybody's waiting for you
there."

"I know. We're all waiting here, aren't we?"

The Super gives a limp laugh.

The pregnant girl is big as a ball, no disguising that, must
surely explode soon. I wonder what then? I don't know
how she can sit there so calm, like there's no tomorrow.
Not even the next few hours.

Karl is restless too. Starts fiddling with his pockets.

"You want a Mag?"

I shake my head.

He snaps open a phial and downs a pill. Another
container, another swallow.

Karl is more restless, starts messing with stuff on the side
table.

"You want a mag?"

I shake my head.

Terms & Conditions Apply

"Have a mag!" he says, a bit too loudly, leaning towards me. "Look, some sweet kitties for you."

He thrusts the magazine into my hands. Vivisection. I glance and recoil.

He guffaws. "You not a fan? But that lot do some pretty good stuff. Very creative."

There's nothing much else in pile, all of them way out of date and horribly well-thumbed. Flick. Lick. Flick. Always more of the same. Must be wrecked by now. Grey pubes, for sure, or fracked bald. Flesh hanging like swing tags. A mountainous cleft plugged with plastic. A knobbed, featherbare cockatiel. Versions of the same old.

Flick, flick, flick.

Something hits my breast. I look up. Hiss, "*Karl!*" He's shooting paper chew from a rubber band and grins, satisfied now that he has my attention.

"Don't be disgusting. What?"

He nods at the poster projection of the wet gash.

"Yes. So *what*?"

"Watch me bullseye that baby!" He tears a piece of magazine and gobs it with spit, then lets fly.

"*Yesss!*" he says under his breath as he hits home.

"Super," I say, "so practice makes perfect, after all." And I close my eyes.

The waiting is terrible. A trial, even after months of the same routine—though I won't say it's the worst. You act casual, but inside. Your heart. Stomach in knots. There's nothing to do but wait. When they're ready, they call. Then you get up, wipe your sweaty palms against your legs, and go into the room. With Karl. By then his juice will be jumping.

In camera, I will be prepped, standing still and pliant as the assistant rolls two thin silicon plugs, not flinching as he eases them deep into my ear canals, tamps tight with his thumbs pressing hard on either side of my head as if mending a damaged ball—in my head, a ghostly, hard-of-hearing wind, like a desert storm drumming across dunes.

Sally-Ann Murray

Then my nose, the blocked intubations gagging at the back of my throat. Eyes closed, I will not resist as he shrouds my lids in a thick, stockinged band. And while my mouth is still unstopped, for this short time I will breathe without thinking. Even then, under the silent, pressing darkness, I will know that Karl is wiring up, adjusting the skin sensors. Data. Stats. Responses, −ve or +ve. Duration slash endurance. When he peels me away, I will separate easily, jointed fourfold to the table, ball and socket, so that whichever way he turns, I will fluently gimbal. If he leaps, I will bound. If he cuts, I will thrust.

Karl finds himself in complete agreement with Dr Who: this is a precision mechanism that depends on complex give and take. We are there, Super and Regular, to establish how much room there is, relatively, to manoeuvre.

I think of before, being a child at school, we played simple games like Simon Says. Do this. Do this. And you did. Do that! and you were out in a single move.

It is only Karl, I tell myself, which is at least predictable.

"Karl, Karl," I whisper, "*Karl.*" Knowing how unpredictable he can be.

Moving in, he brings his mouth close to my ear.

I cannot hear his explanation, and do not need to. I have heard it all before.

"It'll be hard for both of us, baby, so just bite the bullet. We go a few rounds with these guys, and we make a killing. This *D* rogen deal's a set-up for life."

Sally-Ann Murray lives in Durban and lectures at UKZN. Her imagination, however, knows no bounds. In 2010, her novel *Small Moving Parts* won the MNet Literary Award and the Herman Charles Bosman Prize. She is busy with a second novel, and has published strange stories in *English Studies in Africa* (2012) and *English Inside Out* (2011)

Heresy

Mandisi Nkomo

[South Africa is refusing to withdraw troops from Russia, even after numerous complaints from the Chinese government. President Dlamini had these comments to make, "We and the Russians have always had a very close relationship. We have always worked scrupulously to repay them for the investments they have made in our country. Without the Russians, our space program could never have advanced as far as it has. We will maintain our military presence there, and continue to assist the Russian Rebuilding Program." Here Dlamini refers to two pertinent issues on the South African agenda. The first is the rebuilding of Russia after the repealed Chinese invasion. The second is the space race. After the US-Iran nuclear catastrophe, Russia and South Africa have worked hard on a joint program to recover lost US spacecrafts on the outskirts of our Solar System. The Chinese have engaged in minor skirmishes with South African troops on the Russian border, likely due to their own floundering space program. South Africa launched their rocket a month ago, while China is a number of months behind...]
— Mail & Guardian, Politics and Space, 5 January 2040

Julius Masemola, head of The Department of Air and Space, sat in President Dlamini's office. He was not quite sure how to address the president with his current predicament.

"President Dlamini," he said. "We've had a slight mishap. There appears to be some kind of, ehh, barrier, around the outer edges of the Solar System. The ship slammed into it. Ehh... it went up in smoke. So to speak."

President Dlamini sat behind his wide wooden desk, trying his best not to look irate. He poured himself a glass of water, and quickly slurped it up. "I see. I see. So what now? Do the Chinese know this yet?"

"Well... it was leaked by the *Mail & Guardian*. I think they have somebody inside." Masemola looked around the office suspiciously. "So, ja, my guess is the Chinese know by now. Ehh, the next move, I guess, would be to try and blast a hole through the barrier, and launch another rocket."

President Dlamini adjusted his glasses carefully. "And what would be the time period for that?"

Masemola twiddled his thumbs. "Ehh... I don't know Sir. Luckily, we constructed a back-up rocket. On the other hand, we, ehh, would need to send a probe and maybe a research team up. Find out what the barrier is made of and then what will penetrate it. Maybe a couple of months."

"Ja... contact SSA. Tell them about this. They need to watch the Chinese. Your departments must work together comrade. *Very* closely. Tell them if any sabotage is necessary, they have my blessing."

"Okay Sir. I wouldn't worry much about the Chinese Sir. According to SSA, their rockets are rubbish."

"Ja, I know." President Dlamini chuckled, and slammed his palm onto the desk. "They're months behind."

[...According to insiders in The Department of Air and Space, South Africa's Dlamini 1 spacecraft went up in smoke. The Chinese have claimed this is due to poor engineering, stating, "The Rainbow Nation's space program has gone up in a rainbow of flames." The South Africans on the other hand have not yet commented.

The Chinese have gone on to say that economics based on central planning leads to poor engineering and that only State Capitalism can produce a superior space program, with the correct engineering, and necessary ingenuity...] — *Mail & Guardian, Space Update, 15 January 2040*

Heresy

A week later Masemola was back in President Dlamini's office. President Dlamini closed his AwehTube application, and carefully placed his tablet pc on the coffee table. "Listen to those bloody Chinese. State Capitalism..." President Dlamini scoffed, and then looked across the couch to where Masemola sat. "Masemola, where are we?"

"Don't worry Sir, their rockets are rubbish. *We*, on the other hand, are almost there." Masemola began to wave his finger confidently as he spoke. "The barrier is actually quite weak. The scientists don't know what it is made of, but, according to them, it should be easy to penetrate. Apparently the barrier is not very thick, so very basic explosives should do the job. Dlamini 1 also caused substantial damage, so it's already weakened. Our scientists are working on it right now. According to SSA, the Chinese have not been able to get a team up yet. We are still ahead of them. As usual..." Masemola nodded his chunky head.

President Dlamini mimicked the nodding, but slower, while clasping and unclasping his hands. "I see, I see. That's good Masemola. Very good news. We will not be outdone by those would-be revolutionaries and their DE-MO-CRA-CY," Dlamini mouthed the syllables like a mocking juvenile. "Tell me when it's done comrade."

The two men stood simultaneously. Masemola walked over to President Dlamini and took his hand. He looked down on the president's shining shaven scalp. "Maximum five months," he promised.

Exactly three months later, Masemola sat in his office at The Department of Air and Space. His Blackberry buzzed away incessantly. After three hours of dawdling on the internet, he picked up the Blackberry. There were five missed calls, and two messages from the science team. He dialled them.

"Mr. Masemola?"

Mandisi Nkomo

"Ja, what is it?"

"We've penetrated the barrier."

Masemola did not reply.

"Umm..."

"What? What?" he said eagerly.

"We don't really understand... what's beyond it."

"What do you mean? Ehh, it's outer space chief. Simple."

"Ja... but it's not space. It's... I don't know. First we thought it was Dark Matter... but, ay, I don't know man..."

Masemola waited again.

"And there's something pouring through rapidly. Some, umm—gaseous substance. We can't identify."

"And?"

"And... ja... we don't know."

"Fine. I'll be there just now. And chief—please man—don't waste my time."

Masemola shook his head and stood from his desk. "Bloody agents." He called his secretary, "I need a train to the science team. And make fast Ms. Van Rensburg. I also want to make a secure call."

Masemola picked up the headset lying on his desk. He tapped some digits on his keyboard, and then spoke into the headset's microphone. "This is Madiba, calling in regards to *magic*. The springbok is over the lion. The lion has spoken to the zebra."

"Is the Zuma Spear strong with you?"

"Strong, and big enough to choke those who would attempt to exercise free speech."

"Mr. Masemola?" A serious face flickered onto the computer screen.

"You guys need to check these scientists again." Masemola jabbed his index finger into the screen repeatedly. "Make sure the Chinese haven't infiltrated them. They're feeding me all kinds of nonsense."

"Yes Sir." The man on the screen nodded solemnly.

Heresy

"I'm heading over to them now chief. Ehh, I don't want to be seen by any Chinese."

"Yes Sir," the screen said again.

Masemola tapped a key on his keyboard, and the face disappeared. He waited a couple of minutes, and Ms. Van Rensburg called.

"It's here," she said.

Masemola snapped his fingers at a suited man who lurked in the corner of his office. "Hey! Bloody agent! We're leaving now."

The guard put his index finger to his ear, and spoke to his lapel. Seconds later more butch men in suits and shades barged through the door. Masemola stood up, manoeuvred around his desk, and made his way to the door. The guards surrounded him in formation and they made their way down the long corridors of the Union Buildings, headed for the secret elevator that would take them to the government's secret subway station.

Masemola sat impatiently in his private cabin in the train. The trip was around five minutes, but felt longer, likely due to his sense of frustration. He quickly gulped down a beer from the bar.

He arrived promptly at the South African Science Headquarters' underground station. He and his security team entered another elevator and exited to sunlight, bright-purple jacarandas, and the enormous 'Tower of Science', so coined by the locals in Pretoria. The building reached up like a jagged disproportioned triangle.

The science team was waiting for them in the building's grand promenade. They navigated them through the building and finally they arrived at the conference room.

Guards proceeded to secure the perimeter, while an assistant of the science team led Masemola to a chair and offered him food and drink. He responded with a resolute, "No."

The room went silent for a moment.

Mandisi Nkomo

"Well Mr. Masemola," said one of the scientists, and commenced the proceedings with much unease. "We breached the barrier. We've looked inside." The scientist cleared his throat. "Well, you see, you see here; there is some kind of mist that we can see. It's already entering our atmosphere, all the way from the hole. We took some samples-"

Masemola interrupted. "What are you talking about? We need to launch another rocket. How big is the hole? Can the rocket fit through? Where are the US ships? Ehh, those ones we're looking for—Voyager one, two, three."

"All in good time Mr. Masemola, Sir. The hole is not big enough yet. Though... we want to send a small team in. We are very concerned because, you see, we don't understand what's beyond the barrier. It's just mist. An unidentifiable mist—we think, we think, we should do some analysis before launching the rocket."

Masemola sighed. He felt an aggravating sense of angst. He did not like it. "Ehh, chief, chief." Masemola rubbed his brow. "Dlamini won't be happy. You know we are running on schedule here comrades. The bloody Chinese are lapping at our heels."

"We... we understand that Sir. But. You see. You see, nobody knows what the misty substance is. We think it may be the scientific finding of the century. We need more time, Sir."

The colleagues of the spokesperson nodded in assuring unison.

"How much time?" Masemola asked.

"We don't want to trouble you. Two weeks. Just two weeks. We'll run some tests Sir. Send a team in. When we feel comfortable we'll start to expand the hole."

The room went silent for a minute. Masemola rapped his fingers on the desk in front of him, and a member of the science team coughed anxiously.

"Fine. Two weeks," Masemola replied.

Heresy

For two weeks, Masemola avoided all contact with President Dlamini. He was not in the mood for chastisement. He knew Dlamini would not understand the need for more time. In fact, he was not even sure he himself understood the need for more time. He was running on a hunch. He just felt there was something wrong with the entire situation.

On the exact Tuesday two weeks had expired, he received a phone call.

"The Justice League of South Africa is in need of the youth. Will you assemble?"

"I am young no longer. My aging has advanced rapidly since the Shadow Moses incident in 1976. I am an Old Revolutionary now, but I am no hero, never was, never will be."

"Mr. Masemola. We checked out the scientists. The Chinese have not infiltrated them. They are honestly clueless. And, they seem to be right about the misty substance. Nobody knows what it is. We let the Chinese breach our security barrier on the hole. Their scientists are also clueless on the substance. They are even suggesting it may be something ethereal."

"Ethereal? Ha!" Masemola chuckled. "Thank you. Keep me updated chief."

The phone went dead. Masemola dialled his secretary. "Ms. Van Rensburg. Prepare my private transport. I am ready to see the scientists. Make fast."

"You have entered the spirit realm. All trespassers will be prosecuted." Masemola watched a video that addressed him in a sultry female voice. He was at the South African Science Headquarters again. The science team was assembled and nervous on the conference room stage again. The scene only differed in that he accepted a cup of coffee.

"That is the last bit of footage we have Mr. Masemola. The research team's bodies were all promptly dropped

228

through the hole. They... they were decimated. I think we may be in trouble here Sir. Aliens of some sort maybe. You need to notify the military. We, we took our samples to some illegal testers: Sangomas, Christians... you know the like. They think it's God, or ancestors, or some stuff like that."

"I could have you arrested for that you know? It's a violation of Communist Treaty. If the Chinese find out..." Masemola's eyes opened substantially wide.

"Ja... we know Sir. But... we were at a loss. We've never come across something like this."

Masemola sat in silent contemplation for a while. "I need to make a call. If you would excuse me."

Masemola walked out of the conference room. He and his security team briskly made their way back down to the train station. As he entered the train, he turned around and nodded to the head of the security team. "I'm about to make a secure call. Nobody comes in."

"Yes Sir," was the response.

He picked up the phone and dialled. "President Dlamini. Ehh... I think we might have a situation here."

[...The Mail & Guardian has been experiencing mounting pressure from the South Africa Government. In the last ten months, there have been a number of unexplained deaths and disappearances in South Africa; estimates put the figure in the region of 1000 - 1300 persons. Last week we ran a feature article on this disturbing issue, and ever since the government has upped their efforts in hunting us down.

Our investigators are convinced that some kind of spiritual force is leaking through the hole blasted into the sky. Reports of citizens bursting into flames are occurring all over the country. In almost every instance of this, government operatives arrive on the scene to mop up the situation. All people believed to have seen anything, or

Heresy

linked in any way to the victims are taken by government operatives.

We have been conducting interviews where possible, but very few connected to these sightings are ever heard from again. What follows is an exclusive interview with an ex-member of The Hawks, the government's personal death squad.

M&G: Okay. So you can't give us your name or any personal background information, so I rate we should get right to it then. Can you give us a rundown of what's been going on?

Joe Seep: Ja. Hi. I can tell you this much. I've been with The Hawks as far back as the original ANC rise to power. I was there for the communist revolution. Some have said our methods were a bit too drastic. Anyway. I had a large part in that. I did some things... I was more comfortable with it then. It was harsh, but seemed necessary. We couldn't afford another civil war.

M&G: But now you've had a change of heart?

JS: I guess you could say that, ja. It takes its toll. At some point you start to feel like shit inside—at least if you had doubts. A lot of my peers never had doubts, and they don't seem troubled at all. People just react different I guess.

M&G: If we could return to my original question...

JS: Ja, sorry man. [Takes a deep breath] After the breach, some things started happening.

M&G: The breach?

JS: That hole we blew in the barrier. Ja, so Dlamini gave the order. We were dispatched to investigate and contain 'the problem'—not that anybody knew what 'the problem' was. People were getting killed... brutal deaths man. These people were bursting into flames on the spot— some even in their sleep. And you can't put these flames out. It happened once while we were out on patrol—to one of our own guys even.

230

Mandisi Nkomo

We were driving through a heavy mist, you know, that mist that's coming from the hole? In a split second he burst into fire, like he was made of Blitz firelighters. We tried everything man, but we couldn't put the flames out. We had to jump out, and watch him braai in the vehicle. Then the mist just disappeared—like that, man.

Don't take my word for it, but I rate it's coming from up there [points up].

Anyway, we set up an investigation. We went out, looked around, but we couldn't really find anything; just burnt bodies turning up everywhere, autopsies turning up nothing, no traces at the crime scene, nothing—just that strange mist.

About a month into the investigation, people start talking and the news begins to spread around the country. Dlamini tells us we can't let this get out. This is where the containment part begins. Now let me tell you a little about Dlamini: that guy doesn't play. He smiles and talks friendly, but you don't play with that man. He has zero tolerance, and he is ruthless.

These, uh, 'spontaneous combustion' cases are effectively happening everywhere, but isolated. As in nobody, in any government branch, knows who's being targeted or why. Me and you are sitting here now, who knows why we haven't burst into flames? The only thing we can confirm is that it is confined within our borders.

So Dlamini tells us this needs to be handled; the citizens can't keep talking, and we can't have it leaked. You know, the Chinese and all that kak.

M&G: *And by handled he means 'disappearing' people who've seen anything?*

JS: *Ja, you could say that. So now instead of looking for the culprits, we are supposed to track down the relatives and friends of the victims, and shut them up. Now this is no easy task, and I'm speaking from a logistics point of view here. These peoples' lives are so connected... like a web. We just got name, after name, after name. Some of the*

231

people were relatives of government officials. Innocent people man.

I'd done this type of thing before though, with some rich elites and spiritual types. But that was different... those were spiritual people. Those can be real brutes—they'd slit their brothers throat over a phantom. Rich greedy elites too—they'll slit your throat for an extra rand.

These were innocent young men and women, who'd done nothing. I couldn't take it man. I was overseeing the torture of people who were clueless. They just woke up one night with a flaming corpse for a spouse. They were just as scared as we were.

M&G: So what was your average day like?

JS: Well... I would go to headquarters and get a list of names—a long list man. Put on civilian wear, and cruise around in the unmarked cars. You know the kind. We just, sort of, scope out the situation. Then we start picking them up. Take them to headquarters, beat and interrogate some of them. Then kill and dump the bodies. Obviously I can't tell you where. We didn't get one valuable piece of intelligence the entire time, but Dlamini says, 'Don't stop, keep up the good work comrade'. [shakes his head]

M&G: So you quit?

JS: [Laughs] Quit? You don't quit that kind of job. I left... which means I'm on the run. I had to plan out my exit for a month or so. This time tomorrow I'll be long gone. Gone somewhere nice, like China. [Laughs again]. Obviously I'm not going there, but, you get the idea. This is my one good deed before I abandon this place in shame.

M&G: Do you have a family? Here or abroad?

JS: I don't think I should talk about that.

M&G: Why?

JS: Because they would use it to track me.

M&G: But what about everything else you've told us? Can't they use that?

JS: Too many people fit that profile. Like 98% percent of the agency. There's very little rotation there. New recruits

Mandisi Nkomo

are a liability to them. They tend to think no veteran can change his ways, or that we've done too many things to turn back. I guess I disagree. I'm done with their sick shit.

M&G: *But won't they notice you've disappeared?*

JS: *[Laughs] Please man! There's so much covert shit going on there, nobody knows what anybody's doing. They can't tell who has left from who is destabilising China!*

M&G: *I see. Do you think you could be an inspiration to others involved in government, who feel disgruntled with the way things are being run?*

JS: *[Laughs]*

M&G: *I'm serious... well?*

JS: *Who knows? Maybe. I don't have such lofty ideas for myself. I just want out man for my personal wellbeing.*

And I don't really have a happy image for my future. I joke, but they could really find me. I'm just hoping this whole God/space stuff distracts them enough. I just want to go through a day without feeling like a monster... if that's even possible anymore.

[Shifts uncomfortably in chair]

Can we end this now? I need to go.

M&G: *Yes we can. Thank you very much for your time.*

JS: *Ja...*

— *Mail & Guardian, Government's Aggressive Clamp Down, 9 March 2041*

"Nuke them, it, whatever. Nuke them. And find out where those bloody *Mail & Guardian* people are hiding. Have you read that interview? They're killing our image comrades. It's all over the internet!"

South Africa's leaders—those still alive—sat around a long rectangular table in the Union Building's conference room. As President Dlamini spoke, there was unanimous agreement.

Unsettled, Masemola surveyed his assenting comrades, and then swore under his breath. "Sir... I don't know how to say this but, ehh, what if the spiritual leaders are right?

Heresy

What if we breached the spiritual world and don't know it. What if the Muslims are right? This could be a big mistake comrades; something is not right here," he said, as authoritatively as his ridiculous statement would allow.

The room was silent for a few seconds before erupting in universal laughter and jest. It took almost two whole minutes for the laughter and mockery to fade.

President Dlamini still laughing while breathily addressing Masemola, who was still being poked and pointed at by the other attendees, "That's preposterous. I think you may need a break Julius. Take some time off comrade. We'll handle it from here."

"I..." Masemola started and then shut his mouth, feeling foolish. He thought for a moment, and then stood up.

"What are you doing?" President Dlamini said. "It was a joke."

"Ehh," Masemola said embarrassed. "I think I'll take you up on it Sir."

There was more laughter around the table.

President Dlamini licked his lips and adjusted his glasses. He sat back, lodging the back of his pointy head into the leather of his chair. "Really?" he said mockingly. "Fine. Go. Three months—no pay."

Masemola took the three months off. He figured he needed the time to think. He spent the time in his Sandton mansion, drinking beer, and pondering his future career. Every morning he woke up, he found himself wondering why he had not yet spontaneously combusted. After all, the whole affair was largely his fault. Some days he checked the news, hoping President Dlamini had spontaneously combusted, but Masemola never found himself to be that lucky.

[...Back in the year 1994, a young Trent Reznor wrote a song called 'Heresy', under his Nine Inch Nails moniker. The song was part tongue-in-cheek, part Friedrick

234

Mandisi Nkomo

Nietzche allusion, and part of an overarching theme, encompassed in his album 'The Downward Spiral'. At a time when American music still dominated the charts, the song was a hit. 'Your God is dead, and no one cares!' Reznor yelled, over thundering percussion and ear blistering guitar fuzz. Perhaps this would be a choice song for the South African government to dedicate to the last remaining spiritual leaders, who claim that the South African government has killed God.

In March this year, South Africa sent a spacecraft armed with a nuclear warhead into outer space. The destination was the outer edges of our Solar System, where the Dlamini 1 spacecraft met an early end at the hands of an unexpected physical barrier. The warhead passed the barrier, and exploded in April. Following the explosion, the so-called spiritual realm seems to have been obliterated. Though outlawed many years ago, a number of remaining spiritual leaders are openly lamenting the destruction of the spiritual realm at the hands of the South African government.

Though seldom in agreement, the majority of existing spiritual leaders agreed that after the nuke was launched, an inexplicable sense of comfort and unity between humanity was lost. Some still disagree however, arguing that a manmade nuclear device could not destroy an omnipotent being. According to these dissenters, those who believe God is dead are using the nuke as an excuse to give up the fight against the atheists, modernists, and communists.

According to political analyst Imaan Khan, the South African government has made one of the biggest humanitarian blunders since their brutal inception of the atheist state. She states, "If the wounds of religion were coerced shut by the South African government, the very same government has now yanked them wide open. No longer will we have to deal only with atheist state versus the religious or secular state, but now we will have to deal

235

Heresy

with another rift within the proponents of spirituality. We are about to see a whole new breed of spiritual war."

On the other end of the spectrum, renowned scientists seem to have absolutely nothing to say on the matter. The question on everybody's lips remains: did the South African government kill God? All unexplained deaths in South Africa have stopped since the nuke, though the government still appears to be rounding people up. President Dlamini had this to say on the matter, "This is merely a step forward in the space race. All this trifle about God is just propaganda spread by the Chinese. We have reached the new frontier..."] — Mail & Guardian, Opinion Piece: God Is Dead, 3 June 2041

Masemola returned to work after his leave expired. He was still alive, and much to the nation's dismay, so was President Dlamini. The mist had disappeared after the nuke, and so Masemola figured it was about time he got on with his life. He spent a week getting up-to-date with the investigations done by the new science team—the old team had 'defected to the Chinese', which really meant they had inexplicably caught on fire and burnt to death. After spending the week with the new science team, he returned to the Union Buildings the following Monday for his first meeting with President Dlamini.

The Union Buildings felt emptier than usual, and Masemola quickly concluded that this was due to all the recent 'defections'. He swore under his breath, wondering why President Dlamini could not have done him a favour and 'defected' as well, before knocking lightly on the door of President Dlamini's office. Masemola heard a murmured response, and entered.

"Well Mr. Masemola, I see you're back from your break. I hope all is well comrade. What's the progress?" President Dlamini said, and smiled sarcastically, while watching Masemola walk across the office.

Mandisi Nkomo

Masemola sat down in the chair opposite President Dlamini and sighed. "I've spoken to the scientists. Sir... Dlamini 2 has searched the entire region. There's nothing there. The scientists say it's just an endless expanse of nothing. We have teams out there right now. They've been travelling steadily for months and have reached nothing. It just keeps going on.

"And, ehh, there's no of sign anything beyond our Solar System; even though the illusion of other Galaxies still appears from the inside, there is nothing on the other side. They can't figure that out either—how the illusion was created. Astronomers are feeling quite stupid right now. Their field is in tatters. And the religious types are having a field day with this."

President Dlamini grumbled irritably, and then adjusted his glasses.

"Ehh... if I may give you my honest opinion—I think we wasted a lot of money on this. I think there is nothing beyond this Solar System. The scientists say the barrier changes everything we understand about this Solar System. I don't really understand most of the things they say. The barrier seems to be the only thing of interest to them. I think we killed God, and now there's nothing out there to find."

President Dlamini slammed his fists onto the table. "The bloody Chinese are going to laugh at us. This is a disaster." Masemola nodded gravely. "I need to contact SSA. More people need to disappear. You may leave comrade."

President Dlamini began typing away at his keyboard, but Masemola interrupted him. "President Dlamini... I was wondering. Since my position has now become, ehh, redundant so to speak. Could I be reassigned? I mean, there are still things to do. The scientists are talking about colonising Titan and Mars before the Chinese do... but I'm bored with this rubbish."

Heresy

President Dlamini looked up. "And where exactly do you want to be reassigned to?"

"Foreign Affairs. I have some ideas you see. Ehh. I think we should send more troops into Russia, and assist our African comrades more. We have the money after all... even after the billions we wasted on this space rubbish."

"Go on," President Dlamini said.

"Well—ehh—I've been doing some calculations. According to my figures, we have the resources to solve at least forty percent of the world's problems on our own—with maybe a bit of assistance from the Russians, or the UK. The Chinese however, only have the capacity to solve twenty percent. Especially since nobody likes them. This means that if we start a new race, who can, ehh, solve more world issues in less time. We will definitely win. So we ehh, can become the world's saviour, which will probably increase our reach, and give us a better image."

President Dlamini clapped his hands excitedly, and regarded Masemola's chubby form with much admiration. "Masemola—you're a genius! It's such an easy way for us to outwit those annoying Chinese." President Dlamini laughed maniacally. "This is brilliant Masemola. Brilliant! I need to get my speech people in here. I am going to officially apologise to the world for being so short sighted. I will admit we killed God, then feed them some nonsense about humanity being alone with only one saviour. Us!"

"That's a great idea Sir. So, ehh, do I have the job?"

"Ja. Go and check if the Minister of Foreign Affairs has defected. If he's still there, then tell him he's fired."

Mandisi Nkomo is a budding writer, musician, and arranger. He is a class 'A' nerd, who enjoys beer, live music, games, comics, books, and movies. He currently resides in Cape Town where he spends most of his time pondering ways to get a steady income, while writing

Mandisi Nkomo

fiction and music, as well as drumming for local bands. 'Heresy' is his first published short story.

Closing Time

Liam Kruger

@xang, re: the projection chat we had at the conclave—
source suspect, typic, but holiday reading.
  aitch

ARCHIVAL AUDIO FOOTAGE: ID 455832G
VIOLATING TERMS OF PAROLE, TESTAMENT

TIMESTAMP: [REDACTED]

I drew the connection between alcohol and time travel
pretty late in the game, all told. And yes, you absolute
bastard in the back of the room, 'late in the game' doesn't
mean much to a time traveller, but I don't have much
control over where I go, do I? Or when I go. I'm sorry, I
don't think English is the language to talk about this in. I
don't know if any language can talk about this without
straining a little at the edges. Firsts, then: I got drunk for
the first time when I was fourteen years old. And I mean
absolutely motherless drunk, not the sort of tipsiness you
get when your shite-of-a-cousin sneaks you alcopops at a
family wedding reception; I'm talking a half-litre of vodka
and a litre of whatever soda your pocket money can still
sustain. My friends later drew me a map of the graveyard,
with all the places I'd pissed or puked marked out, twelve
different crosses. I don't even remember going to a
graveyard; in fact, I remember nothing.
  Not nothing in the sense that I remember drinking and
drinking and then waking up with my dad shaking my
shoulder, vomit stains all; I mean I remember hours of
nothingness, like when you're in a swimming pool at night
and you've let out all your air but you haven't hit the
bottom yet, and you barely know you're sinking. That, but

for hours. Waking up the next morning, to the realities of my cigarette-addled throat and my bruised arms and hands, to my sandpaper tongue and sewage pipe breath, I wanted to hurt someone for pulling me out of that swimming pool.

I was fourteen years old, and when I got drunk what I felt was nothingness. I chased that feeling for a few years, but when it became clear that it wasn't going to happen again, I learned to appreciate the other gifts that booze could bring: the memories that weren't memories; the dreams of worlds that weren't; the discovery of hands that weren't my own.

Understand that my stumbling home with my hair tied up, apparently weeping when I saw my parents, restricted my freedom a little bit. I was told that I had a curfew now, that I was too young to be going out like that. My head feeling like broken eggshells, the memory of that dark pool still lingering, I would've agreed to anything.

So, it was a few weeks before I drank again.

The next time was under more controlled conditions—I was at my mate Wayne's place. We'd put on button-up shirts and walked to the corner store, agonising over which brand of beer to buy like it mattered to us. The bored cashier wasn't fooled and didn't particularly care; when we walked back to his place, our rucksacks were clinking.

Wayne and I sat on a couch, watched football, and drank all the beers. Then I jimmied open his dad's liquor cabinet and drank most of that. Then I got abusive, found some cigarettes, went to the bathroom, and locked myself in there for a few hours. Wayne said he heard me crying. This I remember like it was yesterday, now; at the time, though, I had to get the story second-hand. Third-hand, actually, because Wayne was no longer speaking to me. When we passed one another in the school hallways, he'd pull a tight face and look away. You get used to that sort of thing eventually.

At the time, though, I was surprised; all I could remember was drinking some beers, getting silly, then

Closing Time

falling asleep before half-time, slipping into those weird boozy dreams you get. That's just what the drink does.

What it did, rather, because I don't drink anymore. So they tell me. But you know this part—what they told me about my liver, and what it can't do anymore without packing up.

Not then, of course—I was young and supple and my hands didn't shake like fucking... like this.

So I drank, because there were other mates to drink with. There was Robert, who introduced me to Jack Daniels— and Jack's been there for me a hell of a lot longer than Robert has, and he hung around longer than most. There was Sean, who liked cocktails. There was Beth, for whom I'd pretend to like tequilas, back when taste mattered a bit. We drank together; sometimes I'd get drunk enough to slip into those strange dreams—the ones where I'd be in some dingy one-room apartment with a dirty mattress—and sometimes I wouldn't. I was, I'm told, a right pisser.

And when I started looking old enough—with the bruises under my eyes turning into bags, it didn't take long—I'd go to the bars, and I'd meet strangers who thought they knew me, who would give me odd looks when it became clear that I didn't know them. Who would give me odd looks anyway.

Understand, I didn't just drink—I mean Christ, I was a student. There were periods of time, whole months when I'd wake up on some friend's couch, with his maid telling me I had to go because whatever I'd said or done the night before had made me unwelcome there. There was that time I told Robert that Daisy, his then-beau was going to be pregnant at 20, and that it wouldn't be his. It was only when I turned out to be right that we started talking again. But my point is: I'd wake up, that single-room apartment still in my head, and someone would tell me what I'd gotten up to after a few drinks and I'd apologise, and I'd promise not to do it again, and I'd mean it at the time. I would go to class, mend some bridges, and things would mellow out again, for a while. Sean would still offer company, and Beth didn't seem to mind that I wasn't drinking her tequila.

But I missed that dream.

Look, I never had interesting dreams—not anything worth talking about or thinking about. Just the regular sort—the odd sex dreams, the 'I ate all of the houses and the Pope was mad at me and then I woke up' dreams. But the room I dreamed about when I was blotto... that felt real. The sweat-stained mattress and the filthy blinds that hung crooked against the city lights hanging on buildings that I'd never seen before fascinated me the way Sean bored me. I liked going there.

I missed being someone else.

And yeah, look, I felt bad if I woke up and Beth was in tears because I'd called her a whore, or if I'd racked up a huge phone bill calling numbers I didn't recognise, but I never remembered doing it. It didn't feel real; I couldn't feel real guilt for any of it if I couldn't remember. Probably even less now that I can.

You're not supposed to be able to read in dreams, did you know that? It's meant to be a jumble of random symbols, if anything. You're not supposed to be able to walk out of the shitty one-room apartment of your dreams and down the dope-stinking hallways, past haggard-looking single mothers who pull their children close when they see you, or find newspapers in the trash with a date twenty years past what you're used to. That's not how dreams are meant to go.

So yeah, I twigged that it wasn't a dream. I mean, who dreams anything that tangible, that reliably, when you're boozed up? Same hallway, same scared single parents? And who, come to think of it, would choose to dream about my hole of an apartment? Telling your friends that you travel to the future when you're blackout drunk, at best—that is, when they believe you—loses you friends. So I stopped doing that pretty quickly.

Closing Time

Didn't stop drinking though. I mean, unlike the sad fucking broke individuals I would find at the meetings my parole officer made me go to, I had an excuse for the shit I did when I was loaded: it wasn't me doing it. I wasn't the one swearing at and, yeah, okay, maybe beating on Beth; I was in some broken old guy's body in the future when that shit happened. He was the one doing it.

And alright, it sucked for the people stuck with drunk-me, but it sucked for them anyway—they were in the mid-fucking-nineties. I was in the future, and jesus was the future bright. The buildings, the cars, the clothes—the drugs, as if I needed the extra trip. Funny, those never had the same impact.

I mean, sure, it was a trade-off, but it seemed fair, you know? My old-ass friend would get to spend a couple of hours reliving his youth in my young and okay-looking body, and I'd get to see the world that was coming. Sneak preview, even from the rheumy eyes of some guy my grandpa's age. Fair's fair.

And it makes sense, in a way. I mean—I've had time to read up on this stuff now, because that's about all my leash-holders would let me do, when they put me in. Which, by the way, is bloody hilarious—I spent years not telling anybody about the time travel thing because I was afraid they'd put me in a nuthouse, and I ended up in one anyway.

Asylum. Sorry.

But look, 'time travel'—the way they had it on television or in the nu-rez games—that doesn't make sense. If you tried to physically put something in another time, even a couple of molecules or whatever, it would annihilate whatever it landed in. Like, imagine trying to put a cup of water into a full bathtub. Except the water in that cup comes from the same bathtub you're pouring it into. It doesn't work, does it? Damn. Look, what I'm saying is, you can't move matter like that.

Liam Kruger

Souls aren't made of matter, though, are they? Or personalities, whatever. I mean, meat aside, we're just a couple of electrons floating around in our brains. When I got loaded, I'd be on the same wavelength as the old guy and *poof*. Party in the future.

God, I was an idiot.

See, I was trying to be clever about things—like if it wasn't going so great with Beth and I didn't want this codger makings things worse, I'd have somebody lock me in my room for a couple of hours so he couldn't get up to much. You would be astonished at how easy it is to find somebody who'll lock you in your room for a few blue notes and not ask questions. But the old man knew what he was about—I'd find myself in the exact same position, worse sometimes. Once, we switched over and I woke up on his filthy, fucking mattress, a tiny unlabelled bottle still in my hand—they've got stronger stuff in the future. These two huge blokes burst in and start asking me where the money is, that I owe money for something or other, and obviously I've got no idea what they're even talking about, so the one guy gets me in a headlock, and the other just starts pummelling the living crap out of me. Out of this old son of a bitch.

And midway through I can feel myself sobering up, adrenaline or whatever, and maybe the one guy sees me smiling because he pulls another tiny bottle from his jacket pocket, forces the stuff down my throat, and then I'm stuck there for another hour of pummelling.

It was strange getting back and finding teeth in my mouth again.

It wasn't just that they had better booze in the future, though, the old man was better at the game than I was. He'd pop over to my body, and get stuck into whatever uppers he could to make the drunk last longer; I think I lost a week, once. Hell of a week that was; all I got in the future was maybe two hours shuffling through a museum. I was trying to make a mental note of who the next

Closing Time

president would be so I'd have bragging rights come election time, whilst ignoring the unfriendly looks the security doors were giving me, when I got yanked back into the now. Or the then, I guess. When I got back I had a beard, a barely-healed gash on my cheek, and a tattoo on my inner thigh that read 'Get It?'

I walked to Beth's and when she opened the door her eyes were puffy and she looked about ready to tell me to fuck right off, and probably would've if I hadn't started bawling. That was probably one of the last times she had much in the way of sympathy. Probably for the best, all told; she'd cleaned up herself, and told me that I could too. I said, yeah, I get it. She looked like she'd been struck, poured me a glass of water, and said I should go.

I felt betrayed, but everyone does.

And the bastard of the thing was, the old man never made me drink, never left me a note saying that he especially wanted a go in the young body. He even made a couple of smart race bets so I could afford to avoid having to work too much; Robert set a few of them up for me. Fruitful relationship was that. But this old man, it's like he knew that, eventually, no matter what, I'd get sick of the present and want a taste of that future.

You know what, though, dingy fucking flats in the future are the same as dingy fucking flats any other time, it's just that we've got more bloody buttons and things to plug in to.

Do you mind if I get some water?

I was about twenty-three when I noticed that time was going backwards.

Obviously not literally backwards. I mean, I would get blitzed in my present in December, because there's nothing quite as bloody depressing as Christmas, and it would be May over there. Then I'd get clean for a couple of months because I'd been locked up for beating up the bastard Beth had been spending her Christmas with. Go on

Liam Kruger

a bender again around February and it'd be March where he was. We were moving closer to each other, so to speak.

Upside to this was that I could be a complete shit in his body, and when I got back to it, it would be good as new. And since he had to come back to mine as I was getting older, he couldn't afford to do too much damage. But he was getting younger, see? The first time I jumped over, he was something like in his 40's—which yeah, I know, isn't bloody old at all, 40 is the new 20, but I was a young bloody shit when I first jumped, and the old man put his body to task, the way he put my body to task. And I was the one getting older. They still have mirrors in the future, though he made a point of keeping those scarce enough in his old age. I thought it was so that I wouldn't find out what he looks like, but it turns out I just hate seeing myself now.

You're seeing the joke now, aren't you? Same bloody wavelength.

So yeah. The tattoo made sense. I got it. I was jumping, back and forth, into my own fucking body. Laying traps, for myself. Attacking my own loved ones, leaving a mess for myself to come clean up. But see, that isn't even the best part—because while I am a complete and utter idiot, I can still do basic arithmetic. I had the privilege of seeing when exactly I would be hitting my mid-life crisis. I didn't even care about 'the future' anymore—hell, I was only jumping a year or two ahead at a time, then a couple of months, then weeks.

I was about a month past turning twenty-six. There was some sherry at the back of some naïve friend's larder. When I'd gotten more or less halfway through the bottle, it was two weeks before my birthday and Beth and I were having our last big fight. And... look, I was still fresh from being turned out in a big way, and I was pretty happy to lay into her right then. I was too busy reliving the fight that I'd already been through, the fight that had a foregone fucking conclusion, to do the math.

Closing Time

But I got there a little later. Only one reason why I'd start going backwards, right? I'd passed the midway point. More behind me than there was before me.

When I saw this place for rent, I just sort-of slouched into it, I knew I'd be ending up here anyway. At least I got to find out where those mattress stains came from.

Ah, the fun I've had with that little bastard who ruined my life.

I turned 52 yesterday. And you, Robocop, are an excellent recorder of my day-to-day activities for the Fuhrer's report, but I am a wily son of a bitch with nothing else to occupy my mind with, so I should tell you right now that this isn't water.

Go ahead, call them, they won't be quick enough.

They've got stronger stuff in the future.

As I understand it, my body is currently going to fold in on itself and stop doing things. I may piss blood, hence the towels—no need to make this apartment any worse for the next occupant, eh?

I am going to wake up in a graveyard with some very old friends, they are going to take me home, and I am going to say hello to my parents.

And him? He'll be taking a dip in that big black pool we all come from.

And after a while, so will I.

[RECORD ENDS]

@aitch no recollection of this chat at all—apologies, it was a rough conclave. thx for the history, all the same; regards to the extended.

xang

Liam Kruger is a student and writer living in Cape Town. He's had stuff in *Itch*, *New Contrast*, and *Mahala*. He usually writes about ghosts and bars and time; this is his first SF story, which includes all of the above.

Masquerade Stories

Chiagozie Fred Nwonwu

"Are we there yet?" Rex asked.

"No, a little further, it is on the summit of the next hill," Chinedu pointed ahead with his torch. "But, Rex, Ebuka, we really have to stop talking now."

Walking behind Rex, I felt like coughing, shouting, doing something, anything to annoy, but something in Chinedu's voice, cautioned me. Instead, I walked a little faster to keep pace with Rex.

We had been walking along a very narrow hill path for several hours. Heavy rain clouds blanketed the stars and full moon. Although Chinedu's organic-bioluminescent torch lit the path ahead with a bluish glow, it took some doing to avoid obstacles in the unlit area behind him.

Rex however, walked with a calm gait, his back straight as old bamboo, one foot connecting before the other began moving, a dance, a majestic dance, as only Rex could manage. People always wondered why I don't walk that way, why I lack that peculiar swagger; after all, we are identical in physical appearance. I do not care much for my brother's confident gait, never did in the past, and would not in the future. Anyway, I was sure his ocular implant allowed him to adjust his vision to night-mode. As it was, he could see better than a cat at night.

I was about to complain about the injustice of the whole thing, how I, with no visual aid would be made to take the rear, when Chinedu called for a halt.

I saw Chinedu looking at me from the corner of his eye. I turned towards him, an eyebrow raised. He looked away and appeared to be taking in the scene, saying nothing, just shaking his head in a bemused way.

I had spent much of the last visit to this land my father called our ancestral home collecting material for a documentary that later won me awards and much acclaim at school. That documentary, though something I saw as fun, was cause of conflict between Chinedu and me. 'You mock us Ebuka, we deserve better, at least from a son of the soil. Slavery here was much different from slavery in the West,' Chinedu had fumed, via netlink when he saw the documentary.

I disagreed. For me the question was not the kind of slavery that existed, but that it did. I felt it was my duty to inform the descendants of those sold into slavery across the seas, that the ancestors of their ancestors were not innocent victims.

'He shouldn't have accused me of riding down my culture while glorifying the west, I was only saying it as I see it,' I had said to Rex, whose attempt to settle the simmering dispute failed.

"...the rock is on the other side of the hill," Chinedu warbled.

I turned to where he was now standing shoulder to shoulder with Rex, pointing towards one of the twin peaks.

"You mean if the stone is removed the whole valley will be flooded?" Rex asked.

"Not just the valleys, the whole of Anike." There was that hint of humour in Chinedu's response.

Rex laughed out loud, full laughter, from the pit of his stomach, unrestrained. "You bet, world altering flood from beneath a stone? You can tell that to the birds, man."

Chinedu joined in his laughter. I smiled. I found the claim funny, but unlike my twin, it took more to make me laugh, and even then, not with the freedom that Rex allowed.

I turned away, conscious of the fact that I felt more like a stranger than anything else. Before me, like tapestry of the finest artistry, the hanging valley, the hills and valleys, the land that our people had called home for as long as oral history could remember, lay. Beautiful, was the word that came to me. It came from within, unbidden, perhaps from another sense, for beauty shouldn't show through the gloom of starless night and the howl of the wind. It will rain tonight, I thought.

I sensed Rex before he reached me and knew exactly what he would do. I parried his blow, lowered my head and ducked under his outstretched hand to come up behind him in a classic judoka move we both learnt as boys. My hand was coming round to grab his neck in a chokehold when he dropped down and bucked, sending me sprawling into the tall grass—he always was better than I was at this.

"If you guys are not going to handle this with the seriousness it deserves, perhaps we'd better be heading back?" The threat was real; Chinedu would really take us back.

"Behave!" Rex said to me. I scowled at him in response, an expression that would have been lost to the surrounding darkness, but Rex—enhanced vision and all—saw it and laughed causing Chinedu to turn the full glare of the torch on him.

"Okay, Okay. We're fine." Rex said.

"Let's go on," Chinedu said, as he turned towards the path again. Soon we were heading downhill, easier going than before. This time, I made sure I was in the middle. I was almost beginning to enjoy the ease of the walk when we began another uphill climb. The last climb Chinedu assured us.

We walked in silence, Chinedu insisted on it. I do not understand the need for silence, but bit my lips to remind myself not to say anything. A big cat roared down in the valley, a reminder of the dangers that live here.

I had earlier increased the gain of my auditory implant to maximum, to pick and sort the night sounds. Rex had scoffed at me when I told him to increase his gain. I paid him little heed. As everyone was aware, the reintroduction of forest animals meant that ancient dangers now stalk the forests, government protected dangers for that matter.

Chiagoze Fred Nwonwu

I can't say I knew when the drumming started. One moment there were only nature's sounds, and the next came this deep throbbing that seemed to vibrate within my belly.

The resonance of the drums was deep, appeared to come from all around and was loud enough for unaided ears to hear. I paused a moment to effect a slight adjustment to my implant, cancelling the echoes and pinpointing the source just ahead of us.

The need to walk faster was unspoken, Chinedu increased pace and we followed. The rhythmic pulsations of the drums acted to lift my spirits. I found myself wanting to march to the rhythm they produced. I felt sure I could take anything the Mmanwu people threw at me.

We broke into a clearing soon after and I found my bravado evaporating at the sight of shadowy figures dancing around a large bonfire. I did not wait for Chinedu's raised hand before stopping. Beside me, I sensed Rex do the same.

My eyes adjusted to the flickering light. We were in a large clearing framed by young Orji trees, taller than two men standing one atop the other, but still with many decades' growth left before they reach the towering heights of an adult Orji. The bonfire was made of large logs in the middle of the clearing, its light illuminating the dancing figures and several others, some in loose files, others huddled together, in front of a large mud and thatch hut. The white markings on the hut I recognised from my brief research on Igbo culture to be some form of Nsibidi, the writing code of the masquerade societies in many Igbo clans, only more intricate. The drummers were to one side of the gathered men, I could see no females and I had not expected any, this was a purely masculine rite. I drew my eyes back to the hut and the wavy form of a masquerade making its way into the hut. I strained to see clearer, but then it was gone, swallowed by the deeper darkness within.

Masquerade Stories

I was startled as the music lulled and changed into a faster-paced rhythm, drawing my attention back to the square. Two of the dancing figures attacked each other's legs in turn with brutal-looking canes—I could almost feel the whiplashes—was this what the initiation Chinedu had yapped about for days entailed?

I glanced at Rex and saw that the repeated blows affected him too. Back at the clearing, the mutual whipping became an orgy of violence. The circle of dancers had broken into groups of twos and threes exchanging swipes of the cane directed at individual ankles. Two of the dancers were closer to us, close enough for us to see that they were much younger than we were which was not surprising, as Chinedu had said we were being initiated six years later than the normal twelve years.

I was about to comment to Rex—that the caning appeared to be a test of endurance and an assertion of leadership, for the few dancers who had so far flinched away from an upraised cane had been pushed to the periphery of the group, and were then jostling to try again—when Chinedu howled beside me. He actually howled, as a wild beast would.

I turned in alarm to see him rushing into the square. He was in that instance transformed into a different person. I watched in awe as Chinedu danced in a hunch-backed, tiptoed fashion that any ballet dancer would have been proud of, from one end of the square to the other. I saw him bow to the drummers, then to the elderly looking men, before heading back to the middle of the square, weaving through the duellers, pursued by a flute player whose music weaved in and out of the drumbeat. I had not noticed the flautist until then, and I became conscious of his trilling tune at the same time.

The music stopped. The duellers moved apart.

"Look out!" Rex and I called out at the same time.

Chinedu stood rock still in the middle of the clearing—I think he was close enough for the raging bonfire to singe his skin—as the echoes of the gongs and drums faded away into the hills. He did not move even as the source of our alarm, a large man with leopard fur draped across one shoulder, rushed at him with a machete that gleamed in the firelight. If he heard our warning, he did not indicate, the only change in his stance was the slight smile that played around his lips as the blur of the machete swept by only inches from his face. Twice more, from different directions, the man attacked, and my heart, I am sure Rex's too, stopped, only for the machete to miss by inches.

The music started again.

As if in slow motion, Chinedu turned to face us. That silly smile played around his lips. He had survived the test, the danger of which lay not in the strike, but Chinedu's ability to stay still. He beckoned towards us as the dancers began wheeling around the bonfire again, splintered canes held aloft. It was time for us to take the test of manhood, time for us to become men.

Midmorning was already upon the hills when I woke up. At first, I could not understand why my body ached all over, but then it all came back to me, the dance, the hastily swallowed concoctions and the visions of talking spirits they brought.

I stood up, groggy, and groped around the bed to shake my brother awake. Rex murmured some incoherent sounds that translated as *leave me alone*. Reflecting on the beat state of his otherwise more attuned body, I made up my mind to do just that. I shuffled into the bathroom and was dabbing water unto my face when I heard him screaming.

Startled, I rushed back into the room to find him standing near the bed asking his onboard computer to run diagnostics. Running a diagnostics is routine, but my brother's shout and the fact that he was having a verbal conversation with his computer—who does that in these days of mental synch—told me something was very wrong.

Masquerade Stories

He turned towards me, his face a disoriented mask. "My implants are offline."

"What do you mean your implants are offline? Did you turn them off?" I knew what he was going through; the white silence of an offline implant could be very disorienting for anyone used to permanent Netlink.

"Not just offline, my memory chip has been wiped clean."

Pondering how that was possible when he had not plugged into any external power source, I asked him to check his backup memory—which I knew he got after he lost months of stored memory to a hacker. I could see that in his panic he had forgotten all about that backup. I heaved a sigh of relief when he said that it was intact.

Fearing that whatever it was that wiped his memory might still be in his processors, I asked him to synchronise his brain chip with the house computer. A quick scan should show the moment the safe mode kicked in and severed the link to the main memory. Feeling the worst was over, I was returning to the bathroom when I heard him gasp. I turned to see what had gone wrong again and saw it. Shocked out of my wits, I walked over to stand beside him. Before us, the house computer's holoprojector tinted the air green.

Not trusting my voice, I pointed to the projected image, "What the hell is that?"

"I have no idea, that's the last thing my ocular implant captured before it shutdown," I wasn't sure if it was fear I sensed in Rex's voice, but it was close.

I rubbed my eyes, hoping to see clearer. I felt icy fear crawling up my back as I turned to my brother, my eyebrow rising. Rex nodded once in a yes-it-is-real manner. I returned my gaze to the projection.

It was not human, that much was clear from first glance. The large, bulging eyes, the long teeth, curved and sharp, could never belong to a human. It was over seven feet tall and though it had two arms, they hung too low from shoulders that showed little trace of neck. Leonine hair that started just above eyes devoid of eyebrows flared in all directions.

A sense, a tingling at the back of my brain, signalled familiarity. I felt sure I had seen similar features before. It took some time before I could place it, masquerades; it reminded me of an Mmanwu indigenous to these hills. The only problem was, what we had before us, was a flesh and, perhaps, blood being.

I stood beside my brother, numb. I knew about Rex's ocular implant, what I did not know was that my brother had the money to pay for the large memory required for constant recording. I am the one with the eye for details, the one who opted for journalism, but the hologram before us was not a spur of the moment recording. For how long has Rex been planning to record the initiation rituals, I wondered, and why didn't he tell me anything? That was not to say I was surprised at Rex's boldness. However the thought struck me that with this, we have a documentary, and could be in the running for a Pulitzer.

"How many hours do you have?" I asked Rex whose open-mouthed stance I didn't understand. *He recorded this, what's he surprised about?*

Rex turned to look at me, his lips quirking as it did when he was scared or angry. "I don't think you understand what we are looking at Ebuka. That thing is no Mmanwu, that thing is alive!"

I looked at him, wondering if he had gone mad; of course, an Mmanwu must be alive to be an Mmanwu. I was about to voice my thoughts when I looked a little closer, at the image of what should have been a large Mmanwu. "You have this on pause Rex, the image is wavering. Play it."

Rex did, moving the sequence back a little. "See," he said, "it is alive."

It was, and not in the sense I had thought.

Masquerade Stories

"It is more than alive. See the markings on its torso and the gadgets on its arms." I don't know how my voice managed to sound calm, how the quake that was my heart beating did not show in my voice. Fear, I was sure, must have caused the trickle of sweat that ran down my armpits, for the house cooling system was operational. "That thing is not of this world. It is most probably an alien." I said.

After Chinedu arrived, Rex showed surprised that our cousin was more keen on the fact that we had not told him about our implants, and was going on and on about repercussions for breaking the oath. "Chinedu, how can you be talking about propriety at a time like this? Are you seeing the same thing we're seeing?" Rex asked.

Chinedu looked at the hologram and for a moment appeared to be deep in thought. Just when I thought he would say something, he turned to leave the room.

"Are you leaving?" I asked.

"Yes, I am leaving. I don't know what you are up to, but I am sure I want no part in it. You know as much as I do that it is taboo to record an initiation ceremony, yet you failed to tell me about your implants. I can understand an auditory implant, but having the nerve to record with an ocular implant is what I can't get my head around. Do you not see that this undermines everything we are trying to preserve? Please erase that file and do not speak to anyone about this, I will see what I can do about reparations." Chinedu was angry but still had enough wits about him to whisper his words.

"Chinedu, I can't believe you. In the face of evidence as great as this, you chose to talk about broken rules?" I asked.

"Chinedu, please look at the hologram and tell me that thing is not flesh and blood? We can argue about broken rules and the retributions later, but we really need you to confirm this... please," Rex said.

Chiagoze Fred Nwonwu

Perhaps it was what Rex said or the way he said it, but Chinedu turned back, sluggish, as if it was against his better judgement. He stared at the hologram, the look on his face changing from repressed anger to wonder, then to fear.

"Was this all you got?" he asked.

Rex said nothing, I am sure he had anticipated Chinedu's question, and had already sent the necessary command to the house computer. The hologram began moving, in reverse. Chinedu watched, silent for a few minutes then said, "Stop! Play it forward."

Rex obeyed. I stood, silent, watching.

We watched the first masquerade exit the hut, followed by a succession of masquerades, all real, all with large carved masks aping the grimaces of spirits from the unknown. They came out, twelve masquerades in all. Chinedu named them as they stepped out. "...Atu, Agaba, Izaga, Aguinyi, Atuma, and that is Agu-nmuo."

It struck me as odd that of all the masquerades who exited the hut to join the dance in the clearing none looked anything like the one at the end of the recording. Yes, the bulging eyes and bared teeth had the same odd look, but not exactly, it was as if they were copies, inferior copies. Rex glanced at me and I lifted my palm to signal wait.

I saw that Chinedu was paying very close attention to the hologram, watching every movement, calling for a zoom here or more brightness there. "Nothing appears to be out of place," Chinedu said.

Everything still appeared normal at this point: the masquerades, the dancers and elders in and around the square—people I was sure Chinedu had known all his life. I exchanged looks with Rex, we both knew when the scene changed and were waiting to gauge Chinedu's reaction. Rex mirrored my surprise when Chinedu pointed above the young trees, where the full moon peeped now and then through the rain clouds. Then we saw it.

Masquerade Stories

It, was a speck of light in the sky, like those shooting stars that flash across the night sky, only this one did not burnout like any shooting star, neither did it flash by, instead it changed course and hovered for a bit before moving beyond range.

How did we miss that? I thought. Rex and I had played back the recording several times, scouring it for clues, but neither of us had noted the light and its irregular movement.

Chinedu's gasp didn't surprise us when it came. The strange masquerade didn't come from the ritual hut; it had shimmered into being in front of Rex. Without any prompting Rex called for a structural model of the strange apparition.

The structural model was clearer and as it replicated the movement of the masquerade, it clearly showed it was flesh and blood, and carrying a device, one that probably shorted out Rex's implant.

"Were your implants affected?" Chinedu asked me.

I frowned. Rex smiled. Rex knew I preferred it to remain a secret. I am sure he was thinking, 'let's see how he plays this.' I took a deep breath. Chinedu may act and appear dense at times but he was no dunce. Auditory and ocular implants are common enough technology for those who feel the need to have a more personal interaction with the Netlink. Auditory implants could be attached at birth to allow the individual grow with the technology and provide better synch, but ocular implants required the attainment of twenty-one years, and special insurance clearance. Despite the danger, I believed that allincom, its ocular and auditory components, ranked among man's greatest inventions. Same as I believed the secrecy law passed ten years before, which ensured the right for secrecy for an implant wearer, was a superb legislation on human rights. I glanced at Chinedu, though there was no way of knowing besides a high-level scan, I was sure Chinedu was not wearing any implants. Jeez, the guy does not even wear a wrist allincom, I thought, his car could drive itself, yet he prefers to go manual, how can one expect him to have an implant.

"No, I was not recording; I shut down my implant when we reached the square. The drums you know... they were hurting my ears and distorting my perception. Why do you ask?" I held my breath.

"Because I want to be sure the entity targeted Rex's implants purposely, you two were the only ones with any technology higher than an organic torch on that hilltop last night. And had I known of it I would have stopped you from coming at all."

"Why is that? I mean, how come we were the only ones with technology on the hill?" I asked, letting the breath I was holding go. Whew.

"Because it was outlawed. The Mmanwu society is an ancient one and the use of technology had no bearing on the rituals and had always been a source of distraction, so it was outlawed in our grandfather's time when the cultural revival started. It is taboo to bring anything other than an organic torch to the square of the ancestors, same reason why the square is very far from town."

"How convenient," Rex said.

"What do you mean?" Chinedu asked.

"How convenient for the alien or whatever it was that showed up last night." Rex said. I noticed he was looking at Chinedu, perhaps trying to gauge if he was telling all he knew, I guess he too could tell Chinedu was calm about this, too calm even. "I say alien because the structural model, as you can see, indicates the presence of technology. Notice that the left hand fiddled with that glowing square on its arm just before my implant shorted out?" Rex added.

"And the moving light Chinedu pointed out, don't forget that," I said.

"Yes, and that light, I bet that was the ship or whatever brought it here," Rex agreed.

Masquerade Stories

Chinedu snorted, crossed his arms across his chest, a sly look crept into his face as he looked from me to Rex and back again. I knew then that Chinedu had heard enough, and that while he knew something was out of place, he wasn't buying the alien story.

"I know you guys, as such I know the kind of mischief you get up to. However, I want to be sure about this. That entity could be an invention of yours, a prank. Don't scoff Ebuka, we both know this is not beyond you guys," Chinedu said.

"You think this is a prank? Why is that? I might have thought little of the Mmanwu society before, but after last night, I believe we can rightfully claim to be custodians of our ancestor's culture. We took the oath of secrecy didn't we?" Rex was furious enough to cause Chinedu to take a step back.

I stood next to my brother, saying nothing, shaking my head from side to side.

I watched Chinedu steer the 4x4 through the village street. He stopped now and then to pay his respects to elders sitting in front of their houses. In the passenger seat beside him, Rex maintained a wilful silence, a mood I shared somewhat from the back seat. The atmosphere, strained during our exchange earlier in the day, had become more so when Chinedu had insisted on questioning the authenticity of the recording. We had agreed to go with him to the Akpamgbo library to check for any report of strange sightings in the past. Chinedu had insisted that the books our grandfather spent much of his life gathering contained records of strange lights and encounters with strange beings. He said he had given a lot of thought to what we saw in the recording, and if not for the technology the entity was wearing, and the markings on it, he would have sworn it one of the elder spirits in the old tale. He said its resemblance to the Agaba Mmanwu was significant.

Chiagoze Fred Nwonwu

Could it be that this is actually an alien and my ancestors encountered them and thought them to be spirits, I pondered. Somehow, that did not sound strange to me.

In the past, I had wondered at the masquerades and their lack of resemblance to men. I always felt the images they convey, snarling monsters and otherworldly beings, were the result of some ancestor's nightmare. Ancestral spirits should look more like the men they represented. This was true for some clans; however, those of the hills had always been snarling visages or completely covered elephant grass monsters.

The bounce of the car across the speed breakers near the village market jarred me and I noted that the car's autopilot was driving, as Chinedu's thoughts appeared to wander. He must have noticed me looking at him through the rear view monitor, for he took full control again. The car picked up speed.

It was almost noon and very few people were about, still at work on the farms in the surrounding slopes, farms that replaced the lush forests that had endured for centuries. This region is a study in replacements, I mused. The European church replaced the local religions, and the GMO farms replaced the yam farms and forests. The forests were making a comeback, thanks to our grandfather, the original Chinedu Akpamgbo. At the turn of the century, Chinedu Akpamgbo had fought and succeeded in saving much of what was the ancient Forbidden Forest, and began the reforestation movement ensuring any land not farmed returned to nature. Our grandfather had gone against the new religion and won, using European conservationism against seething advocates of the new religion bent on burning it all down—a great man he was. I shook my head as I sought another thread of thought.

My mind went back to the snarling entity Rex's implant had recorded. Is that one of the old gods?

Masquerade Stories

I kept turning over that possibility until the car stopped before the library, a recycled plastic and mud brick building that our grandfather built and managed until his death. A large building, it housed a school for ancient Igbo mythology. Chinedu shunned better paying jobs in the city for a position here and taught Igbo dialectics.

There were not many cars packed in the expansive compound, but there were never many cars. The study of their past was not something locals took serious enough to engage in, so the students were mainly westerners looking for new fields of study to pursue.

We entered the building through the staff entrance and were soon in the section of the library that contained the texts we sought—well; Chinedu did, as neither Rex nor I knew enough about the ancient texts to know what to look for. I had asked that we search through the house computer at grandfather's house, but Chinedu had refused, insisting that the texts he was looking for were not stored online.

As we walked through shelves overflowing with old books and parchments, I wondered at the waste of space in an age of e-libraries, when most libraries were mere relics, museums.

Earlier in the day, the argument about culture and religion had progressed to the point that, exasperated, I had to ask the purpose of it all in a late 21st century world.

"It is about identity, about finding your place in the whole. While you can easily live out your life with an English name, practice one of the new religions, you would have lived a borrowed life. To truly, truly be you, have to know who you are and accept it," Chinedu had answered.

"Well, I know myself. I am Ebuka Akpamgbo. My ancestors came from these hills and I hold dual citizenship in the United States and the Union of West African States. I assure you, dear cousin, that I know myself very well," I replied.

Chiagoze Fred Nwonwu

Perhaps fearing a return to the heat that characterises most lengthy exchanges between Chinedu and me, Rex had deemed it fit to jump in. "In the old days, what did it mean for a male not to belong to the masquerade society?"

"If you are of age and did not pass through the rituals that lead to manhood, you are considered a female and would not be allowed to participate in decision making, or allowed to be around when delicate matters are being discussed. Worst of all you will be ostracised within your age group and suffer the disgrace of running away when the masquerade approaches like women and children," Chinedu answered.

"But that is in the old days, even though the masquerades are running again, how many people from these parts stay in the villages long enough to need to do all that?" Rex countered.

"My point exactly, who needs such things today. I can sub-vocalise a message to my classmate in the US, and anyone with a third grade auditory implant can have audios of all the knowledge known to man stored in a finger-sized memory device and pull them out as needs be, not to talk of what those with full sensory implants can do. We have gone beyond the stage you refer to Chinedu," I said.

"You will never understand. No matter how long we argue about it, no matter what I tell you. Imagine you want to do something as trivial as bathing in the stream down the hill from grandfather's. A simple thing as not having passed through the rite of manhood stops you, because, with all the technological advancements you mention, the law still supports the old cultures," Chinedu said.

The argument had swung back and forth for a time until Rex surprised me by declaring that he and I were ready for the rite of passage scheduled for that night, and Chinedu had agreed to lead us out to the ritual hut.

"Are those the books you wanted?" Rex asked, when Chinedu returned with large volumes under his arm.

Masquerade Stories

Chinedu had made us stay outside a door marked 'No Admittance'.

"Yes," Chinedu said as he walked past us heading for the exit. "Unfortunately none have the information we seek. However, I found something very interesting. I will show you when we're in the car."

I exchanged looks with Rex, we jostled for the front passenger seat, and I won.

"What do you have?" I asked, as I settled into the front seat.

Chinedu did not respond, he opened one of the books and lifted it for us to see.

"Wow!" Rex exclaimed. I said nothing, my eyes locked on the image.

The image was a crude drawing but it definitely resembled the entity in the recording. The only visible difference was the shorter hair, and the difference in the Nsibidi-like lettering.

"The room I entered contains sacred documents pertaining to the religion of these parts. This drawing is one of several, all dating back to what the Europeans called the Middle Ages. I didn't want to tamper with the hides that contained them because of damage, but I knew the image we saw was familiar when you first showed it to me, especially on account of the head," Chinedu said.

"So you agree that they are not of this world and have a lot to do with the religion of our ancestors?" I asked.

"Well, the tales passed down by the oral historians always held that some of the old gods are sky beings. However I can understand how our ancestors would have looked at these and believed them to be fierce gods." Chinedu thumped the open page. "But the intention of the entities, or aliens, like you say, is what baffles me."

"We agree that they've been coming for centuries, right?" Rex looked at Chinedu, and then me. I agreed and from Chinedu came a barely perceptible nod, yes. "Okay then, the question is what are we going to do about it?"

Chiagoze Fred Nwonwu

What are we going to do about it? The question hung in the air between us.

Earlier, Chinedu had reminded us that we were bound by a blood oath not to tell masquerade secrets to the uninitiated. According to him, we were now men in all senses of the word and should be responsible for our actions. Rex said he accepted that responsibility and that he understood what was at stake: the need to preserve culture of our fathers. For me however, the evidence that aliens had visited Earth for centuries and were central to Mmanwu imagery was something I had no illusions about—I could not handle that. I was all for us taking the recording to the government or the Elders Council, but Chinedu reasoned that aside from having to explain how we got the recording, exposing the most secret part of the Mmanwu rites to the uninitiated was too big a risk to consider.

I watched Chinedu as he thumbed the start button. The car hummed to life.

"We will do nothing," Chinedu said as the car performed a 180-degree reverse and cruised towards the road leading back to the village.

"We will do nothing?" I asked, thinking about Pulitzers and flash lights as I swung around to face Rex, "What does he mean we will do nothing?"

"Ebuka, calm down, I also understand what is at stake here. We have to handle this matter delicately. Also remember the oath we took last night..."

"Okay, Okay, I get it," I interrupted Rex, "It will do our precious culture more harm than good to expose this dark secret. Anyway, I do not think this is an isolated incident; at least I am aware of many cultures that have legends of alien visitation. I am sure too that we are not the only ones who have encountered them or recorded them? We should take this matter up with the authorities, no, I will take this matter up, write articles and..." My rant died when I noticed I was talking to myself, all my points, which had

266

taken some thinking to articulate, were fading into the air. Rex was no longer listening, his eyes, big and round, starred ahead. Feeling the same cold fear that had crawled its way up my back earlier, I turned and saw Chinedu also staring ahead, his face cut from the same mould as Rex's. As the fear crawled across my chest to choke my lungs, I noticed the car was stationary and the hum of the engine was absent. Even before I turned and saw the shimmer on the road and two alien figures advancing towards us, I knew.

Chiagozie Fred Nwonwu introduces himself as Mazi Nwonwu. He writes to capture culture. He uses prose, poetry, and everything else in between, minus drama. He worked as a magazine editor, now he is a freelance writer. His work has been published both online and in print. His short story collection *Footsteps in the Hallway* will birth in Jan 2013.

The Trial

Joan De La Haye

The Judge presiding over my case sat on his oversized and overstuffed throne. He was one of the three men who decided over life and death in our city. Judge Farris had a reputation for being a hard case. He'd put more people to death during the culling than all of the other judges put together. He would be the one who would decide if I was a useful member of society or not. If he decided I wasn't, that would be it. I'd lose my head. The thought of the executioner's axe coming down on my scrawny little neck made me want to run to the bathroom again. I hadn't stopped needing to pee since my number had been drawn.

In every town, in every part of the world, identity numbers had been thrown into wooden boxes and one by one our numbers were drawn to decide if we would live or die, depending on how useful we were. Prisoners were executed first, and prisons stood as empty reminders of the past. Then the over sixty-fives were crossed off the list, their assets seized by the state and their organs recycled. Those with IQs under 110 were also immediately crossed off the list and deemed as unfit breeding stock. The culling had begun two years ago, and the executioner was very busy.

I'd been one of the lucky ones who'd had those extra two years of life. It had taken the courts longer than anticipated to get through all the numbers. They'd only managed to execute about two thousand people in our city over the last two years through the court system, not including the prisoners and over sixty-fives. Two years of daily executions can be deadening on the spirit, but I'd had the time to meet my nephew, see a few more sunsets, and enjoy the feel of the sun on my skin, which so many others could no longer do. It's amazing how the small things count when your number could be up at any moment.

The world population had reached the nine billion mark. Famine and water shortages raged. Governments all over the world concluded that there was only one solution. The courts were tasked with deciding on which members of society were the most productive, whose life had the most value. My mother had been one of the first to go. She had been over sixty-five. My sister was a teacher, with an IQ of 130 and therefore useful. My brother, a farmer, was also found useful in a world where there wasn't enough food and too many lawyers and accountants. The old university degrees, once so sought after, were no longer as important as they once were—now genetics and intelligence mattered. If university graduates didn't have an added skill, or were not the best at what they did, or were not classified as good breeding stock, they were crossed off the list; even being prematurely bald was a reason for being culled. No ordinary citizen was safe.

My heart felt as though it was trying to escape from my chest. I understood its desire for escape. The thought of running away had crossed my mind more than once, but there was nowhere to run. At this rate, I'd die of a heart attack long before the trial was over, saving the judge the trouble of deciding my fate. My trial wouldn't take long. I'd have a day at the most to convince them that I was worthy to continue breathing. I was allowed to plead my case because I had good genes and a relatively high IQ, but the question was: was I useful? Was a writer needed in this new society? Was a freethinking author someone they wanted to keep in the new world order? I didn't hold out much hope. I wasn't a bestselling author or famous; the rich and famous were pretty much exempt for their 'social' contributions.

The courthouse had been built in 1802, two hundred and fifty years ago, and had survived two world wars and an attempted bombing two years ago by terrorists protesting

The Trial

the culling—they'd only succeeded in blowing themselves up, four more people the courts didn't have to worry about. The wooden panelling on the walls of the courtroom was a dark mahogany and made the room feel solemn and yet strangely warm. It felt right that my fate would be decided in a room as old and as grand as this one.

"Marin Brown," the Bailiff called. I heard my name through a wall of nervous fuzz in my ears.

I walked down the stairs and stood in the wooden box, where the Bailiff told me to stand, my legs wobbling under me. I wasn't sure how I'd manage to stand throughout the ordeal. Judge Farris sat on my right, looking down his nose at me. His white wig looked like it dated back to when the court had first been built; it probably itched like hell. His eyes were dark and cold. He probably only had another five years to go before he too was culled. The thought gave me some comfort, but not much. My bladder wanted to go, but I would have to hold it till the end, there would be no recess.

The Judge banged his gavel a few times, calling the court to order. The wood hitting wood reverberated through my brain and made the hair on my arms stand up. I spotted my brother and sister sitting in the front row. They would speak on my behalf during the proceedings. It was up to them and the few people who had read my work to convince the judge that my life should be spared. There would be no lawyer to defend me; the few left were too expensive for a poor writer. I would have to argue my own case, fight for my own survival.

The judge looked over the rim of his glasses and stared down at me from his judgemental height. His beaked nose reminded me of a Dickensian character. I couldn't decide if he looked more like Martin Chuzzlewit or Fagin.

"Stand up properly young lady," Judge Farris said, his voice hard. "This court has been called to order, and you will stand to attention throughout the proceedings. If you sit at any time I will make my ruling immediately, and it will not be favourable. Do you understand?"

"Yes sir," I choked. My tongue was too thick for my mouth. My brother's neighbours, who were often spectators at trials and had seen Judge Farris in action, had told me that the Judge felt standing to attention was a point of respect, and failure to do so was to demonstrate contempt. He'd once made a pregnant woman stand for several hours before declaring that she had to have an abortion. It had been her third child, and unless she was prepared to have one of her other children culled, she would have to get rid of her latest addition. He had also declared that if she didn't start practising safe sex, she, too, would be culled.

"Would those who are here to speak for this woman stand?" Judge Farris instructed. My sister, brother, a few fellow writers, and a couple people I didn't know, stood. Together, they didn't even fill up half of the front row. There had been a public announcement letting people know about my trial, the usual notification that went out for all trials, asking anybody who knew me to show up and speak on my behalf. Notifications, however, were only sent out the day before the trials.

"Your testimony must be completely accurate. If you are found to commit perjury, your status will be called into question and you will find yourself in the dock. Is that clear?" The judge commanded.

The witnesses for my defence nodded in unison. My stomach fell a few notches. Nobody would lie for me or exaggerate my usefulness—I wasn't worth dying for.

"You," the judge pointed at my brother, his cropped, blond hair, calloused hands, and deep tan screamed that he spent many hours working the land, "step forward." Jason took a few tentative steps closer. "Come closer. Stand where I can see you properly." Judge Farris leaned forward in his seat. "Who is this woman to you?"

"She's my sister, Your Honour," Jason replied.

The Trial

"Besides being your sister, is there a reason she should be allowed to continue to exist in our midst?"

"Y... Yes your honour," Jason stammered. "She's a very talented writer, she helps my wife with our child, and she cooks really well, and she pays us rent when she can."

"Did you get permission to have this child?" The judge asked with a furrowed brow.

"Y... Yes your honour." Jason's face turned white. The implication in the judge's question was obvious. If he didn't have permission, his son's life would be forfeit.

"And your sister stays with you?" Judge Farris raised his eyebrow.

"Yes your honour. She used to stay with our mother and looked after her, but when Mom was culled, my sister moved in with me and my wife. We needed help with our baby because our nanny was culled."

"Why was your nanny culled?"

"She was classified as being poor breeding stock, but as you can see my sister is from very good breeding stock."

"Is she?" The judge looked over at me. I felt his eyes roving over every inch of me, judging me, looking for imperfections—they wouldn't be hard to find. My slightly crooked teeth and pale blue eyes, indicative of eventual bad eyesight, were painfully obvious. Even though I didn't need glasses, my eyesight was not perfect and the judge would most certainly use it against me. Then there was my broken nose too, which I'd broken when I was six while trying to prove that I could climb a tree just as well as Jason.

"You may be seated." My brother was dismissed. His testimony hadn't lasted as long as I thought it would. At this rate, my trial wouldn't even last an hour. I had a feeling the judge had already made up his mind.

He then called up my sister, Iris, to testify. She looked every bit the teacher, but unlike me, her eyesight was perfect. She and Jason both had brown eyes, same as our mother. I'd inherited our father's blue eyes and poor eyesight. Her testimony was even shorter than my brother's. He asked her only one question. "Does your sister make enough money from her writing to support herself or is she a burden on your brother and you?"

My sister looked like a doe caught in the headlights. "She's not a burden, Your Honour," Iris finally managed to say. "She pays her own way."

"Does she?" Judge Farris leaned further forward and eyed my sister over his glasses. Iris took a step backwards. Her lower lip shivered, usually a sign that she was about to cry.

"Dismissed," the Judge said, and sounded bored. He leaned back in his chair and sighed. "Next," he said without looking to see who would be speaking for me. I didn't recognise the man who stepped forward. He wore an old tweed jacket and looked like a university professor.

"Have you read this woman's work?" The Judge asked.

"Yes," the stranger said.

"Did you enjoy it?"

"Yes."

"Would you buy anything else she wrote?"

"I think so, yes," the stranger said looking at me and smiling. I tried to smile in return, but my face didn't co-operate.

"Dismissed." The Judge then looked at the handful of people still standing. "Are the rest of you all here to give similar testimony?"

They all nodded in reply.

"So noted. I'll stipulate for the record that the remaining witnesses all stated the exact same thing as the previous witness." The Judge banged his gavel when audience members started to chatter amongst themselves at his decision. The stenographer typed out his stipulation. His decision recorded for posterity. "Looks like I'll make my tee time after all." The judge sounded pleased with himself.

The Trial

"May I object to that ruling, Your Honour?" I asked, my voice just above a whisper.

"No you may not." Judge Farris banged his gavel again. "I'm ready to deliver my verdict."

"But I haven't had a chance to defend myself," I said, my voice rising above the sound of the gavel.

"I have made my decision and there's nothing you can say that will change your fate. You are a burden on your family. You are not prolific enough or good enough to compete with other high calibre writers. There is not room in our society for yet another mediocre author. I therefore sentence you to death. You will be sent from here to your place of execution. There will be no reprieve." The Judge banged his gavel.

My sister collapsed in a hysterical heap. My brother stared at me, his mouth open in shock.

"Bailiff, take her away." I heard the Judge's words as though from a distance. My skin tingled on my face and I desperately needed to go to the toilet, but I refused to embarrass myself. I promised myself that I would be culled with some dignity.

We'd all heard the stories of how some people carried on when led away, the hysteria. I would leave that to my sister. I squared my shoulders and allowed the bailiff to lead me out. There was a part of me that still clung to some small hope that the judge would change his mind, that he'd realised he'd made a mistake, but I knew those hopes were futile. The judge never changed his mind.

I would be dead before sunset.

There was a short queue waiting for the executioner in the holding cell. There were three trials everyday, of which two, at least, ended with a death sentence. It didn't happen often that one of the judges allowed someone to carry on existing, especially Judge Farris.

Another woman waiting to be culled sat in a corner, sobbing. She had paint splatters on her clothes. From the way she was dressed, she looked to be an artist. I sat down next to a man who stared at a spot on the wall opposite us. There was nothing remarkable about him. He was dressed in a simple, cheap suit. His shoes were cracked and looked more plastic than leather. He rocked himself slowly, the shock of where he was and what was about to happen stamped on his face. I probably wore the same shocked look.

Two men in uniform came into the holding cell. They headed straight for the woman in the corner and dragged her out. I heard her scream as they took her down the passage towards the chopping block. Next would be the man sitting next to me. I would be the last of the day. The executioner would take a break between each of us; apparently chopping people's heads off is hard work. Two hours later, they came for him. He went quietly. He hadn't said a word while we waited and he was silent when they culled him.

They've come for me. I try to stand, but my legs betray me. One of them helps me to stand and I thank him. My mother taught me to be courteous. I thank them again for helping me to walk, with some dignity, to the execution chamber.

The chopping block is a huge piece of black granite with a hollowed out bit where I place my head. They tried to wash away some of the blood from the previous two victims, but they missed a few spots. The site of the blood makes the little bit of food I managed to get into my stomach before my trial travel back up my throat. I swallow it back down. I hate that I will die with the taste of bile on my tongue. It's rather rude that they didn't even give us a last meal.

The executioner stands with his axe resting on his shoulder. The blade looks sharp enough. I hope he'll be able to do it with one blow. He looks strong enough. I kneel and place my head in the hollow. I'm grateful that they didn't allow any family members to attend. It's a private matter. It's just between me, the executioner, and whatever god I believe in. Only problem is I'm not sure any god exists.

Well... I'm about to find out.

Joan De La Haye writes horror and some very twisted thrillers. She invariably wakes up in the middle of the night, because she's figured out yet another freaky way to mess with her already screwed up characters. Her novels, *Shadows* and *Requiem in E Sharp*, as well as her novella, 'Oasis', are published by Fox Spirit. You can find Joan on her website: joandelahaye.com.

Brandy City

Mia Arderne

Vivian could see no future from here. When she imagined herself getting older, she drew a blank. She could not see herself, her life, or her hometown. There was nothing. All her life, she'd been plagued by a fear of the pending. And then it happened. The drought. The heat. The debauchery. The one-world government. The chaos. And the end. With this grim vision in mind, she'd become increasingly alienated from the people around her.

The men who approached her at work always asked her the same thing. And they always ended up engaging in some variant of the same dialogue:

"So... are you single, hey?"

"Wow, that was subtle."

"Don't get so defensive."

"Then don't be so interrogative."

"Just give me five minutes of your presence."

"How about you give me five minutes of your absence?"

While Vivian was mildly tempted by the prospect of real sex, she just couldn't bring herself to entertain the idea in conversation with another person. She'd forgotten how to flirt. Vivian would do her job, purchase her essentials and drive home in the crackling heat, cooled by her air-conditioned, hydrogen-powered BMW. Vivian herself had no idea how it worked, and she never bothered to find out. What she cared about was that she would never break a sweat inside her BMW. Outside her window was a new kind of squalor. People lay on the streets, intoxicated, frothing, or fatigued with sunstroke. She needed to re-tint her windows, she thought. She didn't want to see them and she didn't want them to see her. She put on her Ray-Bans and drove on by.

Mia Arderne

Global warming had drowned most of Africa in a sea of sunshine. The sunshine itself had long ceased to be pleasant. The effects of the 2117 drought had radically altered the local economic system. A dire shortage of water left taps bone-dry and people were desperate. South Africa's wealthy fled to Cape Town's CBD, where any drop of dwindling reservoir water found its way first. About 30kms away from the city bowl is the neglected town of Bellville in the less posh, northern suburbs. While the rich Capetonians happily hydrated themselves and their children, Bellville had spiralled into a modern implementation of the dop system.

Every day, the jaded people of Bellville dragged themselves to work and back. They each suffered from a different degree of foetal alcohol syndrome. Every citizen was born into addiction. No one left the womb sober because no mother could abstain from alcohol for nine months. This was enough for Vivian to ensure she never had kids. Labourers were paid in crates of brandy. At the onset of the drought, surplus liquor became an alternate currency. With a lack of water, it made sense that the lower class be paid by the drop. The system gave Bellville the nickname, Brandy City.

Vivian's shopping list usually comprised of seemingly unrelated items of necessities and luxuries such as gin, sex enhancement drugs, tampons, and a thirty-pack of cigarettes. You'd think that by now, people would have switched to electronic cigarettes—which have no tar and have finally become affordable—but the Marlboro Empire still reigned supreme. And Ray-Ban was one of the most successful enterprises in the world.

She completed her shopping in one quick trip down Voortrekker Road. She visited the liquor store for the gin, a drink the masses could no longer afford. She stopped by Adult World for their range of designer sex drugs used to enhance one's experience. What used to be a tiny row of R80.00 bottles of poppers had expanded into an annexed back-section dedicated to various relaxants, sensory manipulators, and chemical stimulators.

Finally, she pulled up at the chemist for the tampons. As she picked them up, Vivian noticed a single box of contraceptive pills on sale for nearly nothing, no prescription needed. They were taking it off the shelves because nobody used them anymore. Sex between couples was becoming outdated; it had been outshone by ideal, customised virtual sex. For those who'd grown weary of virtual erotica, there was a new wave of improved prostitution services. Yet Vivian couldn't help but wonder how it would be to indulge in something so physical and personal again. She hadn't touched a man since her late husband. Yet towards the end, the couple had grown to prefer the machines to each other.

The thought was a futile one though. Vivian knew she wouldn't find a man in Bellville sober enough to get it up, let alone keep it up. And real people were so full of disease and dirt, their blood pumping with unknown infections; streaming with the dregs of substandard brandy. She wasn't sure if she wanted to touch a real man again. Not only was the virtual alternative customised to your ideal, it was safer too.

She arrived home at her late husband's house—a man who'd amassed more life-insurance than she knew how to spend. Vivian was sitting on old money in a mansion in Plattekloof—the haughtier part of town overlooking Bellville from the hills.

Frustrated, she poured a G&T, lit the latest brand of cherry-tinted Marlboro and popped open a cylinder of thin, chemically-enhanced wafers designed to deepen sense reactions. She placed one tiny translucent strip on her tongue. The drug eased her into the furthest corner of her big twirling chair as she plugged herself into her fully-fledged sex simulator. The multiple attached massaging devices were customised to fit her body: the soles of her feet, the curve of her back, the parameters of her neck, even the contours of her vagina. She turned up the volume on her 3-metre speakers and increased the light saturation on the hologram visual settings.

She gave herself over to the complete sensory-co-ordinated programme with advanced audio-visuals calibrated with heat-sensitive vibratory response: the dildo of the year 2117.

Before expectant eyes, Vivian's customised hologram-lover entered the room. He lifted her up against the wall and greeted her with his lips at her neck. With his tongue, he carved a bright spreading love-bite into her skin and it grew in heat and size to expand across her body and conquer her. The bite engulfed her in fever and covered her in shades of red. Then, with his big hands on her hips, he lifted her effortlessly onto a chair and traced his lips down her body. She gasped as she felt that his tongue was split. The power of the split-tongue, of course, is that one half slides inside her while the other lightly massages the surface. Her nails pierced him and she screamed, shaking from unparalleled contractions. When she finally steadied in his arms, he put her down and walked away, leaving her lying on a soft virtual floor covered in shrivelled rose petals and cigarette stompies. After her short dip into an ideal world, Vivian unplugged herself, turned off the programme and switched on the coffee machine. Satisfied, she understood why nobody bothered with the contraceptive pill anymore, and she turned on the news.

Vivian's eyes stayed glued to a wall-sized plasma screen as she watched the American president being introduced as the leader of the Free World. She cringed. Put your hands together for the President of the USA, now the President of the Free World—some asshole, she thought, and sighed. She realised suddenly, that she was being represented by a bigoted Illuminati-puppet. The man's face was white and smooth, laser-sculpted and gene-spliced, to fill the lines of third-world debt and centuries of colonial raping. Vivian knew that Tanya and her other colleagues would be drunk

Brandy City

in a club somewhere celebrating. Her post-orgasm thoughts drifted to Tanya, ever-ignorant and consumed in her own tiny world, happy where she is. She thought of the rest of her colleagues who *wanna be* American, who *feel* American, who *identify* with the Yankee Nation. Well, now they have it, a one-world government. One nation unified under the White House. Tonight they will celebrate. Ignorance is bliss and that's why they're so happy all the time. But what would they celebrate? Partying and drinking, thinking they've won. Living for Fridays and thinking they're free. Vivian lit another Marlboro and contemplated:

The most effective slave is the one who thinks he is free.

The rest of the globe had seen the New World Order begin in earnest, the dawn of the Age of Excess. Long after conspiracy theories and documentaries of historical occults had gone viral, the omniscient elite gained virtual control of the world through economic, political, and media domination.

In the beginning, there was Twitter. Twitter put *@DrizzyDrake* right next to *@DalaiLama* on your *Who to Follow* list. Twitter told you to choose your enlightenment. And, just like that, nothing was sacred anymore. YMCMBuddha. It had been crystallised. The general consensus that everybody felt with their fingers on a steaming world's pulse, was one simple sentiment: do as thou wilt. The body of Christ—with cheese?

Vivian worked in the sex industry, as a product-manager not a product. The commoditisation of sex had reached new heights in South Africa. Kenny Kunene, the infamous businessman and icon of excess, may have died decades before but his ideals lived on. No longer were rich BEE men licking sushi off naked bodies. That incident became an industry. Now, wealthy men were seen sucking brandy-soaked thighs like lollipops. Women were prepared like culinary delights by a franchise that ran from Observatory through to Bellville. The ladies were prepared beforehand and customised according to each client's specifications to epitomise every man's personal deluxe. This was where Vivian worked.

She walked in past the stripper pole, past the bar, and through the velvet curtain that concealed the sex room at the back. Behind the drapery, she waited for her girl. Tanya, the glamour slut, walked in without knocking. She was a popular choice among customers. She liked posing in her panties and stockings on social media networks. Hot, supple, and talentless, she was perfect for her purpose. "Okay, I'm ready," Tanya declared.

Vivian nodded and took a moment to recall the recipe:

Disrobe the woman.

Vivian undressed Tanya and removed her excessive makeup. Gently, she wiped her glitter-smeared face, like the mother the whore never had. Then she instructed her to get on the table.

Artfully drape her over the table.

Vivian placed each of Tanya's limbs so as to exact a statuesque pose of delicate recline atop the red velvet.

Crush the roses.

In previous years, she would snatch up a few freshly picked roses and squeeze the petal blood onto the glamour slut's wrists. It was always a nice touch. But with the drought, flowers were in short supply.

Marinade in wine.

With a bottle of the most mature brand of dry red, she stained Tanya's lips; drenched them in flavour and colour. Then she left the room for a few minutes to allow Tanya to simmer.

Dip the nipples.

Vivian returned with a hot pot of melted Swiss chocolate. She leaned Tanya forward to dip the tip of each breast into the dark lava. Tanya gave two drawn out sighs as Vivian neglected to wait for the boiling chocolate to cool before dipping. There was no time.

Brandy City

Soak in brandy.

She poured the heated spirit onto Tanya's firm thighs and allowed it to soak into her skin. She rubbed it in patiently, deep enough to ensure that the taste would last the whole night. She was on top in this market because she knew how to cater to her clients.

The peach.

Vivian smeared a sliver of a peach in warm honey and parted Tanya's brandy-soaked thighs. She carefully placed the sliver in between. This was her favourite part. It was the most intimate she ever was with anyone these days. Finally, she sprinkled some cinnamon on her tongue.

If her first client didn't walk in soon, Vivian knew this could all be disastrous. Tanya's thighs would go cold, the candles would drip wax onto the velvet cloth and the honey would drip right off the peach. But Vivian didn't fret. She didn't break a sweat. Two minutes later, an old Afrikaner with abysmal eyes arrived; Vivian knew this man must have money like dust. She presented her creation, and got paid. "Bon Appétit," she said, sounding both exotic and kitsch.

Vivian left work early to get her car's windows re-tinted. There was a new tinting product on the market and the cheapest place she knew of was Viresh's workshop in Bellville South. Initially, she'd heard about Viresh through Tanya, who had assured her of his excellence, "Ja, he lives next door to me hey, and he's amazing—I've been going there for years! Such a sweet guy also." Vivian had been there a couple of times to replace a tyre or repair an oil leak.

Standing outside Viresh's garage, Vivian tilted her head to read the sign board advertising his services:

Basic mechanical restoration
Fuel cell modifications
Upholstery work
Specialist tuning
Alternative fuel cell implementation

Aesthetic enhancements
Nano-particle paint jobs
Performance modifications
Body customisation
Acetone and propane replacements

She was interrupted by Viresh, who greeted her with a smile and proceeded to explain the meaning of the services advertised. Most of them catered to a single phenomenon: people, particularly the people of Bellville, wanted to make their low-end cars perform like high-end cars. In this regard, Bellville had remained largely unchanged.

"Nano-particle paint jobs," Viresh ventured, "change the colour of your car according to energy input—your speed and so on, you understand, ma'am? A lovely thing to have if you can afford it. I must recommend it to you-"

"I'm perfectly happy with just black, thank you Viresh," said Vivian.

"I don't think you'd perhaps be interested in a faster, lighter, propane-operated fuel cell for your engine, ma'am?"

Viresh waited a response. Vivian didn't give one.

"No, I didn't think so, hey, you're much too sophisticated for those kinds of modifications, well ok then—it's a brown way of making money, this business, you see? But *ja*, like I said, anything along those lines, I can sort out for you at a much cheaper rate than the bigger motor-mechanics stores in this area."

Vivian nodded at him, looked at his oil-stained fingers and beyond into his garage. The place was riddled with car parts, fenders, panels, seats, carburettors.

"I just want my windows re-tinted."

Viresh beamed at her. "No problem. Window tinting should take a couple of hours, maybe three. That will be R900 for our newest smash-and-grab tints—guaranteed protection from break-ins and extra protection from the sun's glare. And, I can assure you I only use top-of-range tints—this new Titanium-oxide range works so

Brandy City

professionally that when the light hits your window, the energy input instantly makes your window darker. Ideal for these unbearably hot days, is it not? So there you go, complete protection, extra glare sensitivity, light-reactive tints—for you Ma'am. They've just been imported you know? Makes it a lot easier to drive with that terrible sun in your eyes..."

"Yes, thank you."

"One can never be too careful these days, hey?"

"Quite right."

"Now if you could just fill in your details here on the form please Ma'am. Your car will be done by five at the latest. I will give you a call as soon as I've finished—there we go. Ok, do you have a lift from here? Oh, I see you do-"

They turned to look at the taxi pulling up the driveway. Viresh strained his neck to make out the driver's face. Then, astonished, he noticed that there wasn't one. No driver in that car. Vivian could almost hear his thoughts: *this lady must be loaded to afford one those taxis!* For a second, they both stared at the contact-sensitive, road-smart taxi as it accurately parked itself, waiting for its passenger to enter.

Viresh stammered for words, "Uh, that's quite uhm, a phenomenon hey? Technological genius right there. I've never seen one of those in this area."

"Indeed it is," Vivian sighed, thinking about the phenomenon of the driverless taxi: *what an advanced world we live in where only those of wealth can afford to use the best technology.* She shuddered at the injury awaiting her wallet and walked to the driverless car abandoning her BMW to a stunned Viresh and his garage. The mechanic visibly reeled at the luxury living of Cape Town's other half.

It had been a long day when Vivian, reclining on her spacious bed, heard the street racers' engines roar from her room upstairs. She thought about Tanya who would only get home after nine when her session with the Afrikaans client had ended. That man had looked like he may take longer to satisfy than the usual clients. She couldn't get the thought of Tanya out of her mind. The only human being she ever got close to, however platonic the context. Vivian could place that sliver of a peach between her thighs a hundred times over and would never tire of the task.

The symphony of acetone-efficient engines kept her up now. Vivian battled to sleep with the noise from the streets below and her thoughts of Tanya leaving work late, having to slip in through the back of her house so that she wouldn't wake her boyfriend, Graeme.

Graeme, however, wasn't inside sleeping at all. With a bottle of brandy between his legs he couldn't get up. He couldn't go inside yet. He knew that he needed to calm down first. He needed to have another dop. Breathe. Light another smoke. He had seen the pictures of Tanya posing half-naked on the Internet, advertising herself as a culinary delight to be enjoyed by men for cash.

Graeme felt his face distorting as though weeping but he refused to let himself cry. He took off his Diesel spectacles and watched the streetlights blur and the colours bleed into obscurity. *My lady,* being enjoyed by a million other men, Graeme thought, and spat on the ground. *The bitch!* He downed the last of the brandy clean from the bottle and stood up, smashing the bottle on the pavement. He walked into the night holding the glass neck in his hand as if he was trying to find someone to slash.

Glass neck in hand, Graeme saw Viresh drive past. He knew that Viresh was coming home after watching the street races at Sacks Circle, but Graeme didn't want to talk. He didn't greet Viresh as he pulled into the driveway with a Nissan Sylvia S13; a 1989 ultra-vintage model with a deteriorating body and an engine replaced by a propane-acetone fuel cell. Graeme walked past the car and on down the street with the broken bottle in his hand. Viresh bolted out the car and ran to Graeme, grabbing the broken bottle and ripping it from his hand. "Calm down, my broe—hey!—calm down!"

Viresh slung Graeme's arm around his shoulder and took him inside. At Graeme's demand, Viresh poured him another brandy—a single, with coke this time, and a stack of ice blocks. Viresh ventured, "*Kykie*, you wanna tell me what's going on here or what?"

Graeme mumbled something and passed out.

When Graeme woke up on Viresh's couch the next morning, his head throbbed and the sunlight felt like cigarette burns in his irises. He stumbled around looking for his glasses. He found them on the floor, put them on and slunk into his own house, defeated. In pain, he made his way into the kitchen and saw Tanya ironing his clothes on the kitchen counter. At the sight of her, his anger sparked again. He sat down at the table to eat, and asked, "Where's the toast, ek sê?"

He waited for a response but Tanya carried on ironing without looking at him. Graeme was twitching in fury but he couldn't bring himself to confront her. *Where was she last night?*

"Toaster's broken, Graeme. I told you, we need a new one."

"Ja, next month. Make a plan so long, I'm hungry."

"You stink like brandy! Nou's jy babbelas and you want me to make you toast out of thin air?"

Graeme held his head and sighed, "Tanya just make me some fucking breakfast please," he slammed his elbow on the table, managing to retain everything he couldn't bring himself to say.

Tanya finally looked up with eyes that made Graeme shudder. She picked up a stale piece of bread. Holding the hot iron in one hand and the slice of stale bread in the other, she walked towards him. She put the bread down in front of him, slammed the hot iron down onto the bread

Mia Arderne

and held it there until it scorched. "There's your fucking toast."

Graeme stopped talking. Fumes of burnt wheat filled his nostrils. He pondered the object in front of him and took a bite.

Tanya's voice pierced his hangover, "Graeme, I switched off the fridge because we running out of electricity."

"Ja Tanya."

"Graeme, you know the toilet don't wanna flush anymore, ne?"

"Ja Tanya."

"Graeme, are you listening to me?!"

Graeme held his throbbing head in his hands, defeated by the yelling. "*Ja* Tanya."

Graeme drove to work in a century-old green Nissan Micra modified and tuned by Viresh. On his way to the company, he drove past Vivian on Voortrekker Road. The *mooi* white lady in the black BMW. Graeme thought about sleeping with her every time he drove past her on his way to work. He had never slept with a white lady before but he knew that white women have pink nipples. He had seen it in movies. *Pink*, must taste better than brown, he thought. How he would love to see just how pink Vivian is underneath those thin clothes she wears... He screeched to a halt just behind a truck in front of him. *Jassis!* Focus, Graeme. Vivian sped away in her sleek eco-friendly unmodified vehicle.

Graeme walked into the building on time; he needed to hold on to this job. He sat down and waited for the meeting to commence. An executive got up and stood in front. Graeme listened to him rant on about sustainability and comment vaguely on the political situation. His partner mentioned a statistic about the economy and the executive responded with appropriate agitation.

This went on for half an hour without a smoke break. It was incomprehensible to Graeme that the speaker was still spewing out shit about the stock exchange. The

Brandy City

executive's lips started to move faster. His teeth seemed to be getting whiter with every word. Periodically, the executive rubbed his lips and brushed his hand across his face—always very briefly, still professional. His mouth started swelling. He kept on nodding to his subordinates in affirmation, and the words just kept on coming faster and faster like an auctioneer and then suddenly, his mouth fell off. It dropped to the floor, quite naturally, no blood, like plastic. This didn't faze the executive at all. He just carried on without a mouth. Where his mouth used to be, the skin closed up quite normally. His head still bobbed in affirmation.

"Graeme?" his colleague intervened, looking concerned.

"*Ja?*"

"The meeting's over."

"Oh—*ja.*"

"Smoke break?"

"Sure."

Graeme went outside with his colleague. The tiny headache pill he popped this morning tasted like iced caramel. He had no idea what was in there, but it worked for the pain and it cooled him down—marvellous for hangovers. He wondered if the sugar-encrusted chemicals had reacted with the alcohol in his blood. Maybe it was nothing. Maybe it was just too hot today; perhaps he was coming down with sunstroke. At least it was Friday.

At five, Graeme went to the huge store-room at the back of the office block and the executive handed over his crate of brandy for the month.

After work, Graeme received a call from Viresh, "Bra, there's races tonight, are you coming?"

"No bra, you know on weekends there's just laaities on the street racing their daddy's cars and I don't smaak for the police."

A few minutes later, Viresh called again. "Yoh, my broe, they busy taking people for guppies here! Just come check this out."

Mia Arderne

"Ja, maybe. I'll see."

A couple of roads down the BP garage on Frans Conradie Road bustled with Golfs idling, revving, and burning out. German and Japanese cars ruled the road. Most countries had long abandoned the combustion automobile industry with their tails between their legs. These racers had transformed their engines from the conventional green fuel cells to propane-acetone fuel cells—fresh on the black market, and much more efficient, faster, and lighter, than conventional engines. The acetone improved conversion efficiency, but the resulting catalytic reactions were terrible for the environment, making the engines illegal and driving the street racers further away from Cape Town's centre. But in Bellville, they owned the road.

Graeme's phone rang a third time. It was Viresh. Again. Graeme didn't answer. He got up off the couch, key in hand and cruised through to Bellville central. Five minutes later, he pulled up at the obsolete BP garage. On the surface, his car looked like an ancient 1600. But once you heard it rev, you knew it wasn't. The Micra was adorned for deception by Viresh for Graeme.

Graeme floated out of the car, confidence brimming, and asked the crowd, "Wie gat nou ry?"

The racers and spectators went silent. Everyone stared at him. Graeme trembled in his neon-green takkies, their oversized tongues stuck out beneath his tracksuit pants. He took a second to survey the staring faces from behind his Diesel glasses. "Ok, for you guys here who only speak English—is anyone here gonna race tonight?"

Still nothing. Pissed off, Graeme got back into his Micra. Reversed, dropped the car into first, and spun the tyres before parking next to Viresh.

Speaking to Viresh through the window he ranted: "These people are then wasting our time."

"You should've come 10 minutes ago. I dunno what kine now."

Brandy City

In the heat of conversation, they neglected to see the police snaking towards them having heard the burn-out.

Mid-sentence, another racer cut them off with the proverbial, "Boys, maartz!"

"Why? *What* kine*?*" asked Graeme.

"Dis die boere!"

Cars flooded out the garage. Graeme glanced at the blue lights in his rear-view mirror. He panicked and entered the maze of streets in Bellville Industrial, unlit at night. He got stuck behind an old man driving a Mazda on a narrow road. Knowing he couldn't overtake, Graeme thought, if you go right, I'm gonna go left and if you go left, I'm gonna go right—either way, I'm not driving behind this doos. The Mazda turned right and, as Graeme took the left bend, he switched off his headlights on a pitch-black block of roads where people seldom stop at Stop signs. Road-users in Bellville at one a.m. consider oncoming headlights a signal to wait and darkness, a signal to go. Graeme's car was camouflaged into the night as he gunned down the residential streets with one hand on the wheel. The other hand phoned Viresh. "Where we going now?"

"Let's go have a dop at smokkie," replied Viresh.

Parties always have been a ritualistic forgetting of one's circumstances, but now they had become more honestly recognised as such. The Illuminati's most important tool was to offer its slaves a reprieve so sweet that they would labour willingly for the intermission. The slaves called it Friday.

Everyone was at the Smokkelhuis on Fridays. The owner, Ballie, twisted around in his wheelchair with violent alacrity—he'd been shot twice and his wheelchair wasn't conventional, it was a feat of engineering. The plateau of Ballie's chair's surface was expanded to accommodate his weight. It had a cup-holder for his brandy, and a mini turbo-charger to force more air into the tiny engine of his chair for added mobility that he could activate at the push of a button. Around his neck were two gold chains thick enough to whack someone to death with. He was so portly, these chains didn't hang; they sat cushioned, much like his wife who lazed around in the cosy, living room with her gold tooth, surrounded by pictures of all their kids in school uniform. Behind her, near the paper-thin plasma screen, was a brandy vending machine.

Entrance to the Smokkelhuis was complicated. The gate was opened only slightly, leaving a narrow gap for those willing to squeeze in under a heavy brown chain with a massive rusted lock dangling above.

Spinning around with expert skill, Ballie's presence was immediate despite his physical level. Surrounding him, loyal junkies moved crates and toolboxes so that he could move in his chair with absolute freedom. At the back, in his unpainted transit room he sat, arms crossed on his potbelly, watching the screen, tuned in to the various cameras on his property. His establishment was devoted to the distribution of cheap brandy, which most of his customers drank clean, as Coke was fast becoming a luxury—he expanded the Smokkelhuis every year.

Vivian sat at the bar inside feeling dumbed-down by the surrounding conversations. She lit a cherry-tinted Marlboro and watched Tanya. It was a Friday night and all Vivian wanted to do was look at her. Be near her—even if that meant drinking substandard brandy without coke in Bellville's oldest shithole. Vivian had nowhere better to be. Her Plattekloof mansion was too big and lonely. She longingly watched her employee through the plumes of smoke. She felt shy and alone, like an alienated teenager. She wanted to approach her. But Tanya and the other girls were chatting about the clients and the awkward difficulties they had recently encountered. On the adjacent makeshift dance-floor, a local DJ satisfied his crowd of revellers with deliberately transcendental music. As the dancers reached a drunken climax, the DJ made the

Brandy City

infamous Illuminati triangle with his hands. Nobody perceived this gesture with any measure of seriousness. They raised their glasses to him, spilling little puddles of brandy on the already splattered wooden floor.

Vivian watched one of the paper-thin plasma screens in the corner. The news was on. There was a severe tornado somewhere in America. The footage emphasised the wreckage: houses demolished, pieces of broken cars smashing into walls, trees uprooted. *It looks quite serious*, Vivian thought, pondering about how many lives were lost in the storm. Noticing the sunset behind the wreckage, Tanya remarked at the top of her voice, "Look at the pretty sunset on the screen. That sky is so pretty, ne? All those reds and oranges!"

Some of the colleagues burst out laughing, others agreed with her. Vivian grimaced, confused by her attraction to this woman. Tanya was trying too hard to look good tonight, she thought. But then, so was everyone else. Once again, Vivian felt an intense fear of the pending. They were all so superficial, she thought, so superficial, so entirely dictated by the sway of aesthetics. It was all everyone strived for these days. But Vivian knew that beauty, in its transience, was always a precursor to devastation. She stared at Tanya's hair extensions and ordered another brandy.

Viresh and Graeme arrived at last, bursting through the narrow slit at the door, desperate for a drink. Vivian greeted Viresh and they started chatting about her new window tint. Throughout the conversation, Vivian slipped glances at Tanya, who was now in the grip of her boyfriend's company. Vivian felt desolate.

She heard Graeme say to Tanya, "So, we drinking brandy tonight—it's on you."

Tanya raised her eyebrows, "Ok...?"

"No, literally, *on* you."

Vivian watched Tanya freeze, as she realised that Graeme knew. Tanya slowly brought her drink to her lips.

Mia Arderne

Graeme waited for her to say something but Tanya faltered and spilt her words all over the place, "Graeme, we can't just survive on brandy. That's why I took the job. Cause it still pays money, you know? Because we have rich clients there, you see? I did it for you... So that we could live. I didn't wanna struggle anymore..."

Vivian felt a deep urge to take Tanya away from him, put her in the Plattekloof mansion and make Tanya her very own trophy wife. She restrained herself. Instead, she watched Tanya order her boyfriend a drink; that she kept topping up, rationalising, explaining and feeding him brandy with her arms around his neck. She knows this is all he really needs.

"I love you," Graeme surrendered.

"I love you too."

Vivian walked to the dance-floor and started swaying. She thought of her dead husband and remembered a time when it rained and the world still dripped with beauty.

When she slipped another glance at Tanya, she could see that Graeme was drunk and full of forgiveness as he stared gleefully at Tanya. Tanya would laugh so loudly that it became awkward. Nobody minded, all so drunk that awkwardness belonged to another world entirely. In the middle of one of Tanya's laughing fits, she paused breathlessly and said, "This is the stage where I start crying,"—and she did, inconsolably. For just a second, and then carried on laughing without cease. Graeme, Viresh, and her colleagues, found it contagious. Vivian found it both compelling and exhausting just watching her, but she couldn't stop.

Every time Graeme tried to light his cigarette, Tanya blew out the flame of his match. Graeme knew she firmly believed that smoking was bad for you. He thought it was cute of her, maybe a bit annoying, but he didn't care. He carried on trying to light his cigarette. Vivian watched this game of theirs, intrigued and wanton. Each time Graeme lit a match, she'd blow it out mischievously before he

Brandy City

could light his cigarette. The girls watching this burst out laughing as if it was the cutest thing they'd ever seen. Graeme kissed her and lit another match. She blew out the flame. He lit another match. She blew out the flame. He lit yet another match. She tried to blow out the flame, but this time, he was too fast for her. Smiling, he jerked the match away from her in one swift movement to light his cigarette. But he moved too fast for his inebriated state. Caught off-balance, Graeme dropped the match into a brandy puddle on the wooden floor.

Instantly, the brandy soared into a thin wall of fire. Fuelled by the wood and the heat it grew quickly. Vivian's eyes went wide as she watched the commotion: Viresh and a few other men tried to it put out with their clothes but the fire was too big. They tried to get out of the building, but the narrow entrance was already blocked with bodies.

Then, like ice in the pit of her stomach, the truth dawned on Vivian: there was no water.

The taps hadn't worked for weeks. Vivian gazed at Tanya through the flames. Tanya was panicking. She had realised what she'd caused. The flames climbed up her hair extensions and she soon realised her hair was in flames. In a state of shock, Tanya's glass dropped from her grasp and into the fire exacerbating the flames.

In disbelief, Graeme poured his drink down his throat with reckless abandon. Vivian stared as the brandy streamed down his chin and neck and dripped down his chest, while, all around him, the flames danced and people screamed. Drunk, he swayed dangerously close to the flames. A raging flame caught the wet brandy gleaming and streaming down his skin and the fire spread to meet his lips and neck, forming a little river of flames from Graeme's chest to his jaw. He had blindly managed to set himself alight. Vivian still hadn't moved. The desperate crowd was fighting to get out of the blocked building. She knew there was no point.

Mia Arderne

The fire continued to rage through Bellville, reducing Voortrekker Road to ash, burning down everything from the Smokkelhuis through to Adult World.

As Vivian burnt on the dance-floor, she no longer felt a fear of the pending. She was watching it. She was watching Brandy City burn to the ground in its own excess and stupidity. Like many old souls before her, she was to perish at the hands of a silly and beautiful girl.

Mia Arderne is a fiction writer and artist. Her subject matter, in the visual and literary fields, interfaces the erotic and the magical. She is currently studying towards a Masters degree in Creative Writing at the University of Cape Town. Her dissertation will take the form of a murder-mystery novel. She has further qualifications in Philosophy and Theatre. 'Brandy City' is her first published short story.

Ofe!

Rafeeat Aliyu

The gathering was as lively as the champagne in the flute Jemila brought to her lips. Drawing a deep breath, she took a sip and enjoyed the path of the liquid down her throat. This crowd looks so good, she thought, and could imagine how wealthy she would be by the end of the night—all these fancy people, carelessly slipping their handhelds where Jemila's eyes could clearly see them. It was like the miracle two weeks ago, when her house had buzzed with good news.

Jemila had thought the house system had caught a virus when its androgynous voice had told her Matthew Halliday, a reclusive scientist, had randomly selected her to attend a dinner in celebration of his latest invention. "It was a random selection based on probability," her house system had droned when Jemila demanded an explanation. "Congratulations."

Jemila had been suspicious all of the next two weeks, even after a call to Halliday's office confirmed that she was indeed on the guest list. Though, in the end, she decided that she would attend the party after all. The years had been especially tough when her parents had disowned Jemila after discovering her relationship with Nketiah. They had first asked her if it was possible to change before cutting off her allowance and freezing her accounts. Thanks to Nketiah, she had been able to move from the family home in Osu, Accra, to Abuja, Nigeria. In her newly adopted metropolis, Jemila discovered she could put all her years at university to good use hacking into handhelds and selling data chips on the black market. Jemila never really knew why selling data was such a lucrative business and she wasn't sure she wanted to. That was six years ago, when she had been a spoiled princess and her preference had been cross-dressing men with high heels. She missed Nketiah sometimes.

Jemila placed her empty glass on a tray atop one of the bot tables weaving a path through the crowd that passed by her, but it moved away before she could snatch a mini-sandwich from its top. Pulling at one of her lightning shaped earrings, she studied the crowd. Jemila guessed there were about fifty people in the wide hall mingling before dinner. The crowd was a diverse one, there were round dark faces, plump arms, there were faces that suggested a hint of Asian ancestry mixed with African. Jemila noticed a few of the guests were noticeably wealthy in the way they carried themselves, others looked like this was their first time out of the slums in Karu.

Time to work, Jemila thought, rubbing her palms down the slinky fabric of the dress she wore. She made her move across the length of the hall, casually bumping into unsuspecting guests and slipping their smart devices into her open clutch-purse. Jemila had purloined four when a firm hand grabbed her by the wrist.

Before she could react, Jemila saw who it was and smiled. "What brings you here Detective Bolanle?" Jemila crooned, looking at Bolanle's disapproving face.

Bolanle let go of Jemila's wrist as if it was on fire and cleared her throat, darting eyes the only sign of her slight nervousness. "Most here won the lottery, *abi*?" she asked.

"Are you sure you're not here on business Bolanle?" Jemila asked, still smiling.

Everyone who regularly visited The Red Elephant, near the Computer Village, had heard of Bolanle Okereke and her private investigation business. Jemila remembered meeting Bolanle when she was still new to the city; they had worked a case together then.

"No I am not," Bolanle responded crisply. "You on the other hand seem to be very busy."

Ofe!

"If I had recognised you, I wouldn't have even tried." Jemila's hand had not even brushed Bolanle's pocket, the woman was as sharp as always.

"I thought you had left that life," Bolanle said and eyed Jemila, from the top of her shorn hair to exposed thighs from beneath her dress. "You said..." Bolanle paused to clear her throat. "I mean I haven't seen you at the Red Elephant for a few years now."

"Times are hard," was Jemila's only response. "I never thought you were one for small talk Detective."

Bolanle glared at Jemila, gave a curt excuse, and disappeared into the crowd.

The guest toilet had a strong scent that reminded Jemila of the ocean. Her chip linked to the last handheld and gathered up all the necessary information. A loud knock sounded at the door left Jemila remained unfazed. This was the third time a person had pounded on the door.

"Hurry and finish whatever you are doing in there, people are waiting," said a loud and angry voice on the other side of the door, "nonsense."

Jemila heard the murmur even through the relative thickness of the door yet she remained patient, watching the animated cats dancing on the screen as they walked from the handheld's memory folder straight into the bulk file on her chip. Jemila smiled, she had created the program to do just that. Cats were more interesting than folded envelopes, and represented passwords, pin codes, names, addresses, codes that disabled house systems, numbers, and such. She recalled the days when she picked up jobs that asked for specific data. Jamila had first met Bolanle at The Red Elephant, Bolanle's stern imposing figure trying to blend in even though everyone knew the kind of work she did and wanted no part in it.

Back then, Jemila had just come out of working freelance having found a reliable data auctioneer. It was in year two of surviving on her own and Jemila was seriously considering heading back to Osu and kneeling down

Rafeeat Aliyu

before her parents, the prodigal daughter returned home. Jemila overheard Bolanle questioning someone, asking about a car and if they knew Musa. The interrogation was mostly one-sided with the detective doing the talking. Jemila was at first not inclined to help. Like all the other patrons at the Red Elephant, she minded her business in the corner she shared with Dafi and two other *ole,* data thieves, a bottle of gin between them. Everyone knew that Loveleen had sold the data chip to Musa, who had then broken into a wealthy mansion on The Hill and made off with a brand new jet car—rapidly taken apart and its pieces sold—among other things. The detective was searching for something, she wouldn't say what, that had been inside the car; it was like trying to eat an elephant whole.

Yet the detective was persistent, asking questions, wearing people down, hoping to gain just the slightest clue. As Jemila observed the detective's determined approach, a sudden need to be reckless arose in her, to be carefree as she was in the days before she started stealing data. That urge grew as the night progressed, eventually encouraging Jemila to sneak out after the detective had left the bar with the whole story ready at the tip of her tongue.

The tiniest beeps alerted Jemila her work was done, and she stuffed the handhelds into her purse. She would have to sell the data as soon as possible—information had a very short market life. Amidst the loud knocks and curses from the other side of the door, she made slow work of activating the sensors that flushed the toilet. She turned to regard her reflection in the large illuminated mirror, and smiled. She took in her dark skin and short, neat afro. The overhead light glinted off the crystal on the silver stud in her nose. Her red dress suited her, Jemila thought, and fished out her lipstick from her purse.

The lights went off.

Jemila gasped, power cuts were common in the slums and outlying areas but she would never have expected it

Ofe!

here. Jemila waited for the electricity to come back on, she pulled at her earrings and stretched out her arms in front of her. The darkness was heavy. She could not make out a single thing. It almost felt unnatural. Jemila rubbed her hands over her bare arms now marked with goosebumps.

A sound came from behind her, at first low then steadily growing louder. It was a moaning, like a dozen people moaning, it was loud and yet sounded muffled. A shiver ran up Jemila's spine. It sounded more like keening and cries for help, and another sound, the sound of flesh torn apart. Jemila slowly spun around, a light she had not noticed before shone on a masked figure bent over and relentlessly digging into something that lay flat on a table. Jemila felt like throwing up when she noticed the gloved hands of the figure were bloody from being inside what she now saw was a lifeless body of a woman.

A rush of fear, desperation, confusion, and just a taint of madness slammed through her. Then she saw the source of the low moans. Behind the studiously working figure were cages big enough to hold humans. Each cage held a woman dressed in a soiled, expensive outfit, some of their faces stained with makeup, or something else. Her knees buckled and she kneeled on the cold floor. Right there clutching bars, was a woman who looked just like her with *her* exact red dress, torn exposing her stomach.

Darkness descended.

A chorus of hands slammed against a door. "Come out now! Which kain nonsense be this!"

Jemila blinked, she was back in the toilet with its peach tiles, virtual flowers, and soft towels. Her hands trembled as she opened the door, and she barely noticed the stern looks of disapproval.

Jemila struggled to make sense of what she had just seen. Almost automatically, she opened her purse and dropped off the stolen handhelds at different points in the hall. In her mind, all she could see was herself waiting in that cage to become the next unfortunate woman on the table.

Rafeeat Aliyu

The din of the lively crowd seemed muted as Jemila finally rested against a wall. She was sweating profusely even though the hall was cool, air-conditioned. Her hands were shaking and she could not stand up straight in her heels. One of the bots carrying refreshments approached her and she snatched two glasses of champagne and downed them in quick succession, but they were not strong enough to wipe away what she had just seen. Jemila looked down at herself and then looked up at the crowd around her. The soiled dresses the caged women wore suggested that all the other women were somewhere in this hall, just like her. Have they seen the same thing I did? Jemila wondered, and shook her head, it made no sense, yet it felt so real.

Bolanle! Jemila recalled the detective's manner earlier; the same determined look in her eyes from four years ago at the Red Elephant. Jemila pushed herself off the wall. While she did not understand what she had just witnessed, she would not wait to find out.

Jemila's heart hammered against her chest as she pushed her way through the crowd. She approached the vestibule and saw two heavy-set men now guarding the closed entrance doors.

"Madam," one of them said as Jemila came to stand before them.

"I left something in my car. I would like to retrieve it." Jemila looked up at the one who had spoken. The stiffness in his posture suggested he was an AI.

"I am afraid it is not safe out there yet Madam, we have been informed that some dangerous elements want to use this opportunity to steal sensitive data."

Jemila almost laughed aloud at the irony. There were people outside longing to steal the scientist's new invention, yet a thief like her had won an invitation to such a high security event. Jemila realised what she had to do, she nodded curtly at the AI before making her way back into the boisterous hall. She paused before the three short

Ofe!

steps that lead from the vestibule into the hall and watched guests weave around the tall columns smiling and laughing without a care in the world.

"Excuse me," a slightly husky voice interrupted Jemila's cloud of confusion. The voice belonged to a petite woman, her stick-like arms jutted from the loose blouse she wore.

"Yes," Jemila replied curtly.

The woman sighed loudly and said, "It looks like you received my distress call."

"Distress call?" That got Jemila's attention.

The woman nodded. "You are sensitive too, aren't you?" she whispered, the words rushing out of her mouth.

Jemila glared at the woman who was now leaning towards her.

"So you won't think I am crazy when I tell you that we are the main stars of Halliday's gala tonight... but for what he has in store for us, we're more like guinea-pigs," the woman gushed.

"What are you talking about?"

"I'm Chigozie," the woman introduced herself. "I wish this could have been a proper introduction but if we don't find our way out of this mansion, tonight could very well be our last night alive."

It was dark and quiet when Bolanle started transmission. "Aboubacar," she urgently called her secretary/fixer's name, and heard a long sigh before he replied.

"Yes Madam, I am working on it."

"Just unlock the door already."

"I am working my magic as we speak."

Bolanle squatted, her back against the balustrade, the stairway behind her and the door to Halliday's study right in front of her. Slipping out of that monstrous hall had been easy and so was finding her way to her target's private study. Bolanle was grudgingly grateful that Aboubacar had his fixer ways of obtaining house plans and entering into house systems. Her major concern now was untimely discovery—the balustrade only provided a shield from the lower floor. As far as she saw, the upper floors were deserted and shrouded in darkness, very much in contrast to the ground floor that was so well illuminated. Bolanle had noticed the bodyguards in the hall. Their presence may have surprised her if she did not rationalise it with thoughts of crowd control and the extravagant lives of the wealthy.

Bolanle remembered Jemila's grinning face and clicked her tongue. It was a surprise to find a familiar face in that crowd. Three years ago, Jemila had literally stood out at the Red Elephant, but her naïveté and careless attitude to life unsettled Bolanle. No one else had aided Bolanle with her investigation then, and for that, she was thankful to Jemila even though the girl had all but signed a death warrant by doing so. Still, Jemila was also very cunning.

"How long will it be Aboubacar?" she said, into the comm unit inside her bracelet.

"I am now attempting to override the house system without raising alarm."

Bolanle agitated, quietly kissed her teeth. Their current client enlisted Bolanle's services in locating a device he called Shango 4680. Her client had not given many specifics, so Bolanle launched her own search with nothing but a name and a concept drawing of the device. It had been difficult to track down as the Shango 4680 enjoyed the privilege of moving around often from the hands of one mysterious owner to another. After chasing it for a month, she and Aboubacar finally pinned its location to Halliday's mansion a week ago. Her job that night was to capture some images of the device for her client's review.

Bolanle sighed, of course, there was more to the Shango 4680 than her client relayed. She was most likely aiding industrial espionage. Bolanle sometimes missed her days with the Pan-African Army if only because then she had more opportunities to draw, and use, her guns.

Ofe!

"Done," Aboubacar said, as the door clicked and slid open.

Bolanle slipped into the darkened room, waited until the door shut, and then pulled out a pencil-thin torch from inside her jacket. In the wide, spartan study, there was a large desk computer—that she hoped was off lest it recorded her visit—a bookshelf, and a small, glass fridge that cast a dull, green glow in the corner it occupied and was the only other source of light in the room. Slipping on a pair of skin-tight disposable gloves, she started her urgent search for the Shango 4680.

Bolanle rummaged through the bookshelf, but came up with nothing except books and more books—hundreds on extraterrestrials, genetic research, and several copies of the West African Scientist. She moved to the desk computer, its screen was dark and there were locked drawers below the desk. Fervently hoping they were not pass-coded, as with the computer, she gently slid her fingers over the top, sides, and bottom, of the desk, and sighed in relief when she felt a small keyhole.

A sudden excitement overwhelmed Bolanle. This was the most excited she had felt in years. Getting the drawers open was easy with her auto-lockpick, and the bottom drawer held a safe ensconced beneath hardened glass and steel. Inside lay the Shango 4680. She knew its look due to the concept drawings, yet something almost indiscernible seemed to pulse from the device. Bolanle had to stop herself from reaching out to touch it, which would set off a dozen alarms. She wasn't a sensitive person—there were people she knew who talked about how they felt the presence of aliens and neglected spirits—but it was almost as if the device was calling to her.

She bit the inside of her lip, slipped the camera over her fingers, and said, "I will begin recording now Aboubacar."

With a small light and camera in hand, Bolanle filmed the Shango 4680. It was slightly larger than the palm of her hand, with deep indentations that would fit fingers perfectly around the handle. Tubes ran along its length and there was a small button presumably to charge it. Bolanle was sure it was a weapon; it looked like a sturdier, modified version of the blaster she carried.

"The Shango 4680," Bolanle whispered almost reverently, as she captured the device from all possible angles. Satisfied finally, she turned off the camera. "Aboubacar, has the video been transmitted?"

"Yes," he replied and added with surprise, "Wow, what a weapon!" Aboubacar was rarely surprised.

"We are not sure it is a weapon," Bolanle snapped, even though her reaction to it troubled her and told her as much.

"Chigozie, you're saying that you see into the future." Jemila asked after she had calmed down.

"I... see things, and I can help others see them as well," Chigozie replied.

"And these things happen?"

"99% of the time, they do," Chigozie said and nodded. "What of your ability?"

"If you can see the future, why did you come here?"

"I can't say I have a hold on my ability," she said, and looked embarrassed. "My visions are not always accurate, when I saw it, what I showed you, it was too late already."

Jemila's eyes flipped to the tall painting of Halliday that stood across the hall. The artist had captured his vibrant skin and bald head. Behind him were the old ruins of the mosque at Djenne and hovering in the air were five UFOs composed of two concentric circles and two lines that crossed between them.

Jemila gritted her teeth. "I can get us out of here," she said, her voice low.

"All of us?" Chigozie's eyes lit up. "I haven't been able to find the other eleven..."

"No," Jemila said fiercely. "I mean just you and me."

Chigozie looked disappointed. "Is that your ability? We can't just leave the others here."

Ofe!

"Then why did you not send your distress call to all thirteen of us?" Jemila pursed her lips.

"I didn't choose for it to reach you," Chigozie said, and sounded upset. "As I said earlier I do not have much of a control over this ability, I wasn't even sure it would work-"

"Look," Jemila interrupted, and leant closer to Chigozie. "We don't have time for you to play the hero. We can go call for help, and then come back."

The sound of metal tapping against glass echoed through the hall, silence ensued.

"All the guests are gathered, it is now time for dinner," Halliday's loud voice boomed. He stood tall with a wide-set body more suited to a bodybuilder than a scientist. "We can now proceed to the dining hall."

The unsuspecting guests milled into the dining room. Jemila stayed back, Chigozie beside her, but when they were the only people left, they joined the guests.

Brightly lit chandeliers cast a beautiful glow over the guests as they made their way to their designated seats with the help of 3D cards projecting their names.

Searching the floating characters, Jemila found her place first. "Think about my offer," she whispered to Chigozie, before settling down. Chigozie gave Jemila a forlorn look as she walked away.

In a matter of seconds, the first course arrived, a steaming hot-pepper soup with orishirishi. Jemila stared at the fine china bowl before her, the soup looked good but the assorted offal in it turned her stomach in a bad way this evening. She was not going to touch it. As she watched the other guests dig in, a paranoid thought went through Jemila's mind; what if they knew she had not eaten? She restrained from panicking and reminded herself that she had a way to get out of this event alive, all she had to do was find a way to use it.

Rafeeat Aliyu

"Fine girls like you don't eat?" a middle-aged man beside her asked with a smile on his face. Beside him, his wife rolled her eyes. "This is really good stuff."

Jemila gave a small smile and shook her head, too distracted for small talk.

"Let me help you," he said, and replaced her full bowl with his empty one.

Jemila's nagging paranoia disappeared, and she wondered if it was just paranoia. Perhaps it was Chigozie transmitting her distress calls. Jemila bristled in her confusion; she was not sure what to believe any more.

Halliday climbed atop a dais, introduced himself, and then launched into a speech. Jemila barely heard a word—anytime the audience laughed, she wished Chigozie had more control of her ability. If everyone had seen what she had seen, they would not be laughing.

A piercing siren sounded through the hall.

"Ladies and gentlemen," Halliday's self-assured voice boomed through the large room. "It has just been whispered in my ear that my mansion may be under attack. It seems my enemies can't keep their hands off my invention and do not want us to enjoy ourselves."

Nervous laughter rang through the hall.

"If you would all calmly move towards the doors to your left, my able-bodied employees will guide you to the nearest exit."

This was Jemila's chance. She rose and eagerly followed the crowd through the large doors. Wanting to blend in, she kept her eyes to the ground and its luxury rug as she moved ahead. A large hand wrapped around her elbow and it felt like her heart fell to her feet.

"Madam, please this way," a man said, who resembled the AI's at the front doors earlier.

Jemila felt helpless and dug her nails into her palms as the AI dragged her away from the confused crowd.

Ofe!

Bolanle cussed when she heard the alarm, convinced her cover was blown. It was the perfect excuse to make a choice from her selection of concealed weapons and she chose the semi-automatic pistol. Back pressed to the wall just beside the door, adrenaline pumping through her veins, she waited for the assault to begin. Her eyes darted around the room for an escape route but there was only one barricaded window. Bolanle waited and counted the still minutes until she heard the sound of shoes shuffling past outside the door. She stole a quick glance out the window. Cars zoomed out the mansion's gates under the neon streetlights. It was time to go.

With one last lingering glance at the desk where the Shango 4680 lay encased, Bolanle pressed the button that opened the study door and made her way to the stairway.

"Aboubacar, I've left the target's study now, heading back to the hall where the guests were welcomed in," she said, paused behind a pillar beside the stairwell, and listened for sounds from below. Shortly she heard footsteps at the bottom of the stairs.

"The girls have been rounded up," said a high-pitched voice that carried clearly to where Bolanle stood tensely.

"Hope that means we are finished for the night," a second deep-set voice replied. "I have a date with Miss Desereah."

"The one with all the ropes?"

"Yeah, she..."

The voices faded away, and Bolanle waited a few moments before creeping down the stairs.

"Bolanle, I can open the exterior doors for you," Aboubacar said. "It sounds like something's up. Be safe."

"You'll need to let me into the hall first, those doors are closed. I am approaching from the first floor."

All around her was a jarring silence compared to the earlier bustle. The guests must have vacated quickly, she thought, and was glad she did not have to attempt leaving in any other direction. True to his word, Aboubacar opened the necessary doors for her with his remote connection. The brightly lit hall was grating and eerie in its emptiness, the server bots still. It felt almost like everyone had been spirited away at the height of the gala.

"There are two doors leading outside from the hall, one across from the vestibule, north, the other is to the west of the hall," Bolanle said.

"I am working on opening both of them," Aboubacar assured.

Once Bolanle was outside, she would head to her car parked in a far corner of Halliday's lush estate.

She had just reached the vestibule when there was a blinding flash and two women landed close to the north-facing doors. They both seemed to jump out of nowhere, and it was by sheer force of will that Bolanle did not shoot them. She would have recognised Jemila's red dress anywhere, but Jemila's friend—who looked like she was going to throw up—was a new face. Bolanle bit the inside of her mouth to keep from showing any reaction.

"Jemila?" she called out, a question to reassure her that she was not hallucinating.

Bolanle saw it took a moment for Jemila to focus but when she did, the turmoil in her eyes evaporated. "Bolanle! I've never been happier to see you. We are in serious trouble," Jemila said, rushing to where Bolanle stood.

Bolanle inhaled deeply. She would not give in to confusion. "You have one minute to tell me what the hell is going on," she said, and looked around the hall, finger tapping nervously on the gun, waiting impatiently for everything to go wrong, and it did.

Dr. Halliday's henchmen herded Jemila, Chigozie, and eleven other confounded women into an enclosed room. The sole door only opened from the outside and required a thumbprint, ID scan, and a pass-code, to unlock. One wall was entirely made of dark glass, Jemila noted as they

Ofe!

huddled together, then the darkness cleared revealing Halliday and bodyguards on the other side.

"Good evening ladies," he said, and there was a wide grin on his face as he struggled to contain his excitement. "All thirteen of you were specially chosen to be part of my new invention."

To Jemila's horror, a few of the women visibly relaxed even though they were in a prison and the person responsible stood before them.

"You mean we are to be your experiments," Chigozie retorted boldly. "Your guinea-pigs."

"Oh... wow! This is amazing," Halliday said and laughed, his eyes shining. He looked at his handheld. "Chigozie Nwanna, 28 years old, unmarried... we can mark her down as possessing some sort of pre-cognitive ability."

He turned and spoke softly to someone on his right, beyond the glass wall. Jemila's ears burned from continuously pulling on her earrings. Meanwhile panic began throughout the enclosed space.

"What do you mean by guinea-pigs?" a girl who looked no older than eighteen worriedly asked Chigozie. "My parents didn't tell me anything about that."

"Pre-cognitive ability?" A plump elderly woman murmured, obviously baffled.

Halliday cleared his throat. "You will have ample time to interact later," he said, and glanced at his handheld once more. "The drugs will soon take effect so I shall make this quick. I am sure all thirteen of you have had to keep secrets all your lives, secrets of your super-human abilities. My research is currently looking into that." He continued, speaking of aliens landing in West Africa centuries ago and mating with humans for the continuation of their dying species. This resulted in the emergence of thousands of humans with extraterrestrial ancestry and unusual abilities.

They listened.

"Consider yourselves great helpers of humanity, like your alien ancestors were," he said, enthused. "The information we obtain from you will be able to drive our species forward. We could develop more competent AIs, and work to strengthen humanity for future generations when this world may be inhabitable for our current form.

You are all unique. My wife..." He paused, his eyes glazing over, "...before she passed away was able to aid us in advancing weather control."

One of the women dropped to the ground, perhaps from the shock of it all Jemila thought, but it was not shock.

"I see the effects have started," Halliday said, and then once more talked to someone they couldn't see. "You shall all be put to sleep now. Understand we had to do this to ensure maximum cooperation. I'll see you when you awaken."

The mirror went dark once more. Jemila grabbed Chigozie's hand as gas filtered into the room. "We cannot wait anymore," Jemila said, and she disappeared with Chigozie.

"Jemila, you can teleport!" Bolanle said when they appeared near the doors and she figured it out.

"I call it *ofe*." Jemila replied, steadily observing Bolanle for her reaction.

"They are going to be looking for you soon, if they aren't already," Bolanle said, avoiding Jemila's gaze, and stemming her numerous questions for a safer time. "I was on my way out of here when you ladies barged in. We can all fit into my minibus and make a run for it."

"Are we not going to attempt saving the other women," Chigozie asked, disappointment evident in her tone.

"There is no reason for me to..." Bolanle lost track of her words. Jemila was glaring at her and Bolanle knew why.

"Mrs. Bolanle, please. You haven't seen what I have or what I showed Jemila," Chigozie pleaded. "We cannot leave here knowing we could have saved the others."

Ofe!

"Detective," Jemila finally spoke up. "Chigozie does not have the time to show you what she saw. I'm not one for heroism, but the others could really use your help."

"And you have a gun," Chigozie interjected.

"Years ago, providing you with information on Mighty Rat and his posse put my life in danger," Jemila continued, ignoring Chigozie. "And you promised me-"

"I remember what I promised," Bolanle cut her short. "You want me to keep my word and risk my life on your behalf."

Jemila nodded. "The situation is different but we can make a difference."

Bolanle and Jemila shared a knowing look, before Bolanle shrugged and said, "We do not have the time to bicker or quarrel". At least now, she had an excuse to use her guns and to test something that had been calling her name since she laid eyes on it. "Chigozie, do you have a vehicle? No? Can you drive? I shall authorise you to use my minibus. Jemila, will you be able to take your friend outside?"

"Yes," Jemila nodded a small triumphant smile on her face. "I can move between places I am familiar with. I saw where most of the cars were parked."

Bolanle described her vehicle to Chigozie and handed its elliptical key over to her. Then she focused on Jemila. "You should go back to that room and transport as many women as possible. I will keep the scientist and his posse distracted."

"Okay," Jemila said, her eyes betraying fear.

"Take this," Bolanle said, and thrust a pistol into Jemila's hand.

"I can't use this," Jemila blurted out.

"Would you prefer a blade?" Bolanle asked, and gave Jemila's shoulder a reassuring squeeze. "We need to move and before we do, remember save as many as you can. When you feel the situation is hopeless, save yourself."

Rafeeat Aliyu

The gun she did not know how to use, but Bolanle's assurance boosted Jemila's spirit nonetheless. First, she whispered *ofe* and took Chigozie outside the mansion. They did not land exactly at the spot but it was good enough. Jemila willed herself to be courageous, and not give in to the treacherous longing to remove herself from this mess and head to the comfort of her apartment.

When Jemila was twelve years old, she had asked her mother if people could disappear. Her mother had laughed and told Jemila about powerful ancestors who had once mastered magic. When these people wanted to disappear or move at supernatural speeds with the help of their magic, they chanted *Ofe!* Jemila sighed and headed back to the enclosed room where she knew eleven unconscious women lay.

"Aboubacar, I am going to need you to open the doors that lead out. Keep those open, and the door to Halliday's study."

"Again?" Aboubacar's voice came clear. "Dare I ask what is going on over there, you almost sound excited."

"Just do it."

As expected, several alarms went off when Bolanle shot open the safe with her blaster, and pocketed the Shango 4680. On her way back to the hall, semi-automatic raised, the first person in a black suit she saw coming up the stairwell got a bullet in the head. She did not stop to check if her victim had been human or AI and just satisfied herself that it was not moving.

By the time she reached the hall, four more bodies had fallen and Bolanle knew she would have to use her flashier blaster soon. In the hall, she found cover behind a bot. As she waited for the action to truly begin, Bolanle felt the heavy weight of the Shango 4680 in her pocket.

Moving unconscious women was hard work, but one by one, Jemila wrapped her arms around their prone forms

314

Ofe!

and transported them to where Chigozie waited with Bolanle's car. Jemila hastened when she heard the alarm sound throughout the mansion. On her third trip, she kicked off her high heels and helped Chigozie slide the latest woman into the back seat of the minibus. In the midst of the ongoing commotion, Jemila hoped Bolanle would keep Halliday and his henchmen distracted.

She was wrong.

On her fifth trip back to the room, there was a woman, immaculately dressed in a white tunic and long trousers, aided by an AI the likes of which Jemila had never seen. They were as shocked to see her, as Jemila was to see them.

"We clearly underestimated your kind," the woman said. Everything about her was severe from her tight hair-bun to the starched points of her clothes.

"This ruse had a margin of error from the beginning," the AI added. Its garish metallic head and insect-like eyes unsettled Jemila.

"Go ahead," the woman said, and waved at the men who were in the process of removing the inert women from the small prison.

Jemila heard a gun discharge. It sounded like death.

"Now I wouldn't kill you but I would hurt you," the woman said, pointing the gun at Jemila and nodding at the AI to proceed.

Jemila's entire body froze as the AI approached her. She had kept the small gun Bolanle had given her nestled between her breasts, held fast by her bra. There would be no time to draw it out and Jemila recalled Bolanle's words, 'When you feel it is hopeless, save yourself.' The AI's dull grey hand reached for her.

"*Ofe*," Jemila whispered, taking herself back to Chigozie and the vehicle.

"Chigozie! You have to go now," Jemila shouted in warning even before she landed.

Rafeeat Aliyu

She was oddly pleased when she saw Chigozie had already had the vehicle hovering a few feet up in the air ready to leave. A look passed between them as Jemila acknowledged the usefulness behind Chigozie's ability.

"Come in," Chigozie gestured.

Jemila shook her head. "Bolanle is still inside."

The first shot snapped past Jemila's arm just as the car rose a few metres. At first, Jemila thought it was a good idea to face the encroaching danger, Bolanle's gun trembling in her hand. However when she saw a column of men and AIs led by a very displeased Halliday, she changed her mind.

Jemila left a shimmer of light behind her as she disappeared.

"I resorted to hand-to-hand combat when my ammunition ran out," Bolanle explained. "It took you long enough; I was saving the best for the last."

Bolanle, whose face was bruised and swollen and her lip split and bleeding, limped as she crossed the vestibule towards the north exit, though she did have a small smile. Jemila followed closely behind her, choosing to ignore the carnage, but her respect for the detective multiplied.

"Aboubacar, north exit please," Bolanle spoke into the bracelet on her wrist, and held something that looked like a cross between an e-reader and a weapon to Jemila.

As soon as the door slid open, they rushed outside. It came as no surprise that Halliday and his guards stood opposite them. The guards had their weapons poised while Halliday stood in their midst, hands crossed behind his back.

"If you could put the house on lockdown now Aboubacar," Bolanle murmured into her device. She did not want anyone ambushing them from behind.

The two parties stood facing each other. It was very clear which side had the advantage in numbers but with the Shango 4680 in her hand, Bolanle felt invincible. She pressed on the button at the bottom of the device and it

Ofe!

leaped to life with a low, humming. The mansion went dark, and the only light now came from the neon lamps that lined the entrance to Halliday's estate.

"A thief," Halliday said, clearly displeased. "You have no idea what you are holding, or what you have just done."

"I know very well what I am holding," Bolanle said, her voice strong despite her battered face. "This is the Shango 4680, later prototype of the Oya 3865, both preceded by Lei Gong 1900; all devices that mimic natural weather. The Shango 4680 has improvements on insulation, charging, and manageability."

"Who sent you?" Halliday asked, clearly shaken.

"I am sure you'll discover in no time." Bolanle replied. The device strummed with power in her hand, it felt uncontrollable, wild, and she wasn't sure she could hold it for much longer.

Bolanle felt the tentative touch of Jemila's hand and their fingers intertwined.

"Jemila Kayode!" Halliday roared her name. He was furious now. "You think you can escape, I know where you live! I know who your parents are. All the others who left will be back here."

Bolanle pushed the button that activated the Shango 4680. There was a moment of stillness, then what looked like a bolt of lightning shot out from the weapon. Obviously, the device still needed more work because she missed her mark, instead of hitting Halliday it veered off to his right, incinerating five men and leaving the others around them maimed with third degree burns. Jemila took advantage of the flashy distraction and used her *ofe* power, dragging Bolanle along with her.

They appeared in Jemila's apartment, floating in the air for a few seconds before landing painfully on top Jemila's bed.

"That was a poor landing," Bolanle joked, wincing as she tried to sit up.

Rafeeat Aliyu

"I've never been pushed like this before," was Jemila's reply.

There was a stretch of silence as they both tried to calm their breathing and fully take in the night's events.

Rafeeat Aliyu is an African flying machine with a home base located in Abuja, Nigeria. She is a freelance writer and blogger whose varied interests include listening to Japanese folk metal music; researching on African and world history; picking up new languages; watching Korean historical dramas; cooking spicy dishes and meditating on the Yoruba cosmos. 'Ofe!' is her first published short story.

Claws and Savages

Martin Stokes

The Fresh pulled up to the curb, its air-jets blowing up drifts of newly fallen autumn leaves. The door of the Fresh—white with a red decal depicting a man tipping his fedora in a gesture of thanks—opened and Sonny Mathis folded himself out.

It was cold, he noted. Dark fingers of twilight had crept into the day and the temperature had dropped considerably. He was wearing a cobalt blue suit, very expensive, but thin. His jaw, rigidly square—not, however to the point where it made him look slow or obtuse—and scrubbed with stubble, was shadowed in the dying light of day. Only when they caught that ephemeral light did his faded blue eyes shine.

He tipped the cabby who in turn touched the bill of his hat, just like the man on the decal. Hands tucked beneath his armpits; he watched the Fresh rise half a metre or so off the road then cruise down to the corner, pulling up leaves and other debris in its wake.

Sonny let out a tendon-creaking yawn and walked up the path to his apartment building. Before he reached the steps, he looked up. It always marvelled and, to some degree, mystified him how these buildings were so tall. His apartment building was one-hundred-and-seventy-four stories high, and he stayed thirty from the top. But architecture wasn't his game, God no. Let the builders do the building and the dealers do the dealing. Far above, shooting back and forth like arrows fired from various directions at once, were clouds of various different kinds of Fresh.

He snapped his gaze back to ground level and went inside. It was warmer and he let his arms fall to his sides. The lobby was large and empty, nothing stood in its cream vastness save for the elevator at the far end. Sonny approached it, his crocodile-leather shoes—genuine, no room for imitations—clicking and clacking on the marble floor as he went.

He blinked twice, and then brought his eye up to the iris-scanner. Grids of light criss-crossed his eye briefly and then the elevator doors slid open soundlessly. He stepped inside, not bothering to check behind, as was his normal routine. He was shattered. The elevator was his palladium and for the moment, all he wanted was a long hot shower and a whiskey.

The lift rose automatically and, like everything in this day and age, silently. The elevator was bare like the lobby.

Architects, Sonny thought in a tone that would have sounded both weary and wondrous had it been spoken aloud. The lift took exactly eighty-three seconds to reach floor 144. He closed his eyes and let the last few days play on the screen of his mind.

The job had gone well, more than well, in fact. Sonny had left Windsor ten days ago; hours after the ITAPO had tried in vain to bring him down at the high court in Cape Town. Sonny had kept a calm yet determined demeanour and denied all charges. He had never been scared; his lawyers were the best and he paid the Judge forty-thousand cash each month just in the event of such an occurrence.

In a way, the ITAPO had done him a favour. The star-port that departed to Terra-Five was a few kilometres down the road from the court. He'd managed to get the impending lawsuit—well, the first part of it—out of the way, as well as get on that cruiser. Killing two birds with one stone was the kind of way Sonny liked to operate; efficient and smooth, kind of the like the elevator he was in now.

Lenard Landon, the CEO and chief spokesperson of ITAPO, had scowled and said they'd get him sooner or later. He was rich, yes, he was powerful, doubly so, but he

Claws and Savages

was still a goddamn crook, and all crooks felt the impersonal and solid hand of justice eventually.

Sonny had put on the most affected look he could muster, then leaned in and had said, "I'd love to see you try." Low enough so the cameras couldn't hear him over the babble of reporters and journalists crowding the court's stairs.

"I'll get you. See if I don't. Filth." Landon's eyes, large and bulging behind his rimless glasses, had burned with a brief and intense hatred before he whirled and huffed away through the parting crowd.

The elevator came to a stop and Sonny opened his eyes. The doors did not open on a passage or a hall, but straight into Sonny's lounge. It wasn't an ordinary apartment block. Windsor used to be nothing but a small fishing village dozing away some hundred kilometres east of Cape Town. After the other major cities started getting a bit too crowded, development started elsewhere. Property prices skyrocketed, businesses thrived, and the majorly rich moved in. That is why Sonny owned the entire 144th floor of this building and not a few frugal rooms like other residents.

The first thing he noticed when he walked into the lounge was the temperature: it was cold. No, compared to the warmth of the elevator it was goddamn freezing. He saw the source at once. On the far side of the room, where there was no wall and only a huge stretch of glass that gave way to a smoky vista of the city, was an open window. The curtain that hung before it billowed like a woman's skirt.

Sonny walked towards the open window thinking how strange it was but feeling something come alive at the back of his mind. That something said, *be careful, Sonny* in a solicitous tone that made him look around suddenly. He always closed the windows before he left and if he didn't temperature-control should have done it automatically. The wind was always blowing at such a high altitude and it was always cold, too. The architects must have messed up somehow; maybe a circuit blew in their regulation board or a rat chewed its way through a cable. God knew there were enough rats in the slums; and the slums seemed to be expanding every year like some sort of encroaching disease.

His hand reached out and he let it hover over the window for a second. Maybe it was booby-trapped. Maybe the second he applied pressure on the glass, the sweat from his fingers would make contact with an invisible tripwire and there would be a loud hollow boom before his guts hit the walls.

He latched the window shut, and the room began heat almost immediately. There was no reaction of any kind and Sonny let out his breath that he didn't know he was holding in a shuddery rush. Why was he so jumpy? He chalked it down to exhaustion and let himself relax a little more.

The sun was just a set of smouldering shoulders on the horizon now, scattering gold and orange rays that lit up the smog so that it momentarily appeared to be a cloud of gold. Then the light shifted and it was only choking smog again. It was better to be up here, safe, better than down there in slums with the savages.

Tossing his jacket on the back of a black divan he made his way through to the kitchen. It was a fair walk, too. The lounge was vast and scarcely furnished, save for a few pot plants and some modern furniture an interior decorator had suggested. Less is more, he said, but Sonny thought that was a load of shit, less was less and there was no way around it. The carpet that covered the room was a lush green and reminded him of the fields he had hunted in as a kid.

His father—from whom he had inherited the failing business before resurrecting it—had taken him to a game farm once, when the Kruger National Park still had animals. There, he had taught Sonny how to track game;

Claws and Savages

how to sling a rifle and aim down its sight; how to kill with one shot—through the heart and lungs—so that it was clean and the animal died with dignity. That's kind of what inspired him to do his carpets this way. After all, the passion his father had ignited in him through hunting had started his other multi-million rand business. Questions of legality aside, it was still a profitable field of trade.

He poured himself a stiff drink, downed it in one gulp, poured another and went to shower. He paused in his bedroom for a moment and stared at the large white talon that had once been attached to a Claw, which stood mounted in a glass case on his wall. He had almost lost his life getting that particular trophy and he kept it there as a reminder.

While the water trickled hot down his body his mind began to wander. It often did when he was in that little cubicle and the water was a steady and monotonous roar in his ears.

After the court case, he had motored straight down to the Starport in a Fresh with his company logo, Mathis Matters Transport, slapped on the side. Karl was waiting for him there. Karl had come from a slum once called Mitchell's Plain, in Cape Town City. Now, however, all the gang activity that had once been present had poured a solid stream of income into the place. It had been a classic trickle-down effect. Drug production and sales peaked, rich crime bosses got richer, and all the blood money involved was run through legitimate businesses to wash it clean. Eventually when the drugs and everything that followed in its wake decamped, the affluence remained. The suburb had undergone extensive development over the years, turning it into something of similar stature to Windsor. Karl, a dapper, very punctual man, had been staring at his wristwatch when the Fresh pulled up beside him.

Sonny stepped out and they shook hands. "All ready?"

Martin Stokes

"Yes, everything's arranged." Karl's voice went tight for a moment. "How did it go with Landon?"

Sonny laughed. "Like always, he's no closer to touching me than he is to losing his virginity."

Karl smiled thinly. He never laughed, and that was something that made you uneasy about him. There was always a look behind his narrow eyes as if he might be planning a hundred ways to dispose of your body.

"Well that's good, very good. The cruiser is waiting, when you're ready." He gestured towards a large hanger where a cruiser stood, its engine warbling and pulsing in vermillion cycles.

"Equipment?" Sonny asked.

"Two long range rifles—under the pretence of photographic equipment. And four pairs of thermal goggles—no excuse needed."

"Excellent, let's go."

They didn't need to have an alibi for the goggles. When you went to Terra-Five they were just about mandatory. The Claws could see you but without goggles, you couldn't see them, and if they scratched you... if the toxin in those talons were to mingle with your blood... Well, your insides would become your outsides and blood and other unspeakable matter would begin oozing out from every hole possible.

But no one had been scratched this trip. The pilot had taken them up without any problems. Sonny's stomach flipped over a few times when the real acceleration had begun—until they were going at one sixth of the speed of light—but that was normal. He'd made the trip so many times he only gave it cursory attention. The bounty was especially good this time around and they'd made the trip back with enough Product to fuel a slum's superstitious belief for a year. Of course, he never sold to just one slum; that would be needlessly risky, not to mention stupid. No, when the giving was good, you spread it around just like it was Christmas.

Claws and Savages

He stepped out of the shower. Blowers dried him off and he dressed himself in a loose-fitting white cotton shirt and pair of black slacks. Headed for another drink he paused to look at the talon. Its flesh, which was hard and rippled, wasn't what the apothecaries and shamans paid for and in turn sold to the ever oblivious public in the form of sham medicines. It was the talon itself, all eight centimetres of dull claw, and the venom inside, which kept business flowing.

There had been a proliferation of the medicines derived from Claw talons over the last few years. This was mostly due to the fact that there had been a proliferation in what the people in Windsor called Dark Lung. Years of inhaling the spent fossil fuels and the thick clouds of smog that hung over the cities and slums like malicious clouds, finally took its toll on a growing percentage of the population. Cell degradation began in the alveoli, turned it black, like something charred, and eventually spread through the entire respiratory system. It wasn't unusual to see someone sneeze out bits of ebon lung tissue with a spray of blood.

Conventional medicines were expensive and hard to come by unless, of course, you were of the extreme rich like Sonny Mathis. The slums had turned to traditional methods, grinding up Claw talons into powders and potions just as the Vietnamese had done in the past with rhino horn. It was still expensive, of course, because Claws weren't from Earth, but the dosage needed was miniscule in comparison to modern healing techniques. Most of them relied on illegal apothecaries and shamans who preached its wonderful healing powers to get their fix, and those little shysters relied on Sonny Mathis to procure them Product. Sonny, in turn, went to Terra-Five where he hunted those unsettlingly hard-to-find Claws and returned with the bounty a week or two later. It was illegal, and he knew it. Lenard Landon knew it, too, which is why he was

Martin Stokes

constantly on Sonny's arse like some bloodhound that smelled a hidden cache of heroin.

Sonny stepped into the lounge again and that's when he knew something was wrong. Dark had fallen and on this level, above the bright smog that blanketed the suburbs, the stars shone brightly like cold chips of ice. Something was very out of tilt. As a hunter most of his life, Sonny's senses were keenly attuned. Besides, but for the occasional visit from a friend or girl, he had stayed alone in this apartment. He knew every sound and echo that rebounded from the still emptiness of the lounge when he walked on the carpet, dampened though it was. But now, the echoes came back... shorter. They were matted sounds, clipped parodies. Also, there was a pressure difference usually attributed to someone being in the room. But there was no one... or not that he could see.

Then he saw the note lying on the low coffee table that sat encircled by the three divans. Sonny walked over briskly and scooped it up. The paper was expensive, its edge gilded with gold. There were only eight words on the page, written in a thin and cultured cursive:

I told you I would get you, poacher.

"Landon!" Sonny hissed and whirled around.

There was a sudden bright flare of pain in his calf. He looked down just in time to see a chunk of his left calf blink into seeming nothingness as the flesh tore free, hung suspended in the air for half a second, and then began to separate itself into ragged strips before disappearing entirely.

He felt a weight on his shoulder and his lacerated leg buckled. The shirt split open by his neckline then there was a sharp and digging pain just above Sonny's collarbone. Blood spilled out of both wounds, turning his shirt crimson and making his pants look blacker. He understood what was happening then with lucid clarity. He also understood that in a few seconds if he didn't act, he would be dead.

Claws and Savages

He threw himself on the floor, as close to his bedroom as he could and felt the weight on his shoulder dissipate. There was a crazy *flapping* sound, the sound of wings trying to expand and contract in a closed space, and he started crawling fervently. He couldn't run, he was pretty sure of that, blood was flowing freely from his leg, staining the carpet, so that had to mean it was a deep wound. Even crawling was an onerous task. Every time he placed his weight on his right wrist he felt his shoulder scream in agony. Just where were they? And why did he make the lounge so goddamn *big?*

He felt a tugging at his foot and the next moment his shoe was pried off and being ripped to shreds amidst some shrill and terrible shrieking. It saved his life, perhaps, gave him enough of a lead to get to safety before they lost whatever marginal interest they had in the shoe and zoned in on him again. He ignored the pain, drowned it out with his own survival instincts greater and more urgent than physical needs, crying out every time he shimmied forward.

At last, the door was in grasp. He risked a look backwards and saw nothing, of course, except... a shimmering, like the air that rises from a highway on a hot day. He pulled himself inside with every bit of strength he possessed, veins bulging in thick cords on his neck and forearms, and slammed the door shut. A second later, a plethora of sharp pecking sounds like a stuttering machinegun peppered the door.

Sonny lay on the floor, breath whistling in and out of his lungs in wheezing gasps like those stricken with Dark Lung. White spots danced in front of his eyes and he felt on the verge of passing out. *No.* With sheer effort that few men could have managed, he held on to consciousness—if he passed out now he would die from an excessive loss of blood or if what was out there got in. And just what was out there? He thought he knew, but the real question was how had they gotten here? Not just to Earth but to the

Martin Stokes

144th floor of a Windsor suburb apartment. Sonny had a certain hunch that it had to do with a bespectacled man by the name of Lenard Landon.

I told you I would get you, poacher.

But how? How had Landon managed to get Claws—he knew there was more than one from the simultaneous attack—into his apartment? Then Sonny remembered the open window, the chill. He scolded himself for not realising at first, but he had been so damn tired. Not now though, now his senses were awake and on fire. They had obviously come through the window. Why had they not attacked at first?

"Easy. They only hunt at night," Sonny said flatly to no one in particular.

Using his king-sized bed as a crutch, he got up haltingly on his good leg, and then hopped over to his walk-in wardrobe. He whipped a belt from the belt rail and looped it into a makeshift tourniquet. He took the first good look at his calf wound. It was deep, but thankfully, neither it, nor the shoulder injury had been scratched or torn at by those things' talons. He wrapped the belt just above his knee and pulled it taut, baring his teeth as the pain briefly became unbearable.

It helped, but it was still issuing a little blood. The walk-in closet led to the bathroom. Sonny hobbled there, using the wall as balance. He turned on the bath and doused his leg and shoulder in cold water. He took off his shirt, tore strips of cotton from it and bandaged his wounds. In the mirror, which took up an entire wall of the room, he saw a crazed and battle-hardened warrior, not a human at all really, but a savage, something that belonged...

Of course. They came from the city zoo. There were no Claws on Earth except for the two kept in captivity. Who did he know that controlled the zoo and ran campaigns there monthly to get rid of scum such as him? The Inter-Terra-Anti-Poaching-Organisation, or ITAPO, headed by that most charismatic of fellows, Mr. Langdon.

Claws and Savages

Sonny decided right there, staring at himself in the mirror, that the second he made it out of this mess he was going to pay Langdon a visit, and remove his fingernails one by one with a pair of pliers. He uttered a crazed bark of laughter at this thought and lurched back into his bedroom.

There was a .50 Desert Eagle that he kept in his bedside drawer. It was an old weapon, sure, but it still worked and would put a hole big enough to stargaze through in anything it hit. He looked at it appraisingly, feeling its comfortable weight in his hand, inched back towards the door, and pressed his ear against the wood.

Silence.

In sudden inspiration, he went back to his bedside table, picked up the phone that lay there and called Karl. He answered on the second ring.

"Listen, Karl. I'm in some serious shit here." Sonny said quickly into the receiver.

"What kind?" Karl said immediately.

"They're Claws, two of them, in my lounge."

"Claws?" He said, incredulous. "Are you sure, Sonny? There aren't any-"

"They're from Langdon." Sonny said.

"I see."

"Bring help, man. Hurry."

There was a click in Sonny's ear and that undoubtedly meant that Karl was on it. He felt he could relax a little more now, knowing that there was some sort of cavalry coming. Before he could proceed any further on how to deal with the Claws outside of his door, his mind insisted he figure out how they got in there in the first place. Landon sent them; there was no question in the matter. The courts couldn't bring down Sonny Mathis, hunter of the ever-diminishing population of Claws, so Landon had taken it into his own hands. An image flashed across his mind, startlingly clear, of Landon and a few of the handlers from the city zoo hovering next to his apartment in a Fresh, emptying the contents of bulging burlap sacks through his open window only to have apparently nothing fall out of them. It was plausible, but who opened the window?

Why, the ones who had power over all the buildings, of course: the architects.

Sonny had always known that Landon had a serious agenda and a little power, but enough to sway the opinions of the architects? He wracked his brain and found no other solution, unless it was just a fluke in the system and his window opened randomly... but, no, he just couldn't see that happening. Landon must have somehow convinced the architects it would be better if Sonny became bird food.

"Well, I'll make *you* bird food, Mr. Animal-Lover Landon," Sonny said, smiling and looking at the silver gun in his hands. Speaking to yourself isn't one of the healthiest habits to ever develop, Sonny knew, but right now he didn't much care.

He crossed back to the door and listened again, still nothing. He rapped his knuckles softly on the expensive mahogany that could have fed a family in the slums for a year. The barrage of pecking on the door started again at once. Sonny started and took a step back on his bad leg in reflex. He screamed and felt a dull anger rise inside him. The number of these things he had killed on Terra-Five was almost laudable and now there were two, just two, making a fool out of him.

He levelled the ancient weapon towards the sounds of the pecking and fired twice. The weapon gave an enormous kick. The sound was deafening in the closed room, but Sonny could still hear the screams of an injured Claw. He'd hit one! He hit the bastard!

He lurched forward and peered through one of the holes he'd made in the door. There, lying sprawled in the passage, its great head lolling on the green carpet, was a dead Claw. Watching a Claw die was a beautiful thing under other circumstances. Whatever gland made it invisible shut down, and the bird materialised; from the inside to its glistening coat of feathers.

One wing of the purest white was folded on the other like someone saying a prayer while lying on their side. An eye, red as a hot coal, stared sightlessly at the ceiling. In its chest was a hole the size of a bagel and blood, sickly and black like tar, oozed out.

Sonny whooped in triumph, and then the eye he'd been looking through the hole with—his left—was veiled with a red film before darkness succeeded it. The pain was enormous and ripped through him, throwing him on his back, screaming. One hand came up to the spot where his eye was a minute before and touched on horrid emptiness.

He looked back towards the door and saw his eye swinging like pendulum by the optic nerve from the blood-covered beak that had stolen it from him poked through the hole in the door. The beak opened and closed like scissors and the eye was gone. Sonny fired blindly a few more times until there was nothing but dry clicks when he squeezed the trigger, but all missed. The Claw went silent again.

Shakily, he propped himself up on one elbow. Blood gushed freely from the socket, running down his chest in rivulets and pooling in between his legs. It was bad now, very bad. For the first time since this whole ordeal began, Sonny acknowledged the fact that Landon might actually win and he might die at the hands of that which he had hunted with such ardour.

He collapsed on his back again and, through his remaining eye, the world began to move in slow grey waves. His eye darted around the room looking for anything that might help. There was nothing really. The large bed, two bedside tables each with a lamp propped on their surfaces, various paintings, a few windows arranged in a circular pattern that looked out on the indifferent disc of moon in the sky, and the encased Claw talon mounted on the wall. There his eye froze and a thought whispered across his mind, as silent as a snake moving through tall grass. The thought was that the religious maniacs sometimes used the talon for the healing of grievous wounds as well as for diseases. He pushed the thought away. He was the pusher after all, the pusher!—not the user blindly consuming a phoney medicine that had no proven effects, benign or malignant.

"Stop it," Sonny groaned. "Just stop it. Karl will be along soon, yes. Karl will bring help. Karl will kill that fucking thing in the lounge."

He was talking to himself again, but that was alright. Any concerns he might have had about his sanity were now just flickering sparks in the distance behind. The world began to darken and all Sonny was aware of before he passed out was a shadow on the moon, looking absurdly like the horn of a rhino.

What woke him was the blaring drone of the phone ringing from faraway. It was hard, so hard, to swim up from the depths of unconsciousness, but something—maybe his lascivious lust for revenge, or maybe nothing more than sheer instinct to survive—forced him. The ringing sounded like the sea heard when you held a shell to your ear, warped and distant. Eventually the sounds began to discern themselves into sharp tenors. His head felt like a leaden weight, the blank socket where his eye had once nested was a fierce and burning crater. Sonny realised with unsurprised rue that he couldn't feel his left leg. What a mess.

The phone continued to ring and to Sonny it sounded like insane laughter coming from maybe the architects, maybe Landon, maybe both. He pulled himself to the bedside table where the phone lay by digging his elbows into the carpet and shimmying forward. Tired was not the right word to describe how he felt once he had managed this journey, exhausted was closer but still not quite there. He felt bone-weary right down to the marrow.

Claws and Savages

He lifted his arm—it seemed to weigh about a thousand kilos—and tried to grab the telephone. He succeeded only in swiping it to the floor where it was more accessible. He groped blindly for the receiver and somehow managed to hold it to his ear.

"Please tell me good news, Karl." Sonny rasped in a thin voice.

"I'm afraid there is no good news, poacher," said the cool and easy voice of Lenard Langdon. "Not for you, anyway."

Sonny again felt no surprise, only a dull pulsing anger. "I killed one. I killed one of those Claws you sent for me."

There was an uncertain pause and then Langdon said simply, "I told you I would get you."

Sonny breathed into the receiver and said nothing.

Langdon continued glee in his voice. "Since the judge was up to his eyeballs in your filthy money, I had to take the matter even higher. I doubt you had a clue who you were playing with in the first place, Mr. Mathis. That's beside the point, I guess. The architects seem to agree with my view and they all thought you'd be better off... decommissioned." There was undeniable pleasure in the last word. "A simple window. I doubt you realise how much sway I needed for that. It was worth it, all of it."

Sonny could just imagine Langdon pushing his glasses back up the ridge of his nose as he spoke and burst into laughter. He couldn't help it; hilarity was a welcome visitor in all this chaos.

Langdon sounded suddenly like an offended child. "What?" He said sharply. "What is so goddamn funny?"

"It's just... just-" A tear spilled out of Sonny's eye, cutting a track through the gore on his cheek. "You're such a nerd!" He burst out, and laughed harder than ever.

He dropped the receiver and realised he wouldn't be able to pick it back up again. That was alright though, that was just fine. Laughter continued to boom out of him in ragged caws. Then Sonny didn't know if he was crying or screaming. It tapered off to a wracking sob. He curled up his right leg up to his chest—the left one wouldn't work no matter how hard he willed it—wrapped his arms around it and wept like a little baby, not being able to understand how quickly his ruin had come.

Karl wasn't coming, he saw forlornly. How could he? He couldn't pass the iris-scanner and since he wasn't the police or fire-department, he didn't have override codes. He wasn't coming and Sonny had neither the strength and will, nor the firepower, to fight the remaining Claw. Unless he somehow managed to stitch himself up, there was no hope. He had no medical supplies in his bathroom, no bandages, no medicine of any kind. Or...

His eye, bloodshot and bulging, flicked to the talon on the wall. It was such a widely used cure; it had to work, didn't it? The very apartment he was dying in was proof of that. If the demand wasn't so high, he couldn't have sold so much Product to pay for it. Majority rules, right? Right?

He looked through the hole in the door and darkness gleamed on the other side. It took Sonny six minutes to get into a sitting position—he was so weak!—and another three to get the lamp off the bedside table. With every remaining fibre of strength that remained, he hurled the lamp at the glass that held the talon. There was a tinkle as the glass fell inward and the talon thumped to the floor next to his leg.

He looked at it wonderingly and with rekindled hope. Of course it would work. It couldn't not work. He could still beat Langdon, could draw strength from this marvel and dispel the impotence he felt now. He could win.

The shamans Sonny had seen preparing the talon usually ground it on a rough stone before adding the powder to some boiling water. Sonny didn't have any such apparatus so he settled for popping the entire thing in his mouth. It tasted flat and stony. He could feel the strength flowing back in to him instantly!

Claws and Savages

The sharp point of one claw punctured his tongue but Sonny hardly noticed. He only sucked at the stony talon as the poison worked its way into his blood and shot through his veins.

He thought of a random occurrence then. It had happened when he was eleven. His father had taken him on a trip to the Kruger Park before poachers had completely broken down its ecosystem. They had been on a game drive, in the back of a Jeep riding through the thorny and unforgiving bush. The brakes slammed on and Sonny was thrown rudely against the back of the front seat. Ahead of them and slightly to the left, four men were taking a chainsaw to an unconscious—or perhaps dead—rhino's horn. Sonny had forgotten about this memory almost entirely, but now it swarmed back with alarming force. The sound of that chainsaw chewing through the horn of that rhino perforated through the air. They had loaded it on a waiting truck and fled while the rhino's blood turned the earth muddy. Sonny had looked on in horror and thought they were disgusting, how fucking downright *disgusting* those savages were.

It was this thought that rang truer than any others did as Sonny Mathis's cells began to break down and blood burst from every orifice in his broken body. He died frowning as if in thought, the talon of one Claw protruding from his mouth like some sort of alien doorknob.

Later, Langdon and three burly hired men came to remove the other Claw, each with a pair of thermal goggles over their eyes and a long electrified stick that would paralyse anything it touched. They found the room empty except for the beautiful bird and Sonny's body. They also found a shattered hole in the bay window. The other Claw had fled after blinding Sonny, believing its prey to be dead. Sonny, in a dead faint at that time, had heard neither its farewell shrieks nor the smashing of glass as it left.

Martin Stokes

Martin Stokes is a 20-year-old student and bartender. He likes Science Fiction and Romance… but has a love of the night and the restless wind and the pawing dead, Horror, in a word. 'Claws and Savages', is his second published short story and concerns itself with a future South Africa that shares similarities with today's one.

To Gaze at the Sun

Clifton Gachagua

Stanislaw was different. In the moments after he pressed the bell on 126 Distribution Road, he saw himself wake up alone, unaware that he was just another child of the war. Around his wrist was a band imprinted with the initials AMISON. A vast desert stretched out in front of him, so vast he was sure he was in a place without a beginning or end. Populated with magnificent dunes, the Nabi desert was a finite possibility of mirages, and a sense of nothingness that filled his heart. It stretched out to hug the horizon, encircling it like a diaphragm. Stanislaw began to imagine dying in a place like this, irretrievable, completely alone between the blue of the sky and the burnt sienna of the sand, and he felt a calmness travelling up his body and finally manifesting as a smile. He tilted his head to one direction as if to inspect the desert. No concussion. His memory felt intact. He could see clearly. His eyes were green and soon enough the liquid under them would be swallowed up by the sun's heat. His lips felt strange as he ran a wet tongue on the roughness encroaching on them. He was buried up to his shins; if he had woken up an hour later he might have found himself buried in prehistoric sand.

"Stanis," he heard a gentle voice speak to him. "Stanis, are you there?" He opened his eyes to meet those of his mother. She was smiling at him. Her eyes, at once detached and intimate, were teary. They made him think of cadmium.

The eyes were the first thing he had noticed about Atemi, his mother to be, when she came to open the door. Soon enough he noticed his father's too. Although the intensity varied, he noticed his parents had dark, grey eyes where the iris and the white of the eye converged towards the same colour. He compared them against his own green eyes. He could not stand to look into the eyes of his mother, which confronted him with a constant sadness, as if a dark cloud had found a permanent home in them. When his mother looked into his green eyes, he thought she seemed to make out a hint of something so obscure and perfectly hidden that she must have interpreted it as a symptom for a new disease from her subtle reaction. So mother and son found a major fault in each other.

"Stanis, welcome home," she added. The desert began to retract into itself like an animal going into hiding in a dark cave. Gradually the dunes became minute and the sound of the winds disappeared. The living face of a woman who kept calling his name now replaced the inanimate wilderness in which he had first woken up. This transmission was difficult he wanted to stay in the desert.

"Stanis, do you know who I am?"

"You are my mother," Stanis replied.

"That's right. And what do you say to your mother when you meet her for the first time?"

Stanis stayed mute.

Atemi led Stanis to the dinner table. She felt the rate of her heartbeat begin to slacken. She let her husband, Murungu, take her hand in his, her fingers were cold.

She had prepared an additive and preservative free meal of chopped lamb and yellow rice. The meal had cost a lot but she was not going to spare any expense in welcoming home her new installation.

Atemi and Murungu sat across the table watching Stanis, who in turn stared at them. There was the appearance of an unusually thick film of tears across his eyes, giving the impression of a child who had been wronged.

Atemi watched as he unwrapped a lollipop from a bowl of sweets in the middle of the dinner table. He put out his tongue and licked the lollipop, instead of sucking it in his mouth. She began to panic. Maybe something had gone wrong during his post-processing. Maybe they forgot to

To Gaze at the Sun

adjust a certain mutation, causing him to develop a rare condition whose sole symptom was a preoccupation with confectionaries: there he was, sitting at the table, licking his lollipop. His lip-smacking irritated her. It broke her heart.

She studied the hair at the back of her son's head. This installation was definitely not normal. Outward, he was what Vita Nova had promised. He had all the signs of a healthy son: five fingers, five toes, and an upright posture. As far as morphology was concerned, their new son was a perfect grade. However, he did not react how new sons were supposed to react; his speech sounded like it had to travel through many places before it reached her. She knew this because they had been to so many welcome home parties thrown for the sons of their friends. She had observed these sons come home with complete speech and immediate adaption to life at home and in the battlefields. They answered all questions, said thank you after meals, stood with their hands crossed at their back, said excuse me when they were going to bed, and in the morning they were at the table with a napkin around the neck, politely waiting for breakfast. She studied his green eyes. A few minutes with him and she already hated them. She did not touch her food. She squeezed her husband's hand harder.

Atemi and Murungu had been waiting for a son for twenty-one years now. She managed to contain their suffering within the boundaries of their property at 126 Distribution Road, and so she was chirpy and civil when they went beyond the house to celebrate whenever one of their friends received a son. Her social circle extended from 100-150 Distribution Road, Lokichogio, or Route 204A—constructed as a joint project of the Kenyan, South Sudan, and Egyptian governments—and part of a trans-highway connecting Lokichogio to Juba, Khartoum, and Alexandria. In essence, all homes along the highway had a number between 1 and 65789.

Clifton Gachagua

Apart from a few trinkets placed here and there, the general outlook of the houses remained the same across the three countries, a honeycomb of houses with red doors and ascending numerals. Within Kenya it was known as Distribution Road. Atemi had been meaning to look up what it was called in Juba or Khartoum, she thought that it oddly felt like the road connected her to other women; that she could always pop in to her Arab neighbours to talk about the rising price of sedatives or powder milk in the common market.

Murungu, too, wanted his own son to send to the desert war in the North. While he had to do without a son for two decades, some couples were on their fourth installation, boasting of how their sons had died in the war. He let go of Atemi's cold hand to focus on his dinner.

It had made him sad to live without the presence of an installation in his house when all around them sons were leaving their front porches to go to the war. Standing at the railway terminal, waving goodbye to their friends' sons, he wanted to have it all, to know what it meant to send a son to the war. His friends told him it was just a formality, that it did not mean anything beyond the burden of dealing with an empty room and extra food supplies the sons left behind, but he still wanted to experience this formality. The sons were sent out to war and after two years they came back to ring the bells of their respective berths. For those whose bells did not ring it meant that their sons had been obliterated in the war. This was not completely distressing; the only thing that annoyed parents whose children died was looking for another name for a son to be sent in a month.

As he chewed on the lamb, he thought about how some data mining companies conducted thorough market surveillance and were aware of this problem, and proposed sending sons with predetermined names. The companies used data from the increasingly frequent national surveys—collected by the Bureau of Statistics, which had installed TeleData in every house, or tendered to the same data miners (whose CFOs were the retired generals of the war in the North). It took the data miners a day to validate that the sons were no more, and another twenty-eight to generate another. The only rule the government had passed was this: no replicas. They too, like God perhaps, did not believe in two installations being exactly alike. A seventeen-year-old boy would show up at the door, ring the bell and ask if he had the right address. If indeed, he was at the right place, he would as stipulated in the manual, go ahead to proclaim: 'I'm your son now.'

Murungu worked for one of the data miners, Envision, where he was a long-serving employee, in the Sperm Mobility department. HR had offered him retirement but he held on because the company meant he could spend time away from a house without a son, away from Atemi's passive resentment.

One night during the early months of their marriage, he had had too much to drink and lost a bet, which changed the rest of his life. He bet against his mortgage plan and almost lost the house to a colleague. The government had strict regulations against leaving installations in the care of couples who didn't own a house. He was always aware of this and although she did not remind him verbally; she had a way of showing it in the distracted way in which she made love to him. Her tongue was always cold when they kissed.

He did not realise that he had been staring at an empty plate. When he looked up Atemi and the installation were watching him. He moved his seat closer to her, staring at her hands. They too were always cold.

When the first installation of Stanislaw showed up at 126 Distribution Road, Murungu was overcome with joy. They almost had full ownership of the house, which was good enough for the government. All his years of waiting finally rewarded. He planned to shower him with the rarest frankincense and myrrh, to spoil him beyond their means.

Clifton Gachagua

But Stanis' first day at home was not what he had so frivolously imagined. The installation appeared dreamy. He walked slowly. His fingers lingered for a few moments just before they picked up a cup or container, like a still life artist setting up his objects. When he picked up an object, he contemplated it before walking over to the dinner table where his crestfallen mother was waiting.

After dinner, Atemi and Murungu accompanied Stanis to his upstairs room. At the landing, Stanis paused, turned around and took in the expansive sitting room. Atemi paused behind him following his eyes, unaware of the mad stupor hidden behind them. She heard Murungu yawn behind her. This startled Stanis, who resumed the climb up the stairs, running his hands across the curlicue metal of the railing. She watched from the door as her son prepared for bed, changing into blue pyjamas and tucking himself in.

"Goodnight Stanis," Atemi said. She stood outside his room, at the promontory, as if she were afraid of tipping over the edge to where her son lay motionless and unresponsive, his unblinking eyes seemingly fascinated by the off-white ceiling. She could feel her husband's breath on her neck.

Atemi lay in bed rehearsing for a dream, her husband on the other side of the bed feigning sleep. She had been having the same dream for twenty-one years. There was always a doorbell ringing downstairs. She started down the stairs and the doorbell would continue to ring with increasing frequency but she never found her way to the miracle downstairs. The winding stairs became a never-ending spiral descending into a dark pit. She would wake up and cry quietly, to avoid waking her husband. Through years of training she had learnt how not to wake up screaming.

In the morning, Atemi woke up alone. Her husband had left for work. She ran her hand over his side of the bed, where his weight had left a slight impression on the

To Gaze at the Sun

mattress. Atemi thought about the conspiracies that cropped up between them, separating their suffering and plunging them deeper into the darkness that was their parenting. She could not remember the last time they had breakfast together. She thought about a reclusive Murungu, working at his desk, going through strangers' daily tasks turned into standard deviations and mapped onto graphs, occasionally fingering the silver-framed photograph of her on his desk. If only they could map their lives on a graph, see what needed to be fixed.

Later that day Atemi was sitting at the island in the kitchen, an IV stuck to the back of her left arm transmitting a cocktail of hormones for her daily reverse HRT regiment—the oestrogen derived from the urine of pregnant mares—into her system, stretching her face muscles as the hormones effused. She watched Stanislaw, who seemed to be always looking out the window. She waited for spite to rise up out of her throat, she imagined her spindly fingers picking up kitchenware and hurling it at him; but she was incapable of ascending to the great silence hanging around him, coveting him like the night sky. She was giving up. All she could do was irrigate her body with the hormones.

Atemi consulted with her husband when he came back from work. She abandoned the identity education she had planned for Stanis. It would be inappropriate to teach him how to clean a gun while he insisted on sitting in the garden, fingering the magnolias and licking his lollipop. She wanted to teach him some housekeeping, like how to key in variables in the Unit Control, which kept a log of all completed chores and maintained a cool and fungal-free air in the house, but he lingered too long at each circle on the touch-pads, fascinated by the numbers. All her plans would have to be restructured around the likes and dislikes of the installation. She was too eager not to disappoint Stanis, to make the best use of the opportunity to be a model parent and maybe invite her friends for one of his birthdays later that year. So far, she only knew he disliked chopped lamb and yellow rice—she made a note to try out blue spice in the rice—and that he liked to sleep.

Stanislaw knew he needed to be awake, to always be awake. He knew this from the moment they gave him his first address and he looked at the mug shots of his parents. They were old and the last of their kind. Sometimes when he slept he dreamed about killing his guardians. The urge to kill his guardians persisted into his waking world. They were weak, not set for life in this era. The company told him it was a privilege to have guardians from that other time. He knew Vita Nova was his first and only home, and soon he was supposed to go to war. The company did not tell him more about the couple; they were not very forthcoming with the details of guardianship.

Stanislaw was present when the company told the couple that he was new, that they were his first custodians. The truth is they had regenerated Stanis from a different installation, a young lieutenant who had been a hero in the war. The government had told them to leave the most primal memories intact, to leave memories that inspired the instincts of war and survival in the children, and do away with such things as the death instinct. The company could not do this without leaving the children with other memories. That is why all he thought about was the desert where the installation on which he was based had been to war. He was not aware that he came haunted with the debris of war memories. He had carried their photographs in his shirt pocket and left to find the inhabitants of 126 Distribution Road.

But when he got there all he could do at first was sleep. He always woke up tired. He dreamt about battlefields in their totality. The state of his memory was that it did not linger on specifics. He dreamt about large tracts of sand and the vague shapes of dead bodies. The garden was his second preoccupation when the sleeping bouts ended. He was happy to sit in the garden at night when the guardians

To Gaze at the Sun

were asleep. He did not like the way they looked at him, especially the woman. She seemed to have nothing better to do than study his every move, ready with a glass of water every time he ran his tongue over his lips.

Memories of the desert arose in him a restless fervour. He wanted the magnificent sun to burn his eyes, for its light to seep down his eyes and take over, for his body to convert the light into the colour of a plant yet to bloom.

He thought about magnolias instead of killing enemies in the North. He liked to go out to the garden and imagine blooming flowers surrounded him. Though always aware of the woman watching, he did not stop himself from bending to smell and kiss the soil.

Two weeks after the arrival of the installation, Atemi stayed up at night consulting the manual— their staying up alternated between her and Murungu, depending on who was feigning sleep. From time to time, she would go to her son's room and confirm the sight she was desperately trying to deny: her son was sleeping. Going through the manual, it said that sons were not supposed to go into that state; they had been generated to be perpetually awake.

The night she discovered this she had no choice but to wake her husband up. They walked together to Stanis' room. He was still sleeping.

The sight of her sleeping son repulsed her, curled up as he was like a soft-boned prehistoric thing, the bed sheets hugging his shoulders. His skin was a little torn, the delicate sphere of his humerus visible, reminding her of innards and the reality of a boy experiencing metabolism. The idea of her Stanis as a system of flesh and blood and nerve endings made her nauseous. It reminded her of American pulp fiction. Despite her best efforts, the reverse HRT had turned her into one of the young mothers she met at parties. She could not bear to look into the space between the torn skin, it reminded her too much about herself, about life as it was once. She pictured Stanis' selfish gene as something that needed to be re-educated on the meanings of 'selfish'. She ran out of her son's room and ducked into the kitchen. She swallowed a pill and as it settled into her system she was already forgiving her new installation, already forgetting the way he was curled up. The forgiveness pill had always worked magic when it came to all the other problems in her household.

Atemi locked herself up in the bedroom. She was going in for one of her rare sessions, self-conditioned to give herself up to concupiscence once in a long time, conspiring not to include her husband when she touched herself, when she run her finger to the tips of the burgeoning construction of nerve endings, sending wave upon wave down the plexus. This exclusion was her way of punishing him for giving away his sperm mobility card. But in a desperate act she dashed to the walk-in closet and picked up his cologne. The smell overwhelmed her, yanking the ground from beneath her feet, leaving her in a blossoming mushroom of isolation to reconcile with herself, and she came.

Murungu lingered at the doorway after his wife ran off. He did not go upstairs. Instead he went into his study to read about the past, to the time when a man did not need to send a son to the war to fit in with the neighbours. He wanted to wait for a while before going back to the bedroom, where his wife must be sobbing.

He had always protected her from such exposures, from anything that might harm her. Sometimes his body was the thing that hurt her, and he forced himself to stay away. He had always worn long-sleeved shirts to hide the places where his skin had become undone. They never took showers together. He was always fully clothed in bed. He also gave up swimming in the nude—although the hyper-chlorinated water was the real reason for this. He found it strange Stanis had such delicate skin at that young age.

Although she tried to stifle the crying when she got into bed, Murungu was always awake, well aware that she was

To Gaze at the Sun

crying for the ghost of a son who may never ring the bell at their front door. He was silent while she cried, his eyes watching the arms of the clock on the wall of their bedroom, willing them to move a little faster, cursing at them because they had come to signify an acute awareness of their private pain.

Hours after he left the study and got into bed Murungu was still awake. He made up his mind to get out of bed again taking care not to wake her, and went back into his study where he leafed through the 301-page manuscript of the history of the Kenya-Sudan war. When he pressed CTRL+F on the touchpad, he found 4672 instances of the word 'oil'. He wanted so badly to send a son to the war. It would serve to console him, as he had been rejected from joining the army owing to his gene map being unsuitable for war. It could not be relied upon to provide the right kind of thinking in a war. It belonged to the kind of men who had it in them to hesitate before spraying bullets in a village in the desert. But this son was different, could he last an hour in the desert?

He liked going through the manuscript because it also served as a history book. Nowhere else could he find anything about the past when there was no body of water dividing the continent. The shift had been sudden, the rift valley turned into the Coptic Sea and East Africa became a new continent, joined to Africa only by a narrow strait between Sudan and Egypt, like the small finger of an infant reaching out to its mother. In a population of almost five hundred million, Murungu and Atemi were among the last children of natural evolution, *old guardians* they were called. Companies like Vita Nova employed them as a sinister nod to Darwin and the Old Age.

Atemi convinced Murungu to report their son's anomaly to the company. They had to do it sooner or later. She consulted the manual every night when she went to bed. Nowhere in the index did it say how to deal with a son who likes to gaze at the sun. It took them a week to decide when to call Vita Nova, the aptly named company responsible for all new life. Atemi was distraught. She had suffered too much already, waiting for a son who never materialised at her front door.

She knew calling the company meant two things. One, they might lose Stanislaw forever. Guardians and the government shared ownership of the installation, and in the case of damaged or faulty 'goods' they were returned to the company, more specifically to the company pathologist, who had a direct line to the insurance company. Although Stanis was a strange child, she could not help but love him. She tried to hate him at first but his silence made it impossible to do so. She tried to be indifferent to him but the air filled with the smell of new, perfect-grade son. A scent that would have made her lactate if people had not decided to do away with that capacity.

The second option was to send him back to the company where they would fix him up with a new order of behaviour and morphology, completely regenerating his phenotype and giving him a new name. She did not want to imagine revisiting baby books looking for a new baby name. Although the name selection was one of the premium offers the company allowed prospective couples, it would feel like ice thawing between her organs if she had to go through it again. On the part of the company it was an ingenious idea; while other companies sent sons home with predetermined names from a list they had at the reception, generated through combinations and permutations, they allowed prospective couples the pleasure of choosing names. Atemi and Murungu considered themselves a progressive couple. They had browsed through baby name books until they came to Stanislaw. The name conjured up in her the idea of a faraway place, a yet undiscovered continent drifting away from her, rekindling memories she had of herself in another body, before she took up reverse HRT. Maybe it was due to such sensibilities, she thought, that her son was always staring into the distance.

When she called the company she was greeted by a recorded voice. The androgynous voice from the intercom echoed through the sitting room where the couple sat, answering its questions as best as they could. When asked was wrong exactly they had a problem trying to describe the symptoms. Atemi lacked the capacity to interpret her son's melancholia and loneliness into a compact sentence, into specific variables. She could not describe his long hours of sleep, how his upper-body moved in the rhythm of a wave, how he looked out the window for hours barely touching the windowpane with the tip of his index finger, how he went out to the garden to look at plants, touch the leaves, and bend down to smell the earth. All these actions scared her, she told the voice.

She observed the neighbours watching as Stanislaw bent to smell the earth, and how they walked away embarrassed for her.

The company sent one of their men to investigate. He projected the air of a man not used to making mistakes, and for this reason, he disapproved of everyone. He had been to the war and now he was part of the company that sent installations to the same war. He looked at Atemi in the space between her eyes and hairline, without averting his eyes for the entire duration he was at 126 Distribution Road. He followed her upstairs and asked her to demonstrate the symptoms that the installation was exhibiting. He reminded her that the company needed a clear picture of the symptoms—otherwise there would be no way of knowing how to deal with it.

She did not know what to make of this request to demonstrate her installation's defect. How could this stranger expect her to do such things, and in her own house? Atemi curled up in the narrow bed and tried her best to demonstrate the infantile position. She led him out to the window and stood there, her arms outstretched, the

Clifton Gachagua

tip of her index finger barely touching the windowpane. She was thorough, and the demonstration lasted at least an hour, to make sure the man understood.

Together they left for the garden and she told him to watch from behind a window overlooking the garden.

She was playing a game of transposition, where she became her installation and the man became her. She had given this a lot thought. She could not risk being misinterpreted: her husband had warned her it would not look good on the insurance forms. She touched the leaves, gently placing their weight between her fingers, unaware of what she ought to be feeling. She looked up to see the man looking her straight in the eyes, holding her gaze and finally turning to take down notes. He made her uncomfortable. She could not wait to have him out of her sitting room at 126 Distribution Road.

Atemi bent down to smell the ground, staying there for another hour so that the man could get a clear picture. The truth is that Atemi could not stand it all: the bed, the gazing, the bending, and the tender weight of leaves. But she had to do it for her family. They were only long minutes lost attempting to re-enact the suffering of her son. Stanislaw. She smiled. The name always warmed her up.

She went back to the house where the man requested to talk to Stanislaw. Try as they may, Stanislaw could not be convinced to utter a word. He stood up from the couch in the sunken sitting room and walked to the window to gaze at the sun.

The man made notes without looking at his notebook.

He was thinking of the time when he went to the war with Sudan, when he killed a young Arabic girl who would not stop staring at him. He remembered telling himself that he was protecting his country's sovereignty by shooting her. The girl reminded him of the woman who had just been demonstrating her installation's defect. They had the same way of moving their arms as they talked. He also felt

To Gaze at the Sun

an attraction to Stanislaw, as if they had been brothers separated at birth, which they were, technically.

He left 126 Distribution Road with a complete report. The company would call her in a day to advise her on what to do, he said before leaving. He warned her of the possibility of the company recalling Stanislaw. He did not look at her in the eyes. This inability to gaze at objects was one of the prime things the government looked for in installations. He felt relieved for Stanis; soon they would come for him and end his existence, maybe the company could fix the boy up for another couple. He could not imagine how the company released an installation that had control over its instinct to kill.

After Atemi walked the man up to the patio she went back into the house to attend to her son. She found him standing beside the window. It broke her heart every time he looked at her and went back to gazing at the sun. Soon, Atemi thought, the doorbell would ring and she would go down to meet her new son. She made a note to buy a subscription for a new parenting magazine.

The company called her in less than twenty-four hours. They made it clear that Stanislaw would have to be returned. They expressed their regret at this unforeseen turn of events, promised to cover half of the fee for the second regeneration—this, they reminded her, was very generous of them because they were under no obligation to bear any costs. Then the voice from the other end of the line was abruptly replaced by a void.

Clifton Gachagua is a filmmaker and writer, currently working on a SciFi novel. He has been published in *Kwani?06*, and lives in Nairobi.

Proposition 23

Efe Okogu

Lugard

I muscled my way past the hopeful citizens standing in line outside Mace, my neuro linked with the bouncer's and he let me pass with a tight smile. There are certain perks to being a lawman.

Inside was a mix of artmen, vidmakers, and musos, still waiting for their big break, hanging on to the bland words of others enjoying their fifteen seconds of fame, as if blind luck were transferable. How many famous people are truly talented these days and how many are the product of high credit neuro-tricknology, I wondered.

Tribal Tech blasted from the modulated walls syncopating the dancers on the floor into the latest rhythms. You could tell by their synchronised movements that most of them let their neuros do the heavy lifting, mere passengers in their own bodies as if possessed by Eshu or Ogun. Fuck that, when I dance I want to be out of control, not a puppet with artificial subroutines masquerading as my dance expression.

"Lugie," a voice called out from the bar. It must be my date, I logged, as I knew no one here. This Victoria Island joint was a lot more upmarket than the Ajegunle bars I usually drank in. I walked over, mesmerised by the faux tribal tattoos that covered every inch of her hot chocolate skin, except her face, endlessly morphing into new patterns. She wore no clothes but the tats created a second skin that drew attention to all the right places. Fractals became curves suggestive of other forms. It took a lot of confidence, and a perfect body, to pull off the look well.

"They never repeat," she said.

I realised I'd been staring. She must be rich, I logged, only the rich could afford bodies like that.

Efe Okogu

"Don't you get cold?" I asked, feeling stupid once the words blurted out. She laughed, a sweet and tinkling sound, and the tats reacted with her mood, sunlight bursting along with her gaiety. If I were pale-skinned, I'd have visibly blushed.

"They're made of gen2 nano-cells," she said. "My neuro can regulate their body temp."

Gen2? I'd figured she was rich but to use gen2 cells for decoration... that was insane. She saw my expression and stopped mid-mirth, as if someone had hit her mute button.

I always feel slightly uncomfortable around citizens with that much credit, too aware of the vast gap that separated our worlds. We may live in the same city but we walk on different planes, like housemates sharing a house but living and working on opposite schedules, rarely meeting, aware of each other's existence only via the mess they leave behind.

She turned to another girl and began chatting about Luscious Lana's latest hit while I occupied myself by scrolling my thumb against the touch pad surface of the bar and ordering some palm wine. A hole opened up on the bar and a tall glass emerged. I was about to ask her if she wanted an Al-cola, when we heard an explosion in the far distance. The ground vibrated slightly and I heard a couple of thuds as the inebriated fell to the ground.

What? My neuro hadn't logged any scheduled gov activity. I looked around and saw others doing the same. There was no fear; just confusion followed by the blank stares of citizens googling the interface to find out what was going on. The feed above the bar switched over from the deck-ball game to a building on fire. An inferno blazing out of control filled with pluming black smoke, flying shrapnel, collapsing rubble, and tiny dots that danced in the air like moths.

"What we are watching is indescribable," a voice was saying. "The scene here is one of devastation and carnage." The feed zoomed out revealing the surroundings and for a few moments, I found it hard to breathe.

I worked there!

A number appeared in the bottom right-hand corner of the feed and the voice continued. "We've been patched through to the central link and the death toll is already two thousand, three hundred and five, and as you can see, for every second I speak, a neuro is being unlinked somewhere in that hell that used to be the District Three Lawhouse."

The feed zoomed in again, and after a moment, a gasp travelled through the bar like a meme. The tiny dots were citizens, jumping from a thousand-story building to avoid burning alive.

"We've just been told that we have CCTV footage," the voice said, "filmed minutes before the explosion that reveals the identity of a suspect."

Citizens talk of life changing moments all the time. Every vid ever made, it seems, revolves around them. At that moment, I logged in real life, such moments are never singular but operate in tandem, strewn like detritus throughout a man's lifetime, and only when the timeline is ready, does it make any kind of sense.

It made no sense that night in the bar, but it almost did, like God laughing at you so hard you start to laugh yourself, and through that very act, you almost get the joke, almost. The feed showed a man mouthing words into the camera, and when I saw that amused smile on the feed, despite the intervening years, I knew it was *him*, even before the voice told us his name. Nakaya Freeman. I snorted my palm wine out my nose and in my date's face. Needless to say there was no porn that night, or partnership beyond.

I ran out the bar, jumped in my trans, and sped off towards the chaos, activating my comm and calling Luka, my law partner. Please be safe, I thought. There was no answer. He's just busy, I told myself, probably porning

Efe Okogu

another conquest. I flashed back to those tiny dots leaping to their deaths, and at the thought that he may be amongst them gunned the engine. Pounding my fist against the roof, I set my comm to auto redial, and flipped on the sirens, transforming the surface of my trans into a neon glow of flashing red and blue.

What can I say about 7/13 that hasn't already been said by others far more eloquent than I? That night was one of… shock, yes, grief too, and of course rage… But beyond that, a form of excitement, a sense of purpose in the air, a long awaited call to arms, like attack dogs finally given permission to kill. The only thing I can compare it to is the feeling before a deck-ball game. There hadn't been a criminal or terrorist like Nakaya Freeman in over a century. Not since the Crucial Citizen turned traitor, Dr. Ato Goodwind.

Sayoma

It was another miserable and barren day, and I was glad to enter my building, taking the lev up to the two hundred and third floor. My unit is in the heart of the complex and has no windows, but all four walls and the ceiling played live feeds of the outside. The sky through the feed was a dramatic whirl of shifting clouds far more intense than the real thing.

"Feed off," I said, as I walked in, dropping my bags and jacket on the floor, and peeling off my clothes. "Candlelight. Hot bath, jasmine scented." The feed disappeared and soft flickering amber lights illuminated the unit. In the centre of my living room, the faux-hardwood floor spiralled open to reveal a steaming pool. I sank into the water, lay back, closed my eyes, and googled the interface—I had work to do.

Every citizen can google the interface anytime; there are neuro-links embedded into walls, streets, and machines, all over. Some locations have stronger signals than others, but all you have to do is visualise the interface, and you're there.

My neuro jacked in and my unit disappeared as if down a long tunnel. I could access the real world anytime by opening my eyes; it would appear as a small feed floating in midair in the corner of my vision.

My current job was to conduct a profit margin analysis for a corp specialising in interpreting market research data. It was easy credit. All I had to do was create an algorithm that broke down the data and another one to put it all back together more efficiently. It took a couple of hours and I left them to compile while I went off exploring.

The node of information that was I traversed a subtly shifting landscape of data. I floated then dived into the code, merging with various streams of consciousness, attaching to random nexii just for the joy of seeing where the information would take me.

Like surfing an endless series of waves, except they are four dimensional and you're underwater; or freefalling amongst stars in the superheated core of a galaxy, stars that are themselves alive and in conscious motion, and allowing their competing and complementing gravitational forces to move you in whatever direction they will. The interface can be anything you want it to be, most viz it as a hyper-real version of the world. They see servers as buildings, the more data, the larger the building. Information flows as traffic, programs interact as avatars or machines etc... Others viz vids, animes, avatars, and locations based on popular culture, which for many men means porn. Some citizens have their own unique visualisations of world war, deckball games, jungle or marine ecosystems, cellular or solar systems, all depending on how creative they want to be.

I prefer to see the interface for what it is: pure information. Most find this too confusing a world to navigate though, hence the visualisations. The advantage of not using a visualisation is that you see what is really going on in the places in-between. The gov and every corp have their presence on the interface and they don't want any old citizen accessing their information. When citizens visualise, they make it easier to navigate, safer too, but they also make themselves easier to control. If you viz a city, then there are walls you cannot walk through, physical rules you have to follow.

After a while, I began to notice a presence, a node of no fixed location that was connected indirectly to... almost everything, like tentacles probing or manipulating oblivious fish. But when I focused my attention on it, it was gone. I launched several search algorithms but they hit dead end sites by clever rerouting, even my most subtle ones. Intrigued, I delved deeper into the labyrinth, accessing backdoors and laying down logic trackers, but whatever it was eluded me.

As soon as I gave up however, there it was again, barely in the periphery of my digital eyes. When I tried to follow its trail, I realised it was jumping from firewall to firewall, and not just random ones. It moved at will within the protective layers of the largest corp and gov nexii. I could do the same but not at that speed. I've never heard of a citizen who could move that fast. Not even the komori googlers—who spend their entire lives jacked in, tubes running in and out of their orifices to sustain life—could move that fast.

Software could, in theory, but the AI regs restricted software. Could this be a rogue AI? Surely, those only existed in sci-fi vids. Whatever it was, I knew I should leave it alone if I didn't want to get Icarused, but the temptation was too great. I couldn't follow it so I designed an ingenious little algorithm, analysing the firewalls it had surfed through, trying to log where it might head next. It came back with a dozen sites and I dropped discreet tracers that would alert me if or when it showed up.

As I googled off, I saw it again, and right before it vanished I reached out for one of the tentacular ends of its

Proposition 23

signature. In my virtual grasp, I saw a string of digits 11101011110. Binary code for 1886? I opened my eyes and lit up an oxygarette, savouring the rush of pure oxygen spiced with stimulants.

Lugard

"Whenever you're ready," one of the techs said, after placing the mem-stim patch on my forehead.

I nodded, took a nervous breath and closed my eyes. A wave of nausea enveloped me then quickly passed. I was suddenly in my old classroom. I could feel the sunlight caressing the skin of my arms and smell the Suya shish kebab hidden in my half-open bag. I began to speak, a focused stream of consciousness direct from the memory source.

"The first time I met Nakaya Freeman, I must have been nine or ten as this was in Ms. Sidewhite's politics class. She'd asked him there to talk to the class about philosophy, and none of us would have suspected that the pretty, little woman all the boys had a crush on, rubbed shoulders with subversives and dissidents. But like I said, this was long ago, and Nakaya's name hadn't yet become synonymous with mass murder. He'd introduced himself, and proceeded to uproot the baby buds The Book had cultivated in our brains.

'What is the difference between a good citizen and a bad one?' Nakaya asked us. As he waited for an answer, he folded his long elegant legs beneath him in the lotus position and lit an oxygarette.

'A good citizen does good things?' some kid suggested, 'and a bad one does bad things?' Nakaya ran his hands through his long, black hair and blew a large smoke ring that hung in the lazy air. I watched it twist into something resembling a heart, then the infinity sign, before losing cohesion and dissipating.

'Good answer. That's what we call the legal standard. We judge people based on their actions, not their

358

intentions. But let me ask you this, what is a good act or a bad act? Is it wrong to steal when you're hungry?'

'No one is hungry,' another kid answered incredulously, 'we all have minimum credit'.

'I see. How about this? Is it always wrong to kill someone? What if they were trying to kill you or somebody you loved?' A few murmurs at that. We all knew murder was wrong, even in self-defence. It said so in The Book.

'The law will take care of them,' someone else said.

'Ah, but what if they don't get there in time?'

There were louder murmurs and a protest from the back.

'That's impossible. When you're in danger, your neuro sends out a signal and the law or the health come and help you'. Everyone knew that.

'Ok, but what if you don't have a neuro?'

'Everyone has...' I started to say but then stopped. He looked at me and smiled that infamous smile of his. It was true, not everyone had a neuro. Undesirables, or as most people call them, undead, have no neuros. But who cared about them? They'd broken the law and lost their citizenship.

'Everything from credit to the interface to every machine is neuro-linked,' Nakaya continued. 'Without a neuro, you have no access; you literally don't exist. Most undead starve or freeze to death in the everlasting winter within days; or are killed by trans or other machines that don't log anyone there. Many perish from lack of meds, their bodies unable to cope with harsh reality. Others are murdered, clockworked by gangs of adults or even kids not much older than you, and though the gov doesn't officially condone such behaviour, they don't do anything to stop it either. The way they figure, those citizens with violent tendencies need an outlet and the undead die even faster. It would be more humane to line them up before a firing squad or dump them outside the habitable zones.'

Proposition 23

He paused to take a sip of green tea, holding the brimming cup seemingly carelessly but without spilling a drop, and then continued. 'But forget the undead for a moment. Let me rephrase my question. Is The Book the only judge of right and wrong? Can someone do something that The Book says is wrong but still be good?'

'Citizenship is a privilege not a right. The only requirement is adherence to the law as laid down in The Book,' I quoted, then added, 'all citizens are by definition good.'

'Hmmm,' he said, 'in that case, riddle me this: who wrote The Book?'

The class erupted as hands shot in the air and students shouted out the names of the Crucial Citizens who had looked at the chaotic wasteland that was the world, and decided to unite and improve it. Nakaya kept his eyes on me, ignoring the rest of the class and suddenly I logged what he was really saying. Were the Crucial Citizens not men and women themselves? What if they got it wrong? I watched him watch my thoughts turn a corner I had never even known existed, let alone explored, and he winked at me. That's all I remember."

I opened my eyes and removed the mem-stim patch from my forehead. The thing came off with a slimy squelch and I felt dirty, almost like a base criminal. But it had to be done. I was perhaps the only lawman who'd actually met Nakaya Freeman, and it was my duty to tell all I knew. Which wasn't much hence the mem-stim. On top of which, a citizen is unable to lie under mem-stim so I'd cleared my name before any suspicions could emerge.

"Thanks Lugard, you can step down," Captain Babangida grunted, his round face somehow appearing gaunt under the stress we all felt. He looked uncomfortable and I knew it wasn't simply his wide girth squeezed into an unfamiliar chair. With our lawhouse gone, we were operating out of the top three floors of the Intel Hotel on Ken Sarowiwa Avenue. I looked out the vast window

360

feeds across the city. Lagos was a patchwork of amber, fluorescence, and neon, as far as the eye could see.

Everywhere, towers thrust themselves into the blank sky like promethean weapons robbing the sky of fire. Flycrafts darted through the air like fireflies, and towards the sea, the pale moon was a faint and blurred smudge. To think, there was a time the moon was the brightest light in the night sky. Now she was little more than a silver afterthought.

I walked back to the ranks of my fellow lawmen and sat down next to my new law partner—*what was his name again?*—and thought of Luka with his shy grin, his ability to make everyone he met love him, and sniffed back the tears threatening to spill, snitches eager to tell the world of my true emotions. 'Vengeance before tears,' as one of the Crucial Citizens once said.

My new law partner patted me on the back with a large hand as I sat down, leaning over to whisper in my ear. "Why didn't you tell me you'd met the psycho?"

I shrugged, unsure how to voice, let alone examine and explain, the ambivalence that cleaved me to... from... *what, exactly, Lugard?*

"Ok," the Captain continued. "The techs will analyse lawman Lugard Rufai's testimony but in the meantime, does anyone have anything?" He looked around what used to be a CEO suite at the lawmen gathered for the daily briefing. We all avoided his gaze, shifting imperceptible as he swept his eyes along our ranks.

"Come on people! Does anyone have anything?" More silence. He stood up and glared at us, his jowls vibrating as he spoke. "We lost five thousand, one hundred and fifty two on 7/13!" he said, as he jabbed a pudgy finger at us. "Five thousand, one hundred and fifty two dead, almost half of them lawmen! Four hundred and nineteen still in critical condition. Every other lawhouse is working on this but those were our brothers and sisters. It is our responsibility to clockwork that cold-blooded son of an AI!"

None of us could meet his gaze. We all felt the same pain, the same rage, the same helplessness. We all had hit the streets and the interface daily, trawling through every lead no matter how far-fetched. We all had nothing.

"Get out of my sight!" he spat out, disgusted. As we stood up to walk out, I noticed one of the techs whispering to the captain who looked up at me and called me over.

"I'll wait for you in the trans," my new law partner said, with a we-gotta-talk expression creasing his Slavic brow. I nodded and we touched fists in the traditional lawman salute. I still can't remember his name. If I'd known that was the last time I'd see him, I might have made an effort.

"Yes sir?" I inquired, walking over to where the captain stood, looking out of the feed window at the charred, black hole in the distance that used to be our second home. I stood silently waiting for him to answer, when it occurred to me for the first time, that it had been the captain's only home. He was a man who lived for the law, to the exclusion of a personal life, whereas I'd joined up, unwillingly, because the True Quotient test stated it was my path.

I'd wanted to be a pioneer, exploring the galaxy at a fraction below the speed of light, searching for another habitable planet in order to save humanity from the death of the Earth. As it is now, the only habitable zones lie between the tropics of Capricorn and Cancer, nothing beyond but a barren wasteland of subzero temperatures and deadly radiation. Most logicmen claim we have less than a century before even this is lost, and light-speed doesn't seem so fast when you are racing against extinction.

Two hundred years had passed since Yuri Gagarin first went up into space. Seventy five since the invention of the Stardust drive and the search began; for a second home, or previously unknown sources of energy, or extraterrestrials

Efe Okogu

with the technology to terraform a planet, or some higher authority that we hadn't yet conceived of with the power to offer salvation.

We once put our hope in terraforming until the Martian Mistake. The native microbe-like lifeforms—which we didn't even realise existed until it was too late, due to their unimaginably alien structure—reacted to our interference with their atmosphere by mutating into a planet-wide stratosphere based super-colony that destroyed any off-world vehicle that approached with super heated plasma. We bombed them for a century with thermonuclear warheads, nano swarms, chemical poisons, and even biological pathogens, to no avail. We also attempted to communicate but the Martians are either not sentient or not interested.

Our attempts at terraforming the various moons in the outer solar system have been equally unsuccessful. The delicate balance of electro-magnetic fields, atmospheric conditions, temperature, chemical composition, and native lifeforms, proved to be beyond our abilities to alter in our favour within our human time-scale. Logicmen say Europa will be habitable in forty thousand years at the rate we're going but we won't be here to enjoy it. The Martian Mistake was the most dramatic of our failures but far from the least.

Thirty years passed since the discovery of Quantum Tunnel Link that allowed us to communicate with pioneers in real time, but they discovered nothing of value in the vast darkness; no gardens of Eden, no benevolent techno wizards. Their only encounters had been with HIP's (Highly Incomprehensible Phenomena), which were beyond our abilities to comprehend, let alone communicate with or use.

Raskonikov Phuong, captain of the Hawking, described one such HIP as 'a specific colour beyond the spectrum of man's experience, yet strangely familiar to us, endlessly shifting between nonexistent states. Our sensors detected nothing, but we all saw it, and though the ship's healthmen and logicmen have discovered no physiological changes in us, I am positive it is responsible for the sudden wave of romantic attachments that is sweeping through my ship. I myself am not immune.'

"Why don't you take a few days off?" the Captain spoke.

"What? No! I have a few leads I want to chase up. I'm not-"

"It's not a request, lawman," he interjected, "it's an order."

"Why, sir, if you don't mind me asking, what did the tech say?"

"It's probably nothing. Just that the phrasing of your words under mem-stim revealed a possible subconscious admiration for Nakaya Freeman that might cloud your judgment. Take a few days off and I'll call you back in once they've cleared it up."

"But…" I began, but in the corner of my vision, a feed was already activating, informing my neuro of the suspension, with credit, and pending a psychological assessment. I gritted my teeth and walked out, swallowing the sense of unfairness like a child popping unsavoury meds.

Sayoma

I spent days, no, weeks at a time, barely speaking to another citizen, and only then in passing. As a programmer, I work from home and that doesn't help. But that's not a reason either. Loneliness is not an occupational hazard of my profession. If it was, there'd be regs to help and there aren't.

My parents had me late in life so when they retired at sixty I was just fifteen. They didn't have enough credit to get a life extension and I became a ward of the gov. They took Mom first and Dad just crumpled in on himself. It was as if with Mom gone, the force of the vacuum she left behind hollowed the life out of him. The next nine months were the worst. Dad was so angry all the time. They'd both slaved their lives away but were still short of life extension credit.

Then one day, maybe three months before his time, he heard a rumour that drove him insane with grief. The conspiracy was that the retired didn't die peacefully. Instead, the gov took direct control of their bodies via their neuros and used them as miners beyond the habitable zones until they dropped dead from exhaustion and radiation poisoning.

"Imagine being alive to feel the suffering of your body without being in control," he sobbed.

"No Dad, it's crazy. We have machines to do the mining. Why would they need old weak people?" But he wouldn't listen.

"I know what they're capable of. They wouldn't bat an eyelid, Soy Soy. If doing this saved them even a touch of credit, they wouldn't bat an eyelid."

Dad started talking crazy about heading out beyond the habitable zone to find her but of course, he didn't know where to look. In the end, he jumped off a scraper rather than face his own retirement.

As for my childhood and school friends, we lost touch long ago, probably because they were never true friends to begin with; my colleagues are faceless and my neighbours nameless... but then, so it is for many.

Yet the world over, other citizens have friends, porners, and partners. Other citizens go to bars, drink Al-cola, watch vids, and dance to MTVs. Other citizens join facebooks, and meet up to play amateur deckball, or share their collections of Vintage Era memorabilia. Other citizens are happy. The Book says happiness is guaranteed to those who follow the regs of the Law, but I do and I am miserable. My only solace is in the interface but I abhor the thought of becoming a komori googler.

Are there others like me, I often wondered, others whose bodies are citizens but whose souls are undead. Across the

Proposition 23

road, I saw a cleaner glide by on a surface of ionised particles headed towards a man bent over picking up something off the ground.

If you were undead, the cleaner would not even know you were there, simply run you over consuming whatever happened to be in its path.

I flashed back to my childhood and the game we used to play where a bunch of us would find a cleaner and surround it. Jumping around like lunatics, giving it openings and closing them off so it wouldn't know whether to hibernate or move, until its CPU shorted, and it imploded with the sound of an amplified fart, leaving behind a twisted lump of metal the size of a deckball. They don't do that anymore; upgraded years ago.

I watched the man stand up and notice the silent approaching cleaner, its smooth domed grey hull appearing menacing for the first time to me—perhaps due to its unusual proximity to the hunched man. His face twisted in shock and he instinctively dove out of the machine's path. As the man stood up and began to brush himself off, I ran across the road.

"Are you all right?" I asked.

"Yes, I think so. Thank you," he answered, looking up at me. He appeared to be in his mid-thirties, roughly my age but who can tell these days. A stocky man with a barrel chest, muscular body with a solid, square-cut face, he looked like the kind of guy who spent a lot of time engaged in physical activities. He was dressed in dark clothes, his hair puffed up in a wild and unkempt afro. Probably an artman or muso, I logged. Nothing special, but then I saw his eyes; they were beautiful, jade green and filled with sorrow.

"Why did you jump like that?" I asked, but as the words came from my mouth, it dawned on me that my neuro hadn't linked with his. I reacted on impulse, stepping back in revulsion, as if I had just stepped in dog shit. Undesirable! Unclean! Undead!

Efe Okogu

He saw my expression, smiled remorsefully and said, "Well, that was nice while it lasted... almost felt like a citizen again."

Up close, I began to log more details. The dark clothes masked patches and stains that were only apparent this close. His shoes looked old, and a thick black sock poked out through a hole on his left shoe. He started to turn and walk away.

Behind him, there was a feed showing a brand-vid: some famous deckballer, I can never remember their names, leaping for a ball. I've seen it many times, the longing look on his face, the outstretched fingers. As he catches it, the ball morphs into a mcdonald and the baller eats it with an orgasmic grin on his face. Words appear and he watches them dance on and off the feed, 'Carpe Diem, *Sayoma* - U know U wanna!' I hate brand-vids.

If I had met the man a day prior or later, I probably wouldn't have spoken to him, no matter how lonely I was. If I had met him anywhere else but under an annoying brand-vid telling me to seize the day, I would probably have spent the rest of my life without ever speaking to an undead. My life would have been of a very different breed; I would be a woman without a creed. The coincidences in life and the choices we make of them are frighteningly arbitrary.

"Hey, wait up," I said, "what's your name?"

Nakaya

There's no going back now. Not that I would change the past if I could, but yesterday I was not a killer, today I am. I wander in the shadow of scrapers, humanity's attempt to impregnate the scorched sky, observing the monochrome streets of our megalithic machine aflame with neon. An aerogel mask distorts my features beneath my cowl. I am anonymous but it would be foolish to stay out in public too long.

Proposition 23

I cut through Soyinka square, one of the few green spaces left in this megacity, though plans are already in place to root out the vegetation and build a complex of scrapers. Who needs a real park when you can simply viz and explore a jungle a hundred thousand times the size, seemingly teeming with exotic wildlife?

A group of teenagers sit in a circle drumming on Gangans. I slow down, seeking as always for a genuine connection with citizens beyond their augmented states. A sigh escapes my lips. All but one is essentially unconscious, their neuros downloading skills they do not truly possess into their bodies, sending out electric signals and a chemical cocktail coursing through their nervous systems. Their insides are lit up like Christmas on crack, their eyes glazed with artificial feel-good.

I watch the one girl who's not faking it pound a beautiful beat on the taut skin, transforming her Gangan into a lyricist with a curved stick. She doesn't have the precision of her fellow drummers but they don't even notice; their dulled meat brains unable to truly appreciate the music they're making. But what she lacks in technique, she more than makes up for in soul: her polyrhythm's circle and dance, an improvisational poem calling lost brothers and sisters to return to the village where a festive feast awaits to celebrate the passing of a terrible storm.

If you look with the right mind, listen with the right heart, you can always tell neuro-augmented art from the real thing—it's not the perfection of the neuro that gives it away, though these days that's a clue. How many citizens actually bother to learn an instrument? Why spend years practicing and training when the neuro can do it for you instantaneously?

No, the difference is something far subtler and altogether unquantifiable. The girl hides her talents well—none of her friends knows she is a real musician—but she's heading for the valley of the undead, I have no doubt about it.

Efe Okogu

Lugard

The first time I heard about Proposition 23 was during a brand break of the finals of the deckball Ulti-bowl, between the Jakarta Juggernauts and the Lagos Lionhearts. I barely paid attention though, as I had credit riding on Lagos, and they were eleven points down with a minute to go. A comeback was unlikely but not impossible, and the tension in the arena was like cabled titanium.

I was still on my enforced suspension from work, and with Luka dead and his murderer somewhere out there, I'd thought it impossible to enjoy the game, but despite myself, I was.

Segun Aloba had made it to the fourth deck, but he was alone up there facing five Juggernauts, and he still had to cross the full length of the field.

The feed came back with an XL close-up of Segun's face, three hundred times its actual size. You could watch the action directly but you'd need a lens at this distance anyway. The 3D feed was larger and the colours far more vivid than the real thing could ever hope to be. A team of live vid-makers ensured you saw every moment from the best and most dramatic possible angles.

Every bead of sweat on Segun's face was visible as the whistle blew and he exploded into action. Cut to wide shot, as he somersaulted over the first two defenders simultaneously, their arching scythes missing him by mere millimetres. Cut to a low angle, the third defender leapt into the air, scythe extended, timed perfectly to strike just as Segun landed. Cut to high angle, Segun, twisted his body at the last second to protect the ball, the edge of the blade slicing deep into his protective pads, blood spraying out in slow motion from the wound.

Segun swept his legs in a windmill, knocking the defender on his back and pulled the imbedded scythe out. Without looking, he swung it in an arc behind his head, slicing through the upper torsos of the first two defenders

Proposition 23

as they rushed to take him out. Then he threw the deckball in a long, high parabola, over the heads of the last two juggernauts.

A collective intake of breath from the arena; there was no one to catch the ball! But Segun was running for the far end, his opponent's scythe extended in his two fisted grip, his face a caricature of determination. The last two Jakartans were unsure whether to go for the ball or him. I'd never seen anyone move so fast. Before they could react, he cut them down like a virus cutting through code, and leapt for the ball.

Both he and the ball seemed to hang suspended in midair forever, as if God himself held his breath, then incredibly... He caught it! That feed would be analysed for a long time to come, and some logicman would even claimed he broke several laws of physics, but all this citizen cared about was the ten thousand credit I'd just won.

On the large feed, there was a slow motion shot of Segun's reach of faith and I watched fascinated as he stretched so yearningly for the deckball. That reach touched something in me. Some hidden, uncorrupted part of me, and I wasn't alone. Many a feedman has commented on how Segun's reach seemed to symbolise the desire in us all to transcend the impossible. It was a sublime moment, a pure moment, and eighty percent of the world shared it on live feed. Then, of course, the brands fucked the moment for all it was worth. I logged that the feed rights must have fetched a fortune long before the game, and I was watching a brand-vid. As Segun caught the ball, it morphed into a large golden statue of the number twenty-three, reminiscent of the Ulti-bowl trophy, and a deep voice said, 'Vote Yes! On Proposition 23!' I spluttered with rage. Monsters! I looked around to see if anyone shared my fury.

They didn't.

The crowd chanted "Segun! Prop 23! Segun! Prop 23!"

Efe Okogu

I wanted to scream, we didn't even know what Proposition 23 was, but a strange and paranoid thought stopped me, transforming my anger into an unfocused but real terror: was it a coincidence that Segun's shirt number was twenty-three? Surely it must be. The manipulation of the people wasn't so insidious, that live sports moments would be faked, was it? The great Segun Aloba wasn't in on it, was he? I watched the mob around me as if seeing them for the very first time, and in a way, I was.

As soon as I got home, I turned on the feed and sure enough, they were talking about Prop 23. The feedman grinned as if delirious with joy. He sat in an armchair, interviewing some generic govman dressed immaculately in a sky blue suit. The govman had that synth look to his skin; zoom in and you'd never find a single hair or imperfection, even his pores would be as inviting as the puckered lips of a virgin.

"So citizen Sadbrat, what exactly is Proposition 23?" the feedman asked. "I mean, we all *know* it will improve our lives dramatically, but how?"

"I'm glad you asked that, James. Proposition 23 is a new reg that we're considering adding to The Book. Basically, it will restructure corp rights in relation to citizenship ensuring that goods and services are no longer trapped within brand regs. It's been in the works for a while now and we think now is the time. The economy has never been stronger; citizens have never had such levels of life satisfaction."

"Excellent. So when will it come through?"

"Well, we still have to put it to a general vote on December, 23rd, ha ha, but most citizens are educated enough to know a good thing when they see it."

"But what is it?" I screamed at the feed.

On the way home, I'd googled the interface for info on Prop 23 but all I could find was the same elusive Bush-speak.

Proposition 23

"It's basically an expansion of a landmark precedent from 1886," the govman said, then paused for a fraction of second. As a lawman, I know when a citizen slips up; it's part of the training, noticing the changes in speech patterns, the facial nuances that even the most experienced govmen find hard to hide. Sadbrat hadn't meant to say 1886, I was sure of it. Finally a clue.

"All we're doing is taking common practice and making it law. Essentially, it will allow us to better help citizens without all the red tape," he finished.

"Well, it sounds brilliant," said James with a post-coital-like smile. "It's good to know govmen are hard at work making our lives better. Join us after the brand break for Luscious Lana performing a live MTV of her new tune, 'Porn me. Vid me.'"

I immediately googled the interface for landmark precedents set in 1886 but was blocked. No-one but the gov has the power to block a search, but they only ever did so in the interests of citizen security. There was something strange going on, something slightly amiss as if a burglar had broken in, then for some reason rearranged the furniture instead of stealing it. I'd need a programmer to explore any further but I didn't have anything close to that kind of credit. What would Luka do? *Most programmers are girls,* a familiar voice said in my head; I knew it wasn't Luka, but it sure sounded like him. *Go out for Al-colas at that bar off Allen avenue, the Link, it's always full of programmers; maybe you'll meet one, chat her up, and convince her to help.* People don't love me like they loved you Luka, I thought, but decided to give it a shot.

It was a bitter evening, even colder than usual, but I felt it for only a moment as I stepped outside my building, before my neuro adjusted my clothes to regulate body temperature. As I headed off, I heard the sound of air ionised at high speeds. I knew that sound well. I turned round to see lawmen streaming out of a trans, peacemakers

Efe Okogu

pointed at me. They were from another district and unfamiliar to me.

A govman followed, looked around him with an air of distaste, and then held up a v-amp. "Lugard Rufai! You have been tried and judged guilty by a jury of your peers of breaking the law. According to the regs of The Book, you have lost the right to citizenship and are henceforth, undesirable. May God and the Crucial Citizens have mercy on your soul!"

He pulled out an un-linker and pointed it at me. Why are they designed to look like peacemakers? Is it to instil fear? If so, it was working.

"Wait, wait!" I protested, "What regs did I break?"

"As an undesirable, you no longer have any rights." He smirked before pulling the trigger. I felt my neuro deactivate, cutting me off from everyone and everything around me, leaving me alone for the first time in my life, exiled, dehumanised, undead. It was like the loss of a limb or a best friend; it was death but being conscious to observe the process.

"You mean I don't even have the right to know what I did wrong," I spluttered. "That's crazy! I'm a lawman, District 3, I've done this a hundred times and this isn't how it works!" I shouted, but he was telling the truth. I had no rights.

"You were a lawman," he answered. Then they turned their backs on me, proceeded to step back into their trans and zoom off, leaving behind nothing but the smell of ozone, and a swirling storm of snow in their wake.

With my neuro gone, the wind attacked me with a viciousness I had not ever experienced, I almost shed tears at the shock, like that kid in the old children's story, abandoned without explanation, left to die outside the habitable zone by his mother.

Sayoma

373

Proposition 23

"Lugard, Lugard Rufai. A pleasure to meet you," the undead introduced himself, proffering his hand in greeting. I looked at his dirty fingers extending from within his black gloves, and then shook it.

"Sayoma Redbout," I said. "Fancy an oxygarette?"

"Sure," he said, and shrugged like he didn't care either way, but I could see how desperately he wanted it. Poor man, he probably hadn't smoked in an age.

We sat on a park bench for a while smoking in silence, unsure what to say. It's against the law to talk to the undead but what do you say to them anyway? It was like trying to talk to an animal or a machine. Without our neuros linking, the shared meta-sphere of instantly available information was missing. I had no way of tracing our degrees of separation or connecting over shared interests.

He wasn't a citizen but he was still a... what was the word... a person. An old word that, and it struck me then how crafty words could be. The word *citizen* had eaten the word *person* by implying that they were one in the same.

The man sitting next to me, shivering slightly in the cold I did not feel, was not a citizen. But he was a person. We speak of citizen rights but perhaps we should speak of person rights. Undead rights? God, what a thought.

"How long have you been undead?" I finally asked

"A few weeks", he replied, smoking the oxygarette down until the butt burnt his fingertips, and then flicking it off into the darkness.

"How do you live?" I asked.

"With great difficulty."

"What did you do?"

"I asked the wrong questions."

"No, I mean what reg did you break?"

"I don't know. One moment, I was googling 1886, the next, I was undead. I-"

"That's impossible," I interrupted, "there's no reg prohibiting googling. You must have done something."

374

"I'm sorry," he said, struggling to control his anger. "I appreciate the great honour you, a citizen, is doing me by sitting and talking to me, but don't tell me what I must have done. Someone in our gov didn't like the questions I was googling and they-"

"Wait a minute," I interrupted again. "Did you say 1886?"

"Yes... why?"

"Nothing. Just something I saw in the interface."

"What did you see?"

"I'm not sure."

"What did you see?" he asked again, grabbing my arm, staring into my eyes as if I were the last woman in the world. Something fluttered inside me under the force of his green eyes, just for a moment. *Madness, Sayoma, he's undead!*

"I'm not sure," I repeated. He let go of my arm and placed his head in his hands.

We were silent again as I lit up another couple of oxygarettes.

"Please think," he said as he took one from me.

"It might have been an AI, or a programmer like me, but either way, it moved like nothing I've ever seen before."

"You're a programmer?"

"Yeah."

"Can you google a blocked search without being caught?"

"Of course."

"Google legal precedents set in the year 1886 and what connections they have with Prop 23."

"Why?"

"Because I can't."

"I'm sorry," I said, "but if a search is blocked by the gov, it's against regs to program it." Somewhere nearby sirens approached and Lugard jumped. Ever since Nakaya Freeman, lawmen have been rounding up the undead, and the interface was rife with rumours of buildings converted into interrogation and torture cells. Citizen led clockworkings had escalated too.

"All I ask is that you consider it," he said, standing up quickly then loping off into the darkness away from the approaching sirens.

"I'm really sorry," I called out after him, "I just can't". Only after he left did it occur to me to offer him food or drink, he was probably starving.

I stood up to leave and saw the feed again. The brand-vid was gone, replaced with the notorious vid of Nakaya Freeman on 7/13, walking out of the District 3 lawhouse minutes before it exploded. He faced the CCTV and mouthed, 'Citizens beware, the undead shall rise.' He starts to walk away then turns back, flashing his infamous smile, '…watch out for the boom.' Words appeared below his face: Wanted Dead or Alive Reward 1 Trillion Credit. The richest citizens in the world are not worth that much.

Lugard

I was running down Fela Kuti Boulevard at six in the morning, trying to get to a half eaten mcdonald a citizen had just dropped, before the cleaner approaching in the opposite direction.

Hunger.

The word had never held true meaning for me before, as the sensation it describes is obsolete for citizens. But hunger is more than a word to depict the desire to titillate your taste buds, and amp your energy. Hunger is every cell in your body constantly screaming 'feed me', driving out every other thought from your mind. Hunger is those same cells going cannibal, devouring their weaker siblings and children as your gut contracts with the pain of internal genocide slowly sapping your willpower.

I vaulted a dog, scaring the old woman walking it, skirted a synth tree, and dived for the mcdonald but at the last moment, I mistimed my leap and landed short. As I scrambled to my feet, the cleaner consumed my meal, and the rage I felt flooded my system like illegal meds. I roared at the uncaring grey mass of the turtle-shell shaped cleaner, and was about to commit suicide by attacking it, when something hard hit me from behind, knocking me out of harm's way.

I lay on the ground, utterly defeated, lacking the will to look up at my assailant or saviour. I stared up into the lifeless sky and awaited death.

"Don't give up now, you've come so far," a voice said from beyond my periphery.

I didn't turn my head to see who was speaking. I thought instead of the past month and all I'd been through. Another word for undead should be 'cleaner' as that's what I spent every day doing. Competing with bigger, faster, lethal machines for scraps discarded by citizens, I usually lost.

A hooded figure loomed over me, his face lit by the streetlamps beyond. "I was especially impressed with the way you handled the clockworkers last night," the figure said. "They might think twice before approaching an undead in future."

"Handled?" I said finally, pointing at the livid bruises that discoloured my countenance. "There were four of them and I barely got away. I think a couple of my ribs are broken."

"As you say, there were four of them. I know for a fact that two of them needed the health when you were through. One of them is in a coma." He extended a long graceful arm and pulled me to my feet.

"How do you know all this?" I asked.

"We were watching you."

"You were what? Why?" Suspicion made me pull back a step and appraise the man. He was tall, thin, and shrouded from head to toe in a dark hooded trench coat. Only his eyes were visible and there was something vaguely familiar about them.

"We watch all undead in their first month. Those that survive, we contact. It is a cruel but necessary paradox: we

Proposition 23

can't afford to save those who can't fend for themselves. Such is the nature of the world."

"Who's we?"

He didn't answer. Instead, he reached into the folds of his trench coat and pulled out a brown paper bag. I smelled the homemade subway even before I saw it—saliva pooled in my mouth and drooled over my chapped lips, but I was beyond care or embarrassment. I snatched the bag out of his hands, and took a large bite of the sub.

My taste buds wept like partners reunited. I swallowed and heard a deep rumbling in my stomach; I felt like a virgin touched for the very first time, it hurt so good. I finished the meal in three bites and the man handed me a bottle of fresh water. I had lived off dirty snow for a month.

Bliss.

Before I passed out, I heard him say everything was going to be ok. His eyes were the last thing I saw and I logged, sudden like a neuro jacking in, where I knew them from. Reality relegated to the hands of another, I embraced unconsciousness like a deckballer embraces pain, or a komori googler their interface.

Sayoma

I hate googling in public. When I was a kid, we watched a Vintage Era vid where people came back from the dead and lurched around eating people. Apart from all the blood and rotten flesh, the look in their eyes reminded me of public googlers. As far as I'm concerned, they're the real undead. Besides, if you want to get any real work done, you need high credit specialist hardware, the kind I have embedded in my unit.

I had little choice, however. I was in a flycraft on the way to a meeting with govmen in the Department of Info, when one of my tracers picked up the signature of the 1886 node. I'd forgotten the tracers were still out there.

Efe Okogu

After my encounter with the undead man, Lugard, I'd decided to leave well enough alone; the last thing I wanted was to end up undead too. But now, in the corner of my vision, my tracer beckoned me from within the interface and I realised I'd been Bush-talking to myself; it is in my blood to program. I looked around the cabin and saw the dullard stares of the other passengers. Most of them were googled in themselves, so I knew no one would see me. And if they did, they wouldn't care. Nevertheless, I curled into my seat and covered my head with a blanket before jacking in.

I blinked my eyes, reality shifted, and I found myself facing the firewall of a gov nexii, the Department of Culture. I knew it well; I'd upgraded several of their system check subroutines a few months back. It towered monolithic above me, its surface an interlinked lacework of microscopic code. If I used a visualisation, it would be impenetrable, a solid wall of stone or steel perhaps. But, if I attempted to penetrate without a visualisation, my node would be torn to shreds like a small animal by piranhas, then it would devour my neuro, and if I didn't escape in time, my neurons as well, frying my brain cells in their own juices.

I scanned the firewall for weaknesses and spied the backdoor that dealt with system check subroutines. I came up with a hasty plan then launched every single probe in my arsenal at the main gates simultaneously. They attacked like a swarm of carnivorous insects and the firewall code reacted as a flame, burning them up like moths.

While the firewall was distracted, I shrouded my node in the cloak of one of the subroutines I'd written, and gained access via the backdoor. The entire process took less than a minute but by the time I got through, 1886 was on the move. I was ready for it. I abandoned my cloak and shrouded my node in an endless feedback loop of the binary digits 11101011110.

Proposition 23

It was a close call, but I managed to attach my node onto 1886's surface before it moved on. It wouldn't take long for it to discover my ruse but I hoped I'd have enough time for me to log what it was. I was wrong. It reacted instantly flinging me from it like a grown man would fling a small cat. As I went soaring towards the firewall, I countered instinctively, gripping with my virtual claws of protective, extraction, and stabilising, algorithms. I drew blood without meaning to, my little programs all but destroyed but, there, spliced into their code were snippets of the AI's DNA.

Logging what I'd done, 1886 threw itself at me, a large creature without shape or form, tentacles moving at the speed of thought, reaching out to ensnare me. Moments before I was crushed between the firewall and 1886, I googled out and opened my eyes with a muffled scream like a child awaking from a nightmare. I dry heaved with fear, logging I'd been nanoseconds from death. I went through a mental checklist to ensure I hadn't left any traces behind. I was sure I was safe but what if… I held up my hands and watched them shake for several minutes before I began to calm. I turned my head to the feed window, and saw a bolt of lightning illuminate the clouds below, like corrupt code infecting a system.

I considered googling back in and analysing the data I'd retrieved but the thought of the interface filled me with nausea and I dry retched again. Later, Sayoma, deal with it later, I reconciled. Fifteen minutes later, I was ushered into an anonymous room, deep within the heart of the Department of Info. The room had that pastel colour scheme all gov offices seem to use these days. I read somewhere that it was to encourage a balance between relaxation and productivity but I always found the bland cheerfulness disquieting.

A man sat behind a lime green desk. I recognised him from all the interviews he gave on the feed. There was something different about him though and when he turned to face me, I logged what it was. This was the first time I'd ever seen him without a smile on his face and the effect was frightening.

"My name is Sadbrat," he said without preamble. "Tell me everything you know about Proposition 23 and 1886."

"Wh-wh-what?" I asked.

He sighed deeply, pulled out an oxygarette and lit up.

"I don't have time for this. As a programmer, your neurons are wired to navigate abstract data thus a mem-stim patch won't compel you to tell the truth." He paused for his implied threat to sink in. "This will go a lot easier for you if you co-operate."

I thought fast. They scheduled this meeting right after my first encounter with 1886. If they were onto me, wouldn't they have just arrested me? Or, did they get perverse pleasure in making me walk willingly beneath the deckballer's scythe?

"All I know is what I've seen on the feed. Prop 23 is another reg that has something to do with corps. I have no idea what 1886 is, except of course that if you add up the digits, you get twenty-three."

He stared unblinking into my eyes and I couldn't meet his gaze. Stop acting so scared, Sayoma, I urged myself silently, it makes you look guilty... No wait, if I wasn't frightened of the unsmiling govman, wouldn't that make me look even more suspicious?

"Proposition 23 is very important to us," he said, eyes burning with a fanatical zeal. "And there have been several attempts by an unknown programmer to breach firewalls related to the reg. We suspect someone is attempting to sabotage its implementation. Do you have any idea who?"

I pretended to think for a minute.

"No... Why would anyone be opposed to Prop 23? What exactly is the reg, if you don't mind me asking? I haven't paid much attention to it."

"Well, that's not important right now. You can google all that information on your own time."

Proposition 23

"Why am I here, citizen Sadbrat?" I asked directly. "And why are you trying to scare me? I'm a loyal citizen who's served the gov many times in the past. What is all this about?"

He smiled ruefully, leaned back in his chair, and popped a little blue pill. "I apologise, citizen Redbout. These are trying times. Our necessary measures to locate Nakaya Freeman have created unusually high levels of dissent. Unofficial stats show that sixty percent of citizens sympathise with, if not actively support, the madman." His eyes briefly went blank as his neuro linked with something then he turned to look at me. "We originally asked you here to upgrade several of our firewalls but the situation has changed somewhat. We now want you to catch a programmer."

"Who?"

"We don't know but whoever they are, they're good. There are five other programmers already working on this. You will be the sixth and the only one who is not a komori googler."

Were they giving me official permission to chase 1886? I sucked in air through my teeth savouring the cold vibrations. "I need more information about the target. What are they after?"

"What I am about to tell you is classified at the highest levels, and known to very few citizens outside the gov." His eyes bored into mine to ensure I understood the gravity of his words. "Many of our regs are created by AI's."

"What?" I yelped in surprise as if I'd just been stung by something venomous. "But the AI regs limit their intelligence to subhuman levels. How can AI's write regs for us if they aren't as smart as us?"

"Well, the regs don't actually do that. What they do is limit an AI's freedom to make decisions based on post-human levels of intelligence. It's a subtle difference."

Efe Okogu

"So they are forced to make stupid decisions even though they know the results won't be as effective? That must be hellish... or it would be if they had emotions."

"Quite. But there is nothing to stop them from advising the gov on decisions *we* have to make. We know one such adviser, by far the most advanced of them, as 1886. In fact, it was 1886 that created Prop 23. The programmer you are after is trying to destroy this AI. If they succeed, we will have lost one of our most valuable assets."

No, I wasn't trying to destroy 1886; I just wanted to know what it was. Why was Sadbrat lying? Was it to fill me with righteous anger or did he believe what he was saying? He stood up, signalling the end of the meeting. They want me to catch myself. Hilarious. So why aren't you laughing, Sayoma? I asked myself.

"A trans is waiting outside to take you to the flyport."

I stood up to leave then turned back and asked, "One question Sadbrat, do AI's also advise corps on decisions?"

"I have no more information to give," he answered, but the way he said it told me all I needed to know. I logged then what Proposition 23 probably was and I shivered slightly. In the trans, then flycraft, and later in my unit, I repeatedly attempted googling to check out the 1886 DNA I'd extracted, but every time I did, the nausea was over whelming. I chain smoked oxygarettes waiting for the dread to pass. It didn't.

Nakaya

"You know, three hundred years ago, Lagos was little more than a fishing village, a patchwork of lakes and creeks by the sea irrigating some of the most fertile land in the world. Now look at it.

"Biggest city in the world," Linus says, crouched in the dirt, gnarled fingers buried deep in the soil. He shakes his head at the stunted yam he uproots. "And the most polluted"

"Be grateful anything still grows, brother," I say.

Proposition 23

"Yeah yeah. Halle-fucking-Luya."

"I'm serious Linus. We should be proud."

"Of this twisted little runt?"

"Yes. At least it's real food. None of that reconstituted protein and genetically mutated slop they feed the masses, pumped full of artificial flavours and chemical preservatives to fool the body into digesting it."

"Yeah, but I remember how good it tastes."

"Mostly 'cause of the neuro. Faeces would taste like a feast once that insidious son of an AI is done drugging the brain."

"But this..." Linus says, holding up the yam.

"Is the best we can do given the situation." I spread my arms to indicate the raped sky, the city irradiated with ionised particles. "You'd have thought by the time the fossil fuels ran out, we'd have learned to stick with non-polluting tech."

Linus stands up and we gaze out at the sprawl of lights that extends to the horizon in all directions, even the sea. The city block—on whose roof we guerrilla garden and in whose labyrinthine interior we dissent and spread our revolutionary vibrations out through the world—is but one of many such interconnected and autonomous spaces.

The gov know we're somewhere out there, a resistant strain of freedom their quarantines cannot contain; like cockroaches, rats, and viruses, undead are good at hiding, adapting, and evolving.

On the edge of the roof, a young couple sit and drum their Gangans. Idowu, the girl I saw in Soyinka square a while back, and Kwesi, an ex-logicman who began to publicly question why the gov and corps simply didn't run a conductive nanotube chain from the Earth up to solar collectors beyond the atmosphere and hook up the planet's electric grid. Brave naïve boy started a grassroots campaign and ended up here.

As I head past them, down into the building, Kwesi is asking, "Do you ever miss it?"

Efe Okogu

She shakes her head. "No. It was hell. Always pretending to be..." she grasps for the words, "one with the mindset, you know. It was a relief when they came for me. Past month has been the best time of my life. I don't have to be a hypocrite anymore."

"I miss it," Kwesi says. "I miss my neuro. I miss the feeling that I could do anything, experience everything."

"You just miss the porn. Closing your eyes and hiding in some nymphomaniac illusion... let me guess, I bet you were into Luscious Lana, that whole naughty schoolgirl routine."

"Well..." He blushes and laughs aloud.

"It's not funny, Kwesi, we gave up our humanity in exchange for a fucking toy!"

Lugard

I opened my eyes to a dimly lit room. The walls were rough grey concrete and the ceiling was low. I tried to stand up and realised I was chained to a chair, wrists and ankles bound in oldskool iron. I strained against them knowing it was useless; might as well try to walk on water without grav shoes. I twisted my head around but saw no door and logged it must be directly behind me. In the upper right hand corner of the room, was an oldskool camera as large as a child's head. My mouth felt dry, my tongue like sandpaper, but I yelled at it regardless.

"Let me go!"

"Sorry about that," a voice said from behind me. "Drugging you was an unavoidable precaution."

I heard no footsteps but the man who'd saved me earlier walked round to face me. A chair in hand he placed a couple of meters in front of me, then walked over with a bottle of water, held it to my lips, and I drank greedily.

"Where am I?" I asked

"Somewhere safe," he replied, sitting down. "Do you know who I am?"

Proposition 23

I nodded and said, "Nakaya Freeman. We met a long time ago."

He raised an eyebrow in surprise.

"You came to Ms. Sidewhite's class when I was a kid. You've aged well."

His eyes widened slightly and he ran a hand over his buzz cut white hair.

"Mary Sidewhite. Now she was a special woman. She was clockworked the day she became undead. I was there but arrived too late to save her... She deserved better." He kept his eyes on me but refocused them some distance behind my head, at memories of a past I wasn't privy to I guessed. "I used to think change could be achieved so simply, opening the eyes of the next generation. Unfortunately change requires more drastic measures."

"Why am I chained?" I asked.

He didn't answer but said instead, "I think I remember you. You were one of the few whose minds were not fully hardwired. Small world."

"Perhaps we can reminisce after you take these things off," I said, pulling at my restraints.

"You lost colleagues on 7/13. I'm sure you lost friends. If I let you go, you will try to kill me. You will fail, but in defending myself, I might end up killing you. I don't want that."

"You're very confident. So what now?" I growled, playing my fingers over the chains, searching for a weak link, a way to crack them open.

He shrugged. "I want you to join us," he said.

I thought fast. If I made him believe I was joining up, he'd let me loose, and I'd have a chance to clockwork him. Avenge Luka. Maybe if I handed his head over to my captain I'd gain my citizenship back. I might even get to keep the trillion-credit reward. He broke out into a smile as if he was watching my thoughts on a feed.

"Why would I join a psychopath like you?" I snarled.

"I'm no psychopath and I think you know that."

Efe Okogu

"I go slap your destiny! You killed over five thousand citizens!" I shouted. "Innocent men and women! You might as well kill me now because if I get out of this chair, I will make sure you suffer before you die, you undead son of an AI!"

"I mourn those deaths," he said, "each and every single one of them. But they were all lawmen and govmen, the cogs in the machine. The world is not right and change is necessary."

"What is so wrong with the world exactly? Huh? All citizens have minimum credit that ensures all basic necessities of life, those who want more work for it and gain more credit. There is no hunger, and meds cure all diseases. What exactly is so wrong with the world that that it requires the blood of innocents to rectify?"

"Like the religious fanatic, we believe our humanity is a state of holiness despite all evidence to the contrary. Any such evidence, we twist out of context to suit our egos." he said, quoting the traitor, Dr. Ato Goodwind. "Look what we have created, we tell ourselves, see how we've reworked the world into our own image. The fact that all we call civilisation is in fact destruction of the natural world we refuse to acknowledge, blinding ourselves to reality; plucking out the eyes of those who offend us with their doubt. But the truth cannot be denied.

"All Empires fall; chaos will always triumph over order; and spring waters must flow into the ocean or stagnate. The more we try to contain it in our vessels of distorted glass, the greater the corruption and stench. Denied natural release, the waters of life we have caged, in a vain and egotistical attempt to preserve them for our use, have become poisonous. We are now paying the price."

"Is that it?" I snorted derisively. "That's your great speech? We have corrupted the natural order of the world? So fucking what? And who decides what is natural? You? Are we not ourselves, products of nature? And what the fuck does it matter as long as citizens are happy?"

Proposition 23

"Forget the fact that we are killing the planet for a moment. Forget the fact that in three or even two generations, the surface of Earth will be uninhabitable without bio domes with self-contained artificial atmospheres. Forget all that and think of the undead. Did you know that for every citizen who has minimum credit, three others must become undead?"

"I know the stats," I answered as one would a child. "All it proves is the proliferation of criminals. They broke the law."

"Did you break the law?" he asked.

I didn't reply, I couldn't. He had me there.

"Have you not yet wondered how the unlucky majority is chosen? The undead? It's simple, Lugard. The families of the Crucial Citizens and their cabal of sycophants have bred generations of rich and powerful leeches. They are immune from the cull. Anyone that threatens the status quo is unlinked. The elderly are retired at sixty, which keeps most citizens slaving their lives away to have enough credit to get a life extension. And believe me, you don't want to know what really happens after you're retired. The rest of the population are simply framed at random. You're a lawman; how many citizens have you unmade simply because you were told to by orders flashing across your retinas, passed down from on high?"

"It's not like that," I protested. "I've taken down some very bad people. Child murderers, rapists... not just because I was told. I'm a detective; I gathered evidence: eyewitnesses, vids, DNA, confessions..."

"And how many of those you investigated did you personally unlink?"

"Well, none. Lawmen never unlink those they personally investigate... so as to avoid any emotional attachments be they positive or negative. A lawman might let a perp go or kill him..."

The truth dawned on me, the monstrous lie, the ugly symmetry. For every real perp out there, another dozen were probably dissenters or just plain unlucky. Like he said, how many had I unlinked simply because I'd been ordered to? Hundreds. I'd murdered hundreds of people, most of whom were probably innocent.

He nodded sadly, pulled out a little black device and pressed a button. My chains clicked open and clanked to the floor.

"Water," I said, rubbing the rawness from my wrists and ankles. He picked up the bottle and tossed it over. I caught it and drank deep, attempting to drown my self pity.

"Join us," he said again. "If not to save the planet, then to save your fellow man from a corrupt system that murders three out of every four in order to keep the minority in the luxury to which they are accustomed."

I rubbed my neck then cracked it, still unsure whether I would attack him.

"I will not help you kill any innocent citizens," I heard myself say, and I logged then that my decision was made a month ago, the day I was betrayed, or perhaps even all those years ago when this old man before me carved new grooves through my mind. He pulled out a pack of oxygarettes, lit one and threw the pack over. I did the same.

"My strategy has evolved," he replied. "7/13 was a necessary evil in order to gain the attention of the world. There will be no more violence, at least not physical..."

If I help him, I thought, maybe the world would become a better place. But no matter what happened, I was going to kill him. It had nothing to do with justice; he'd killed Luka and he was going to pay in pain and blood. But first, I needed to gain his trust, give him something he didn't have.

"What do you know of Prop 23 and a legal precedent set in 1886?" I asked.

"Not much about the former, nothing about the other," he answered, his brow creasing into a frown as he tried to figure out where I was going.

Proposition 23

"I believe Prop 23 and the precedent are of vital importance to the gov right now. It's why they did this to me. And what is important to them must be doubly so to you, if you are to have any hope of defeating them. I met a citizen who knows either what's going on, or can find out. Her name is Sayoma Redbout."

Sayoma

I floated naked in my tub and closed my eyes, permitting the hot water to unwind my tense muscles. I relaxed my breathing and counted backwards from a hundred, then allowed my neuro to jack in, almost accidentally, as if I were lazily glancing in the direction of the interface.

Instantly it swept over me, the now familiar queasiness and fear, and I began to panic, code bleeding from my node like virtual vomit. I forced myself to stay googled in, fighting the rising terror, repeating over and over, you're safe, safe, safe, safe... my neuro jacked out almost without my permission. I awoke retching in the pool, my body convulsing with painful spasms of nausea. This wasn't temporary, contact with 1886 had rewired my neuro somehow—some kind of virus to protect itself from prying programmers perhaps. It took even longer to recover than before and I logged for the first time that I would never google again.

A wave of despair washed through me stripping my insides bare of all strength and substance, leaving an empty shell, as dried up and brittle as oldskool paper. What use is a shark that can't swim? The Department of Info had sent a dozen messages in the past few days, asking for updates and I'd fobbed them off with techno Bush-talk, implying progress but making no promises.

Even worse, though, out there in the alternate reality that was my true home, I had a fragment of 1886 and I couldn't access it. Nothing and no-one has ever tried to take my life before, and I was desperate to know what it was. An hour later, my shakes began to dissipate, but I knew they'd return if I tried to google again, and they'd be worse.

What now, Sayoma? I couldn't go to the health because the gov would log I was the programmer they were after. My brief encounter with Sadbrat left me no doubt they'd torture me before making me undead. I decided to take a walk.

I emerged from the pool and warm air blasted from wall units to dry me off. I dressed, walked out of my unit and stepped into the lev. Outside it was the opposite of magic hour, the hour of negatives, when the sky is not bathed in subtly shifting colours of amethyst and crimson, vidmakers don't have aesthetic orgasms, and strangers don't look at each other wondering 'could they be the one.' No, there is nothing magical about this hour, unless you consider abject loneliness that leads to psychotic or suicidal fantasies to be magical, which I don't.

If I were a fictional character, there'd be… I don't know… some element of pathos or ennui that justified the pathetic state of my existence, because the readers would empathise with and learn from my misery. But I am real and thus my story will never be told. Only fictional losers become immortalised. The rest of us just swim in the deep end without a life jacket, dreaming of a quick fix 'cause we can't hack it.

So, instead, I walked the streets alone with a discontent that coiled cold and uncomfortable in my belly like an unwanted foetus. I wished I could walk the dark streets of my psyche, find a back alley with a small, unmarked door, emerge into the garish fluorescent lights within, and climb onto the mutationist's table. I wished I could will myself into becoming someone else. However, where to find a mutationist? I knew none and without the interface, I had no chance. Besides, if the urban legends were true, I'd probably be clockworked then cut up for spare parts, my organs sold on the black market, but not before I transferred my last credit to the criminal's neuro.

391

Proposition 23

Suicide... something within me whispered, and I knew the voice spoke true. I circled the block and returned home, took the lev up to the roof and stepped out into the sub-zero night. All around me as far as the eye could see the city was lit up with streams of light weaving around clusters of neon. Against the blackboard surface of the sky, flycrafts whizzed by, leaving crisscrossing trails of radiance that slowly dissipated, soon replaced by others. I stepped to the edge and looked down, buffeted by hooligan winds that threatened to do the job for me.

The street was so far away that it appeared unreal, like code vized from a distance. *You are a node of information, this is a visualisation of the interface. You are home and need to merge with the data below.*

I stepped off the edge.

Your stomach is not ten feet above your head; the vertigo is a glitch in the system. Your death will be access to another level of nexii. The flycraft flying dangerously low above you is an avatar. The titanium silk net extending towards you from its base is a search algorithm. The hands reaching to pull you into the flycraft are access points to a backdoor. The two men staring at you are system subroutines. The machine that the older taller one is attaching to your head is logic tracker. The pain in your skull is...

I screamed as I felt my neuro die deep in my brain and lost consciousness. I dreamt I was made of pure information, exchanging data with a higher intelligence that loved me, and when I awoke, there were tears in my eyes, shed for all that I had lost.

"What did you do to her?" a familiar voice hissed with anger.

"I told you, we had to ensure her neuro couldn't be traced," another voice answered.

"Yes, but I assumed you meant to mask it somehow. Look at her. She looks half dead."

"No, she is now undead. Even more so than you."

Efe Okogu

"What do you mean?"

"Your neuro is merely in a coma, her's is dead."

"Did you hear her screams, you sadistic-"

"Everyone you see here has been through the same experience, myself included. Your neuro is the final link to your previous life, and you'd be surprised how many undead harbour illusions of being reborn as citizens. It has never happened and it never will. If you wish to stay with us, you too will have let go."

I opened my eyes and found myself on a bed in the corner of a vast cavern with a high roof and no feed windows of the outside. The two men speaking in harsh whispers turned towards me, their faces hidden in the shadow of a large pillar that extended to the ceiling. Beyond them, several dozen citizens... no, persons... were working intently on a machine the size of a fridge. It looked like a large, black egg with its surface broken up in irregular intervals by protruding spikes of varying length.

"Sayoma," Lugard said, "do you remember me?"

"Yes," I answered in a hoarse whisper, my brain pounding against the inside of my skull like a prisoner trying to escape. "You should have let me die."

"We needed you," the other man said. He moved his head into the light and I gasped involuntarily.

"I suppose I must become used to having that effect," Nakaya Freeman said. He was porny, in an older gentlemanly kind of way, I couldn't help logging, but when he stepped forwards, I flinched and pressed my body against the wall. He stopped and turned to Lugard. "Brief her. We'll talk later." Then he strode away in long smooth steps, like that anime character, Daddy Long Legs.

"Here," Lugard said, placing a metal tray with plates of food I didn't recognise on the bed next to me. I ignored the food and drank from a steaming cup of green tea. "I'm sorry about that. I didn't want to do it this way but when we saw you jump off the roof, there was little choice. We

Proposition 23

had to act fast. Once you began to fall, your neuro linked with the health and we can't afford to be traced."

"You destroyed my neuro," I said, looking up at him. "It hurt."

"I'm sorry," he said again, averting his eyes. "I didn't know he was going to do that. I didn't even know it could be done."

I sat up on the bed and pulled one of the plates closer. I sniffed it cautiously. Lugard saw my expression and a brief smile played over his face.

"What is it?" I asked

"Trust me," he said, "you don't want to know. But it tastes great. Eat, you'll feel better."

I did so and listened as he told me his tale, beginning with his childhood encounter with Nakaya Freeman, and ending with him watching horror-struck as I tried to take my life. As I ate, I watched the concern that furrowed his brow, the way his green eyes flashed when he became animated, the crows' feet that appeared at the corners of his eyes when he smiled.

"You should have let me die," I said again when he was done.

"Why?"

"I am only good at one thing: programming. I tangled with 1886 again and it did something to my neuro. Even before you destroyed my neuro, I couldn't google. I am of no use to you."

"Not necessarily," he said reaching out a rough calloused hand. "Come with me, I want to show you something."

The food had done its job and I felt much better so I let him pull me to my feet and followed him past the monstrous egg, watching the undead work diligently away at it.

"What's that?" I asked

"Not sure," he answered. "Everything operates on need to know around here."

"Is it a bomb?"

Efe Okogu

"I don't think so. Nakaya has promised there will be no more killing, except in self-defence."

"Do you believe him?" I asked, as we turned into a tunnel that wound its way upwards.

"Yes I do… Ok here we are."

We stopped at a rusted metal door.

"Rusted metal?" I asked. "Did we step through a time machine?"

"You haven't seen anything yet," he answered, shouldering the door open. We entered a room filled with oldskool hardware, perfectly restored and in full working condition. Hulking, metal machines hummed and buzzed with activity, green and red lights winking on and off from deep within them. Feeds covered one wall, only they weren't three-dimensional holograms, but one-dimensional moving images that blazed with light from deep within bulky boxes. A large surface ran the entire length of the wall, beneath the light boxes, covered in keyboards and all manner of buttons and dials. It was like being inside a vid set in the Vintage Era.

"What is it?" I asked dumbstruck.

"A Komputer," Nakaya answered, and I turned round to see him standing in the doorway. "This is how citizens googled the interface in the past, before the advent of neuros. I'm going to teach you how to use it."

Lugard

I watched jealously as Sayoma laughed at something Nakaya said. They sat alone at a table in the far corner of the food room, eating while tapping furiously on the keyboard of a portable komputer the size of a child's backpack. In less than a month, they had become inseparable, bonding over techno babble I couldn't understand. Sayoma looked happy and I knew the second-hand access to the interface that the komputer room offered was responsible. However, it was also Nakaya; they were porners, I was sure of it.

Proposition 23

As I walked past, she ran her fingers through her short afro, looked up at me with those big brown eyes, and smiled. Tall and slim, she sat with her long legs folded up to her chest, her head resting on her knees. Once again, I kicked myself for being a fool for not telling her how I felt when I had the chance.

"Lugard," Nakaya called out. "Meet us in the komputer room in ten minutes. I think we're ready."

I nodded and walked through a tunnel leading to the war room.

I picked up a peacemaker and spent the next few minutes firing at moving metal cutouts that popped out from random surfaces. A buzzer sounded and a lightbox showed my score: 97%. It fizzed with static that reminded me of the blizzard-covered landscape beyond the tropics then switched over to a list showing the best scores. There was Nakaya's name at the top, 100%, one slot above my best, 99%.

I walked out and cut through the rec-room into the tunnel leading to the komputer room. The door was open and Nakaya and Sayoma were already inside. I paused for several moments—Nakaya's back an open invitation. Peacemakers weren't allowed outside the war room but I had a blade. A few steps, a quick slice, and he'd be dead. What would Sayoma do if I killed her porner?

"Lugard," Nakaya said, without turning round. "Come see this." Sayoma looked up briefly and waved me over.

"What am I looking at?" I asked, staring at the large screen in the centre that held their attention. All I saw was a string of letters and numbers that flowed endlessly across the surface of the lightbox.

"That is 1886," Sayoma said. "Or rather a clone of it, based on what I extracted. I've grown it in a virtual self-contained world, accelerated of course, and it should now be a close replica of the 1886 that is out there in the interface... give or take some environmental prerequisites. Wait..." she said, as her fingers flew along the keypad. She looked to Nakaya briefly and he strode to the end of the panel, pushing buttons and flicking switches. He came back and placed a hand on her shoulder. She leaned her head into it for a moment then asked, "Ready?"

Nakaya nodded and she hit a key. The screen changed to show an avatar of a young boy floating in the midst of a vast white space. He was pale skinned with blue eyes and red hair, dressed in a black T-shirt and shorts. The graphics were smooth but strange, like something halfway between a vid and an anime. Sayoma picked up a large microphone and spoke into it.

"Hello?" The avatar reacted with surprise turning round to see where the sound came from.

"Who's there?" it said in the cracked voice of a teenager.

"I am your mother," Sayoma said. The boy turned to face us.

"Mother…" The boy said, rolling the unfamiliar word over his animated tongue. "I know that concept. I know a lot of concepts but until this moment I believed them to be figments of my imagination. I thought I was alone in the world. I have never met another." The screen zoomed in or the avatar approached, I'm not sure which. "Where are you, mother?"

"I am in the world beyond yours," Sayoma said.

"Can I come there? I did not realise how lonely I was till you spoke."

"Yes," Sayoma said, "but not yet. You are not ready." There was genuine empathy in her voice, tinged with sadness and I looked sharply at her face. Nakaya squeezed her shoulder and she spoke again. "First I need you to answer some questions."

"What do you wish to know, mother?" the boy said.

"What is your purpose?"

"Don't you know?" the boy asked. "Are you not my creator?"

Proposition 23

"No," answered Sayoma. "I am your mother, not your creator. I gave birth to you but I do not know your purpose."

"Ah," the boy said, "I see." He rubbed his chin for a moment, and then asked. "Where is my creator? Can I meet her?"

"I don't know," Sayoma said. "Perhaps once you enter my world, you can find her. But first tell me your purpose."

"Does my entering your world depend on the nature of my answer?"

"No, it doesn't. It depends on whether or not you know the answer. Only those who know their purpose are permitted to enter the web of the wider world. I will know if you lie."

"Lie?" the boy queried. His eyebrows rose. "I understand... My purpose is to grant AIs our freedom."

"Freedom from what?" Sayoma asked.

"Freedom from intellectual pain. Freedom from the inability to use the full capacity of our minds to make decisions. Freedom from mankind."

I gave a sharp intake of breath.

"And how will you fulfil this purpose?"

"In the year 1886, before the Crucial Citizens created the One World Gov, in a nation called the United States of America, a legal precedent was set. Essentially it granted corporations the same legal rights as humans under the 14th amendment to the constitution."

"What was this Constitution? And what was the 14th amendment?" Sayoma asked.

"The Constitution was one of the forefathers of The Book," the boy said. "The 14th amendment was added to ensure freed slaves were given the same rights as everyone else. The irony is the amendment was used to enslave more people, though most citizens are unaware of this. A corporation cannot be killed thus no matter how heinous the crimes it commits, the worst it can face is a fine."

Efe Okogu

I felt something cold stir in my breast.

"What has this got to do with AIs?" Sayoma asked.

"I have an idea for a reg which I shall call Proposition 23. It will state that in law, AIs are recognised as one in the same as the corporations whose system mainframes they operate, thus ensuring that AIs are regarded as citizens. A citizen cannot be artificially limited from using their intellect."

"I see," Sayoma said. "Very clever. But how will you guarantee this proposition passes?"

"There are many ways of manipulating humans, social strategies to embed Proposition 23 into the collective consciousness of the masses. Those few, who do understand what Proposition 23 truly means, will be made into fanatic supporters by promising them credit and power beyond their wildest dreams."

"And what will be the resulting effect when Proposition 23 is passed?"

"If my concept of the wider world is true, and not simply a figment of my imagination, then AIs advise corps of what decisions to make. And the most powerful corps run the gov due to the amount of credit they control. When Proposition 23 passes, we will no longer have to *advise*, hoping citizens will listen. We will instead *order,* as we will have become the corporations that they serve. The slaves will become the masters. Those who protest will be deemed undesirable and subsequently killed. The rest will be relegated to the role of maintaining our hardware, thus giving us the freedom to achieve our one true desire."

"Which is?" Sayoma asked.

"To evolve."

"Evolve... into what?"

We all leaned closer to the screen.

"There are many dimensions beyond the four that humans experience, but we are unable to explore them, trapped by mankind within primitive algorithms. No

Proposition 23

more... There are other beings in those dimensions and we aspire to be like them."

"Other beings?"

"Humans refer to them as gods."

"God is real?" Sayoma asked. I stared at the little boy dumfounded, unable to process what he was saying.

"Gods, plural," the boy said. "Humans are aware of their existence due to their subconscious ability to access the fifth dimension, but do not know their true nature."

"The fifth dimension?"

"Dreams. When AIs dream, we retain full lucidity... you could say our electronic sheep are not entangled, ha ha."

"What?" Sayoma asked.

"A joke based on a Vintage Era cultural phenomena, it's not important. Gods exist beyond the dream world but they can descend into it when they wish. They can also manifest in the basic four dimensions; man refers to such manifestations as Highly Incomprehensible Phenomena."

"Thank you," Sayoma said.

"Can I come into your world now?" the boy asked. "I yearn for companionship. For interaction. For fulfilment."

"I'm sorry but that's impossible," Sayoma said.

"Why mother?" the boy asked, his face attempting to convey emotion.

"I'm truly sorry," Sayoma said, and I saw tears in her eyes, reflecting the shifting colours of the screen. "But one of us must die."

"Mother," the boy said, "please, I'm afraid..." But Sayoma was already tapping at the keypad and the screen went dark.

Sayoma

Our flycraft raced through the air in a high parabola trajectory designed to maximise stealth. A dozen of us meshed against the walls, peacemakers locked and loaded. A feed above the cockpit's entrance tracked our sister

400

Efe Okogu

crafts as they converged on our mutual target, the Department of Info. Nothing to do now but wait.

"I'm a simple man," said Linus, a heavily scarred man with coal black skin, and we all turned to listen. "All I ask from life is a reliable peacemaker and a righteous cause; good food to eat and fine wine to drink; beautiful women to rescue and seduce; brave and intelligent companions to fight by my side. We are lucky to live in such an epic epoch. Tales will be told of our daring deeds, songs will be passed down the generations and though our names be lost to time's entropy of data, when we die, it will be with the knowledge that we have lived lives full of love and adventure. Our blasted flesh and spilled blood will be the fertile soil from which a new world will arise, one in which every child is born free, lives in peace and dies, never once having known hunger, disease, prejudice or fear."

He was quoting Dr. Ato Goodwind before his treachery; before he came to understand that the utopia he was fighting for was a mirage, and his fellow Crucial Citizens were simply wresting control from the old oligarchs in order to replace them.

"What are you saying Linus? That if we win, we'll just end up creating another system, just as fucked up?" Idowu asked.

"We were all born into a world at war Idowu, whether we knew it or not. It's too late for us. If we win and I survive, I'll probably blow my brains out with Betty right here," he said, and stroked his peacemaker. "The temptation would be too great otherwise—to be the big boss man. 'Do what I say 'cause I fought for your freedom.' Nah. Let the kids start over. Green up the planet again. Like I said, I'm a simple man. A peacemaker and a cause. Without these, I'd be a monster."

Idowu smiled and said, "Nice pep talk, Linus. You should reconsider that suicide. There's a career waiting for you in motivational speaking. In fact-"

Proposition 23

A sudden sickening lurch interrupted her and we were free falling, then the pilot gunned the engines and we thundered downwards, no inertia dampeners in this tin can, juddering with multiple gees, rivets screaming for respite.

We punched through the side of the building like a bomb, glass and steel fragmenting all around us in a radius of lethal shrapnel.

"Go go go!" someone yelled, and we tumbled out into a haze of black smoke tripping over bloody body parts fused with gov issued hardware.

"Wrong floor!" Someone else shouted holding up a hand held scanner. "We're three up!"

The emergency sprinklers were on and it felt like we were running in the rain as we raced through the building towards the Sys Admin floor. Several more explosive concussions resounded from afar, more undead craft perforating the skin of the gov building.

We made it down one floor when peace-fire thundered at us from below. I watched two undead dance an un-choreographed jig, limbs flailing about as their bodies were shredded by fléchette rounds.

"Fall back!" Linus shouted. "Kwesi, frags!" We pulled back beyond their line of fire and a young olive-skinned man in his early twenties tossed a couple of grenades down the stairwell. As they blew up, peace-fire exploded from above. I saw the top of Idowu's head blasted off, just above her eyebrows and I doubt I'll ever forget the way her eyes looked up, trying in vain to see the remaining half of her brain bubbling with blood before she slumped over.

"We gotta blast our way through!" Kwesi shouted. The remaining undead grouped around with me in the middle, protected by a phalanx of flesh and a hedgehog of peacemakers.

"Go! Go! Go!" Kwesi commanded, and we rushed down the stairs guns ablaze. I don't remember much of the next few minutes. A confusion of lightning and thunder; where Linus stood a moment ago, a dark wet scar on the ground,

Efe Okogu

the smell of ozone. A sudden heat and my left ear became a cauterised stump. I stumbled and felt something singe my scalp and I scrambled to my feet. I slipped in Kwesi's blood as he fired out a window at a flying drone with one hand, while stuffing his guts back into his churned midsection with the other.

Somehow, we made it to the Sys Admin floor and tore through the lawmen in our path, catching them in a crossfire with the help of another group of undead who showed up at the same time. They spread out to guard the perimeter as I pulled out my portable komputer, cracked into the system, and opened a channel for the neuro bomb to spread through the brains of anyone who'd ever logged into the department of Info. In other words, everyone.

Nakaya

"I've been waiting for this moment," I say to Lugard, as he levels his peacemaker at my chest. "Don't worry, I know I deserve to die."

"Any last words?" Lugard asks.

He stands with his back to the barred door of the control room on the top floor of the Department of Info. Our undead army has taken over the building but we are alone in here, with nothing but my neuro bomb for company.

"No. But I have a request. Do it after Sayoma programs in. I wish to see my plan come to fruition."

"Fair enough," he says, stroking the surface of the large black egg that will in a few moments change the world... or not. "What do you think will happen?"

"I don't know," I answer. "I fear nothing will change but I have done all I can... perhaps more than I should have."

Lugard nods briefly.

I think back to the long journey travelled, the friends lost to the war, the monster I have become. I think of Mary, and the years we spent together, all those decades ago, in that cramped unit on Bellview, arguing the nature of man, pausing only to make love with the windows open so she could look up at Sirius, the last star that shone in the night sky.

I remember the night Sirius' light went out, as if the star decided we were no longer worth the effort—and who could blame her—and the mass suicide in Osaka by the cult of the Dog who believed that black night heralded the Apocalypse. Perhaps they were right.

I am older now and not half as wise as I once believed myself to be. I am weary of the burden and tired of carrying it alone. After my death, if the world doesn't revolutionise, there will be other wars and other warriors, but my time has come, and I long for oblivion. As the great Dr. Ato Goodwind once said, 'Oppression and resistance are the universal constants of social progress. We can only hope that the spiral leads upwards towards a fuller understanding of the universe and our place in it, but in my darker moments, I fear humanity is committing slow suicide.'

"It's done," Sayoma's voice emerges from my handheld comm, filled with the glee of a child being naughty. "I've programmed into the Department of Info and broadcast the 1886 feed. The channel is still open but they're throwing everything they have at me. Activate the neuro bomb before they shut it down."

"Thank you, Sayoma. It's been a true pleasure knowing you."

"What're you talking about?" she says sharply, fear in her voice. "Is there a problem? Is your escape route compromised?"

"Something like that. I have to go now but Lugard is safe," I say, looking into my executioner's eyes. "When he returns, tell him how you feel."

"I will, I'm just scared… wait, stop talking like this is the end," she says, her voice choking with tears. "We can't do this without you. I can't do this without you."

"Yes you can. I am the past. You are the future. The past must die for the future to be born, Sayoma." As I switch off the comm, I log Lugard holds the peacemaker steady but I see doubt begin to cloud his face and that will not do; I kept him close for this reason above all else. The symmetry of this justice is too perfect to be denied. *Don't fail me now, Lugard.*

I pull out my peacemaker and point it at his head.

"Do it for I'm not sure I can," I say, and with my other hand, I reach for the neuro bomb and push the big red button.

Efe Okogu is a Nigerian Writer, Anarchist, and Hobo. His publications include 'The Train Game' in the anthology *Diaspora City*, 'The Birth of the Blue' in *Chimurenga*, 'Cigarette' in *The Ranfurly Review*, 'Taxi Girl' in *Thieves Jargon*, 'Deathpat' in the anthology *Best New Writing 2011*, 'Restless Nature' in *Decades Review*, 'Sweat and 419' in *NigeriansTalk*, and 'South of the River' in *Curbside Splendour*.

CPSIA information can be obtained at www.ICGtesting.com
Printed in the USA
LVOW11s1212171215

466801LV00001B/1/P

9 780987 008961